Mosquito Pass

A.C. Foster

Mosquito Pass

Previously published as The Scarab's Touch

For my first writing teacher, Mrs. Nunnally.
I doubt you will remember me
but I never forgot you.

A.C. Foster

Shanghai
February 1932

PROLOGUE

His first awareness that a combatant had engaged his aircraft was when the console in front of him suddenly had parts flying off of it. The enemy fighter shot past his left side, giving him a fast glimpse of the machine that nearly killed him in his twenty-eighth year of life. Lieutenant Yoshiro Kanji of the Imperial Japanese Navy banked hard right and dove. The plunge out of the sky probably saved his life, but it also sent him into a dizzying nose first corkscrew straight towards the hard earth below. It took a very long minute for him to regain control of the fighter and climb back into the sky.

Ten minutes later and satisfied that no one was shooting at him anymore, he looked at the neatly furrowed slice running across the forearm of his flying suit. The bullet had sliced through the leather, missing the skin and bone beneath by the narrowest of margins.

Kanji raised his arm above the edge of his biplane's cockpit. The hard blowing icy air rippled and pulled at the damaged sleeve. He flexed gloved fingers and marveled at the sight of a perfectly untouched arm. An instant before the unexpected attack began, if he lifted that same arm to scratch an itch or adjust with his goggles, his predicament would be considerably worse than it was now.

Kanji lowered his arm out of the slipstream and took a double grip on the joystick. Holding the stick with both hands helped him control the shaking in his limbs. It wasn't that he was afraid. It was surprise and adrenalin and an unhealthy dose of winter altitude in an open cockpit making his hands shake. That's how he would remember it. He was never afraid, and the shaking was caused by the icy wind. He tried to clear his head, to think rationally, and solve the immediate problem.

The Nakajima was in bad shape. Bad enough that he was surprised the wood and canvas biplane still flew. Three seconds in someone else's gun sights nearly shot both him and his A2N out of the sky. The console in front of him was gone; shot to pieces and looking like someone with anger issues had taken a fire ax to it. Canvas flapped from torn wings as wisps of blue smoke leaked out of the big radial engine.

Not only was his bird limping in the sky, Kanji had also lost his bearings. Getting shot at for the first time in his life had disoriented him. One problem at a time, Kanji told himself. He needed landmarks.

An angry wasp settled a few dozen meters off his wingtip. Saitama, his wingman, his fighter unmarked by the enemy's fire, waggled double wings and waved a glove above his cockpit.

Kanji returned the wave but didn't wag his wings.

Saitama was the newest man in the squadron. He was hardly more than a boy, and would no doubt expect him to know the way home. Kanji needed to think. In his head, he played back the preflight briefing instructions. Directions, time to target, landmarks, course home. He tried to picture the world as it was before he was falling out of the sky. It was all scrambled together now. Looking at the ground, he compared what he saw beneath him to the photographs from the preflight briefings. The harbor, with its piers and warehouses and the coast road running north were his landmarks.

Saitama kept even with him and waited.

Kanji always had an innate sense of direction. He hoped he still did. All he had to do was concentrate and stop his damned hands from shaking. The *Kaga Province* was out there somewhere over the horizon waiting for her planes to come home.

Lieutenant Kanji waved a gloved hand at his wingman, pointed to his ruined instruments and then east, out to sea. Saitama nodded his head, changed his course to follow, and took his station above and slightly behind his wing.

Pulling a splintered piece of wood away from the spot where his oil pressure gauge used to be, Kanji held it to the wind blowing through his cockpit. The wind tore through his gloved fingers at over one hundred knots. It caught the splinter and sent it sailing past him to drift slowly to the ocean's surface far below.

He swallowed, tried to find enough saliva to spit the bad taste out of his mouth, failed, then adjusted the goggles on his face. He looked left and right, above and below, and over each shoulder. Except for Saitama, the skies were empty. He hadn't seen the others from their flight since the enemy fighter jumped their formation. For all he knew, the rest might be landing right now or they might be dead.

Shot to pieces and he never touched the trigger to his guns. Not once. He hadn't been looking, hadn't expected another fighter to come diving out of the sun and now, here he was in a wounded plane with his instruments gone. If he died today, there would be no one to blame but himself.

The rhythmic screaming of the A2N's Kotobuki radial engine had an uncertain clank in it. The whole airframe felt tired. Saitama, still flying close to him, throttled back his engine to keep it from leaving the damaged plane behind. The unnatural clattering from the power plant was not good news, he knew, and the *Kaga* and the safety of its flight deck were still somewhere out there in front of him. Still over the horizon.

The East China Sea looked very empty. He looked over the side of his cockpit at the bright blue water a thousand meters below. An oily bluish plume of smoke stained the view.

If the engine stalled now, and by the sound it was making it just might, and he had to take to his parachute, he would freeze in minutes once he hit the cold ocean water. Better that, he told the wind screaming past his face. Better that than the less than welcoming reception he could expect from the Chinese on the mainland.

He needed altitude. Altitude increased his glide range. Pulling back on the stick, he nudged the throttle lever forward. The Nakajima's damaged engine missed, the prop refusing to turn faster in the cold winter air. Gritting his teeth, Kanji eased the short lever back to its original position. It would have to do. This was as high as he was going to get.

Saitama flew a slow three hundred and sixty degree circle around his struggling airplane. After completing his circle, his wingman gave him a thumbs up. It was encouraging whether it was accurate or not. Saitama returned to his station as the two planes flew eastward.

Farther out to sea. *Kaga* was out there somewhere.

He wished he had more altitude.

The minutes ticked away. The oily smoke coming off his engine looked darker and was thicker now. The A2N had an unsettling vibration. He could feel it in the soles of his boots resting on the rudder pedals; a toe-numbing buzz that he never felt the engine making before. His goggles were stained with oil and he could taste petroleum when he licked his lips. Giving the lenses of his goggles a quick swipe with the back of his glove made the world go blurry as the oil smeared across the glass.

How much longer would the engine continue to run? Long enough, he hoped. Kanji rubbed his hand along the leather wrapped edge of the cockpit and again looked down at the ocean far below. If he ditched, would he drown before he froze to death? Would he even know the difference?

"Get me home," he told the Nakajima, "and if you cannot get me all the way, get me close enough." He had always been a strong swimmer.

The Nakajima's engine missed a beat. The vibration in his feet got worse.

Saitama edged his fighter closer and wobbled his wings. Lieutenant Kanji followed the pointing finger of the other pilot to a small, dark object floating just below the horizon.

A ship.

Beyond it, he saw more ships. They found their home and he wasn't going to drown. Kanji smiled for the first time since the bullets almost killed him. He tasted the oil spraying from the Nakajima again. No, he wasn't going to drown or freeze in the China Sea. Not today.

Ten minutes later, the pair of fliers circled the *Kaga* as Saitama lined up for his approach and matched his course to the long white wake streaming away behind the carrier. Kanji pulled his limping fighter out of the way. Damaged airplanes always landed last. It was naval aviation's version of the emergency room's triage. Save the ones who could be saved first, then try to save the others. Today was Kanji's day to be one of the others. He knew the rules and took up his position, making a low, slow circle three hundred meters off the ship's port side.

Saitama's A2N touched down on the long, straight wooden deck. The hook trailing from the rear tail section of his fighter caught the second cable and brought the fast moving little biplane to an abrupt stop.

Crewmen on the carrier's flight deck could see the trail of blue gray smoke coming out of the other fighter still circling and could hear the laboring stutter being produced by its engine. Saitama's plane was guided quickly out of the way and onto the elevator, vanishing below to the sound of warning bells clanging loudly throughout the ship. *Kaga Province* was prepping for a crash.

Kanji pulled out of his turn, flew a short distance in the opposite direction of the ship's heading, flew over the top of the trailing destroyer, then turned again to line up on the carrier's wake. He started his approach. Pushing the fighter's nose down a touch, he began the mental calculations and judgments necessary to land a fast moving object onto a much slower one. Picking his spot between arrestor cables one and two, he adjusted his approach again and watched the waving paddles of the landing officer. Both paddles waved upwards. He touched his throttle to run his engine up a little more and raise his approach angle. It was no good. The engine lost all its muscle and the extra fuel dumped into its cylinders proved fatal. The big radial gave a hammering, loud bang from deep inside its mechanical heart as something, maybe a part of the cylinder head itself, blew off taking a jagged section of the cowling with it.

The screaming, vibrating roar that filled Kanji's world since he left the flight deck was gone. Instead, he heard the whistle of the wind cutting through the guy wires and struts of the A2N and the klaxon of his ship wailing its alarm.

His alarm.

The Nakajima was falling out of the sky at last and the tons of steel floating in front of him no longer represented shelter. In an instant, it had become unyielding death. He was going to hit the flight deck with a dead engine and there was nothing he could do about it.

Kanji felt his heart pounding in his chest. "Damn you," he screamed as the A2N lost altitude far too quickly. He yanked the joystick all the way back to his crotch. "Fly."

The broken fighter didn't fly. The A2N dropped out of the sky towards the ship. It slapped down onto the wooden deck with a solid crunch, missing the unforgiving steel curl of its trailing edge with no more than two meters to spare. He hit hard, the impact making him bite through his lower lip. The fixed undercarriage of the A2N crushed upward and folded beneath the Nakajima with a mangling crack of wood and steel. The fighter slid belly down across the deck, making a fast jig to the right and sending the ship's flight deck crewmen scattering. Bits and pieces of the propeller, fuselage, and lower wing broke away from the destroyed fighter and flew across the deck of the *Kaga Province.*

Kanji gripped the sides of his cockpit and held on. Stunned by the hard collision, he was only partially aware of what was happening. The broken plane kept going, tearing its way across the carrier. The flight deck was a straight line, but the fighter wasn't sliding down the length of the ship. It canted far over and was dragging its way in a diagonal slash towards the unprotected edge. The Nakajima tilted then went over the side. Still strapped into his seat, Kanji dropped five meters straight down, crushing his wrecked airplane onto an antiaircraft mount and killing three of the gun crew standing at their station.

The A2N finally stopped moving. He spat out a mouthful of blood from his torn lip and pulled his goggles off his face. He was hanging sideways in his harness, still stunned by the hard strike of his landing when the WOOSH of fire engulfed the front of the wreck. With the flames came the terror. Panicking, he released the harness and gripped the side of his cockpit. Get away from the flames, a voice in his head screamed. Kanji grabbed something solid and pulled ignoring the sudden jab of pain from his leg. He pulled as hard as he could, but nothing moved. The lower half of his body was caught in the tangle of wires, struts, cables and fuselage that made up the remains of the fighter.

The ship's flight deck crash alarm screamed. There were bodies moving in and out of the surrounding smoke. Crewmen tried to get closer. Voices shouted. Kanji tried again to pull his body free of the wreckage and again, nothing moved. He was stuck tight; wedged like a rat in the jaws of a trap. A wave of heat washed over him. The fire made a horribly frightful sound as it consumed the wooden frame of his airplane. The flames were so close he could feel the blistering heat rising like a volcano beside him.

"Oh no," he moaned. "Not like this."

A face, an unknown seaman holding an extinguisher, came closer, moving through the twisted debris of what used to be a wing.

"Hurry," Kanji screamed. "Don't let me burn." His gloved fingers slapped at the flames as the blistering heat singed the leather covering his hands. He could feel his legs starting to roast. The pain had an agonizing grip on his mind. Relentless, unforgiving pain.

Lieutenant Yoshiro Kanji screamed something, something beyond words. A fear greater than the sudden attack by the enemy fighter took control of his mind. He panicked, pounding his fists against the twisted and broken cockpit that was now his coffin.

One of the *Kaga's* seamen, seemingly unafraid of the white hot heat coming from the burning fighter, grasped the shoulders of his flight suit and pulled. Another doused the flaming wreck with a cloudy white spray.

Kanji could see the face of the unknown man with the red bottle of fire retardant in his hand. The volcanic heat of the flames burning all around him seared the sailor's face into his nightmares for the remainder of his days.

Puget Sound
Two years later

CHAPTER 1

Harry Watkins leaned to the right of his boat's wheel to look down the passageway behind him and into the main cabin below. His boat, *Scarab,* sounded unnaturally quiet with the engines dead even with the soft rain making gentle taps upon the woodwork above his head. From roaring, vibrating mechanical power to near silence floating on the swells gave the boat a very different, constrained feel. Helpless. That's what it felt like. Harry hated the feeling.

He had felt it all day.

Roscoe Harrison, his mechanic, was somewhere down below in the boat's cramped engine compartment. He could hear grunts from him now and then as the older man tried to fix whatever stopped them in the middle of the Sound. It happened right as Harry pushed the twin throttles forward. They hadn't made it much more than a half mile from Wing Point when both engines gave up the effort. Number one missed, lost speed, and died. Number two went a few seconds later, leaving Harry, his mechanic, and the boat drifting on the swell. Neither engine would restart. They hadn't moved since.

He went on deck to get the anchor in the water since the rocks lining the shore of Bainbridge were not that far off. The wind would have the boat on them soon enough if he didn't. It started raining again. It was a cold, wet, dreary day and the unexpected breakdown put the finishing touches to a perfectly terrible afternoon.

Harry could hear noises coming from the small space where the engines made their home. Taps and bangs, but nothing from Roscoe. Twin screwed boats weren't supposed to lose both engines at the same time. It wasn't natural. Try explaining that to his dead boat.

The sleeves of Roscoe's coveralls showed fresh gasoline stains from his current battles with a stripped brass fitting. The fitting finally gave up the fight and he had the new fuel filter almost ready to go. Squatting in between the big eight cylinder motors, flashlight held between his neck and shoulder, he was doing his best to tighten the threads on the new fitting. The filter was in an awkward spot and he was having a hell of a time getting his wrench on it. At his feet, the stopped up and completely worthless piece of crap filter that caused all the problems rolled back and forth as their boat moved with the swell.

Of all days, he thought, it had to happen today. The wrench tightened the fitting another half turn. Five more minutes, Roscoe thought. Five minutes and he'd be done and maybe Harry wouldn't be too late.

Harry was feeling time tick away. He was going to be late, very late, and today was a day he couldn't afford to be off schedule.

"How much longer, Roscoe?" he yelled over his shoulder.

"Hit the switch on number one again," came the muffled reply from below.

Harry stood from the helmsman's seat and leaned over the wheel to reach the engine controls. He pressed the start button for number one and listened to the whirr of the engine turning over underneath him.

"Wait, get off it," Roscoe shouted from his cramped space between the engines.

Harry, releasing the start button, sighed with exasperation and slumped into the swivel seat behind the wheel. "C'mon Roscoe," he said mostly to himself. "I can't spend today drifting on the Sound."

The clatter of a dropped wrench followed quickly by a string of colorful swearing came up loud and clear. Not long now, Harry thought. When Roscoe started cussing, the repairs were moving along.

The lighthouse at Magnolia Bluff northeast of him was hard to see. The hard drizzle and gloomy winter gray skies made the point of land come and go in his vision. He could just make out the bright eye of the light going by on its slow rotation. He scanned the horizon, looking for anything that might be coming towards them. The water around him was mostly empty as far as he could tell. It would be just his luck to get run over by a freighter after the morning he had. A westbound ferry coming out of Seattle's municipal docks was due north of Duwamish Point three or four miles away. There was also an ancient looking coal burning tug, black hulled with red topsides and with a long black exhaust oozing into the drizzle, heading their direction. If the old tug turned for the Bainbridge Island channel, it might cause some concern. For now, it didn't matter much; too far away. Besides, it was probably bound for Seattle's wharves. Good luck to them. There wasn't much business there, the longshoreman's strike having paralyzed most of the west coast.

He didn't see anything to be concerned about. They were far enough out of the way with thirty feet of water under the keel, nothing was coming toward them, and the anchor had a good bite. Roscoe would have them moving again pretty soon.

He opened the wheelhouse's rain smeared side window and checked the water to his west. The approaches to Bainbridge were empty save for a fisherman far over near the rocks. Leaning out the window, he looked at the sky beyond the house's overhead protection. The clouds made a solid wall of dull white above him. The rain, not falling as hard now, was ice cold on the skin of his face. He saw a darker cloud was coming down from the north. More rain was coming with it. Already, the lighthouse's sweeping beam had disappeared from view, lost in the quickly approaching shower.

He'd had better days, but at least it was almost over now and he managed to keep the boat. That was something, after all.

The rain fell harder, and he closed the wheelhouse's window. His fingers touched the bronze builder's plaque screwed to the bulkhead. Watkins Yacht Building, Bainbridge Island, Washington was spelled out in proud letters.

Joshua Tatters, the Kitsap County Sheriff, an old issue in his life, smirked when he locked the entrance gates to the boatyard.

"Justice is a funny thing, ain't it, Watkins? It's a damn sure a funny thing. Guess none of them old fast money acquaintances of yours would help bail out one of their own, what with the changing times and all. Yes sir," he added as the lock snapped shut on the gate, "justice is a damn sure funny thing." His blue suit needed pressing and his vest had the remains of yesterday's lunch stains still on it, but the badge shone brightly where it was pinned to his lapel.

"Are you done?" Harry asked.

"Me? Done? No, I ain't the one that's done." The sheriff rubbed his hands along the bulge of his stomach. "That would be you." His smile was all cheap dentures and bad breath. "You're done."

The metallic snapping sound of the padlock's jaws closing the doors on his grandfather's business was one he would not soon forget. His grandfather's life's work was gone and the man locking the gate had enjoyed doing it. The worthless old bastard couldn't be trusted to find the keys to the county jail cells, but he knew how to do foreclosures. He had done them often enough these past three years and more.

Harry's hand rested on the rail that ran across the front of his wheelhouse from the chart table to the helm. Yes, at least he kept the boat. *Scarab*, launched almost a full year ago now, was the last hull Watkins Yacht Building had built or would ever build. She was a beautiful sight with fifty feet of double planked mahogany hull painted a shining white and a bright red boot stripe around her waterline. Her topside bright work varnished to a golden brown glow and dark blue canvas trim stretching over the open afterdeck made her a delight to look at as she powered across the water.

Her buyer, a Hollywood motion picture producer, put down a hefty deposit on the boat with the rest payable upon delivery to Long Beach, California, but that was before. Before the heart attack sent the Hollywood man to his final curtain call and before lawyers and the damned sheriff came calling.

Harry phoned the producer to arrange the delivery details. The man's widow told him about her late husband's sudden death.

"I'm sorry for your loss," he said. The widow's reply hadn't been good news.

"What boat did you say and how much of a deposit was there?"

It all went downhill fast from there. *Scarab* would indeed be the last hull launched by Watkins Yacht Building. Lawyers, bankers, sheriffs and bad hearts in California saw to that.

"Hollywood," he whispered. The mahogany wheelhouse chair gave a commiserating groan as he took his seat once more. "Never trust a man who dies on you before a deal is done," he said aloud while looking at the bronze plaque.

All his worldly goods were afloat with him now, and if Roscoe didn't figure out what made the engines die so suddenly, he might be forced to signal for a tow. The tug would be close enough in a few more minutes. His arrival in Seattle wouldn't have the exact flair he was hoping for, but it was better than a slow drift to nowhere.

But that wasn't going to happen. Roscoe cussed again. He must be almost done.

"One more time. Hit number one," came up from below.

Harry leaned over, wiggled the lever to the transmission from old habit, eased the throttle slightly forward, and pressed the brass button again. The engine whirred and cranked with all the expected thundering power. Number two started just as smoothly. The white faced displays on the engine gauges quivered with life.

Roscoe, after closing the access hatch to the engines with a loud bang and with coveralls smelling of gasoline, came up from below, grabbed his slicker and immediately went outside to the foredeck.

Harry pushed both transmission levers into the forward position, listened to the change in sound as the engines engaged then pushed his throttles forward another quarter of an inch. *Scarab* eased forward, bouncing through the low waves and no longer floating like a tethered cork.

Roscoe crouched next to the partially slackened anchor chain and released the stopper with a practiced tap on the retaining ring. Stooping over, he worked an arm's length iron bar back and forth slowly winching up almost fifty feet of chain as *Scarab* slid slowly through the water. The anchor chain rattled and ground its way back aboard slipping down a pipe in the deck to coil in its locker below until the anchor itself, dripping seawater and mud, broke the surface.

Harry gave the engines more power. Roscoe braced his feet against the movement of the boat as the bows dipped low once, pushed through a crest of a wave, tilted to one side for a moment, then quickly picked up speed. The rain began to fall harder.

Roscoe wiped his face and spat over the side. They were underway again and maybe Harry wouldn't be too late. Maybe just a little late and that wouldn't be too bad. Anybody could be a little late.

Roscoe, a compact and powerfully built product of the fishing fleets in the area, had the coarse face of a man who spent his life working hard for his living. As he almost always did, he sported a faded black cloth cap over a head of cropped brown hair that had never been more than an inch long. He was getting on in years now and the hair was sprinkled with a generous amount of gray. He scratched absently at the three day stubble growing on his cheeks and looked at Harry standing behind the glass windows of the wheelhouse. He was embarrassed. Embarrassed that his engines failed on a day when they couldn't afford the delay.

It was just one of those things. Something stopped up the fuel line right where it came out of the port tank. If he had known that was all it was, he could have switched the engines over to the starboard tank and they wouldn't have wasted all this time at anchor. It was a simple thing to do, and he was wondering at himself for not having thought of it to begin with. Chalk it up to the unfortunate doings at the boatyard earlier in the day. His thinking was distracted by things that weren't his concern. That must have been what it was. Still, the timing was bad. They were his engines. Maybe not on paper, but everybody on board the *Scarab*, all two of them, knew those power plants were his.

Roscoe made his way towards the wheelhouse as the boat hit a wave with force. Cold spray dampened both him and his spirits. It was turning into a raw day on the Sound.

"Fuel problem, Harry," he said as he came inside. "Just one of those things. Could 'a happened any time." There was no point in mentioning the time he wasted in finding the problem.

"It happens," Harry said. "Go grab a towel and pour yourself something hot." He glanced over his shoulder at the old tug. It was closer now, but still too far away to matter.

"I ain't that wet. My slicker got most of the water."

Spinning *Scarab's* wheel to port, Harry started his run for the eastern shoreline. He planned to tie up at the old sawmill's dock on Lake Union, but that wouldn't work now. They would never clear the Ballard Locks and make the run down Salmon Bay in time. A pier somewhere on Elliott Bay would have to do. With all the trouble with the longshoremen's strike, there wasn't a lot going on at the commercial piers. They should be able to find a spot. He could grab a streetcar to the city from there. "We'll go to the city wharves and see if we can tie up there for the night. I'll need you to stay with the boat this evening if that's okay?"

Roscoe bobbed his head up and down. Asking if he would stay aboard was Harry's way of being polite.

"One of those things, Roscoe. Bad timing for a breakdown."

Two hours was a long time for someone to wait. He hoped Drake had waited. Checking the compass, he steadied *Scarab* on her course and gave the engines all they had; too fast for the visibility caused by the rain, but he had lost a precious amount of time. The water flew in a soaking white spray from the boat's bows as she accelerated past eighteen knots. Down below, racks of plates and cups rattled their protest. One of the stateroom doors shook loose and started banging against the bulkhead as it kept time with the rolling motion of the boat.

Roscoe looked at the spot where they were anchored and listened to the sounds coming from his motors. He could tell more about how his boat was behaving by listening to their sound and watching how quickly they pulled away from a spot on the water.

Scarab was running healthy again.

They were fully out in the Sound now and the swells increased. Roscoe absentmindedly wedged himself more solidly against the side of the house as *Scarab* yawed more noticeably against the running sea. He was wondering about tomorrow. They would be okay, he felt sure. Him and Harry, they had always been okay. The sound of his engines increased to a pulse changing rumble after Harry leaned on the throttles. *Scarab* sounded like she was doing her best to climb out of the ocean's grip as she went thundering away to the southeast. A clogged fuel line. Nothing much at all.

Harry was thinking about tomorrow as well. All of his tomorrows. He had two hundred and sixty-four dollars in a cigar box in the owner's cabin, two pairs of shoes, a few miscellaneous belongings, his foul weather gear, and a stack of lawyer's letters half a foot thick waiting for him below and not much else.

And Roscoe. He had Roscoe.

When he finished with the sheriff earlier that day and walked down his grandfather's dock for the last time, Roscoe was onboard fooling with the mooring lines.

"Roscoe, I can't."

"Tanks are topped off, batteries are charged up, and I pumped the bilges this morning. There're eggs, bacon, coffee beans and red beans aplenty in the galley to see us through the week. I put my kit up for'ard in the crew's berth like before and she's ready to head for Victoria or Portland, whichever. It don't matter to me at all. Either direction."

Harry hadn't said anything more. Roscoe was like him. They were both in the same boat. Literally. *Scarab* was all either one of them had left.

Roscoe turned his back on Harry not wanting to say anything more. He pulled a blue bandanna out of his pocket before wiping at the crystal clear salon windows.

All his worldly goods in one spot, Harry thought as he looked ahead into the rain willing the turn to the pier to come closer with all his might.

"We've been in worse spots before," Roscoe said. "Your old granddaddy had a good run with the business. Why, I remember back during the Great War when I was on the *Grouper*."

Harry's attention went elsewhere as his old friend's memories played out. He'd heard all about the two years Roscoe spent in the North Atlantic and the best damn sub chaser the navy ever built long before he shaved his first whisker, tasted his first burning sip of whiskey, or kissed his first girl.

Whenever Roscoe hit a rough patch, he remembered 1918. As a boy, Harry was sure Roscoe sank every U boat the Germans had ever launched and was awestruck at the sight of the scar on his chest; a permanent souvenir left by some enemy gunner in a faraway battle. The scar was straight over his right lung and, as Roscoe told him many times, "Everyone except my old skipper, Mr. Thornton felt sure it was going to kill me."

But it hadn't.

Roscoe moved on to discussing the coldest winter he had ever seen. Harry wasn't listening and didn't notice. Seattle's waterfront on the eastern shore of Elliott Bay was straight ahead and his tomorrows.

He was very late.

*****

Yoshiro Kanji rubbed his eyebrow with the tip of one finger, closed his eyes to better concentrate on the scratchy, far away voice speaking through the telephone and tried to be patient. When the connection with Japan had finally been made, his first words down the long lines stretching to Hawaii and beyond were a crisp, four word sentence.

"I am in contact."

It was the agreed upon signal. He was in contact. All that was needed now was the anticipated reply from their side of the Pacific. The static filled connection forced him to listen very closely to hear the muffled, half understood words being spoken into his ear.

"Can it be done?" came faintly over the line. The words themselves sounded like they were fighting to be heard over the background noise.

He thought something else was said, but the words were lost in a high pitched electric squeal. Outside, the rain fell harder.

"I said, can it be done?" the faraway voice repeated, cutting him off before he could answer. It did no good to tell the old man on the other end there was a time delay. Such things were beyond his understanding.

Yoshiro Kanji considered his answer carefully. So much was riding on the decision he was about to make. He could still say no, make some excuse and go home, become a farmer or fisherman or some other nameless, faceless nobody, and, and what?

He could not say no. No, was never really an option. He was in contact.

Lieutenant Kanji opened his eyes, closing the inner vision he had of the men in that room speaking to him from so far away. He was standing by one of his hotel room's windows. Across the street, a tall concrete and glass building, almost a twin of the one he was in now, stood silently in the rain. He had been looking at the building for twenty minutes, but hadn't really looked at it at all. His vision and his concentration were focused inwards, towards the barely heard voice so far away. The telephone's tube-shaped earpiece was in his left hand, jammed close against his ear as he tried to separate static from words. Perhaps he should have sent a cable after all? Too late now for second guessing.

He squeezed the black, elongated candlestick shaped body of the phone held between him and the cold glass of the hotel's window, as if his grip could wring the interference out of the connection.

The room was only seven years old; the hotel having been built during the economic boom of the last decade. Its better rooms had private telephone lines installed. Private, meaning he did not have to stand in the first floor lobby shouting his words into a public phone but the line still passed through the hotel's operator. He had to choose his words carefully, even if the language wasn't English. Anyone could be listening.

The operator would be somewhere on the ground floor behind the front desk with her cords and headset ready, he supposed. Perhaps she was listening to their words or perhaps not. It didn't really matter if she listened. It was not her attentions he feared.

The American authorities had no reason to know he was even here, but it would be foolish on his part to assume there was no danger. He had done nothing illegal. Not yet. For now, he was just another guest in the hotel. One who preferred the unusual extravagance of an overseas telephone call to sending cables.

They told him to play the part of a wealthy man, a man with means, and gave him the bank account to live the part. Pretending to be rich with someone else's money had proved to be an easy burden.

It took three hours for the operator to make the connection. Plenty of time to consider the answer to the old man's question, the question that had to be asked, and here it was before him. Can it be done? His life spelled out in four words.

"I believe," he said slowly and doing his best to pitch his words to carry along a few thousand miles of copper wire, "there is every chance for success if we apply ourselves in the proper quarter."

A scratching hiss came through the phone's receiver jammed against his ear. His unblinking eyes looked at the rain striking the windowpane of his room, unseeing and unaware of anything as he waited for the old man's reply. His silent concentration was competing now with a low buzzing whine coming out of the handset. It reminded him of a sewing machine running very fast. He resisted the temptation to say something more. They had his answer.

He thought he could almost make out other faintly heard voices on the other end of the line. Dissention or agreement? He couldn't tell. His breathing stopped as he waited for the reply.

How many were in that room? Not many. His father would be somewhere in the room certainly, and perhaps that colonel, the one who sounded so skeptical of his success. The army wanted results, but the generals were unsure if his mission was a sound one or not? They would not tolerate a mistake and would not contemplate exposure of their involvement.

But they most definitely wanted to know the answers. He wondered if he still had the navy on his side?

A glance at his watch told him it was past eight in the morning their time on the far side of the Pacific. His tomorrow had already begun there.

"Yes," came the reply in his ear, for once as clear and sharp as if the old man were standing next to him. "Proper quarter. That is certainly the correct approach. Tell us when you see the mountain and keep to the path."

The line went dead, and Yoshiro Kanji replaced the earpiece in its cradle. Seven thousand kilometers away and it was virtual instantaneous communication. He was American enough in his thinking to be impressed with their new Trans Pacific telephone service. It was an amazing accomplishment.

When he placed the telephone back on its stand in the short, dim hallway behind him, his reaching arm caused the sleeve of his shirt to ride up slightly. The scar tissue from the burn, the burn that had almost taken his sanity and his life, showed cleanly at his wrist. This would not be another Shanghai, he told himself. Not this time. Proper quarter, he thought. Keep to the path.

Exhaling a long deep breath, he turned stiffly away from the telephone. With slow, deliberate steps he limped to the far wall's row of windows retrieving the cane that was now a permanent part of his life. Reaching out with his arm to touch one of the cool glass panes, he felt the now familiar stiffness of the scar tissue move along the length of his arm. It almost felt normal now. Or if not normal, expected.

Looking through the glass at the rain blurred street eleven stories below, two double lines of cars moved slowly along Fourth Avenue beneath a crisscrossing spider's web of trolley cables and power lines. A beautiful cream white convertible accelerated quickly, then cut in front of a line of crawling automobiles. There was a single open parking space in front of the hotel and the convertible meant to have it. He didn't recognize the make, but it looked like something designed more for a land of permanent sunshine rather than Seattle's dampness.

He liked his cars and this one was made to attract attention, bad weather or not. It was a big, long two-seater; a *cabriolet* a salesman would call it, with a retractable rain soaked brown canvas top. The front was long, very long, and he wondered what kind of power the engine beneath a hood like that would make. The tail end of the automobile came to a sharp point between the large rear fenders accenting the designer's fine lines.

What could they do, those powers far away across the ocean? What could they do if he took the money out of the account and bought a car like the one on the street below and simply disappeared?

Nothing.

Not to him. But if he did that, instead of a wounded hero with the scars to prove he had served the Emperor, he would forever be a miserable thief and a coward to all those voices far away across the Pacific. That he could never do. Those voices so far away knew that already or they would never have sent him here.

The white convertible won its race for the last remaining parking space. A man, the hotel's doorman, stepped into his view from the window holding an umbrella for the convertible's driver. A blonde haired woman in a shiny red coat and wearing a matching hat got out of the car. The red hat and coat stood out sharply against the gray drab pavement far below. The passenger's door opened as well but the angle from his window was too sharp for him to see who was riding next to the driver. A taxi drove by. Water sprayed from its tires and onto the woman's legs. She twisted around in a vaguely familiar movement. It was graceful the way she did it like a dancer's practiced movement for an admiring audience. Pure reflex. The doorman's umbrella held high, showed a quick glimpse of a young woman hurrying in from the chilly wet outside.

He was too far from the street to see clearly but there was no mistake. She was here. Six years and eleven stories in the air and he could tell.

Lucy had arrived.

Yoshiro Kanji leaned his forehead against the cold pane of glass and watched as the umbrella disappeared beneath the hotel's waterlogged awning. His edgy nervousness caused by the overseas call disappeared. He smiled. How exactly did one define proper quarter?

As a young man, his father sent him to be educated in America. He had, in fact, spent more of his life on this side of the ocean than the other. It was because of his years in this country that his English was no longer blemished by even the slightest hint of a foreign accent. In many ways, he was now a person with his feet in two very different worlds. America, like his scars, felt almost normal.

The wearer of the red raincoat was Miss Lucile Jones McAllister of the Kirkland McAllister's. She was also the sister of one Donovan McAllister. He met the brother when he was an undergraduate at Stanford. Lucy, as the sister liked to be called, came along a couple of years later.

He was smiling still as he pulled on his coat, found his gray hat bought that morning from the shop on the corner, and tested the strength of his leg unsupported by the cane. The limp was better now. On some days, he didn't think he needed the stick. On others, he couldn't walk without it. Like his scars, he had grown used to the feel of the ivory handle in his hand.

As always, his first step with the twinge of pain in his hip reminded him of the crash. But that was long ago now and the memory of watching the deck of the *Kaga* race up to meet him, although still vivid, didn't haunt his dreams like it once had. At least not as often. Especially not today with old friends only moments away.

The door to his suite closed softly behind him. Locking the door with the key, he turned for the elevators at the end of the hallway. His cane tapped softly against the carpeted hallway. Pushing the call button mounted on the shiny plate to his right set a bell to ringing somewhere far below. He waited for the cage to climb to his floor while he adjusted the knot in his tie. The elevator ghosted to a stop at his floor and a man of thirty hard years and wearing the hotel's livery opened the brass barred door. He stepped inside.

"Down, please."

The door closed behind him and the attendant pushed the control lever over to one side. The elevator dropped to the level of the lobby. When he walked out of the cage, there was no "good day, sir" or "careful of your step, sir." He was used to that by now and hardly noticed anymore. Common staff, those faceless people who did the demanding, unrewarding work in American society, seldom spoke to Asians.

Lucy McAllister paused at the threshold of the large modern glass and steel doors of the hotel and looked around her for a moment. "We couldn't have met him somewhere else?" she asked her brother.

Donovan McAllister, his dark blue coat with its pair of gold striped epaulets glistening with raindrops, followed his sister through the hotel's door. The heavy wool collar snapped tight as he jerked at the corners making drops of water fly off in every direction. "That dammed fancy car of yours leaks more water in than it keeps out." He ran his hands down the front of his coat undoing the brass buttons and shaking off raindrops as he spoke. "What's wrong with the Bergonian? I thought you liked this place?" Donovan, wearing the blue uniform of a Coast Guard officer, removed his white hat and shook raindrops from the cover. "Besides, this is where he said he was staying."

Lucy dropped the key to her automobile into her purse and snapped the clasp closed with a click. She wasn't pleased with how much water found its way beneath the top of her father's beautiful gift right now either, but she hadn't agreed with anything her brother said since she left kindergarten. "If I could have gone faster, the rain couldn't have gotten in."

"Any faster, and I wouldn't have gotten in. Really Lucy, if you're going to drive a car you shouldn't jump out in front of traffic like that."

"There was plenty of room and I got the spot, didn't I?" Of all places, she thought, how odd that Joe Kanji would choose this particular place for dinner. When she was told they were to meet here, the Bergonian, she almost made some excuse not to attend. She still hadn't decided if she was going to stay long or not. Donny could grab a cab home, one that wouldn't get his precious uniform wet. But she was fond of Joe once and it would be good to see him again even if it was in the one building in all of Seattle where she would have preferred never to set foot in again.

So, she came.

Taking off her raincoat, she handed it to the hatcheck girl for safekeeping. How many times had she done that before, she wondered, given her coat to someone standing behind the counter after coming in from the rain? More times than she could remember. She smoothed a few wrinkles out of her dress, wiped the water off her legs from the taxi with an offered cloth, then turned to face the main entrance to a hotel she remembered so well.

The Bergonian's designers did their best to bring light and sunshine into the lobby of their hotel. The entrance was tall and spacious, with a long line of windows designed to magnify the natural light from the street outside. The floor was a pale gray marble with darker lines of charcoal making random patterns in the stone. Lucy's heels clicked across the floor as she made her entrance.

The girl checking coats was pretty and Donovan leaned over the counter to get a better look at her legs as she hung his sister's coat beside the others in her keeping. Lucy left him to his admirations and went deeper into old memories. Her brother would either be a few seconds or half an hour, depending on how well the young woman's legs appraised.

The Bergonian hadn't changed much since the last time she was here. The same old oversized chandelier still hung from the ceiling. Its crystal petals, lit by several dozen small electric bulbs, glistened and shone brightly in the large room. There were fewer people wandering around inside than she expected. Another sign of the times, she supposed. Her gaze glanced to her left at the hotel's ornate fireplace done up in white marble. That was where it had ended.

She sighed. It was too wet, too cold and too late for thinking about that all over again. Better to think about old friends showing up out of the blue and the good times they had at school.

Past the fireplace and around the corner from the wide front desk was the hallway leading to the entrance to the old pharmacy. Workmen had removed the paneled bookshelves that hid the hallway for more than a decade. That, at least, was different.

"Worst kept secret in town," she said to no one in particular. The unobtrusively located bar was no longer pretending to be a pharmacy anymore, a pharmacy whose doors were never open during drinking hours. It was an honest bar once more, all pretenses to other uses gone since December.

The desk clerk had all the tools of his trade expectantly near at hand. Registration book and fountain pen were to his right. Room keys were in their slots behind him and the little brass bell for tormenting the lesser staff was on his left. The clerk had a good head for faces. He remembered the attractive blonde dressed all in red with navy trimmings from somewhere. He couldn't place the when or the where.

"Good evening, madam," he said. "Welcome to the Hotel Bergonian."

Her eyes glanced at the racks of keys lying in their slots behind the clerk. The brass gleam of a room key could just be seen in its small rectangle of wood. Six eighteen, the fourth room on the right as you stepped out of the elevator. The key turned easier in the lock if you pressed down on the knob. Did hotels ever change their locks, she wondered. She smiled at the fussy little man behind his high desk. "Miss Lucy McAllister and Mr. Donovan McAllister for Mr. Joe Kanji, please."

Lucy McAllister, thought the clerk. Of course. He should have remembered that name. He would have known her instantly if he hadn't been distracted by that unpleasantness with the third floor maid. And what timing. He had only minutes ago discussed the eccentric tendencies of their wealthy Japanese guest with Mrs. Jelps, the hotel's talkative operator, and now in she walks and asks to see the millionaire.

"Lucy McAllister," said a voice behind her.

Lucy turned from her review of hotel keys.

"Joe," she yelled loud enough to cause both the bellboy and the doorman to look her way. "My god, I was going to say you haven't changed at all but not even I could pull that lie off. What happened? You're limping like a stray dog that's been hit by a bus."

Joe smiled. As always, Donovan's sister was never at a loss for words. Time, he saw, had improved on an already attractive woman. The nineteen year old he knew at Stanford had disappeared. The hair was shorter. Probably a change in the current fashion. She wore red well, he thought. It suited her fine complexion and curling blond hair.

"Lucy, you look divine in red. No, it was not a bus and I am much better now. You should have seen me nine months ago."

She held out her hands at arm's reach and Joe took them in his. The curved ivory handle of his cane balanced on his forearm.

"Six years and you still look like the pride of Stanford. Where is Donovan? Is he not with you?"

"Trying to get his trousers pressed."

"He is what?"

Lucy nodded with her chin in her brother's direction.

"Joe Kanji, all the way from Hawaii and in the flesh," Donovan said coming up behind them and tucking a small, folded piece of paper into a breast pocket. Donovan shook Joe's hand and looked at the black walking stick. "You never said you were hurt." He looked older, Donovan thought. Older by more than the six years that passed since he'd last seen him. Injured, too. "It's been too long," he said. "Are you okay?"

"It is good to see you again, Donovan. I was about to explain to Lucy, I lost an argument with an automobile on a bad road outside Honolulu." Joe let go of Donovan's hand and balanced his bad leg with the cane. "It is far better now and the doctors tell me I will be climbing mountains in no time at all."

Joe looked at Donovan's attire. "A uniform? I did not know you were in the navy." His briefing mentioned nothing about Donovan McAllister being military. He wondered if this would require him to alter his approach.

"Coast Guard," Donovan said. "See those two stripes?" Donovan held his arm out before him with the sleeve bent at the elbow. "That's my rank. Lieutenant Junior Grade."

"Donny chases gangsters," Lucy added. "And hatcheck girls," she said with a tap at her brother's coat pocket. The white piece of paper was just showing and Lucy's finger sent it sliding down out of sight. "I swear," she said, turning her attention back to Joe, "I've never seen a man so fond of his gin and so sad to see Prohibition come to an end. He'll never forgive Mr. Roosevelt for taking away all his fun."

She looked intently at Joe Kanji and, like Donovan, saw someone very different from those far off days at university. Lucy pointed to the entrance to the old pharmacy and, waving a hand in the general direction said, "The bar is open. Let's go sit down, Joe. You can buy me a drink and tell us all about your travels. Here, take my arm and lean on me." She winked one eye at Joe. "We'll let the patrons comment on my scandalous behavior."

Joe smiled at the quite lovely Lucy McAllister. It wouldn't do, of course, and Donovan was bound to object if he offered to take his sister's arm. "I can manage, Lucy. Thank you for the offer of an arm to lean on."

"Sure you can manage," she said quickly as she slipped her arm through his. "You look like you about managed to kill yourself."

"Lucy, I think Joe is right about—"

"Clear a path for us, Donny, would you dear? See if you can grab a table near the front."

They walked into the newly reopened and now very public bar with the desk clerk looking on. As soon as they were out of sight, he turned to the bellhop and said, "That's him, Kanji, the millionaire from Japan." His voice had an excited tone to it and was squeaking a notch too high.

"He called overseas. Japan. Can you imagine? He talked for almost twenty-eight minutes. Mrs. Jelps told me the time not two minutes ago. Twenty-eight minutes," he said with a staccato tap of his finger on the counter, one tap for each word.

"That don't make him a millionaire," the bellhop said. "Just means he don't know a thing about working for a living."

"Wait till those boys over at the Olympic find out about that. I'll bet you no one in Seattle has ever called across the Pacific before."

The desk clerk turned to straighten the room keys laid out in their little boxes behind him. "Never would have believed it."

"He didn't impress me much." The bellhop grabbed the evening edition of the paper, skipped the front page headlines and went straight to the sports page. He left the front counter and its clerk for the comfort of the shoeshine chair. He never had cared much for excitable fellows like the desk clerk.

When he was in the public's eye, Donovan McAllister never sat in a chair. He occupied it. He was occupying one now in the bar at the Bergonian with Lucy, Joe, and an audience of unknown strangers. One or two of the patrons stared when his sister walked through the entrance of the old pharmacy arm and arm with an Asian man, but no one said anything. Most of the bar's customers were more interested in savoring the joys of legal drinking after a decade of playing hide and go seek to care much about who walked in with whom.

Donovan found an empty table not far from the pharmacy's entrance and within shouting distance to the mustache wearing bartender busy behind his counter. He didn't recognize the man wearing a derby hat, white shirt, starched white apron and black bowtie. Whoever he was, he had a look in his eyes when he noticed Donovan's uniform. The government might have changed the law of the land, but old animosities took more than Congress to properly heal.

And he recognized Lucy.

His sister and the bartender exchanged a few words together; Lucy speaking across the bar and the derby hat listening to her with both hands resting on the polished wood in front of him. The hat bobbed back and forth in agreement with whatever she was saying.

Donovan didn't like it; the idea of his sister being recognized by bartenders in public houses. There was something unseemly about it. His sister had her ways. First, she walks in arm in arm with a half lame Joe Kanji then she has a conversation with a bartender. It wasn't the sort of public behavior a McAllister woman should be exhibiting.

A woman in a maid's uniform walked by carrying a tub filled with soiled dishes. The tub snagged against her apron and pulled it taught against her breasts as she carried the heavy weight across the room. Donovan's attentions wandered away from his sister's behavior in public as he stared at the pretty young girl's figure. By the time she disappeared through the door to the kitchen, Lucy finished her catching up with the man behind the bar and joined them at their table.

It was during the second round of drinks that Lucy convinced Joe to tell them about his accident. Joe told his story, the one he would tell anyone who asked. A car wreck was an easy explanation if anyone wanted to know. In a way, it was only half a lie. He *was* in the condition he was in because of a wreck.

Donovan only half listened. After his ride through the city earlier with his sister, he didn't want to tempt fate by talking about automobile accidents. He had one arm of his dark blue uniform coat dangled over the back of his chair. The other arm was making expressive gestures in the air as he tried to attract the attention of their waiter. The Bergonian's bar was a fashionable place for the after dark set and their waiter was having a hard time keeping up with his thirst.

"That is really all I remember," explained Joe. "One minute, I was looking out my window at the view. The next, I am waking up in a Honolulu hospital. They said my car was a total wreck and the other driver had not stuck around to wait for help to show up." Joe sipped his bourbon. Donovan wasn't paying much attention, he noticed. Just as well. Lucy had her chin resting on her palm with her elbow sitting on the tablecloth. Iridescent blue eyes paid very close attention to his story. "The other car was blue," he added. He liked the color blue.

"You were lucky." Lucy glanced at her brother whose attentions had wandered far from their table. "Wasn't he lucky, Donny? He could have been killed." Donovan had drunk too much, too early again, but she knew better than to remark on it. It would just cause unnecessary friction between them and the evening was going well so far. That was a good phrase to describe her and her brother's usual activities together. It hadn't always been that way between them and maybe her long stay away from home mended whatever caused so much friction before. She hoped so, anyway.

"I tell you," her brother said with a whirl of his arm. "It's a lot of damn stupidity. It's those fellows down in San Francisco I blame. If you're not satisfied with what life's given you, then do something different. There's no call to go and start a longshoreman's strike from San Diego to as far north as you can go. It's hard times out there and they are hurting the common people more than they know."

Lucy looked around the room and its total lack of anybody her brother was likely to classify as common. Joe seemed to be enjoying the evening well enough, she noticed. He was sitting very straight in his chair with his cane between his knees and his hands resting on the ivory handle. She stood quickly and reached for her bag.

"You boys carry on with your civics discussions. I'm going to go powder my nose." She would like to have heard more about Joe's adventures abroad, but Donny was determined to hold court. He would start lecturing his captive audience on all that was wrong in today's world at any minute. She'd heard it all before.

Joe rose stiffly from his chair as Lucy stood to make her departure from their table. Donovan kept his seat, not thinking a sister qualified for excessive displays of manners. A small crowd of locals and hotel guests made a maze of immobile figures as she weaved her way between them. More than a few of the bar's patrons followed the tightly fitting red dress' departure with their full attention.

"Lucy looks marvelously well in that dress," Joe said. Like most of the single men in the room, he didn't look away until she disappeared in the direction of the lobby.

"Hmmm, I suppose she does, yes." Donovan finally caught the eye of their waiter. A medium height awkward looking young man with slicked down black hair and a long white apron, a match to the one worn by the bartender, approached their table. "Another round," he said, as he tried to get a better look at a woman just beyond his field of view. "Gin Ricky for me. Bourbon on the rocks for my friend."

The woman got a few steps closer to their table. She was tall and slim with a black and white checkered hat on her head. Donovan could see the hat, but the waiter blocked the rest of her from his sight. He leaned over in his chair to get a better view as the waiter picked up their empty glasses.

"I'm glad she came out tonight," he continued to Joe while canted over in his chair. The legs looked promising. "She's been in New York, you know?"

The waiter vanished into the crowd and the young woman moved past their table. The hat turned sideways and, lifting both arms in front of her, fended off one of the bar's friendlier patrons as she tried to make her way deeper into the interior of the pharmacy. Donovan, smiling as she squeezed by their table, noticed there was no ring on her finger. The checkered hat's brim almost touched her shoulder, casting an attractive shadow about her features.

"No, I did not."

"No you didn't what?" Donovan asked.

"I did not know she was in New York."

"Yeah."

The hat with its pretty shadows, joined another man at a corner table. "Isn't that the stupidest looking hat you've ever seen?"

Joe followed the direction of Donovan's eyes but didn't see any hat particularly more unappealing than any other.

"She was seeing some banker or stockbroker, something financial anyway. I thought I had finally gotten her married off. She's only been back a few weeks. The old man was so happy to see her back home, he bought her a new car. An Auburn. Pure bribery. I told him so, too. Did you see it? It's parked practically in the front door. Giant white convertible?"

"I believe I did. It is a beautiful machine."

"Yeah well, don't let her talk you into going for a ride in it or your other leg will be broken. My sister only knows two speeds: fast and collision."

"Has she hit a lot of other automobiles?"

"Well, no, not yet. The old man should have bought her something a little less powerful, that's all."

Their waiter returned with fresh glasses. Donovan toyed with a slice of lime floating in his drink. "Hell, she could have done perfectly well with my old Buick." A large swallow of gin disappeared down his throat.

"I see," Joe said, not asking whether the beautiful white car would then have had a different McAllister maneuvering it through Seattle's traffic. "She has grown up remarkably well."

Donovan grunted.

*****

The rain stopped falling but a north wind set in behind it making it feel much colder than what the thermometer's mercury showed it to be. It was that in between weather. The kind that was difficult to dress for. Too warm to bother with an overcoat but too cold to be without one. Harry made do with just his jacket and a hat. He didn't expect to be outside long and his appointment wasn't very far from where they tied up. Harry jumped for the pier almost before the engines died and headed straight for the streetcar stop on Front Street.

The day having surrendered to the night, a long row of streetlights lit the way before him as he walked quickly up Fourth. His hat was pulled down low and tight and the collar of his coat was turned up against the chilly wind that kept finding its way beneath his shirt. The overcoat might have been a good idea after all.

The doorman at the Bergonian opened the same steel and glass door he opened for Lucy McAllister. Harry hurried through the lobby heading straight to the front desk. The clerk raised a hand.

"Mr. Watkins. Good to see you again."

He turned the collar of his jacket down and gave his tie a quick tuck to make sure it was straight. "Hi Jimmy."

"Johnny," the desk clerk said.

The bellhop standing at the end of the check-in counter snapped a wrinkle out of his paper's crease.

He did a quick survey of the lobby. He didn't see Drake. He didn't really expect to. Not here. "Has a man named Drake left any messages for me?"

Johnny turned his back on Harry to examine the rack of room keys behind him in their little wooden cupboards. "I believe that gentleman checked out earlier. No messages. Mr. Watkins," he continued, turning back to face Harry, "about your bill."

But Harry Watkins had gone, walking quickly past the same marble fireplace that had briefly held Lucy McAllister's attention. He never gave it a second look.

A workman in coveralls and cloth cap was putting tools away. "No more hidden doors," he told Harry. "You can go straight in now."

"Mysteries revealed," Harry said. He pushed his way past groups of drinkers, businessmen celebrating the end of the week, hotel guests and a good sampling of the city's more affluent members. The old pharmacy was doing a brisk business. He recognized one or two faces in the crowd and shook hands with someone he would swear he had never met before. Whoever he was, he apparently remembered him well enough to call his name as he passed. Harry kept going.

He agreed to meet Drake in the bar at five and it was touching seven now. Quickly scanning the row of business suits all standing in a long line at the bar he didn't see the set of shoulders he was looking for. Elbowing his way up to the long counter itself, he caught the eye of Lou, a pharmacist to anyone who asked a few months ago but now a barkeep once again.

"Hey Lou," he shouted over the voices talking animatedly on either side.

"Well, speak of the devil. How'ya doin' Harry," Lou shouted back loud enough to be heard over the general clamor of a bar filled with a Friday night crowd. Lou wiped a shot glass clean with a towel. He leaned towards Harry with a bartender's ready expression.

"Lou, was there a gent in here earlier? Fat guy. Back east accent asking for me?"

"Sure was. He was standing right over there." Lou pointed with a dimpled chin towards the other end of the bar. "Whiskey and water, no ice. Asked me himself if I had seen you this evening. I think he's gone now." Lou sat his clean shot glass next to a dozen gleaming copies and reached for a beer mug. "Where you been, Harry? You haven't been in here in weeks."

Harry took his hat off and ran his fingers through straight, dark hair and studied the varnished wood grain of the bar. Too late, he thought. He was just too late. Settling his hat back on his head, he pulled the brim down low over his eyes and leaned his body against the bar.

"Want your usual?" Lou asked.

Harry nodded. "Make it a double. It's been a double kind of day."

"Coming right up." Lou turned to the stacks of bottles behind him and pulled one out from the back row.

"Well, if it ain't Al Capone himself," said a loud and sarcastic voice from somewhere behind him.

Harry's eyes focused on the long mirror lining the back wall of the bar. The angle was just right for him to see the table directly behind him and the face that matched the voice he just heard. He saw a blue uniform coat and a smaller man in a gray fedora. The fedora had its back towards him. If he hadn't been searching the row of men standing at the bar when he was elbowing his way towards Lou, he would have seen him sitting at the table. He turned around and leaned his elbows on the bar behind him. "It isn't a real good time right now, Donovan."

Donovan, both arms hooked over the back of his chair, had the posture of the freshly crucified. His expression had all the disdain he could muster. "Hey Harry," he said with an upward tilt of his head, "how's the boat business coming along? I hear not so well or I hear things worked out fine, depending on your point of view." Donovan took a long swallow from his glass.

Harry's elbows slid off the bar. His whole body tensed. What was Donovan McAllister doing in the Bergonian? And wearing his uniform, too. Times really had changed. He leaned forward when a hand reached across the bar and grabbed his sleeve.

"Harry," the bartender said as he leaned towards him. "We don't want trouble. The place just opened up all legit and everything."

Harry tried pulling his arm out of Lou's grasp. The grip tightened.

Lou said in a loud whisper, "The owners won't like it, and you know who they are. Here, here's your whiskey. Let it go. This one's on me."

Harry took the glass from Lou then took a long drink. He felt the warm burn go down his throat. McAllister was supposed to be in Port Angeles. Not Seattle and for damn sure not the Bergonian.

Lou let go of Harry's arm but stayed close by on his side of the bar just the same. It wouldn't be the first time he'd seen Harry Watkins take a hard swing at the mouth sitting at the table. Where the hell was Roscoe Harrison? Roscoe wasn't likely to let Harry bust up the place. He hadn't seen him come in with him and, come to think of it, it was the first time he'd seen Harry in his bar in years without that old tree trunk shadowing his every move.

Joe Kanji, feeling he might perhaps be behaving rudely to someone Donovan was speaking to at the bar, took this moment to stand and introduce himself.

"I don't believe I have had the pleasure? Yoshiro Kanji, Nippon Heavy Industries." Joe looked into the shrouded eyes of the newcomer and wondered if he had missed something in the short conversation.

Harry, momentarily taken off guard by the oriental man suddenly standing up in the middle of his argument, woodenly shook the offered hand. "Harry Watkins," he muttered. "Watkins Yacht

Building."

"I see you and Donovan have met. We were about to have dinner. I can highly recommend the halibut. Would you care to join us?" As he said this, Joe twisted around slightly to offer an open seat at the table, then said, "Oh, Lucy, you are back. We seem to have run into an old acquaintance of Donovan's. Mr. Watkins, I believe?"

The room seemed to be shrinking ever so slightly for Harry. The oriental was saying something about fishing and the guy standing next to him at the bar was laughing loudly at the punch line of his neighbor's joke. He could feel Lou standing behind him like he was about to grab him in a choke hold any second, and now his eyes were seeing someone he never thought he would see again.

Lucy walked slowly through a crowd of people and came straight towards him. She was wearing a dark red dress with a single row of small blue buttons coming down from the collar. It suited her figure well and showed off all the right curves. She always looked good in red, he remembered. A soft brimmed hat the same color as the dress and with a dark blue ribbon around it was tilted slightly to one side accenting all those yellow curls coming out from beneath it. That look was on her face, the one he could never quite figure out. Like she was trying to decide if she wanted to scratch your eyes out or scratch your back in the morning. She had a poise about her that made men like him watch. He remembered it very well. Just like he remembered those sapphire blue eyes that were looking at him through long eyelashes. Donovan said something. Harry didn't notice.

"So, shall we make it a foursome?" Joe said, looking back and forth from Harry to Lucy to Donovan. Neither the man at the bar nor Donovan answered him. Joe sensed a change in atmosphere. He wasn't sure where to go with the conversation when Donovan began speaking.

"Hell, Joe," Donovan said. "I doubt a bankrupted," he began, then stopped. His sister's red dress made its way through the crowd, a crowd that parted before her like the Red Sea before Moses. "Wonderful," he grumbled as he reached for his drink.

Lucy walked past their table and moved to a spot at the bar inches away from where Harry was standing. She leaned in and said past his shoulder to the still apprehensive bartender, "Lou, I'm empty.

Fix me another, would you?"

Lou looked at the back of Harry's head and wondered if he shouldn't just grab him now before the trouble really got started. "Sure, Miss McAllister, coming right up."

No one spoke. In the corner of the bar, someone sat down at the piano and started tapping a few of the keys. Light applause came from a few of the patrons. The musician ran his fingers up and down a jazzy rift. The rest of the band members joined him on the bandstand.

She was so close Harry could smell her perfumed scent even over the cigar of his noisily laughing next door neighbor. The rest of the alcohol went down in one swallow and he made that reflexive face men do when they drink a hard shot of whiskey. The back of his hand made a self-conscious swipe across his mouth as the burn ate its way down his insides.

Lucy reached for her glass as Lou finished his mix almost but not quite touching Harry as she stretched her arm past his.

The band started warming up.

She tasted her drink. Two red tipped fingernails held the swizzle stick out of the way. Her lipstick left a blushing kiss on the edge of her glass as she sat the cocktail onto the polished surface of the bar.

"Hello Harry," came softly to his ears. "Long time."

CHAPTER 2

It was the scramble alarm. The wailing siren screamed and screamed. He had to run to keep up with the other pilots in the squadron. The siren was ordering them to their planes, but something was wrong. The A2N's controls were right in front of him only something was wrong with them. What was wrong? He couldn't remember. Something happened, something bad, and the controls weren't working. The biplane rolled. He couldn't make it stop as the spinning earth raced to embrace him with bone shattering force. The face was there again, the face that always held the fire extinguisher. Why wouldn't he come closer? Couldn't he see he was on fire?

Joe, lying face down in his hotel room bed, jerked awake. He opened one bleary eye and tried to focus his vision on the sound that awakened him. The squadron's scramble alarm clanged away on the bedside table. Reaching out with a burn scarred arm, he made an ineffectual attempt at silencing the clock and missed. Resting his hand on the edge of the table, he gathered his willpower to make a second try. The alarm kept ringing; each note a small torture to endure. His hand grabbed the clock by its little brass bells and squeezed. The windup machine strangled, twitched and finally went silent. Blinking his eyes for a moment to try and clear last night's cobwebs, he rolled over and sat up in the bed.

"I'll never drink again, I swear," he said as his pounding head reminded him that alcohol came with a price other than monetary. A glance at the hotel's freshly murdered clock told him it really was eight in the morning. He had some fuzzy recollection of setting the clock late last night before passing out in his bed. Last night, he drank far too much. Of that, he was certain, and the pounding force of his headache wasn't going to let him forget it too soon.

Donovan developed a strong thirst after last night's dinner and insisted his old friend, or victim, Joe thought now, help him enjoy the delights of the Bergonian's new, completely legal nightclub. As he swung one good and one not so good leg over the edge of his bed, reached for his cane and limped his way towards the bathroom, he smiled; smiled despite the pounding ache inside his skull. He'd been asked to the McAllister family home tonight for a party. Some social get together arranged by Donovan's father in honor of Lucy's return. The aching head was worth it.

Pulling the chain on the toilet's tank and wishing for a tall glass of bicarbonate, he still wasn't sure what to make of Lucy's mood change last night. She was almost somber for most of the evening but became the virtual life of the party after the misstep with that boat fellow.

Joe opened the tap for the bathtub. Water swished onto the white porcelain and, despite the increased pounding in his head telling him movement was undesirable, he reached far enough down to stick the rubber stopper in the drain.

Last night, he was unsure of whether to ask the man to join them for dinner or not. Lucy said something while they were standing at the bar and, whatever it was, the stranger didn't seem to take it well. The tall man slammed his empty glass down on their table, then followed it with an unfriendly glare at Donovan.

"I don't fish," he yelled at Joe before turning for the exit and leaving without a backwards glance.

What did he mean about not fishing? He still didn't know what to make of that.

Lucy watched the stranger's sudden departure for a moment, but just for a moment before coming back to her chair, twirling a swizzle stick in her glass. Joe thought she had a pleased look in her eyes.

"See that, Joe," Donovan said, pointing a finger at the receding man's back. "There goes what's known as a family embarrassment."

"He is illegitimate?"

"What? No, not like that. I knew his father well."

Lucy let out a loud and full bodied laugh. "Careful, Donny. You might damage Harry's reputation."

Donovan glared at his sister. "It's not me that wrecked his reputation. Harry Watkins did that all by himself and I disapprove of you whispering to him at the bar. People notice these things."

"Where's that waiter?" she said, looking around the room and ignoring the look Donny gave her. "I've changed my mind, boys. I'm starving and I think I'll stay for dinner." Turning a brilliant smile on Joe, she added, "Did I hear you say something about the halibut?" For the first time all night, she didn't feel haunted by old memories sitting at a table in the Pharmacy. "That is," she added, "if your offer still stands?"

"It would please me greatly, Lucy if—"

"He turned out bad is what I'm saying," Donovan said.

"How do you mean?" Joe asked.

Donovan leaned closer to Joe and continued in a confidential voice. "He's a bootlegger. Or he was." He pounded a clenched fist once against the tabletop, making Joe's whiskey slosh out of its glass. "Roosevelt may have changed the law, but it doesn't change what people like Harry Watkins turned in to." Donovan looked down at the table for a moment. "Good family, too. He went bad."

Lucy leaned towards Joe and said in a conspiratorial whisper, "What did I tell you about Donny and Mr. Roosevelt? He's lost all his F-U-N." She rocked back in her chair and smiled while looking at her brother with practiced indifference. "Now Donny, you're spreading tales to our guest and you know you shouldn't. You and your revenuers never proved a thing about Harry. Not a thing at all and you know it."

"I'm not a revenuer. Bunch of damn glorified tax collectors. I'm an officer in the Coast Guard and I enforce the law where a revenuer wouldn't know how." Donovan looked at Joe sitting across the table, then touched the two gold stripes sewn onto his uniform coat's sleeve. "Coast Guard. I know you don't really understand."

Joe's hand rubbed self-consciously at the scars on his wrist. His face showed no expression whatsoever. Donovan was drunk.

"It's different." Donovan looked at Lucy, then back to Joe. "She doesn't understand what went on out there in the dark, but I almost had that man many a night. Red handed, too," he said, an intoxicated slur in his words. He took a long drink from his glass and stared with an unfocused look in Joe's general direction. "He's a small time gangster. I put the cuffs on better ones than him." Donovan made a jerking motion with his thumb over his shoulder. "Out there."

"In the dark," Lucy finished for him.

"Many a night. Better men than Harry goddamned Watkins. My dear sister thinks it was all fun and games. Cops and robbers playing cowboys and Indians. Gangsters." Donovan half suppressed a belch. "Bastards, all of them."

Joe turned and looked in the direction of the long departed Harry Watkins. "A gangster. Was he carrying a gun, do you think?"

"Oh, he has a gun," Lucy murmured, then immediately burst into laughter. She was beginning to feel the effects of the bartender's trade herself.

"Harry Watkins is just another crook. Like that one over there." Donovan's chin motioned towards a group of men sitting across the room from them. "He's one of Watkins' types, too. Damned revenuers couldn't put him where he belonged."

Joe followed Donovan's eyes to a table against the far wall. The room was too dark for him to see them well. Four men sat in a crowded huddle.

"I'm surprised Watkins didn't go over and join them," Donovan added.

"Those men are gangsters?" Joe asked.

"Criminals. Just fucking criminals. Like Watkins."

"Donny," Lucy said.

"What?"

"Please don't use that kind of language."

"Pardon my French." Donovan took another swallow of his Gin Ricky.

"So, now I have seen an American gangster."

"He's nobody now," Donovan told the bottom of his glass.

They ate their dinner as a four piece jazz band entertained and the patrons came and went. Lucy ordered the halibut as Joe recommended and seemed to find each forkful something worth smiling over. Donovan had a steak and two more Gin Ricky's. Theirs was the last table to leave the hotel's bar. Lucy had to help Donovan to her car. Joe hadn't been in much better shape himself.

"Think you can find your way to Kirkland?" Donovan asked. "You have to catch a ferry."

"Lucy gave me a map," Joe replied. She had drawn it for him on a paper napkin.

"That's good," Donovan mumbled as his sister slammed the car door closed.

"I hope he doesn't get sick in my car," Lucy said. "You are coming tomorrow, aren't you, Joe?"

Oh yes. He was coming. It was why they sent him here.

Joe eased his way painfully into the welcoming caress of the bathroom's steaming tub. It was filled with scorching hot water. The soaking heat always helped his hip afterwards. This morning, he was hoping it would help his pounding head. Sinking chin deep into the near scalding water, he closed his eyes and savored the feeling of the heat against his skin. After his bath and some breakfast, he would take a long walk to work the stiffness out of his bones.

*****

"Stop that damned shaking," Donovan groaned, emphasizing his point with an eyes closed windmill sweep of an arm.

"Get up. It's almost noon and pop says it isn't dignified for a grown man to stay in bed so long."

"Millie, you poke me one more time with that finger, so help me, I'm going to slug you."

The finger immediately poked him in the ribs. "Rise and shine."

Donovan sighed with resignation, knowing his morning's peace had come to an end. He opened his eyes and rolled over in his bed. "Since when do you come into the room of a sleeping man? Suppose I was indisposed?"

"Suppose I hadn't been pounding on the door the last ten minutes? Indisposed. Is that what you call someone who comes stumbling down the hallway in the middle of the night?"

"For Pete's sake, you little monster. Take pity on the dying and go away. I didn't stumble in the hallway. I tripped over someone's shoes." Donovan yawned and groaned before adding, "Yours, no doubt. What time is it?"

"Time to rise and shine. That's what time it is."

Donovan sat up in bed, scratched at the bristles on his cheeks, and looked sleepily at his youngest sister. For a moment, he thought it was a brunette haired version of Lucy standing beside his bed in a long white skirt, white blouse and a sweater draped over her shoulders.

"Is that coffee?" There was a steaming cup sitting in a saucer on his nightstand. He ran his tongue around the back of his teeth, tasted something unpleasant, and reached for the cup. "Millie, you're an angel of mercy." His hand shook, making the cup rattle in its saucer. Hot brown liquid spilled over the side.

Millie, the monstrous angel of mercy, her duty done, stood back from her brother's mess of tangled sheets and said, "It lives again."

"Weren't you going on sixteen yesterday?" Donovan closed his eyes as the pleasure of hot caffeine filled his system.

"That is so quaint," Millie replied with an exaggerated drawl in her voice. "I was sixteen five years ago."

"Four years ago," Donovan said between attempts to drink his way awake and squinting his eyes at the overly bright glow coming through the window.

"Five years ago next month."

"Look at that," he said, ignoring his sister's arithmetic. "The sun has come out." Donovan lifted one hand to shade his eyes from the blistering glare shining in his room. "Would you close those damned curtains? My eyes can't stand the pain."

"It's a beautiful day outside. Hardly a cloud anywhere." Millie put her hands on her hips. "Too bad some of us missed half of it."

Donovan looked at his sister standing in a painful ray of sunlight, noticed her attire, and said, "Isn't it too cold for tennis?" It's damn sure too early, he thought.

"No, it's glorious," Millie said as she yanked the curtains closed over the bedroom window. "Lucy bet me she can beat the socks off me and I'm about to show her my new and improved deadly serve. That woman won't know what hit her. We're playing for high stakes." Millie, sweeping an invisible tennis racket through the air, said in a lower tone, "Tennis is my game, you know?"

"No, I didn't know. What's the purse?"

"If I lose, I do her laundry for a week. If I win, she has to let me drive her car. Poor, poor Lucy. She doesn't know Clarence and I have developed my backhand into a thing of awe." She swept her invisible tennis racket through the air again and smiled with anticipation of the match.

"Clarence?"

Millie paused in mid swing. "Not important."

"Is she up yet?" Donovan sat the cup on the bedside table. He doubted it.

"Lucy? She's been up for hours. She and Papa were having breakfast when I came downstairs. That's when she made her fatal challenge to my tennis game. I can feel that steering wheel in my hands as we speak."

Donovan wouldn't have gotten up to have breakfast with their father for anything, and he didn't want to think about food in any form. "Lucy's got a pretty strong serve. You better be on your game, kid. Have you seen how much laundry she goes through in a week?"

Millie picked up her brother's crumpled trousers from the floor and tossed them onto his bed. "We'll see who is on whose game." With that, she turned and walked out of the room still lit brightly by the late morning sun shining through the room's thin curtains. "You'll have to make your own lunch," she called from the hallway outside his doorway.

"Not hungry." Donovan pulled a blanket around his shoulders and put his feet on the cold floor. "Too damn cold for tennis. I don't care what she says." His wristwatch showed the time to be eleven thirty, late even for him to be crawling out of bed, and he was sure his father would give him his opinion about that. His father gave him his opinion about most things he did. The bedsprings squeaked as he stood, then reached for his wrinkled trousers. When he gave them a hard shake, an envelope fell out of the pocket and landed on the floor. For a moment, he thought about pushing it under his bed with his foot. Instead, he picked it up, folded it in half and shoved it back into his trousers' pocket.

He was trying hard not to think about his immediate future; a future defined by the very official typed words inside that envelope. His six year career was coming to an end that paper said. He wasn't sure how he would tell his father the news. They weren't chasing rumrunners anymore. What was a prison sentence a handful of months ago was legal again. The country didn't need picket boats or the officers and men who manned them to keep the smugglers at bay.

The smugglers weren't the only ones who lost their market. Lieutenant Junior Grade Donovan McAllister, United States Coast Guard, lost his as well. The only thing he knew for certain was a lot of his fellow officers were going to be looking for work. There was a good chance he might be one of the lookers before Millie made it to twenty-one. What would his father think of that?

"Is he awake?" Lucy asked as her sister came bounding down the kitchen stairs.

"Finally at last. Where's Papa?" She wanted to ask for an advance, a very small advance on her salary. She refused to call it an allowance, thinking the term too childish. Their father kept an office in the house and she helped with his paperwork from time to time and occasionally fussed about his desk. Honest work. Nothing at all like an allowance.

"He said he had a tee time after lunch. Oh look, it's the troll from under the bridge. Are we feeling like we look this morning?"

Donovan came down the same set of stairs Millie sailed down seconds before, but he wasn't sailing. Not even close. His tread was heavy, and he held onto the rail as if he might collapse and roll down the flight at any moment. "That goddamned bathtub gin at that fleabag hotel has poisoned me."

"Donny, your language please. Millie is in the room."

"Lucy, you didn't just say that?" said the youngest sibling in the house. "When did I become twelve again?"

Donovan wearing last night's undershirt and the wrinkled uniform pants fresh from the bedroom floor skulked his way to the stove, reached for the percolator and refilled his empty cup before sagging slowly down onto a kitchen chair.

"Did I hear you say the old man is playing golf?" He was glad his father wasn't home. His spirits weren't up to a moral discussion this morning.

"You just missed him," Lucy said.

"Where's Bertie?"

"Aunt Bertie is off today. It's Saturday. I think she's coming in this evening." Millie glanced at Lucy for confirmation.

"Bertie said she would be in later for Papa's party. I think she's cooking something," Lucy said as she looked around her at the mysteries of a kitchen and all that went on there.

Bertie had been with them since Lucy was a child and although she tried to make her understand the joys of eggs and flour, it had never taken root with her. Only Millie still referred to her as Aunt Bertie when she wasn't present. Neither Lucy nor Donovan would dare call her anything but Aunt Bertie to her face even though there was no family relationship.

Millie sat across her brother's lap putting both hands on his shoulders. "Donny, Papa said I could go to the movies tonight with Julie and Elizabeth if I wanted."

Donovan tried a cautious sip from the hot liquid. "You'll miss Lucy's party."

"I really don't want to miss it but…"

"She's got boy troubles," Lucy said.

Millie gave her sister a look that said be quiet without any words. "Papa's invited the Chandlers, all the Chandlers, and I can't be here this evening."

Donovan glanced at Lucy. "Who's the gentleman to be avoided?"

"Clarence."

"Not Deadly Serve Clarence?" Donovan asked Millie.

Millie smiled sweetly, as if she was trying to explain issues far too complex for someone at her brother's level to understand. "It's a situation."

Lucy snorted.

"What's the movie?" Donovan asked, thinking he really didn't want to know any more about his sister's situations.

"Clark Gable."

"That's an actor, not a movie."

"Says you," replied Millie. She patted the front of his shirt. "I'm a little short this week."

"So I can play both benefactor and rescuer from situations all at once." Donovan fished around inside his pocket. "Here, buy the girls some popcorn while you're there," he said, handing her two crumpled green bills.

Millie, kissing her brother's cheek and springing up from his lap, bills in hand said, "I knew you would understand." Turning to Lucy, she added, "Ready to lose that bet?" She didn't wait for an answer before turning and walking out the backdoor relishing in her Saturday morning's accomplishments.

"Did I really let you drive me home last night in that ghost of Moby Dick? Kanji must have spiked my drink when I was in the head."

Buttoning her sweater, Lucy grabbed a canvas bag with a pair of wood handled rackets sticking out of it and headed towards the door. As she passed the table where her brother was sitting, her hand made a try at smoothing down his light brown hair.

"You're an easy mark, Donny. Millie fleeced you with a smile and a cup of coffee." She closed the door behind her.

Donovan listened to his sisters laughing about something as they walked towards the garage. The sun was shining through the square windowpanes and Bertie's lace curtains. The bright light only hurt his eyes a little now. His morning afters never lasted very long. Sitting in the peaceful quiet of his family's kitchen, he tasted the bitter heat of his coffee. Outside, Lucy's automobile growled to life.

"You haven't seen her serve yet," Donovan said to the empty kitchen.

*****

Joe Kanji felt much better. The pounding in his head receded a little more with each step he made along the seldom level contours of Seattle's roadways. His walk took him up Westlake Avenue almost as far as the southern tip of Lake Union. The morning was still a day for a warm coat, but at least the clouds had disappeared from the sky. Mt. Rainier sleeping under its white blanket of snow stood guard on the skyline in volcanic glory.

If this were summer, Joe told himself, he would try his legs on some of the mountain's lower slopes. By summer, surely he would be strong enough for the attempt. By summer, he thought. No, he would be long gone before summer ever made it this far north.

It was a perfect morning for a long walk. A month ago, he would never have been able to walk half as far as he had today. Six months ago, he feared he would never walk again. A year ago, he was barely alive. Now, today, he could look at a snowy mountain and think about walking along its forested trails. Progress came to those who earned it.

Tomorrow, he would try for the lake's shoreline. He had mountains in his future and did not plan to lean upon a cane for the rest of his days.

By the time he made it back to the front door of the hotel, his steps were slower and his left foot occasionally dragged along the sidewalk. The elevator ride to the eleventh floor passed in silence. When he walked into the hallway, he was careful to move as normally as any other man until he heard the cage door close behind him.

His suite of rooms was half the size of his parent's home in Osaka. The hotel's decorator did them in art deco color contrasts and stamped chrome accents. An oversized radio in a polished, chest high black cabinet stood against one wall. Twin sofas, bold splashes of green and maroon and each long enough for four people to sit comfortably, made parallel lines in the center of the room. Between the sofas, a low, knee high table burnished obsidian black was almost as long as he was tall. He liked the table. It reminded him of home.

The radio was turned down low. Duke Ellington's *Mood Indigo* was just finishing as he entered the room. He liked American music. American music and American machinery. That made him think of Lucy in her red dress. She was an altogether different kind of American machine. Ellington's song over, a new voice cut in full of deep tones and crisp syllables.

"And now, a word from our sponsors."

He switched off the radio and, leaning hard on his cane, tapped his way across the room to the windows, the same windows from which he had gazed upon Japan with the help of one very long copper wire. The front desk told him his room offered a view of the mountains. Until today, all he had seen were gray clouds and concrete. But not today. Today, the view from his window looked like something an artist painted. There were dark mountains to the west splashed with snow and a large bay filled with ships anchored in ice blue water. It reminded him of a postcard. All it needed was a stamp.

If the Americans put him in prison, would he be able to see the same mountains from his cell? Doubtful. Did American prisons even have windows?

The view made him melancholy. Too pretty. Things would be easier if he was looking at a rubbish filled back alley or a factory's smokestacks. He tapped his way back to the low table and decided not to think about prisons. The papers and documents intended to draw the eyes of overly curious maids were still strewn across its surface.

There was a soft knock on his room's door. When he opened it, the boy entered with a tray holding a kettle of hot water and a cup and saucer. Joe tipped the boy, then closed the door. Sitting on one of the long sofas, he measured a spoonful of his own personal supply of tea leaves into the cup. American tea was definitely one of the things he did not like about this country.

The scattered papers were from a leather valise sitting on the floor. The valise's top opened like some great fish about to devour unsuspecting prey, or the hinges of a trap ready to crush the bones of the unwary. Either metaphor pretty much described what he was doing now.

The valise's contents, neatly organized stacks of documents, correspondence, business invoices, inventories, bank statements with the current rates of exchange and various manufacturing requirements were old news to him. Reading through them again made him feel like a nervous actor trying to memorize the lines to a play. Act One was over. Act Two was about to begin.

About half the papers were written in Japanese script, gibberish to the casual observer, but many of the assorted pages were in English. There were detailed instructions concerning his authority to negotiate on the behalf of Nippon Heavy Industries, what expenditures he was authorized to spend, bank account numbers and lists of contacts known in the area.

He poured hot water into the cup.

Most of it was all show for nosy customs officials, curious eyes of anyone involved in law enforcement or the even more curious eyes of hotel staff. The bank statement was real as were the totals listed on the bottom line. It was a sizeable amount of money, far more than he would ever earn, and it was his to do with as he saw fit.

Sipping his tea, Joe skimmed through the papers in front of him. His was not a criminal activity, not in his eyes, but if he were found out, if the truth of why he was here was discovered, he was sure the Americans would not agree with his definition of legalities.

Jail. Handcuffs. Trials. All were possibilities and all equally upset his peace of mind. He would rather be shot than arrested, interrogated and locked away in some forgotten hole where mountain views were things of fantasy.

Last night, he found out his primary contact, Donovan McAllister, was one of those Americans who put criminals in prison. Nothing in his preparatory intelligence reports mentioned anything about that. He hadn't even been told his primary contact wore the American Coast Guard's uniform.

Donovan could wear his uniform. Joe Kanji could not.

If Donovan was to be his enemy, he would rather they both know it and face each other like honorable men, both prearmed with the knowledge. Did that make what he was doing easier or harder? He didn't know.

His father told him he was the perfect man for this and was his chief sponsor with the General Staff. He spoke faultless English, knew the American mind, had shown valor and courage over the skies of Shanghai and bore the marks to prove it. Perhaps most importantly of all, he knew the son of the man who would know all the answers. His father said many things to make this mission a reality.

Few in America paid attention when a Boeing built biplane jumped a flight of three A2N aircraft in the skies over Shanghai. Two years had gone by and no one on this side of the Pacific even noticed.

The Empire noticed, and specifically, Joe's father noticed. So had Nakajima. It was their bird that was shot out of the sky.

The Army was itching for an all out assault into Northern China. Their sources in Washington said the new American president favored the Nanking government. There were rumors the latest fighter plane to be bought by the American's Army Air Corps might find its way to the Nationalist. The airplane, a very advanced all metal monoplane designated the P-26, was already operational and in service with the Americans. He saw it with his own eyes flying at Hickam Field. It was unquestionably a major advance over the fighter that caused such an upset in Shanghai.

Was it superior even to Japan's newest, the A4N? Nakajima didn't know. No one did.

Joe sipped his tea.

American machines. The A4N was supposed to be his country's best and already they were concerned it might not measure up to what America had in the sky. There were rumors of engine problems with his country's newest fighter. The Americans in the Philippines would have a window of opportunity against his homeland. That window could just as easily be opened for China despite the American government's talk of neutrality. When the Army decided the time was right to cross the borders into China, how long would American neutrality stand?

Joe didn't think it would last long. Neither did his father. A battle was coming. He was sure of it and although he felt no animosity towards this country, it was coming and Lieutenant Yoshiro Kanji was already on mission. The arrow's tip.

He looked at his left shoelace. It had become untied during his walk and he had left it that way until he could find a place to sit before trying to retie it. The arrow's tip still struggled to keep his shoelaces tied on long walks in the sunshine.

He was as informed as the Imperial Japanese Naval Air Service could make him and had the funds available to back up his mission. War planning wanted to know everything about the new airframe coming out of the production facility outside Seattle. Lieutenant Yoshiro "Joe" Kanji, a member of the elite *Kokutai* and lately released due to injury from his fighter squadron aboard the Navy of the Greater Japanese Empire's fleet aircraft carrier *Kaga Province* was on a different kind of mission. One, his father said, only he could do.

So, they sent him to America; to this cold, rainy city in the far corner of their country to find answers to Nakajima's questions. He had his orders. His duty was clear, and he knew the risks involved.

Thumbing through the papers lying on the low table one last time, he gathered the pile into a stack and pushed them into a corner. The small twenty-five caliber automatic was a hard lump in his hip pocket. If the Americans came for him, he wouldn't hesitate. Better a corpse than a convict.

And then there was Lucy McAllister. The fascinating Lucy

McAllister; the teenager he used to look at in fast glances when no one was watching. He always found her so incredibly different from the women of his country. The teenage girl might be gone, but the difference hadn't gone anywhere. He hadn't told his father or the navy about the attractive blonde sister of Donovan McAllister. It was a fair trade in information. Or perhaps a fair trade in the withholding of information. They hadn't told him his friend from his days at the American university wore this country's uniform.

Joe poured himself another cup of tea and wished again his window's view was of alleys and smokestacks.

*****

Roscoe scooped up Harry's discard almost before his fingers left it, sticking it in the middle of the fan of cards in his hand. "Gin," he shouted as he laid his cards down on the dinette's table. "Ha, Lady Luck loves me today, yes she does. What're you holding, Harry?"

Harry spread his cards on the *Scarab's* galley table as Roscoe did his sums with the nub of an old pencil. It was the fourth hand in a row lost to the pirate sitting across from him and the game was losing its luster.

The boat was tied up next to an old rickety pier just north of the United Warehouse Company's dock. Harry's grandfather tied boats up here before the turn of the century. The pier wasn't far from where Blanchard came down to the train tracks and, although still a commercial pier, it was seldom used anymore. More than the normal number of ships were anchored just beyond the fingers of piers and wharves that lined the shore of Elliott Bay. The longshoremen walking the picket lines kept them from unloading, which meant Harry, well known to the harbormaster and also well liked, was allowed to tie up there. At least temporarily. He pushed a pile of discarded cards to one side.

"You ain't quitting on me, are ya?" Roscoe consulted the point totals. Harry might be able to find his way from here to Anchorage blindfolded in a blizzard with anything that floated, but he couldn't tell a winning hand of cards to save his soul.

"Time to go to the sawmill, Roscoe. We should have already left." He was wasting time tied up here hoping Drake might wander down to the dock, see the boat, and come calling. He hadn't.

"Are you going to try to find Drake tonight?" Roscoe scooped up his cards from the table and put them back into their worn cardboard pack. There was a small ledge above the galley's table, and he shoved the well-used deck into its usual spot. Ready whenever Harry felt like getting skinned again.

"I guess he gave up on us." Harry left the galley, going aft and up the three steps to *Scarab's* salon.

Roscoe went forward to his quarters to grab his coat. By the time he pulled it on, crossed through the galley and into the salon, Harry had an engine cranked. Opening the port side door, he stepped out into the cooling late afternoon air as the second engine rumbled to life. The sun was already slanting away westwards towards the mountains on the opposite horizon and a chill was sure to set in for the evening.

Last year, Roscoe thought as he looked at the sun still shining gloriously above a thin line of clouds, he was glad the days were so short and the nights long. But that was last year when he and Harry had business in the night.

Stepping off the boat and onto the pier, he noticed the heavy planks were about at the end of their useful life. He certainly wouldn't want to haul freight down them. He stomped his boot on one of the more suspect boards and wondered if it would last until summer. Probably not. Whole pieces had rotted out and fallen away. As he made his way along the rickety boards, he kept one eye on the creaking planks beneath him and the other on the life rail around his boat. If the pier gave in on him, he didn't want to go for a swim in an ice cold bay.

Reaching the end of the pier, he examined the varnished stern of their boat. Both of *Scarab's* exhausts were bubbling out their exhaust from the heat exchangers. He ran the engines for a long time last night, checking and rechecking to make sure everything was right this time. Even though Harry hadn't said so, he blamed himself for the breakdown that made them miss their appointment. He listened for a moment to the sound coming out of the pipes for anything that didn't sound exactly as it should. They sounded perfect; a rumbling, well-tuned, powerful growl. He couldn't say the same for the varnish on the boat's stern. It wasn't the burnished mirror finish he liked to see, and he would have to wax it again. The nine inch blue letters spelling out 'SCARAB' weren't as shiny as they could be, either.

Roscoe was particular about his boat's appearance. Looking around the shabby pier, he thought it was too bad the other folks around here didn't feel the same.

"Let's go," Harry called from the wheelhouse's window.

Roscoe grabbed the line and pulled a little slack towards him, slipped the eye over the cleat and tossed the rope onto the *Scarab's* deck. Jogging down the pier to the next line and still hoping the whole thing didn't collapse and dump him into the bay, he tossed the second line onto the boat's foredeck.

"All clear," Roscoe shouted before jumping aboard his floating home as the wind caught the boat and *Scarab* drifted free from her moorings. In reverse now, the boat backed out and away. Picking up a boathook and standing on her port side, Roscoe watched to make sure they didn't accidentally scrape anything on the way out. Roscoe cleared his throat and spat a well deserved expression of his opinion of the pier into the water as *Scarab* backed farther out.

When they cleared the last of the rickety planks, Harry went ahead on both engines long enough to check her sternway. The chilly north wind pushed them farther off the pier as he backed the starboard engine again with the port still going forward.

Scarab began a slow clockwise rotation turning a one hundred and eighty degree half circle to point her bows away from their overnight berth. Shifting his starboard engine out of reverse and into forward to match its sister, he gave the boat more power and pointed his bow in the general direction of Alaska. With a rumbling vibration causing the galley crockery to shake and rattle and with a trail of churning water behind her, they pulled away from the docks lining Seattle's waterfront and motored past Smith Cove.

Harry looked out the wheelhouse windows at Roscoe standing on the foredeck. He was flemishing the mooring line in a tight, flat spiral just like he'd done a hundred times before. His deckhand looked at the shipping anchored in Elliott Bay. A couple of steamers, a yacht about half the size of theirs, an old tug that needed painting, and the usual scattering of fishing boats were all riding at anchor.

What was he going to do with Roscoe? The business was closed now and even though he couldn't really remember a time when he wasn't around, how long could he keep him here? How long could he even keep the boat? His old friend, probably sensing he was being watched, turned and looked at him standing behind the wheel.

Lifting both arms with a smile on his face, Roscoe said, "Beautiful."

Harry couldn't hear him. His voice didn't carry over the sound of the engines, but it wasn't hard to read his lips.

Yeah, it was beautiful. A beautiful day after an ugly night.

Scarab cleared the harbor itself and ran out into the deeper water of the bay. The boat took on a rolling sway under his feet as he adjusted his course. The compass mounted inside its brass binnacle spun slowly past west and onto northwest. Cold spume from the waves crashed across the bows.

Roscoe made a hurried retreat down the starboard side. Four Mile Rock was a mile ahead on his right and two miles beyond that, the West Point Lighthouse. The starboard side salon hatch opened and closed.

Roscoe, pausing at the forward entrance to the house shouted, "More coffee, Harry? I was thinking of putting a fresh pot on the stove before it got too rough out. The weather's getting cold again."

"Sure, that would hit the spot," Harry said to the unseen Roscoe. "I think you're right about the weather. It's damn sure colder than it was this morning."

A schooner was southbound. He adjusted his course to give them more room in the channel. Harry pushed himself up into his seat and eased off his throttles a half inch. The schooner passed him going the opposite direction.

The helmsman, standing behind his wheel under the weakening sun was buttoning up a blue woolen coat. He would be reaching for a slicker before long, Harry thought. A cold night to stand watch on the deck of a boat. That was for certain.

A year ago last November. That's how long it had been. It was during his third losing hand at gin rummy that he finished counting back the months. November before Thanksgiving. Someone told him she caught a train for New York. He hadn't believed it at first. Hadn't believed Lucy left without a word.

Donovan McAllister.

The only thing they ever fought about was Donovan, but that time, that November, Donovan had it coming.

In the Bergonian's lobby, a fire was burning in the white marble fireplace. He remembered the fire very clearly.

"Are you insane?" Lucy screamed at him. "That was my brother."

Harry looked at the back of his hand. The knuckles were red, but not nearly as red as Donovan's nose. "I don't give a damn who he is. I never have and neither has anyone else. Your brother's a drunk who brags to anybody who'll listen about how dangerous he is."

People in the lobby of the Bergonian were staring at them, but Harry hadn't cared. Lucy, she had never cared who stared at her. What else was said that night was lost in the blur of time. Lucy turned away from him, crying. She never cried when they fought. He reached for her shoulder, about to say he was sorry or say whatever she wanted to hear, but she shrugged him off.

"You can be a real bastard sometimes, Harry Watkins."

Lucy walked out of the hotel, pausing only long enough for the doorman to whistle for a taxi.

He hadn't seen or heard anything from her since. Not until last night. In the Bergonian again and looking just like he remembered. Only the outfit had changed.

Roscoe stomped his way into the wheelhouse with a mug of steaming coffee in each hand. They had done this together for a long time, running up and down these waters, but they both knew those old days were just that now. Old days. The times had changed.

"You've been quiet all day," Roscoe said.

Harry was looking ahead, trying to see the buoy that marked the turn from Shilshole into Salmon Bay. He had done this so many times before, he could probably make the approach to the locks with his eyes closed.

"I saw Lucy last night when I went to the hotel. She was in the Pharmacy."

Roscoe turned away to look out the starboard windows as the lighthouse passed astern of them. "Is that right? There's somebody we haven't heard from in a while." For a moment, he couldn't think of anything else to say. If Harry looked over his shoulder at the starboard side windows, he would have seen the reflected face of Roscoe with a grin from ear to ear. "She got a ring on her finger yet?"

Harry remembered the red nail polish and the swizzle stick in the drink Lou made for her. There was no ring. "I didn't look."

"Well," Roscoe said, still grinning, "that's just about the best thing I've heard all week. Yes sir, that's just prime." He pulled his blue bandanna from his pocket and started polishing little round circles in the glass.

"Will you stop that infernal glass rubbing? I said I saw her. That's all."

"What did she have to say?"

"She said hello. I didn't stick around."

Roscoe, a big believer in fate, understood now why his engines shut down so suddenly. If they hadn't broke down, Harry might have done his business with Drake, left the Pharmacy and never seen Lucy McAllister at all. Fate. "We'll be seeing her again, won't we." It was a statement, not a question. He stopped cleaning the glass and rubbed his rag over the compass dial in front of Harry.

"Not sure I'm staying on the Sound," Harry said. "I might head south for warmer weather. I hear Costa Rica's nice."

"Costa Rica," Roscoe said. "I've been there. Pretty women, palm trees, sand and mosquitoes in the wet season like nothing I've ever seen before. They got yellow fever down there."

Scarab dug her bows into an oncoming swell and spray shot across the deck.

"But there's lots to be said for the senoritas," Roscoe added. "I remember one—"

"She was with her brother."

Roscoe noticed a bit of grease that needed removing from underneath a fingernail. Harry adjusted his course. Both men swayed in time to the movement of the boat's hull beneath them.

"Well," Roscoe said at last, "you can't hold that against her. Nobody gets to pick their relatives. Has he gotten over that little dust up we had yet?"

"Don't think so." Harry leaned over *Scarab*'s wheel and wiped the back of his hand across the windshield smearing condensation across the glass. "You would think from his attitude, it was me who clocked his buddy that night."

"Wasn't my fault. All I did was offer to buy him an illegal beer." Roscoe leaned forward with his rag and wiped at the smear Harry left on the glass. "And I might have mentioned something about revenuers, people who shot guns at me and what part of my anatomy they were free to wrap their lips around. Besides, I'm not the one who hit her brother square on the kisser. You did that all on your own."

Scarab bounced hard into a wave and healed far over. From the galley down below, the sounds of dishes in danger of turning into shards of glass made Roscoe wince.

"That was probably your plate." Roscoe turned for the steps leading below.

"Probably right." Harry adjusted his course slightly to make his boat hit the oncoming swells at a better angle. "Easier to break 'em than wash 'em."

"Did she ask how I was doing?" Roscoe called from below.

"I said I didn't stick around."

Roscoe stayed silent.

"It doesn't mean anything's changed between us," Harry shouted loud enough for anyone on board to hear. "Besides," he said in a much lower voice, "she's the one who left." Harry pushed his throttles forward and *Scarab's* pace picked up considerably. "And those engines don't sound right at all," he added back down the passageway.

"Uh huh," came from below. "Things sound pretty good to me."

Harry could hear Roscoe singing something from the boat's galley. His mechanic had always liked Lucy.

CHAPTER 3

"Straight sets," Lucy said to the woman sitting across from her. "The last time we played, she could barely get the ball over the net." Lucy tasted her Gibson in its tall highball glass. "The little minx. I lost the bet and now I have to let her drive my baby for a day."

"Where is our Millicent?" Mrs. Chandler said as she twisted around in her seat to survey the room's guests. Twisting wasn't something that came easy to a woman of her bulk and she tried to avoid doing it. She hadn't seen the youngest McAllister girl all night even though she was keeping an eye out for her. Still not seeing Millicent amidst the guest, she focused her attentions back to the oldest sister.

Lucy took another sip from her drink, then sat the empty glass on the small table between their chairs, being careful to use Bertie's coaster. For twenty years, Aunt Bertie had been relentless about the evils of little rings left on the polished wood. "I should have known I was being chiseled."

Mrs. Chandler didn't approve of women drinking, especially unattached women. Nor did she care for women engaging in wagering, married or not, and considered giving Lucille a short sample of what she considered proper behavior for young ladies. Mrs. Chandler, a woman who never failed to be the oldest member of any room she was in, scanned the McAllister's parlor to see if any of the other ladies present might share her opinions. There was no one in the room with whom she could commiserate. Even Bertie, a sensible woman, was nowhere to be seen.

It was a large social gathering. The rooms were filled with people, most of whom were strangers to her. At least a dozen of the McAllister guests were lounging or sitting nearby and there were more in other rooms. Too many of the young men in this particular room were openly ogling the form of Lucile McAllister and that dress.

She had never seen a woman exposing so much skin in all her days. Lucile was practically naked. Mrs. Chandler wasn't sure if it was a display of bad manners on the part of the men, or bad taste on the part of Lucile. Drinking, wagering and wearing clothes like that might go over in New York. She knew all about New York, never having been there, but it wouldn't go over in decent society. Mrs. Chandler made a mental note to let Bertie know about Lucille. It wouldn't do, and she was considering taking her into a quieter room and warning her of the spectacle she was making of herself before the party ended. Maybe she should find Bertie and the two of them could explain proper decorum together. And perhaps suggest a shawl for Lucy's bare shoulders. "Clarence was expecting to see Millicent this evening," she said, not wishing to discuss tennis wagers any further. "He will be disappointed if he doesn't get to see her."

Mrs. Chandler reached across the ornate table and gave Lucy's arm a soft pat. Perhaps she did not know about Millicent and her Clarence's near understanding. She smiled knowingly and wondered if now was the best time to explain how things were between the two of them.

"Millie's missing tonight's shindig," Lucy said. "She promised some friends of hers she would meet them for a movie. Said she forgot all about Papa's little get together." It was Lucy's turn to smile knowingly at Mrs. Chandler. "One of those unfortunate situations."

Lucy, catching a quick glimpse of Bertie walking towards the kitchen while carefully balancing a silver tray covered in empty glasses, thought it was a good time to follow her. She stood with a smile and nod to the female member of a bygone era and said,

"Won't you excuse me?"

The shimmering sequins sewn into the bodice of her dress sent tiny darts of light bouncing into all corners of the room. The swaying movement of the dress, acting like a private signal to an attentive audience, caused three young men to clear their throats expectantly. A fourth, standing by a window adjusted the knot in his tie. Another hopeful, standing close to where the two women sat, stopped pretending to appreciate a painting of red and yellow flowers. Its spray of colors were of intense interest to him for the last ten minutes. They all began their initial engagement approach aimed at the curly haired blonde in the heart stopping dress that showed more than it concealed.

"Maybe we can send Clarence along after them? Young ladies would appreciate a chaperone like my Clarence," said the still sitting Mrs. Chandler as she reached out to touch Lucy's arm a second time.

The watching men in the room paused in their advance upon the shining light coming from the dress.

Lucy paid no attention to the men arranged around her but Mrs. Chandler had. Like moths to a flame, she thought and wished she had a flyswatter.

"Where can that grandson of mine be?" Mrs. Chandler leaned as far back in her chair as she could, trying to locate the missing grandson lurking in the hallway. She frowned, deep wrinkles running down each side of her mouth. Too many bodies blocked her view.

"I'm sure you're right, dear." Lucy thought the woman was on the verge of shouting Clarence's name throughout the house. "But I have completely forgotten which theater they were going to."

Joe Kanji found a place to park his rented car not terribly far from the McAllister's front door. He dressed with particular care for this night. He knew perfectly well Donovan McAllister went out on a limb by inviting him to his home. The Seattle social circle wasn't known to be welcoming to Asians. Not to their homes. He also knew he was playing a part. This was the only first entrance he would ever get to make. Tonight had to be perfect.

His tailored suit made from the best English wool cost more than his first automobile. His shoes, stiffly starched shirt with fashionable attached collar and dark gray silk tie were all brand new. Joe drew upon his bank funds to purchase a heavy and very noticeable gold chain for his pocket watch. The chain formed an expensive crescent across the front of his vest. His father would call it unnecessary extravagance. The final touch to his ensemble this night was the most expensive indulgence of all.

The first day he arrived here, he commissioned an article of jewelry from a shop on Pike. He paid for the jeweler's work earlier in the day. It was a perfectly enormous ruby set in white gold. The stone was offset to one side and, shining outward from each side of the stone's surface were sixteen linear rays made from smaller rubies. The rising sun anchored his new tie and competed with the sequins in Lucy's dress for the room's available light.

He felt a little like he was attending a masquerade ball with all his accouterments of wealth. Before leaving for the McAllister's home, he debated with himself whether he had overdone his appearance. But in the end, he decided he couldn't overdo things tonight. Wealth, or the appearance of it, would be the steel in his armor against the house's other guests. He had to look the part.

At his knock, an older gray haired woman in a plain dress and holding a silver tray in one hand answered the front door. She looked fairly shocked to see him standing on the stoop.

"Mr. Donovan McAllister's home?" he asked the woman. "He is expecting me."

The woman stood aside and, after pointing to a coat rack in the hallway where he hung his overcoat and hat, she closed the door behind him without a word and disappeared into the house. He didn't have to go far into the home before he saw her.

"Good evening, Lucy."

Lucy spun, the bouncing reflections of light spinning with her. The reserved face of Joe Kanji in a very nice black suit and vest with thin silver pinstripes came towards her. His cane marked time beside him.

Lucy retrieved her glass from the coaster, wondered briefly if she should introduce Joe to Mrs. Chandler if for no other reason than to see the reaction on the old woman's face, but decided not to. Who knew what she might say to him?

"Uh huh," she said to the older woman, not having any clue what words she might be agreeing to, and left Clarence Chandler's grandmother sitting by the fire. Taking Joe's free arm, she whispered, "Wonderful timing. Rescue me, won't you? That old bitty will be asking me why I'm not wearing stays in another minute. Did you just get here?"

Mrs. Chandler watched the back, or lack of back, of Lucile McAllister's flimsy emerald green dress as she walked away. "Dressed like that," she said to no one within hearing, "and talking to a foreigner, arm and arm, too. That's what comes of girls raised without a mother's influence." Mrs. Chandler wasn't at all sure her Clarence needed to be spending so much time around that Millicent girl after all. Birds of a feather was the old saying.

The ice in Lucy's glass tinkled. "You look very dapper with your cane tonight. Do you keep it to lure unsuspecting women?"

Joe, usually a mask of impassiveness, looked intently at the diamond and gold necklace resting in the bare cleavage between Lucy's breasts. He had never seen so much of her so exposed before. "Are canes the in thing these days? I didn't know." He tried to not lean so heavily upon the ivory handle, hoping it made the walking stick look a little more like a fashion accessory rather than a third leg.

"It makes you look mysterious. Every woman likes a good mystery. Didn't you know?"

"Perhaps I should change my story for needing it? Tell women I was hit by a charging rhino while on safari rather than a charging Chrysler at a stop sign?"

Lucy laughed. "Now you're getting it."

"My dear Lucy, where did you find that dress? Did you wear it just to start a scandal?" Joe pulled his eyes away from Lucy's plunging diamonds and followed along beside her, the cane swinging nonchalantly in one hand.

"Like it? I saw it in a shop window in Manhattan and had to have it. Papa was amazed when he saw me in it."

"I can certainly understand his amazement."

She did a quick twirl as they stood at the entrance to the parlor. The room's lights, caught by the emerald colored sequins sewn along the bodice, danced across Joe's eyes.

A clock in the hallway chimed the hour.

Mrs. Chandler, not caring to look at Lucille McAllister's naked display in front of a house filled with men, instead watched the logs burning in the room's fireplace. She set her teacup delicately back onto its saucer and thought about how she was going to straighten out this kind of behavior with Bertie. The clock in the hallway continued to mark the hour. Ten chimes. Certainly late enough. It was time for her to gather up her grandson and go home.

"What's your poison tonight, Joe? Have you bumped into Donovan yet?" Lucy looked around the room, seeming to notice for the first time that her brother was not present.

A solid brigade of her father's younger coworkers looked back at her.

"He was here a minute ago." She deftly failed to make eye contact with a single male member of any of the room's attendees. "He probably went outside to sneak a cigar or a kiss from that silly nitwit Inga. Heaven help me, and Mrs. Chandler is worried about my morals?"

Lucy swirled the ice in her glass and kept any further moral comments to herself.

"I do not think I am drinking poisons tonight, thank you. I still have not recovered from last night's attack on my liver. Coffee will suit me fine if you have any made." Joe looked around him. The house was filled with guests. Most of the men were watching Lucy with something very close to open desire. The women present were looking at the men staring at Lucy. More than one or two of the room's guest were positively glaring at Joe with something approaching hostility.

"Nonsense," she said, oblivious of anyone's stare. "All first time visitors to my home drink when I drink. C'mon, fellow voyager. Take me to the bar and tell me again about Hawaii."

The brigade of young men, their mutual advance to engage the enemy repulsed before it began, watched and wondered at their loss. A young man with rusty red hair in a tweed jacket elbowed his neighbor. "Helen of Troy couldn't hold a candle to that one."

The neighbor, both hands stuffed deep in his pockets and watching the rhythmic sway of Lucy's hips as she left the room said, "Was that old man McAllister's daughter?" When Lucy was completely out of sight, one hand pulled free from his trousers' pocket and a long, thin finger smoothed the pencil thin lines of his mustache.

"The platinum piece?" answered the tweed jacket. "One of them. There's a brunette around somewhere, a few years younger and not quite as well amplified, if you get my drift. The brunette's a lot friendlier."

"You get invited here a lot?" asked his neighbor. He gave the competition standing next to him a glancing appraisal. He didn't think the McAllister daughter had recognized him.

"Not exactly invited. I drive the old man down to the field now and then and I've taken him to the train station a few times. The blonde's been gone for a long time. East coast, I think? Or Chicago. Her name's Lucy and the other daughter is Millie."

"You don't say," said the neighbor as he walked across the room. "I think I'll go pour myself another scotch."

Joe watched Lucy mixing some gin concoction and felt his stomach twist. She deftly skewered a pair of cocktail onions onto a toothpick then dropped two ice cubes into a glass.

"Men fresh from an African safari don't drink coffee at my party. Bourbon was your downfall last night, wasn't it?"

"Being a big game hunter has its disadvantages," Joe said. "Bourbon will do."

Lucy poured his drink. "Hair of the dog," she said, then clicked her glass against his.

Looking past him, Lucy's face showed pleasant recognition of someone across the room. "Edith. Edith Carmichael. Is that you?"

And just like that, she was gone leaving Joe standing with an untasted drink in his hand. Mingle. That's what they called it. A verb meaning to enjoy the company of others at a social affair. Another man approached the drinks cart and Joe stepped aside.

"Know her well, do you?"

The question sounded more like an interrogation rather than social prattle. Joe examined the ice cube floating in his glass. Hair of the dog, Lucy called it. "We met on the Serengeti."

Taking his bourbon, he decided to explore the McAllister home. A short hallway ended in a formal dining room, its center dominated by a large dark table with seating for twelve.

On the far wall was an oil painting of the McAllister family of more than a decade ago. He moved closer for a better view. A man, the father himself, was seated just right of center wearing a dark suit and tie. His sideburns were gray and his dark hair was parted down the center, cut very short on the sides and slicked close to the scalp. Next to him sat a slightly built blonde woman with keen, intelligent blue eyes; Lucy's mother in a sky blue dress that looked like the ones worn by women before the Great War. The resemblance to Lucy was very prominent, Joe thought, although the physical Lucy was stronger framed than this woman. She was wearing a wide brimmed hat with a spray of feathers. A diamond and gold necklace was around her neck. It looked just like the one he had seen earlier resting so beguilingly between Lucy's breasts. Lucy's mother however, wore the diamonds with a dress that covered her all the way to her throat.

Behind the two seated parents stood a teenaged Donovan with his own hair slicked flat to his head like his father's, but combed to one side instead of the center part. His left hand rested on his father's shoulder while the face in the painting returned Joe's look of appraisal. It was the Donovan McAllister that Joe remembered from Stanford when they were both first semester freshman, or almost. A few years before that time, perhaps? Donovan had aged a lot since he sat for the painting.

Next to Donovan and behind the mother stood his sister, Lucy; the battles of adolescence not yet begun. Her nose and cheeks were dusted with a touch of tiny freckles. The lace collar on her blue dress did not suit her, he thought. He couldn't imagine the grown version of Lucy wearing lace unless it was the kind a gentleman seldom saw.

Lastly, seated on her mother's lap was a little girl in chestnut pigtails wearing a blue dress to match her sister's. Her hands held a dark, furry bear wearing a sailor's uniform.

The other daughter, Millie, thought Joe.

"Those were the days," Donovan said, coming up beside him and looking at the picture. He offered Joe his hand.

"Hello, Donovan," Joe said as the men shook hands. "I was admiring your family's home. It is a compliment to your father's success. Your mother was lovely."

"She was, wasn't she? We lost her to the Spanish Flu in '18 right after she sat for this." Donovan looked fondly at his parents captured forever in colored oils. "She never got to see the finished work. Everybody says Lucy is the spitting image. Millie took after the old man, like me." He turned to say something to a passing guest in the hall then, looking at Joe, "I see you found the booze. Seen Lucy yet?"

"She was just here. I believe she is catching up with an old friend. Is your father enjoying the party?" Joe asked delicately.

"The old man? Don't make me laugh. He's upstairs hiding from the masses."

"Ah," Joe said. "I was hoping to pay my respects. Old Japanese custom."

"C'mon then. I'll introduce you. Wouldn't want to break old customs."

Joe tapped his finger along the handle of his cane. The father.

Donovan stepped into the hallway then paused, waiting for the slower going Joe to catch up. "Can you manage stairs with that rig?"

"It will not be an issue."

Donovan kept going down the hall Joe had just come down earlier. Lucy had disappeared. He followed as Donovan made his way to the center of the home and to a large staircase. His untouched glass of whiskey was left sitting on a hall table.

"The old man likes to throw these parties for the boys out at the field," Donovan said. "Then he sits in his study and waits for everyone to leave."

He walked up the stairs one slow step at a time as Joe climbed beside him refusing to wince even slightly.

"Don't let him spook you if he stares." Donovan thought for a moment before going on. "What I mean is, don't take it personal. I don't think we've ever had a Japanese visitor before."

Joe thought what his own father's reaction would be if he was to bring a gaijin like Donovan into their home in Osaka. He smiled. "I am looking forward to meeting your father, and I am sure he and I will get along famously."

The pair reached the upstairs hallway.

"Down this way," Donovan told him.

*****

Harry Watkins stepped through the double wide doors of the *Full Moon Bar,* felt the bite in the night air, and immediately turned up the collar of his raincoat. It rained while he was inside and he was beginning to wish he picked a different evening for a pedestrian's tour of Seattle's dives. The rest of the population didn't seem to be noticing.

It was a Saturday night and despite the wet, Seattle's theater district was open for business. A sea of umbrellas marched along the sidewalk moving in time with a rhythm controlled by corner traffic signals.

Fifth Avenue from Pike Street north was lined with overhanging signs lit with rows of bright white electric bulbs. The marquees advertised the latest examples of Hollywood magic, like lures designed to draw the eyes of the masses. The city's after dark offerings of entertainment venues were mixed in among daylight businesses now shut tight waiting Monday morning's arrival. Shoe stores, a hardware store, clothing shops, produce and butcher's shops all had no interest in the damp passersby on the boulevard this evening.

The *Full Moon* was the last place on the list for the night. He'd been everywhere he could think of trying to get a line on where Drake might have gone. All the regulars in the old haunts hadn't helped at all. No one had seen him. Not even the liars who would see anybody you wanted for a couple of bucks or a free drink. Harry was beginning to believe that when the fat man told him he was leaving if he didn't hear from him by Friday evening, he meant it.

He could always try the Pharmacy again. It was just bad luck he ran into Donovan sitting in the bar. Donovan never went to the Pharmacy. It had to be because of Lucy, he reasoned. Only Lucy would go back there.

Harry checked his wristwatch. Almost ten and the night was in danger of turning miserable. His gray raincoat glistened with reflected light from the streetlights, marquee signs and headlamps from the passing cars.

Earlier, while not paying attention to where he was walking, he stepped square into the deepest part of a freezing cold puddle of muddy water. His left foot was soaked to the ankle and felt like a block of ice in his socks. Standing on the curb at Fifth and Pike, he watched the approaching automobiles, hoping to see one with the sign on top saying TAXI. Two went by but either didn't see him or already had fares.

A maze of streetcar power lines stretched up and down the

avenue, but the rails were empty. A cold gust of wind whistled past his ears and he pulled his hat down a little tighter. His breath came out in a cloud of cold misery and he thought wistfully of Acapulco and warm, tropical heat. He was a long way from where they had moored their boat. It was at least fifteen or twenty blocks to Lake Union and the sawmill. The thought of having to hoof it on a cold rainy evening with one wet shoe was not exactly how he wanted to end his Saturday.

When the Coliseum Theater let out a crowd, his odds of successfully finding a cab diminished as the growing number of pedestrians filled his corner of the pavement. The rain came down with an attitude and Acapulco got farther away from his reality. Harry pinched his collar closed with his left hand and waved his right into the oncoming headlights. He didn't see any taxis.

"Might as well go to the Pharmacy," he said, half to himself and half to the rain gods. It was on the way to the boat, anyway. Turning his back on the headlights, he headed for Fourth and Olive. He'd look in the lobby and check the bar before grabbing a cab. As he turned for the walk up the hill, he collided with a very plump young woman bundled in cashmere and struggling with an uncooperative umbrella. She had just come out of the theater entrance behind him, propelled out into the rain by the exiting throng before she could get her umbrella up. She didn't look at all happy about the damage being done to her hairdo.

"Pardon, miss. Didn't see you." Holding his collar closed and not at all happy about the weather himself, he started picking his way through the crowds. The Bergonian would at least be dry.

"First you don't show up for my birthday party, then you disappear entirely and now you've ruined poor Julie's stockings," said a woman's voice behind him.

Harry stopped. He turned to look at the young lady speaking from under the shelter of an umbrella. "I don't think your brother would have been too happy if I had showed up, now would he?" he told the pretty young girl.

"It wasn't Donny's birthday party, Harry Watkins, now was it?" Lucy's little sister came closer and held her umbrella above both their heads. Reaching an arm around his back, she pulled him towards her and, standing on her toes, brushed her lips against his cheek. "How have you been, Harry? I forgive you for not coming."

The crowds were still pushing out of the Coliseum, and the pair were being shoved from every direction. Someone ran into Millie's back and before Harry could move, she glued herself against him.

"You're all wet, Harry," she purred privately. "Want me to dry you off?"

"I'm soaked clear through," he said.

"Even better," Millie said with a smile.

"What have you done to your eyebrows?" he asked as he tried without much success to get some space between his torso and hers.

Millie, with a fast glance at the staring plump Julie and her other as yet unnamed friend said, "I've always worn them like this. You like them, don't you?" Her free arm went around his neck as she leaned her upper body away from him. She wanted him to get a better look at her new eyebrows in the glow from the street's electric advertisements, but the rain spoiled the effect. Abandoning her attempt at looking glamorous, she ducked back under the protection of her umbrella. Millie looked around Harry's shoulders at the glowing blue sign behind him. "Buy me a drink? It's freezing out tonight and we can catch up."

Harry laughed, thinking she was making a joke. A cloud crossed Millie's features.

"Your friends are too young to be drinking with strangers met on a rainy night. Besides, the *Moon* is no place for a lady of your age."

"Oh, we're—" the unnamed girl behind Millie began.

"Too young," Harry finished for her. Taking Millie's arm from around his neck, he said, "Good night, ladies. Millie, you are a handful and I'll buy you that drink sometime, I promise. You're looking more and more like," he almost said Lucy, but changed it in the last instant. "Like a ravishing beauty every day. I'd stay and talk but," Harry squinted into the rain, "it isn't a good night for catching up. Another evening." He tipped the soggy brim of his hat to Millie and the two girls. Leaving the shelter of Millie's umbrella, he started back up the hill.

"Looks like you could use a ride," came Millie's voice from behind him.

Harry stopped. With a squinted eye, he examined the night's sky again. It had turned into one miserable evening to be caught outside. Pneumonia weather. If he went to the hotel, the clerk was sure to ask about his bill. Harry thought about the shoebox back on the

Scarab, the total amount of his life savings contained inside the cardboard bank vault, and how much a taxi ride to the lake would cost him. Silvery spikes of rain fell steadily through the glow of streetlights, headlamps and marquis signs. Too much of the ice cold water was finding its way down his back. Millie was still standing where he left her and as dry as a bone beneath her umbrella. Her two cohorts were behind her, each looking over one of her shoulders. The offer was very tempting.

"C'mon Harry. Don't be stubborn. Elizabeth has her dad's Ford."

The face to Millie's left bobbed up and down a few times in an affirmative motion. Millie put one hand beyond her umbrella's protection, as if she was checking the weather outside. The rain bounced on her palm. She looked at him with what she hoped was her best pout.

The pout worked.

"Sure it won't put you out? You haven't even asked where I'm going."

"No trouble at all," Millie said, half twisting around to glance at Elizabeth and giving Harry a view of her profile outlined by automobile headlamps. She was fond of her profile. "We can at least get you to the Bainbridge ferry. Beats walking. I'll even share my umbrella."

"I'm not going to Bainbridge. I've got a boat on Lake Union."

"Even better," Millie said. "We have to go that direction, anyway."

"Alright, ladies," he said as he ducked his head under the offered umbrella. "Where's your car, Elizabeth?"

Millie put her arm through his. "It's not far."

The four of them, Harry and Millie leading the way and the other two girls behind, walked the two blocks to where a dark green Tudor was parked at the curb on Seventh. Along the way, Millie introduced Harry to Julie with the ruined stockings and Elizabeth, the holder of the car keys. Harry opened the passenger door and stood aside for Millie and Julie to crawl into the back. Millie, supple as a house cat, slid past him and into the back. The not so supple Julie balked at the narrow opening between the door post and the seat. Embarrassment loomed.

"C'mon Harry." Millie patted the fabric of the seat beside her.

"I won't bite."

If he gave Julie a shove, he was sure she would fit nicely in the backseat. Ice water falling out of the sky ran freezing fingertips down his spine as he ducked into the shelter of the automobile's backseat. Millie didn't scoot over very far, and he had to sling his left arm along the back of the seat. "Got enough room?"

"I'm just fine." Millie put her folded umbrella on the far side of the seat. This was so much better than fending off the clumsy attempts at romance from Clarence Chandler, she thought to herself.

Elizabeth closed her door behind her, turned the key, pulled the choke and stepped on the starter. "Everybody comfy?"

"My, it sure turned nippy out tonight," Julie said from the front seat. She wiped at the inside of the windshield with a gloved hand as the car's power plant came to life.

"Very nippy," Millie whispered into Harry's ear.

The Ford lurched forward with a jerk as their driver, Elizabeth, steered them out into the street.

"Which way, Mr. Watkins?"

"Head for Eastlake. I'm on the water," he told her.

When they turned onto Olive and drove towards Howell, Harry craned his head past Millie to look in the direction of the Bergonian. He thought he saw a few people standing outside the main entrance, but it was too dark to tell if any of them might have been Drake. Where the hell had he gone to, anyway? As the car made its turn, his eyes turned with it until he was looking through the rear window of the Ford. Millie's face was in the way and suddenly, he was very close to her. In the darkened interior of the car, she didn't look very kidlike at all. Elizabeth shifted gears making the transmission groan. He wasn't sure, but he thought he heard a low groan from Millie as well.

She could feel Harry's arm behind her head as it rested along the top of the seat. His hat shaded his features and she couldn't quite see his eyes, not clearly anyway. They were just a shinier spot in the darkness beneath his hat's brim, but she could tell they were looking at her. Harry had never looked into her eyes like that before. "Like what you see?" Her voice was almost a whisper.

"Elizabeth," Harry said. "Are you sure I'm not putting you out?" He turned away from the rear window's view and concentrated on things in front of him. It was a good thing he had taken it easy on the *Full Moon's* whiskey because he had liked what he had just seen in those eyes.

"You're not putting us out, Mr. Watkins. Besides, it's raining," Elizabeth said as she steered the car around a curve.

The windshield wiper made swish-swash sounds as they drove out of the city. Harry and his three young escorts left its lights behind them as they went past rows of wooden homes lining Howell and on toward the intersection with Eastlake. Elizabeth hit a crossing for one of the streetcar lines and bounced the Ford hard over the tracks. Sitting as close to Harry as decency allowed, Millie used the bouncing rear end as a perfect excuse to rub her thigh firmly against his.

Harry kept his eyes on the windshield, watching the twin beams of light shining out in front of them as they found their way through the falling rain. "Rough road," he murmured.

After struggling to see for nine or ten blocks, their driver was forced to abandon vanity and put on her glasses. She hadn't seen the tracks in the road at all. The other occupant of the car's front seat, Julie with the damaged stocking, turned around and, with an arm over the back of the seat, hadn't stopped talking since Olive.

Harry was glad she was talking. Looking into Millie's eyes was disturbing. What was it about the McAllister women that made things so difficult? For a moment, he had wanted to kiss her. She hadn't seemed like anybody's younger sister with her face inches from his and a grown woman's look in her eyes.

"I'm cold, Harry." Millie curled herself a little closer to his body as Julie prattled on about her issues with Myrna Loy and how she wasn't a very good leading lady. She was only half listening. Movies were far from her mind right now. Harry felt very warm sitting so close beside her.

They drove up Eastlake until the rainy drive changed from suburban homes to the more secluded forested area close to the lakefront.

"It's right up here," he said to Elizabeth as she wiped at the fogging condensation on the windshield. "On the left. The gravel road. See it?"

The car lost speed. "Right here?" Elizabeth asked.

"Uh huh. Drive straight down the hill."

The car turned to the left and Millie leaned hard against him as the car swung into the turn. He could feel her breasts pressing against his chest. It wasn't an accidental lean caused by a sharp turn. It was a long, deliberate push against him. Almost home, he thought, and a good thing, too. Millie was getting older every time they hit a bump in the road. Acapulco, he thought to himself. "Don't pull up to the gate," he told Elizabeth. "Follow the curve around to the right."

"Here?" Elizabeth said again, reaching to turn off the wiper. The clouds had run out of water for the moment.

"It goes to the right a little farther down."

The end of a tree branch hit the passenger side of the car and Elizabeth, catching a lower gear, drove a little more to the left side of the lane.

"Just ahead. There's a place to turn around at the bottom," Harry told her.

The headlights swept around a sharp bend as the dark surface of Lake Union stretched out before them. All along the hills on the far side of the lake were little stars of light from scattered homes and occasional streetlights. The road ended a short way farther on in a wide, tree lined clearing with just enough room to turn around like Harry said.

At the end of the drive, the first thing the passengers in the Ford saw was a small shack lit by a single yellow bulb fixed to a short pole. Harry was very glad to see that light and the box shaped building beside it. He preferred to think of the building as a boathouse, but he was more charitable than most. The gravel track ended at the building's front.

Elizabeth brought her father's Ford to a stop in front of the shack and pulled the hand brake. Its loud grind as the lever's pawls engaged announced their arrival to everyone inside the cab. The glow of her headlights shone into a wall of trees not very far in front of her. She mentally measured the distance while wondering how she was going to manage turning the car around in such a small area. The shoreline was very close and accidentally backing the car into the lake looked easy to do.

Beside the boathouse, a T shaped pier pushed out into the dark waters of the lake. Harry's boat was tied up at the end. *Scarab,* looming like a solid shadow in the faint, pale light was completely dark. It didn't look like Roscoe was home.

"Well, ladies," he began.

Elizabeth killed the Ford's engine. Julie opened her door and stepped into the chilly night. As he pushed the seat a little forward so he could squeeze out through the passenger side door, Elizabeth turned off the headlamps, opened her own door, and joined Julie on the gravel. Millie followed Harry out the passenger side, again sliding out of the Ford like a house cat and feeling very good about her evening.

"Ladies," Harry began again as both Elizabeth and Julie headed for the pier. Millie followed them across the gravel towards the boathouse's circle of yellow light. Harry sighed, looked at his wet shoe and said, "Watch out for mud puddles."

He followed the girls down the pier taking off his hat to rub the back of his neck.

"It's bigger than the one you had before, isn't it, Harry?" Millie asked as he caught up to them.

"Which one before? You mean *Seahorse?*"

"You have more boats, Mr. Watkins?" Julie asked.

"Harry's in the business. He builds them all the time, don't you, Harry?"

All the time, Harry thought. "*Seahorse* was a little smaller. You've got a good eye for size, Millie. This one's fourteen and a half feet longer and about four and a half feet more beam. We built her to order for a," Harry looked at the three young female faces looking at him in the reflection of the boathouse's yellowish light. He tried to think of a suitable word for the dead movie maker. "A buyer who didn't hold up his end of the bargain."

"Can we see it?" Millie asked.

Lifting the wooden life rail up and out of the way by its hinges, he stepped onto the deck of his cruiser. The port side entry door was directly across from the rail's hinged opening and, after slipping his key in the lock, he swung open the varnished wooden door. Reaching through the opening into the boat's interior, he found the bulkhead light switch to the salon sconces. *Scarab's* very plush main cabin windows glowed bright with electric daylight. Harry moved out of the path of the girls still standing on the pier.

"In we go, ladies," he told them. "Watch your step. There's a gap and a step up," he said, pointing at the spot where they needed to set their feet. He followed them inside, pulling off his raincoat and laying it and the girl's coats over the storage cabinet to his left. "Welcome aboard the finest example of skilled workmanship ever produced by Watkins Yacht Building," Harry said as the girls looked about themselves.

"It's beautiful, Mr. Watkins. I had no notion. Does it have a name?" Julie asked.

"Call him Harry," Millie said. She moved across to the opposite side of the salon. Reaching for the neck of the bottle sticking up from the built in liquor cabinet, she asked, "Got any ice?"

The bottle was halfway out of its rack before Harry caught her hand and put it back in its place. Millie smiled at him over her shoulder and continued her inspections.

"The boat's name is *Scarab*, like the old Pharaoh's jewel," Harry said to his visitors. "Up those steps behind you and through that door is the wheelhouse and down those steps forward to the right are the side by side galley and dinette. Just past that, the head. Farther up are the crew's quarters where my mechanic sleeps."

"Mr. Harrison is still with you?" Millie asked.

"Yeah, we're kind of used to each other. Behind you and down the steps on the starboard side is the passageway to the cabins and access to the engines. Owners' quarters are all the way aft. Right before that is the guest cabin and the second head. We built her with a shower," he added. Harry smiled and put his hands in his pockets, thinking this would impress female visitors. It was the first boat he had ever owned with a shower. He was very proud of his shower, but telling his visitors about it didn't seem to make much of an impression.

"Don't they always have showers?" Julie asked.

"You can feel it moving," Elizabeth said, looking at Julie. She had removed her glasses and had both hands palms down out in front of her as if trying to judge the very slight rise and fall of the deck beneath her feet.

"It's too cold for showers, baths, or anything else to do with water," Millie added. "Where's the heat, Harry?"

A very pretty stainless steel heater with brass trim running across its front was mounted on the bulkhead in the far corner. Harry went to it and opened a box of matches.

"No, they don't all have showers. The buyer requested it." Opening the fuel valve, he made a couple of short pumps on a little brass plunger, then struck a match. Slow heat gradually filled the room. "If you went outside and followed the deck around, there's a wide open space covered by a removable canvas cover running back to the stern. It's nice when the weather cooperates. The buyer wanted to be able to sit in the sun on nice days." And he wanted to take showers, the chiseling bum, he thought to himself.

"Nice days," echoed Julie, as she rubbed her hands up and down her arms before going over to stand by the heater.

"Can we have a little music?" asked Millie, looking at Harry. "Does it have a radio?" She ran her fingers along the wood trim bordering the interior bulkhead.

"Under the liquor cabinet, there's a radio built inside. It was shipped out from Chicago special when we were finishing the joinery."

The cabinet was two steps away and, bending over, he opened a louvered wooden door and turned the power on to the device. An amber glow illuminated the large dial as its electrical heart warmed up.

Elizabeth, done with her measuring of the boat's movements, took a seat on the long sofa lining the aft bulkhead. She ran her hand along the fabric of the settee. A little chime went off somewhere below and forward of where she was sitting; three pairs of dings, followed by a single ding then silence. Elizabeth looked around her. "What was that?"

"Seven bells," Harry answered. "It's a nautical clock. Belongs to Roscoe, my mechanic. He likes the way it sounds." Harry closed the cabinet door in front of the radio. "It's an eight hour clock instead of twelve like a regular one in a house. Seven bells means eleven thirty."

Elizabeth shot bolt upright from the settee.

"Eleven thirty? Is it fast?"

Harry looked at the Hamilton strapped to his wrist. "No, it's right on the money."

"We're going to miss the last ferry," she said. "We're going. We're going right now. Good night, Mr. Watkins."

"Call him Harry," Millie said with a sharp look at Elizabeth who was grabbing her coat. "And we've got plenty of time."

Julie and Elizabeth disappeared out the door, crossed to the pier without a pause and headed towards the car at a fast walk.

"I guess the evening has come to an end," Harry said to Millie.

"Guess so." Millie handed him her coat, then turned around. "I'm glad we bumped into you tonight." Her arms went down the warm sleeves as he helped her into the wool. She moved out of the boat's interior and onto the narrow deck outside. It wasn't a very wide space. Harry followed her out.

They were very close to each other. Millie moved her body closer to his and tilted her face to look him in the eyes. "Alone at last," she whispered. He wasn't wearing his hat now and she could see his face clearly in the darkness. Julie and Elizabeth were almost to the car. "That's right, Harry."

"What's right? I didn't say anything." He heard the sound of the Ford's doors opening, but he didn't look at the car.

"I think you did. I think you just now noticed I'm a grown woman." Millie lifted her chin and smiled.

She was right, too, Harry thought. He *had* just noticed the kid who used to trail behind her sister with awkward knees and chocolate on her fingers was long gone. The kid had turned into a very attractive woman. The diffused lighting coming from the boat's interior gave her soft brown curls and pretty face a glow that a Hollywood starlet could hardly match.

"You can kiss me goodnight if you want to," she said softly as she leaned against him.

Yes, she was much older now, and he could feel her body's subtle movement as it pressed against his. But it wouldn't do. It wouldn't do at all. If this went on much longer, he might begin to press back.

"Good night, Millie. Thanks for the lift. I would have had a miserable walk back and I'll buy you that drink on your twenty-first, I promise." Leaning over, he kissed her on the forehead then spun her around by the shoulders. She needed to go before he lost an internal battle with himself. He damn sure didn't need to be looking into those eyes anymore.

Millie's body went rigid.

"Oh Harry, not you too. Everybody thinks I'm still a damned child." She stepped over the gap between the boat's side and the edge of the dock. She didn't look back as she marched down the pier. The Ford's engine rattled, coughed and cranked followed immediately by the headlights shooting twin white beams into the gloom.

"My sister's back in town, by the way," she yelled over her shoulder. Reaching the car, Millie stopped, turned around for a moment then looked at the boat. Harry thought her fists were clenched but couldn't be sure. The Ford's door slammed shut and after a couple of stabs at the trees, Elizabeth got it turned around and headed back up the hill.

"Goodnight, ladies," Harry said to the night as he closed the salon's door. "Feel free to come by and test my shaky morals anytime you're in the neighborhood."

An unknown singer's voice mixed with a fair amount of static poured out of the radio's speaker. Its tubes had finally warmed to their operating temperature. Harry's tubes were pretty warm, too.

Reaching for the same bottle in the cabinet's top that Millie had tried for earlier, he exhaled a long, slow breath. Pulling the cork on the fifth of *Black & White,* he turned over one of the crystal glasses and poured a stiff shot. The scotch had a welcome burn as he sat on a soft chair in the salon. He kicked off his shoes, then pulled off his socks and held his foot closer to the warmth of the cabin's heater. Leaning back with his drink in his hand, Harry closed his eyes and tried to think of something other than the way Millie's body felt when she pressed her body against his. A clarinet played something. He tried to remember the name of the tune when outside, he heard the Ford coming back down the gravel lane.

"Oh for god's sake," he muttered and squeezed his closed eyes to tight slits for a moment. He tossed back the last swallow in his glass and went to the door. He was going to have to be mean to a kid he happened to be very fond of. As he stepped out onto the cold exterior deck of the boat for the second time, the car was turned around and going back up the gravel road. Roscoe was doing some carnival version of a waltz with a closed umbrella for a partner half way down the pier.

"Why hey, boss," he said, all but falling off the wooden planks when he noticed Harry. "I went down to Barefoot Nessie's for a little while. Ran into an old friend." He waved a hand at the red taillights disappearing around the curve.

Roscoe walked past him and into the salon smelling heavily of a Saturday night on the town. As he went past Harry, he tossed the umbrella near the settee.

"I borrowed that," he said, pointing to the one thing Harry wanted more than anything else in the world an hour earlier. Then, looking at Harry's bare feet added, "You'll catch cold running around like that in this weather. It's been raining." Roscoe added his own vocal trumpet to the clarinet on the radio and did a quick side step, back step, then forward again dance move that almost upset his balance completely.

Harry looked at the discarded umbrella lying on the salon's deck. "Thanks for bringing it back."

Roscoe stumbled and lurched his way over to the steps leading below going down to his quarters without another word. Harry closed the salon door. At least he looked like he had enjoyed his evening. He was glad someone had.

Two nights and two McAllister women, he thought. The crystal glass was sitting on top of the cabinet. Empty. He decided he might as well have another go at the *Black & White.*

*****

The second floor of the McAllister home consisted of five bedrooms, a full bath, a hall closet and a study. On one side of the staircase, down the length of the upper floor's hallway and past the bedrooms were the back stairs leading to the kitchen. On the opposite end was the study. It had originally been a second master bedroom but was converted years ago when Donovan's mother was still alive. Donovan could still remember a few fuzzy childhood memories of his mother sitting in a bright shaft of sunlight in that room. Sometimes in his memory she was sewing while sitting in a chair. Sometimes she was standing in front of the big double windows that looked out onto the front lawn of their home.

Donovan led the way up the stairs, stopping every couple of steps to let Joe catch up to him. "Want to race?" he said jokingly.

"Give me a few more weeks, and I will give you three to one odds." Joe lifted his leg gingerly, moving slowly and being careful not to fall. First his right leg stepped up, then his left. He could feel his forehead beginning to perspire with the effort. His right hand used the balustrade for support while his left had a death grip on the handle of his cane. This was good for him, he told himself. The next set of stairs he climbed would not be nearly so difficult. He was glad Lucy wasn't here to see his difficulty at climbing stairs.

"When I'm in town, that's my room over there." Donovan jerked a thumb over his shoulder towards the row of bedroom doors. "My sisters are the ones across from it and that one's a spare."

Joe made it to the top of the staircase without incident.

"The one on this end belongs to the king himself."

The entry to the study was shut tight. That was like him, Donovan thought. Invite half the names in the phonebook to a party, then go to your room and close the door. He thought about throwing the heavy, oak paneled door wide open and walking straight in with a quick, "Hey Pop, meet one of my old friends from college." Thought about it, but didn't. Instead, he knocked twice just like he and everyone else in the McAllister household did and waited. "Last chance to run for it, Joe."

"Come in," said a heavy resonant voice that was low but easily heard from the room's interior.

"Too late," Donovan said. He turned the knob and pushed the door open. As he crossed the threshold of his father's study, behind him, the noises of a house filled with guests faded away. In this room, all was library-like quiet. The elder McAllister and an older gray haired man in his sixties were standing behind and slightly to one side of his father's desk. The desk with its carved, kneeling dragons on the corners, each holding the heavy tabletop with darkly varnished talons was a new addition to the room. The two high backed red leather chairs sitting in front of it sat right where they were for at least a dozen years. His father was on the right beside the dragons with the gray haired man closer to the dark glass of the window. The man was vaguely familiar, probably someone from the field. Half the people in the house were his father's coworkers. Donovan couldn't recall his name at the moment or where he'd seen him before. Whoever he was, he was handing a double barreled shotgun with the action broken open back to his father.

"Ah, Donovan. Come in, son. You remember Wilson, don't you?" Archibald McAllister didn't look at Wilson as he made the introductions. He only glanced at his son for a moment before the shotgun took all of his attention. "Close that door, would you? Lord above us all, I can't stand all the racket they make. I don't know why Lucile invited so many people."

"She's a beautiful piece, Archie."

Archie McAllister turned sharply towards Wilson. "What's that?"

"Just beautiful," Wilson said. "You knew what you were doing when you bought it. Well worth the price. Well worth it." Wilson leaned his head back and peered at the blued barrels through the lower half of his glasses. "We'll have to see if you can hit anything with it sometime."

Wilson looked like a man made for golf course deals and dinner party negotiations. With the gun no longer in his hands, he pulled the loops of his gold rimmed spectacles away from his rather hairy ears then tucked his glasses into the front pocket of his jacket. He raised a friendly hand towards Donovan. "Ah, the young bull of the family has—"

Whatever comment Wilson planned to make about cattle died in his throat as Joe Kanji followed the family's young bull into the room.

"Mr. Wilson," Donovan said. "Sure, I remember. I saw you at the club's New Year's party, didn't I?" He had no recollection of meeting him at the club, but it was a safe bet he was there. Everyone his father knew was there on New Year's drinking French champagne by the case and cursing the memory of Prohibition.

"I, uh, yes, the club on New Year's." Wilson's voice lost its force and the smile on his face changed to a look of surprise. Golf courses and dinner parties hadn't prepared him very well for the sight of an Asian man walking into Archibald McAllister's study. He needed a moment to collect his thoughts. "Yes, New Year's. I remember." Wilson recovered his composure and the jovial smile came back to his cheeks. "You were with that brunette. She was some number, wasn't she, Archie?"

Archie didn't answer. Or return the smile. He didn't approve of his son's constant pursuit of women and couldn't have described the brunette Wilson was referring to if his life depended on it.

Joe's cane made no sound as the tip sank deeply into the rug beneath his feet. Almost half a year of his life spent preparing for this moment, he thought, as he followed Donovan into the room. Half a year and two steps and he was finally here.

Donovan closed the door quietly behind them, isolating the four men completely from the celebratory clamor in the rest of the house. "That was Lilly. She was a big fan of New Year's Eve champagne."

Lilly, her blouse unbuttoned and with both breasts on prominent display had thrown up in the backseat of his Buick. Happy New Year. He hadn't bothered with her again.

To Joe, the change in atmosphere in the home, from downstairs socializing to upstairs fraternizing was very noticeable. One minute, he was just another guest at a party. A moment later, the party was forgotten.

The study was the room where the patriarch of the McAllister family spent most of his home hours. It looked very different from the other more public parts of the house he had seen. The room was quite large and took up most of the second floor's front corner. The walls were paneled half way up in a dark wood with complex patterns of molding accenting every angle. The upper halves of the walls were papered in a soft tan color with repeating patterns of gentlemen hunters shooting at unseen birds. The tall windows flanking the desk would make the room very bright on sunny days. Beginning about knee high from the floor, they reached all the way to the ceiling with heavy green drapes so dark they were almost black bordering each side. Tonight, the drapes were open, making the windows look like a pair of ebony mirrors. Joe could see his reflection looking back at him from within the darkness of the glass.

On his right was a recessed bookcase filled with the spines of old leather bound books. Some were stacked in neat rows. Others were lying on their sides as if returned in haste by the reader. He thought they had the appearance of expected ornaments in a gentleman's study. In the far right corner stood a glass curio cabinet taller than he was, with its interior lit by an unseen light in its top. The cabinet was divided by glass shelves. On each shelf sat one or two model airplanes. He doubted they were mementos of childhood toys. The lower glass shelves and the very top shelf had various biplanes on them. The middle shelf held a solitary model of a blue and yellow single winged airplane; a pursuit plane to use the vernacular preferred by America's Army Air Corps.

The opposite side of the room on his left had a small fireplace piled full of logs that were burning warmly behind a brass screen. A small oval shaped rug like one might see on the floor of a hunting lodge was in front of the screen. A dog, some big, dark, long haired variety unknown to Joe, stood up slowly and trotted over to Donovan for its required inspection of the newcomers.

Donovan scratched the top of the dog's head for a moment. "Hi Bouncer," he said to the dog. "Now go lie down."

The best part of the dog's bounce had left him several years ago. Like his owner, Donovan's father, age was rapidly catching up with Bouncer.

"Papa, Mr. Joe Kanji. We were at Stanford together. Joe, my father Archibald McAllister and Mr. Wilson." Donovan turned from Joe back to his father with a flat smile on his lips.

Joe bowed slightly at the waist with his eyes looking keenly into Archibald McAllister's. Lieutenant Yoshiro Kanji, reflected in the room's mirror-like window returned the bow.

The shotgun in McAllister's hands snapped closed with the barrels locked into the ready position.

The gray haired man named Wilson was right, thought Joe. It was a beautiful example of the gunmaker's art with a finely burled walnut stock and engraved receiver. It was the type of workmanship his own father in Japan would appreciate.

"Mr. Kanji," Archibald McAllister said.

The way he said it, Joe could not tell if McAllister was asking a question or making a statement.

McAllister pulled the foot long forearm away from the bottom of the paired barrels of the shotgun and dropped it quietly into a velvet lined case sitting on his desk. His thumb pressed the release lever on top of the gun's action, breaking the shotgun down into its two main parts; barrels in his left hand, shoulder stock and action in his right. Both pieces followed the forearm into the case. He closed the lid with a soft, caressing touch before stepping away from his desk. McAllister moved decisively towards Joe and offered his hand.

"How do you do?" he asked. "Archibald McAllister."

Wilson remained where he was, standing silently in front of the window's dark glass.

"Yoshiro Kanji. My American friends usually prefer Joe."

McAllister's grip on Joe's hand was firm as he looked directly into his eyes. "Joe it is then."

Joe, leaning on his cane more than usual and thinking he was going to have to practice walking up flights of stairs, produced his business card. Looking intently into the older version of Donovan standing before him, he paused for a moment. "Nippon Heavy

Industries," he said in a very smooth, measured voice.

McAllister's eyes flickered for a moment. He took the small white card from Joe's hand and laid it on the desk next to a bronze figurine of a golfer forever teeing off. The card joined a small stack of identical little white cards leaning against the golfer's legs.

Wilson stared at Joe as if he were a circus performer. "He sounds like he's from Kansas, Archie."

Archie McAllister half turned towards Wilson as if he had only now remembered he was still there. "Wilson," he said, "would you mind if I did a little catching up with my son and his uh, his guest?"

"Oh, sure, say no more, Archie. I need to locate my wife, anyway." Wilson was a man used to graceful exits from boardrooms and McAllister's study was very much the boardroom of this home. "Donovan, good seeing you again." Both men shook hands. "Mister, uh, Kanni?"

"Kanji."

Wilson shrugged his shoulders. "Close enough, hey?" he said as he passed Joe. He hadn't offered to shake hands.

Archie McAllister followed Wilson across the room and opened the study's door. The sound of a woman's laughter drifted into the room from somewhere downstairs as Wilson left with a good natured wave and a salesman's natural smile.

"Have a seat, boys," Archie McAllister said as the woman's laughter disappeared behind the closed door. "Joe, you look a little done in."

"He was in a car wreck in Hawaii, Pop. Busted himself up pretty good."

"The worst is behind me now," Joe said softly.

"Sit, please." McAllister motioned both Joe and Donovan to the pair of red leather arm chairs in front of his desk. "It must have been some wreck."

"It was. I was not looking where I should have been. By the time I saw him, it was too late. He hit me very hard but I lived and will be as good as new. Eventually."

Archie returned to the place where he was standing when they first came into the room. He gazed into the darkness of the window for a brief moment. The reflected Lieutenant Yoshiro Kanji gazed intently back at Joe from the opposite window.

Clasping his hands behind his back, he said, "Where did you say you two met again?"

"At Stanford," Donovan answered. "Joe got me through trigonometry with a B and I got him through, well, Joe got me through trigonometry." Donovan reached over to bump Joe's undamaged leg with a good natured fist.

"And you've kept in touch all these years?" He was still looking at the night sky through his study's window. Below him, the street with its half circle drive in front of his home was filled with the automobiles of his guests. The rain stopped, he noticed, or perhaps it was only catching its breath for the next round.

"If I may," said Joe. "No, we have not." A dark shaded desk lamp shined its light on the cased shotgun, a pile of rolled up blueprints and a stack of manila folders. "I have not seen your son since graduation." Joe looked away from the papers and rolled blueprints to watch the straight back of Archibald McAllister before going on. "My purpose in returning to your country is purely commercial, representing Nippon Heavy Industries. Perhaps you have heard of my employer?"

He kept his attention focused on the back of Archie McAllister. In the corner of his eye, he saw Donovan's head turn to face him. He told Lucy and her brother he was taking a long vacation to restore his health. It was only a small lie, one that was wrapped deep within a much larger one. Donovan wouldn't care he didn't think. Work. Vacation. Play. It was all pretty much the same thing in Donovan McAllister's world, anyway. The lines certainly blurred. He liked Donovan, but this moment was why he was sent here. His mission had nothing to do with whom he liked or disliked or to whom he told the truth.

"Donovan," Archie said, turning away from his study of the world outside his window. "You know I completely forgot with Wilson coming in and all, but that young woman you brought up earlier. What was her name?"

"Inga." Donovan's face turned cautious. Inga had insisted on a tour of the home and nearly walked into his father's room unasked. He seldom introduced his women friends to his father and wouldn't have brought her up to meet him by choice, but Inga could be demanding.

"Yes, I think it was her. She came in right before you knocked. Something about looking for you everywhere. Did you see her?"

Donovan gave the closed door behind him a hormonal look. "I left her about a half hour ago standing in line for the bathroom." He leaned closer to the chair next to him. "Do girls in Japan line up to pee, or is that just an American female thing?"

Joe smiled at his friend, but offered no answers.

"It was just a few minutes ago when she was here," continued his father. "I'm certain it was the same young woman. Run along and see what she needed." Archie stepped towards his son, one hand reaching for his arm. "A gentleman shouldn't make a lady wonder where he has disappeared to at a party, hmm? I'll send your friend down after you in a minute. I have a tremendous curiosity about Japan, you know." McAllister helped his son out of the chair and moved him towards the door.

Donovan sighed. "I wonder what she wants now?"

"You'll have to go find her and ask." The sounds of the party once again briefly interrupted the quiet solitude of the study as the door opened and closed.

Joe tapped his finger along the ivory handle of his cane. "You maneuver very well, Mr. McAllister."

He sat straight in the leather chair with hands resting on the end of his cane while facing the cluttered desk as Donovan's father stepped into his view. Joe did not look at him, preferring instead to stare at the rolled blueprints lying just beyond his reach.

"You've got your nerve coming here," Archie McAlister said. "To my home," he added angrily.

Yes, thought Joe to himself, I do. "The American government's attitude towards business with my benefactors is not encouraging. The Washington endeavors have not met with success, as I am sure you are aware."

Joe, making a conscious effort to relax, eased himself deeper into the soft leather. His gaze left the papers on McAllister's desk and moved slowly to the eyes of the man standing in front of him. "It was felt a more direct approach to someone," he paused, thinking of the best way to say what was coming next. "Someone experienced with our mutual requirements would be more beneficial." He lingered briefly on the word mutual knowing its meaning would not escape McAllister.

"And so, you decided to drag my son into your underhanded bullshit? I thought we made our decision plain and simple. Simple enough even for you people to understand." McAllister leaned heavily upon the closed wooden gun case on his desk. "I should put the dog on you."

The dog, sensing perhaps he was being called upon, thumped his tail several times against the floor but gave no signs of moving from the warmth of his rug and the fire.

"Going through my son? You people, by god," McAllister continued, slamming his balled fist down on the lid of the gun case. "My own son used as a, a—"

"A pawn?" Joe finished for him. "More like an avenue than a pawn, McAllister. Your anger is misdirected. Donovan has no knowledge of the extent of your helpfulness towards my benefactors in the past."

Joe sat impassively in his chair as Archie McAllister's cheeks changed rapidly from a slightly flushed pink to scarlet red.

"And why should he?" Joe continued. "There is no reason for him or anyone else to know what his father has done." Joe looked at the displayed wealth in McAllister's private world nicely tucked away within his very lovely home. "Comfort has a price, does it not? And we all have our secrets to keep."

Archie McAllister's left eye twitched. He looked at the seemingly frail invalid sitting across from him without comment. Neither man spoke. The room was very quiet except for the sound of the logs burning in the hearth ten feet away. McAllister sat heavily in his chair. A loud, prolonged squeak broke the near perfect silence in the room.

"You've got stones. I'll say that. Look," he began in a more reasonable tone. "This isn't '28 anymore. Congress has tightened up the laws and what your man in Washington asked me for can't be done."

"Your company provided a P-12 to one of the Chinese factions easily enough. That was done. This is not so different."

"It's damned different and you know it. Boeing didn't make that deal happen. Uncle Sam did. We provided a product. Besides, it wasn't a P-12, it was a—"

"I know what it was," Joe said, interrupting McAllister. He flexed his wrist and felt the scar tissue stretch beneath his sleeve. He knew very well. "A Model 2-18."

The 2-18 was a civilianized version of the Boeing biplane. The

Chinese simply reinstalled its missing guns and turned it into a P-12 again.

"Officially," he said, "not a fighter at all and yet, it was flown by a reserve Army Air Corps pilot. Lieutenant Short by name."

McAllister grunted. "We should be able to do some business with the 2-18. Still, it would be tricky." McAllister leaned back in his chair and touched a finger to his lip. "It might be difficult to get past those watchdogs on Capitol Hill. You boys shouldn't have invaded Manchuria. That pissed everybody off and just makes it harder to conduct commerce between nations."

The nation of McAllister leaned forward, resting his elbows on the surface of his desk. The tips of his fingers touched each other almost prayer like. "Interested?"

"No, I am not. The P-12 holds no interest for me or my associates. We are talking about the P-26." Joe pointed his cane at the blue and yellow monoplane in McAllister's display case, the one he noticed as soon as he came in the room. The Army Air Corps' newest pursuit plane sat all alone on its glass shelf.

"And my company has no interest in doing that kind of business with your associates," McAllister said. "I feel comfortable in speaking on their behalf in this matter."

"We did not speak to your employer in 1928, did we?"

"That was different. We weren't talking about new airframes then. It was only a few drawings. Besides, I really didn't do anything all that out of the ordinary. It was all strictly business."

"Yes," said Joe. "A few drawings and how much did you sell them for again? Eight thousand dollars cash, wasn't it?"

McAllister stood slowly from behind his desk. The chair squeaked in symphony with the movement. "You seem to be very well informed, Mister," McAllister's hand snatched at the white business card lying against the legs of the bronze golfer and quickly read the name, "Yoshiro Kanji. You didn't cross the Pacific, ingratiate yourself with my son and worm your way into my home to talk about allegations impossible to prove, did you?"

Joe stood slowly from his chair as well, partly because he did not wish to be spoken down to by a standing McAllister and partly because his hip was beginning to ache badly. Moving to the corner of the room, he bent to look at the airplanes sitting on their glass shelves.

"This thing that you say cannot be done, what would it cost Nippon Heavy Industries if it could be done?"

"More than you've got. Listen to what I'm telling you. Eight grand was for old ideas. Old plans. No harm in turning a profit on something like that. The Twenty-Six is different. It's brand new. Come see me in six or seven years and we can talk."

Joe's nose nearly touched the cool glass of the curio cabinet. The display model was a very good representation of the P-26 and right then, he wished more than anything to be flying the real machine. Ever since seeing it in the skies over Hawaii he had wanted to fly it. Looking at it here behind its thin glass wall made him wonder if he would ever feel the thrill of being in the air again.

Anyone could tell just by looking at it that it was advanced well beyond the A4N. Nakajima's newest biplane was a product of the last age built on the wood and canvas ideas of the European war of almost twenty years ago. This plane was the future. Its low slung single wing was like nothing he had ever seen before, something no one had ever even imagined in a fighter. The Navy thought it was faster than anything either service could put up against it. It would change everything and in doing so, make everything else obsolete.

The future. A wholly different class of fighter.

He gently tapped the display case's glass sides with the handle of his cane. "The economic realities of the world are what they are, McAllister."

He did not look at the man as he spoke, but Donovan's father standing behind his desk looked at him. Joe could feel his eyes. This was the moment, the moment of it all.

"I understand you completely. Offering eight thousand dollars for something like this would be insulting." He turned away from the brightly lit display case with its miniature copies of all the designs McAllister had a part in making. The old desk with its dragons carved into the corners was between them. Its rectangle shaped top reminded Joe briefly of that day when he approached the *Kaga* for the last time. "What do you think something as new as the Twenty-Six would be worth?"

"I told you," McAllister growled, ignoring the question. "It can't be done."

Joe began a slow walk towards the door, the same door he came through a few minutes earlier when he was still just a friend of

Donovan's and its noisy hallway beyond.

"The business climate is so precarious these days, and nations will always argue over politics. You Americans think it is wrong for Japan to be in Manchukuo but have no doubt of your own right to be in the Philippines. Politics. America defeated the Spanish and claimed Manila as a prize; a city you gained by force of arms. I do not think our positions are so different."

"Leave my home, Kanji. Don't show your face here again."

Joe noticed an oil painting on the wall next to the door for the first time. It was a painting of a fisherman's boat washed up on shore and beaten by many years of ocean waves.

"And yet," he continued, ignoring the words spoken behind him, "no matter the politics, a man still has to provide for his family's needs, does he not?"

"Do not involve my son in your doings, do you hear me?" McAllister said. His voice had a threatening edge in it.

"I have at my disposal," Joe went on, "a very large sum of cash. It was entrusted to me by my employer." The painting wasn't a very good one. "We are interested in the purchase of certain drawings, plans and specifications of a very new and modern design of an airframe developed by your employer."

Joe, leaning heavily on his cane now, turned slowly from the painting to look once more at the father of his friend. "Top speed. Armament. Payload. Range. Operational ceiling. Engine specifications. Those kinds of details would be worth a great deal to us."

"I don't have access to that kind of information and even if I did—"

"You have the information," Joe interrupted sharply. "The Twenty-Six was your project."

"I told you. This isn't 1928 anymore."

"Blueprints are especially valuable." His injured hip throbbed with fresh pains. Worse than it had in weeks. It was time for him to go. "Since your Congress has blocked your employer from taking advantage of our offer to buy, we thought perhaps you might be interested in another very profitable opportunity. How did you phrase it? Strictly business?" Joe turned the knob on the door but did not open it. "In 1928, we made you comfortable. Today, we can make you rich. That is clear enough, is it not? How would it feel, do you think? To be rich, when all around you in the world everyone else is so poor. Think on it and I am sure you will see how the impossible is really quite possible after all." He opened the door and the sounds of the party below invaded the room once again. Voices, their sounds flowing up the staircase and down the hall, invaded the sanctum sanctorum of McAllister's boardroom. "I can be reached at the Hotel Bergonian," he said as he left the study.

"Do not come back to my home again, Kanji," McAllister shouted.

Joe closed the door to the study and the sounds of the party wrapped around him. Had the house been quiet, McAllister's shouted last words would have been heard by everyone, but with the noise of partygoers on the lower floor, they were swallowed up so that only he and the dog heard them. He was gripping the ivory handle of his cane very tightly as he left the room behind him and approached the stairs. His heart was thumping in his chest as he made his way down the wide staircase. Despite his best efforts, he could not keep a grimace off his face as he negotiated the steps. He delivered his message and his offer. It was time for him to leave before the old man upstairs made good on his earlier threat to put his dog on him.

Reaching the bottom landing after a very slow descent, he saw Lucy's blonde hair and her very revealing green dress across the room. She was facing away from him and hadn't seen him struggling with the stairs. He was glad of that. He looked intently at the naked smoothness of her pale back as she talked animatedly to an overly determined looking young man standing in front of her. The man had his hands in his pockets and looked as if he was sharing some great confidence with the strikingly beautiful woman in green sequins. Lucy didn't seem to be following the young man's point and appeared to be trying to see around him into the next room.

Joe walked slowly towards the pair half listening for the sound of a dog's growl behind him or the cocking of a shotgun's hammers.

"It's particularly visible in the night sky after a good rain has come through, like we had tonight," said the unknown young man to Lucy. "If you'd like to see what I mean, I have a car."

"Oh, hello Joe. Where did you disappear to?" Lucy said as Joe made his slow approach. "Would you look over there?" She waved a hand at her older sibling. "What is my brother doing? He's been crossing the house like a basset hound sniffing for a rabbit. Donny," she called as he made a near pass.

Donovan, seeing his sister and Joe, gave up on his quarry. Joe thought he looked a little anxious.

"Donny, did you know Edith Carmichael was married?"

"Who?"

"Edith Carmichael. Stringy brown hair, terrible complexion. She used to play the piano." Lucy crossed her arms in front of her dress. The young man with his hands in his pockets chewed his bottom lip while openly staring into the bunched up fabric in the front of her dress.

"She's been married for almost a year. A year, Donny."

"It's particularly striking to see it after a good rain has come through. My car is right outside." The young man looked away from Lucy's open display of cleavage. He noticed Joe for the first time.

Joe nodded.

"It's really beautiful by moonlight," he continued, ignoring Joe.

"You haven't seen Inga, have you?" Donovan asked his sister.

"You mean the Trollop of Beacon Hill? Donny, really."

Joe smiled.

"She came through a few minutes ago heading for the front room and trailing a school of sharks," Lucy said.

Donovan, smelling the blood in the water himself, left for the front of the house.

"I know just the spot," the young man said again.

"My brother, the basset hound." Lucy sighed with exasperation. "Benny," she said to the young man, "give it a rest. There's no moon tonight, anyway."

Joe took a step forward, placing himself between Lucy and the moon gazer. "I am going back to my hotel, Lucy. It was a lovely party, but it is time for me to go."

"So soon?"

"It is late, my dear, and I do not want to miss the last ferry." He tapped the shaft of his cane against his leg. "And my leg is being bothersome this evening."

Lucy looked Joe up and down. Her eyebrows bunched with concern. "We can get you a chair to get off that leg if you'd like?"

"Thank you, but I really must be going. Will you tell our friend the basset hound I said goodnight and thank him for the invitation to your home."

"Would you like me to call you a cab? Or maybe we can get Donny to pry his hands off Beacon Hill's boobs long enough to drive you back."

Joe smiled and shook his head. "You have a flair for understatement."

"Sometimes my brother tries my soul. I swear he does."

"A cab is not necessary. I hired a car. I can manage perfectly well if someone has not blocked me in."

"I'll walk you out then. Can't blame you for leaving. The party is dying anyway."

"Lucile." Archibald McAllister stopped halfway down the stairs.

Lucy, Joe, and Benny all turned to face him.

"Donovan's friend is leaving. You, what's your name?"

"Benny, Benjamin Parks, Mr. McAllister. I work at Assembly Three." Benny's thin mustache twitched. "I was just telling Lucile what a lovely—"

"Take my daughter into the other room. There's a warm fire burning. She looks cold."

"Papa, have you met Donny's friend, Joe Kanji?"

Benny placed his hand on Lucy's elbow. "Shall we?" he asked sweetly.

"Hands off the goods, Benny," Lucy said. She pulled her arm out of his.

"I'm walking Joe out, Papa. He's not getting around so well and I'd hate to see him slip in the driveway."

"I left my hat and overcoat hanging on the stand," Joe said in his usual quiet tone.

McAllister looked at him from his vantage point on the stairs as if Joe were a stray dog that had dug under the backyard fence.

"Good night, Mr. McAllister. I found the company very rewarding," he told Lucy's father.

McAllister glowered, but did not say anything.

"Lean on my arm, Joe. I'll walk you to your car."

Joe didn't need the arm for support, but he delighted in the touch. "It must be the damp. I usually get around much better than this."

Lucy patted his arm. "You're doing swell."

The half circle drive in front of the McAllister home was bumper to bumper with the cars of her father's guests. As he passed them, Joe's hand used the fenders to steady his walk.

Somewhere in the house, a woman laughed. Lucy glanced behind her at the now closed front door. "Donny's a terrible host," she said with a touch of exasperation in her voice. "He's spent the whole night chasing after what he's always chasing." Lucy rubbed her hands over her bare arms. "I should have grabbed a coat."

"Would you like mine?" Joe unbuttoned the front of his overcoat.

"No, that's okay. I'm not that cold." Goose bumps lined her arms and her breath was a thin fog in front of her.

"I am told the Bergonian puts on a marvelous breakfast on Sunday mornings. I was wondering if you and Donovan would care to join me?"

"You obviously have my brother confused with someone else," she said with a quick laugh. "Donovan and Sunday mornings? I don't think those two words are heard very often in the same sentence. How about I bring my sister instead?"

"I have never met your sister before."

"Well then, you'll be in for a treat. I'm letting her take me for a ride tomorrow. I have to pay for my sinful wagering. It's supposed to teach me a lesson about gambling."

"What is the lesson?"

"Don't lose when you gamble."

He laughed politely at her joke. "I would be delighted to host the beautiful McAllister women at breakfast tomorrow."

"A final meal for the condemned. We'll be there. She says she can drive. Lord, I hope so."

"Your father did not seem pleased to see me speaking to you just now. I do not wish to cause you problems with the family patriarch."

"My father sometimes confuses me with his little girl and sometimes, I have to remind him of the grown woman." Lucy touched her mother's diamonds.

"That's quite a necklace. It is the same one your mother was wearing in the oil painting, is it not?"

"Aren't you the observant one? Did my brother show you the painting?"

"He did." The material of her dress was very smooth as it caressed the swell of her breasts. The shimmering cloth was thin and the night air was having its effect. He looked away before Lucy noticed him staring. Joe opened the door to his car. "What time shall I expect you?"

"Nine thirty or ten. That work for you?"

"That sounds fine." He glanced briefly again at the stones lying demurely between Lucy's breasts still kissed by the chilled night air. "I look forward to seeing you and your sister tomorrow," he said as he slid behind the wheel of the car.

*****

Millie and Elizabeth dropped Julie off in front of a home blazing with light and angry parents.

"Drive," Millie told Elizabeth as soon as their unlucky friend was out of the car. Julie's father was coming to the curb and nothing good could come of that. Elizabeth stepped on the gas, knowing full well her own father would be waiting for her when she finally made it home. Eleven o'clock was her witching hour and her parents were very strict.

Unlike Julie's house, Millie's home slumbered in unbroken darkness. She wasn't going to take a chance of someone hearing the Ford pulling up to the curb. The Ford was half a block from her home.

"Let me out here," Millie told Elizabeth. "Remember," she told her with a conspiratorial whisper. "We missed the ferry, and that's why we're so late. Don't say anything else."

"What if Julie's mom calls mine?"

"Improvise," Millie said. "Call me tomorrow."

It was going to be a long time before Elizabeth was allowed out again. Even longer before she was allowed to use the family car.

Heading for the back door, she moved as quietly as she could with shoes in one hand and her clutch purse in the other. The old wooden door stuck when it touched the jamb. Silently, she gritted her teeth, then closed her eyes to better feel the door's moods. If it made any sound at all, a rattle from a glass pane, an unpredictable squeak or heaven forbid, a thundering loud bang as it closed the last bit, she would be found out. Or at least she might be. It didn't rattle, nor did it squeak. The kitchen door ghosted closed with hardly a sound behind her as she gently and slowly pushed it too. Millie smiled in the darkness. The hardest part was behind her.

With the backdoor opened then closed with a skill to rival a cat burglar, she stood very still and listened to the sounds of the house. All was silent except for the hallway clock. The slow, measured ticks were barely loud enough to be made out from where she stood. The kitchen faucet was leaking again. So much for her brother's repairs. The drip's cadence-like advance falling on some unseen dish kept time with the clock as she waited and listened for anything out of the ordinary. No one was coming to investigate. No one heard her. She made it indoors and the house still slept.

Playing burglar wasn't something she did often. She only dared it on those times when her father was away on business and the hard sleeping Aunt Bertie had the household watch. This was attempt number four. It would be just her luck, she thought, to be caught coming home late on the one occasion when it wasn't done intentionally.

The youngest McAllister did a slow pirouette in the near jet black darkness of the kitchen. The night's rain clouds blocked out even the light of the stars from coming through the windows, but the room was as familiar to her as any place could be. Still, she took no chances. With her hands out in front just in case some idiot left a chair in her path, she crept slowly and carefully towards the back stairs. Her stocking covered toe touched the upright of the staircase's first step. Old practice told her to step high and over the second step with its notoriously loud squeaking board. In a quiet house with a young woman coming in past curfew, a squeaking board would sound like a cavalry troop sounding a charge. If she were coming down to the kitchen at three in the morning for a glass of milk and fell halfway down the stairs, no one would hear a thing.

Reaching the second floor without any bugles announcing her presence, she was glad to see there was no light coming from under anyone's doors. She stopped biting her lip for the first time since coming home and tiptoed down the darkened hallway.

Her father's room at the far end of the hall was lost somewhere in the gloom in front of her. It was a long hallway and there were two bedrooms between hers and her father's. Her bedroom, the second door on the left, had a crystal doorknob that was loose in the mountings since forever. Given a chance, it would rattle, but she had lived behind that door ever since she was a child. She knew better than to give it a chance. The door opened with barely a sound as she slipped into the darkened room as quietly as a cat in search of a late night meal. Taking absolutely no chances now that she made it free and clear, she took her sweet time making sure her own door closed without a sound by holding the glass knob turned all the way in and lifting it upwards. Once the door was closed, she released the knob slowly and shuddered with every squeak of the old spring inside the latch.

Victory was hers, even if the enemy would never know it. Millie made it undiscovered back to her home, back to her room, and back to her bed.

She dropped her shoes on the bedroom's floor, no longer feeling the need to be deathly quiet within the confines of her own palace. Groping in the darkness, she found the metal coat hook on the back of her door. After hanging up her coat, she pulled off her hat, ran a hand through her hair then tossed the hat towards the vicinity of the dresser. Her fingers went to the top button of her blouse, the one she sewed back on after that idiot boy Clarence Chandler broke it. Harry would have never broken a button on her blouse. Harry would have…

"You're home late," said a soft voice from behind her.

Millie jumped. She couldn't have been more startled if a mouse ran across her foot. Reflexively, she clutched the front of her blouse and blushed red in the darkness, as if her thoughts about Harry were known to the world. Dreamy imaginings of Harry Watkins vanished.

"Jesus, Lucy. You scared me half to death," she said in a loud whisper.

Lucy stood close against the wall in black pajamas and robe. The dark silk made her almost invisible in the room's shadows. Switching on the bedside lamp, she wrapped her robe tighter around her against the chill in the room before sitting on the foot of her sister's bed. Millie finished unbuttoning her blouse, slid the heavy fabric off her arms, and opened the wooden door of her grandmother's wardrobe. Not seeing a free hanger and not really caring, she dropped it in the bottom of the old cabinet.

"What are you doing in my room?" she whispered. Lucy's

presence made it seem like a good idea to resume her earlier cat burglar mode. She regretted the careless dropping of her shoes on the floor. A foolish extravagance of sound, she now realized. Her palace of refuge was once again a bedroom in her father's home.

Lucy examined her younger sister and wondered just how much kid was still there. Before she left for New York, Millie would never have dreamed of sneaking in or out of the house.

"I heard a car turning around down the street. I knew it had to be you." She looked at the curtained window of her sister's room as if she could see the empty street outside. "I'm an old expert at sneaking into this house."

Millie reached behind her and unbuttoned the back of her skirt, bent over, and stepped out of it. She froze in her movement. "Does Papa know I'm late?" Millie knew with certainty she was grown, but wasn't nearly so certain if she was old enough to be immune from her father's rules. Not yet. If he found out his daughter was not behaving as he expected, things could get difficult.

Lucy shook her head. "I hardly saw him out of his study all night. He only came down for a minute to say goodnight to a few people when the party was ending." She paused to look around her sister's room. Millie's bedroom was a disordered collection of piled clothing, stuffed animals, shoes, their grandmother's wardrobe, a dresser and chair and various magazines of the glamor promoting sort. "Do you ever put anything away?"

Millie tossed her skirt onto her discarded blouse, stopped, then felt the hem. It was still wet from the night's rain. She draped it over the back of her chair to finish drying. "Was the party any fun?" she asked as she pulled her slip over her head.

"Edith Carmichael got married. Someone named Webster." Lucy lifted one leg from the floor and hugged it close to her body. She rested her chin on her knee as she tried to think of Edith as a married woman. She couldn't remember a time when Edith even had a boyfriend.

Millie balanced on her left foot with the right on the edge of her chair and unsnapped her stocking. "Who?" she asked, switching legs. She tossed all the hosiery in a pile across her skirt and looked at herself in the dresser's mirror admiring the benefits of all those hours on the tennis court.

"Edith. Just forget it. Somebody I used to know."

Millie turned sideways and stood on her toes for a moment, one hand resting on the taut, flat surface of her stomach as she examined her profile in the mirror. "Do you think I look like Jane?"

"I don't know anyone named Jane," Lucy answered.

"Jane. You know. Tarzan and Jane. Maureen O'Sullivan, for goodness' sake. Didn't they have movie theaters in New York?" She reversed her position to examine her other side. "Someone told me I would be the spitting image of her if I put on one of those little outfits she wears in the movie." She was so pleased by the comment she let Clarence put his hand under her blouse for the first time and paw at her breast. Clarence's unpracticed groping broke her button.

"Maureen couldn't hold a candle to you." Lucy tried to think of something else to say before she came to her point for being here. "I like those shoes. Are they new?"

"You stayed up this late to tell me you like my shoes? God, it's freezing in here." Millie pulled a drawer out of her dresser and rummaged through the garments stuffed inside. Reaching behind her, she unhooked the snaps of her brassiere and tossed it on top of her slip.

"Have you seen my gown?" She rubbed her hands along cold arms. After looking through the chaos around her, she found what she was looking for under her sister. "Move your behind. You're sitting on it."

Lucy pulled the flannel decorated with little pink flowers out from under her. "It's impossible to be in this room and not be sitting on something. Has Bertie seen this place?"

Unfolding the gown, Millie fished around for the sleeve openings. Lucy's black silk made the flannel seem very drab. Putting her arms through the sleeves, she pulled the flannel over her head.

"Why are you back so late?"

The white gown with the little pink flowers bunched up under her arms. "Double feature." The nightgown slid over her breasts and fell to her ankles. Her sister was giving her one of those looks as if she knew everything that happened to her tonight. "We missed the ferry," she added.

Lucy caught the subtle change in Millie. Her sister was lying. "Clarence was asking for you tonight."

"Clarence is a boy."

There was someone new in her life, Lucy decided. What would Mrs. Chandler make of that? "Who is he?"

"Who is who?"

"Clarence's replacement."

Millie remembered the look in Harry Watkins' eyes when they were in the backseat of the Ford. He wanted to kiss her. She'd seen it. "Nobody." She started brushing her hair.

"It's a good thing I was born yesterday, else I might think you were being very vague all of a sudden."

"I'm not being vague. I just came home later than usual." Millie tossed her brush onto the dresser.

"It's almost one o'clock."

"It is barely past midnight and you've stayed out later than that plenty of times."

"I'm grown."

"So am I," Millie replied.

"Yes, you're all grown up. That explains the tiptoeing through the house."

"That just means I'm smart. Some things fathers shouldn't know."

Lucy smiled. She couldn't argue with that logic.

"Is the heat on?" Millie asked her sister. The room's temperature was a safer topic than where she was tonight. Propping one foot on her chair and lifting the flannel's long bottom out of the way, she rubbed lotion on her shins and calves. She finished with her arms and hands. The bedroom took on a strong scent of tropical flowers. Her nighttime rituals completed, she made a fast dash for the warm covers of her bed.

Lucy still sat at the foot wrapped in her dark silks.

"You didn't answer the question. Who is he?"

"Out past midnight and a new mystery in her life," Millie said in that sarcastic voice sisters use on each other when they were annoyed. "Are we worried about my reputation all of a sudden?"

"No, Millie. I'm not worried about your reputation. I'm worried because instead of telling me why you're out so late, you made up a tale about double features."

Millie sighed. "If you must know, it was Harry Watkins' fault. I've been with him since the rains came through." Millie reclined against her pillows, doing her best imitation of how she thought a freshly deflowered woman would look. "Now he could be a girl's Tarzan," she said in a dreamy voice.

"Ha ha, you're terribly funny."

"Laugh if you want, but it's his fault I'm so late." Millie shrugged a shoulder. "I didn't want to tell you."

Lucy watched her sister. Millie wasn't telling tales. Not this time. "What?" She rose slowly from the corner of the bed. "What do you mean, it was Harry's fault?" She couldn't hide the surprise in her voice. The black silk robe, shimmering wraithlike, billowed around her as if some unseen wind had suddenly blown through the small bedroom.

Indifferent to the silky wraith in front of her, Millie sighed, hugged her arms across her chest and smiled at nothing in particular.

"Millie," Lucy whispered. "Don't think I won't drag you out of that bed." Lucy's voice rose in volume as the beginnings of a shouting match welled up in her.

"Shhhh," Millie hissed. "You'll wake Papa, you goof." She didn't like the look in her sister's eyes. For a moment, she was afraid she was going to test her theory about falling down the back stairs and no one hearing it.

"He's a grown man," Lucy said. She wanted to scream, but kept her voice under control. "He's not one of your boys."

"I'm not a child anymore."

Lucy tried to imagine Harry Watkins being with Millie. Would he do that? She crossed her arms. "Spill it. This time, skip the Tarzan and Jane lullaby."

"We ran into each other in the city."

"Go on," Lucy said icily.

Millie thought about Clarence Chandler's bumbling attempts at seduction, broken buttons and all. She wished again Harry *had* kissed her goodnight. She made a show of straightening the shade on her lamp.

"After the movie. Tonight. That's why I'm so late. He was outside the Coliseum looking like an adorable half drowned puppy." She stretched out under her covers, then pulled the quilts up to her neck. "Julie, Elizabeth and I gave him a ride back to his boat." She smoothed a crease out of her quilt and puffed the pillows under her head. "You should see that thing he has now. Bigger and prettier than the one he used to have. I forget the name exactly. Something like scar or scary. It was mighty fine whatever he called it."

"You took the ferry over to Bainbridge?"

"No, not way over there. He had it up on the south end of Lake Union, right off Eastlake. Or maybe it was the east side? I wasn't paying all that much attention to where we were going. Harry and I were sitting in the back and I wasn't looking at the road. I think he's living on it. It looked like it anyway."

"By one of the sawmills? Out in the trees?"

Millie yawned. "I didn't see a sawmill. There was hardly any light at all and I was more interested in looking into Harry's eyes than sightseeing." Millie tried the dreamy look again, but Lucy wasn't biting this time.

"Uh huh. The three of you ran into him at the Coliseum?"

"It was just a ride."

"Why did you say such a mean thing to me? You know what Harry and I are to each other."

"No, Lucy. I don't know that. You haven't mentioned him once since you got back." Millie nodded her chin at her sister's shimmering silks. "And I don't think it was Harry who bought you that get up you're wearing, was it?"

Lucy felt her cheeks getting warm. "It was a Christmas present," she explained. "We were good friends."

"Sure. A good friend who bought you silk lingerie. Black silk lingerie at that."

"They're pajamas," she said defensively. "What's wrong with black? I like black."

Millie rolled her eyes. "Jesus, Lucy. You really do think I'm still twelve. Christmas present pajamas have candy canes or Santa Claus riding in a sleigh on them and are made of cotton. Black silk means, you know."

"It means no such thing. My choice in pajamas is none of your business."

"My double features are none of your business, either."

Lucy tried a different track. "Why did Harry need a ride? Where was his car?"

Millie considered for a moment. "You know, I never thought to ask."

"Did he say anything about me?"

"He had other things on his mind. Besides, you've been gone a long time."

"He didn't mention," Lucy paused. "Never mind. It's not important." He didn't have to ask about her. But Millie was right about one thing. She had been gone a long time. She turned for the door.

Millie switched off the lamp. "Tomorrow, I drive, right?" she said to the darkness. "We had a bet and you lost fair and square. Just because I spent time with Harry, that's no excuse to welch." Harry or not, tomorrow was her day in her sister's beautiful new car.

"He's a little old for you to have a crush on, don't you think?"

Millie thought about Clarence, the way he groped her breasts, her broken button, and about boys in general. No, she didn't think he was too old, but Harry still thought she was too young. "I don't have a crush on Harry." Lying was easier in the dark.

Lucy opened the bedroom door almost as soundlessly as Millie had and said quietly, "No, I'm not going to welch. Tomorrow you drive."

"Night, Lucy. Sleep well," Millie whispered. She even managed to say it sweetly. In the darkness, the crystal knob and its loose mechanicals protested as Lucy closed her door. She was feeling pretty good about things.

CHAPTER 4

Sunday morning showed all the promise of being a glorious day. The clouds had gone completely with the sunrise, and the snow-heavy shoulders of Mt. Rainier dominated the southern sky. The hills on the far side of Lake Union were sharp and clear in the early light and the lake itself was a beautiful eye hurting sapphire blue. Winter was in retreat this morning and if the sun stayed out, there was every possibility of a warm day ahead. Or at least warmer than yesterday. Roscoe and Harry, standing on the stern of *Scarab*, looked out over the near mirror smooth surface of that sapphire pool.

"Well," Roscoe said, "all I'm saying is, it was nice of them to give you a ride all the way back here. I wouldn't have wanted to walk that far. Not in the rain."

"It quit before we got halfway," Harry said. "Besides, I'd just about convinced myself to square up my bill at the hotel or grab a cab back to the boat. It damn sure would have cost me a lot less aggravation."

"A night at the Bergonian would have been good for you, Boss. Hot bath, clean sheets and your morning coffee in a clean cup. Been like old times."

Harry wished he had taken that advice now. Temptation had a powerful grip. He felt it squeeze him very hard last night when he caught himself looking the wrong way into Millie's eyes. She seemed a very different girl sitting in the back of that Ford.

Her sex.

That's what he was thinking about. Those eyes looking into his and the feel of her pressing against him every time the car hit a bump just about made him forget whose sister she was. Millie had always been the kid who wanted to race you to the front door or try to trip you when you weren't paying attention. But last night, with Millie sitting so close beside him and feeling her body pressed against his, he paid attention. Something told him Millie wouldn't be challenging him or anyone else to foot races anymore. He was tempted. Very tempted.

"What was that?" His friend was talking about something and he hadn't been listening.

"What do you mean, it cost you?" Roscoe repeated. "They billed you for a lift?"

Harry pushed his hat back on his head as he leaned on the railing of their boat. "No. Not like that." He tasted the coffee in his mug and watched a powerboat go by far out on the lake. The boat was a fast machine; a runabout painted dark blue with a long enclosed bow ending in a sharp wedge. He'd built one something like it himself. A runner's boat made to go faster than whatever might be chasing it. This morning, it was in a hurry to get to Ballard. He knew the boat although he never had any direct dealings with the owners. He did his best to avoid those types when he and Roscoe were running whiskey down from Canada. Pure criminals had owned it; people who would kill you or do business with you depending on what kind of opening you gave them.

He never thought of Roscoe and himself as criminals. Not the pure type, anyway. They never killed anybody, double crossed anyone or let the lifestyle consume them. Running hooch from Canada kept his grandfather's business afloat. But there certainly were times when he dealt with the less desirable thieves, murders and run of the mill scum who filled the docks and wharves around the Sound. He always tried to keep them at arm's length or even better, keep a cutout man between him and the darker side of the business. Harry's cutout was Drake, but Drake wasn't to be found and nobody needed an ex rumrunner on the waterfront anymore. Everything was changed now.

Two years ago, the owners of that particular dark blue speedboat had never been afraid of the word criminal. It was what they always were and always would be.

"Isn't that *Jacks or Better* tearing it up over there?" he asked Roscoe with a nod of his chin.

Roscoe squinted in the direction of the boat.

"I thought the Coast Guard caught her going into Port Townsend last fall?" Harry asked.

The rumble of the boat's oversized engines echoed around the shore as both men watched the old rumrunner plow across the smooth water. The sound of the speedboat seemed out of place on a peaceful Sunday morning. Still too loud, Harry thought. That's what got her caught. Even sitting at idle, you could hear those power plants for a mile or better on a quiet night.

"Yeah, that was *Jacks*," Roscoe said. "Ain't she a beauty? I could listen to those engines scream all day long. They had boiler plate put in behind the wheel back in '30 or '31. That's what somebody told me once, anyway."

"I wouldn't have done that. Must have cut at least five or six knots off the top speed," Harry said. "Besides, plate or no plate, a cutter's deck gun would have sent her to the bottom quick enough. I'd rather have the extra throttle." The sound of the engines faded to a distant growl on the morning air and quiet came back to their part of the lake. "You know who owned her, don't you?"

"I know." Roscoe spat into the water below them and watched the circular ripples denting the surface. The wake kicked up by the *Jack's* hadn't reached them yet.

"Maybe they were worried about hijacking? Plate would have come in handy if somebody started shooting, but I still think I would rather have the extra speed," Harry said.

Roscoe touched the old scar on his chest. "I don't know. There are good points and bad in that argument. I think I'd like the armor plate myself. Especially if I was working with that outfit," he added in a quieter voice. "I heard some nobody down Tacoma way bought her at auction. Wonder if they left the plate in?"

"Doubt it," Harry said. "No reason to anymore."

From their vantage point on the stern of the *Scarab*, there wasn't much to see of activity. A few old relics from the Great War were anchored not far away. They sat there for years and by the look of them were never going to move again. The old lumber mill they were tied up next to was closed down on weekends. Even during the workweek, it wasn't all that busy. Unless things turned around pretty quick, the mill would close for good before the end of summer.

Harry's family did business with this particular mill since his grandfather started Watkins Yacht Building. Odds were that a good portion of the wood used to build the very boat he was standing on came from right here.

"How many boats have we tied up here all totaled?" he asked Roscoe.

"Counting *Scarab,* three, I think."

Three boats. *Jupiter* became too well known, so they scrapped it. *Minotaur* almost outlasted prohibition and was the fastest boat he had ever been on. A perfect design for an illegal trade. Some Canadian bought it for half of what it was worth. A few bullet holes in the hull caused a drastic depreciation of its value.

"What about *Seahorse?*"

"That old bucket? Don't think so," Roscoe said. "Why?"

"Nothing. Something Millie said last night."

The long wooden pier on Lake Union didn't belong to him, but it might as well have. No one but he and Roscoe ever used it. The boathouse on the shore was filled with all the junk they owned that wouldn't fit onboard. The boathouse looked shabby in daylight with its drooping lamp pole and peeling paint. Last night, in the glow from the Ford's headlamps, it looked mysterious and filled with ambiance. The ambiance faded with the sunrise. Harry wondered if the ambiance he saw in Millie last night survived the rising of the sun or if the change would be permanent.

"Harry, I was thinking." Roscoe examined the grounds in his mug for a moment before going on with whatever he was thinking.

Harry had gotten used to that a long time ago. The more important the subject, the longer Roscoe would consider before speaking his mind.

"I've been thinking about transportation," he said at last.

"It's a moving subject, Roscoe."

"Yeah, well, we ain't doing a lot of moving these days." Roscoe thought that was enough conversation on the subject for now and decided to let the idea sink in.

"Something on your mind?" Harry asked at last.

"Well, it's just, we can't be walking all over the county. I think we should get another car."

Cars weren't exactly a pleasant topic of conversation. "I've got a car. It's right across over there." Harry pointed towards the west. "Other side of the Sound. Go ask the sheriff to show it to you. Hell, maybe he'll let you borrow it. It's a swell 1930 Plymouth coup, red with the spare mounted on the fender and electric windshield wipers on both sides. Both sides," Harry said again. "Runs like a top and it's the only one like it on the whole island." He poured his grounds into the water, creating a muddy brown smear on the blue surface. He'd spent more on lawyers trying to keep that car than what the thing was worth, but in the end, the car was forfeited along with almost everything else he owned. "You remember it well, I'm sure."

"They ain't going to take *Scarab* too, are they, Boss?"

"Nah, they got all the blood out of me they wanted. They didn't find the boat on the books because the lawyers had it listed as sold to that dead guy down in California, delivery pending. Never thought I'd see a silver lining on a corpse." He tapped the bottom of his cup on the wooden rail. "But they damn sure took my Plymouth." He liked that car. Next to his boat, which was supposed to be sold, it was his most favorite possession.

"I got a little put back," Roscoe said. "I've been saving ever since your old granddad hired me." He was entering the dangerous ground now and had to be careful how he phrased his approach. "It beats walking, having a car, I mean. The only reason I hadn't picked one up already is on account I was waiting to see what we decided about what we was gonna do. You know, for a living and all."

Harry studied the open face of his friend. Roscoe's face was like a road map of his life. There were deep lines across his forehead and a white scar ran through his right eyebrow; a memory of somebody's knuckles. It was a face Harry had seen all his life. He supposed he always would be seeing it. Roscoe was his constant in a turbulent time. But what exactly *were* they going to do for a living?

"Roscoe, if you were to get an offer from somebody, something a man could live on, I wouldn't expect you to turn it down. In fact, I'd be sore if you did. A car would come in handy going to and from work or if you had to go out of town for a job."

"Why Harry, what a notion." Roscoe took his rag out of his pocket and rubbed it along the top of the teak railing. "Jobs ain't all there is. A man's got to have a feeling like he belongs."

"You going to start writing poetry now?"

Roscoe ignored the question. "We belong, Harry. You and me. It ain't so much because of a job, needing a car and all I mean. It's just I'm not real fond of walking. You know that, and if we were planning to stick around these parts, a car would be a nice thing to have."

"One of those old back alley scoundrels you know got something for sale you want?" He couldn't help but smile at the roundabout way Roscoe had of coming to a point. If he wanted to buy somebody's old farm truck to get around in, it was his business. He guessed Roscoe was looking for financial advice on how much he should pay and didn't want to ask.

"No, Harry. None of my running buddies. But the Kitsap County sheriff does. They're going to auction that nice red Plymouth of yours tomorrow and Martha Ann Hines, you remember her? She told Jake Thompson down at the filling station the sheriff wants it for his nephew. I'd like to buy it. Make it ours again."

The wake from the long gone *Jacks or Better* hit the hull of *Scarab* at last. The shining white boat tied up next to the old sawmill rocked rhythmically on the water. Harry quit smiling.

"You want to buy my car?"

Roscoe raised his hand. One finger pointed to the heavens as if he had a biblical point to make. "Now Harry," he began. "Let me explain my position."

*****

"Jesus, Lucy, I know how to start a car," Millie told her sister.

"Humor me." Lucy pointed a gloved finger at the slot on the dash. "After you turn it on, you push the start button until the engine catches. Make sure it is in neutral when you do that. Or you can hold the clutch down, but sometimes, if it doesn't start right up, your leg gets tired."

"Are you going to teach me how to tell time, too? Crank this baby up," Millie said. "I'm ready to go."

"Fine. Pay attention and watch how I do it." Lucy started her car, found reverse, and eased the spotless cream white Auburn out of the garage. "You have to watch behind you when you back up."

"You're unbelievable." Millie shook her head. "I *have* borrowed Donny's car before."

"You haven't borrowed mine before. This is a heck of a lot more car than that hack Donny drives."

The Auburn eased gracefully down the long drive. When they reached the street, Lucy pulled to the curb. The car barely came to a stop before Millie was out her door and around to the driver's side.

"Scoot over," she told her sister.

"You know I haven't even let our brother drive this car, right?"

"Well, maybe Donny should challenge you to a tennis game. Scoot over," she said again.

Lucy slid across the seat to the passenger side. "Be honest Millie. You have driven a car before?"

"Dozens of times."

Lucy gave her sister a silent stare.

"I can drive, alright."

"Fine. We're going to go slow until you get the feel of things, and just around the neighborhood."

Millie slammed her door shut, adjusted the mirror, and gave the gas pedal a quick tap. The twelve cylinder engine rumbled with power making a tingle go through her fingers as they rested on the wheel.

"Ohhhh yeah," she whispered. "You should have asked around, sister. I've crushed everybody I know on the tennis court."

No kidding, Lucy thought. "Put it in gear and let's go." She looked down the driveway. "Think we should have closed the garage door?"

Something in the car's insides gave an unnatural grind as Millie worked the stick around trying to find first. "Too late for going back." She found her gear. The Auburn pulled away from the curb. Making the first right, the women eased slowly down the lane. Alder trees, still slumbering their way through winter, lined the road on both sides. Their bare branches extended over them forming a cocoon-like tunnel as the automobile toured the neighborhood.

Sunday was a good day for learning how to drive. The roads were mostly deserted and traffic was at minimum levels. The sun was out, so they left the top down. It was cool, but not too cold for comfort.

"Watch where you're going," Lucy said. It was the fourth time she said it.

For her day behind the wheel, Millie chose a camel colored beret pulled to one side of her head with matching gloves. Berets were all the rage ever since the Clyde Barrow's gangster girlfriend Bonnie made the papers wearing one. She thought the color was a good choice for the Auburn's tan leather interior.

Raising her hand above the glass windshield to feel the force of the wind pushing against her palm, Millie said, "I've got both eyes wide open." She hadn't stopped smiling since she first revved the engine.

A half hour later, after driving up and down the hills of Kirkland, Lucy felt less apprehensive. She was giving her sister lessons in good driving habits almost continuously since they left their driveway. Lucy tried to be patient with her instructions. Patience was not something that came naturally to her. The instructions part never gave her much of a problem.

"Where to now?" Millie asked as they made their fourth pass by their home. She was ready for the open road. "Doesn't matter where we go," she said with a bright, flashing smile. "Any road's a good road."

"The ferry," Lucy said. "I promised an old friend we would meet him for a late breakfast."

"What old friend? You aren't trying to set me up with someone, are you?"

"Don't be silly. Whatever would I tell Mrs. Chandler? It's one of Donny's friends. We knew him in college. If you came to Papa's party last night, I would have introduced you."

"If I had come to the party last night, whatever would I have told Mrs. Chandler?"

"I'm sure you would have thought of something." Lucy pointed towards the intersection in front of them. "Slow down. There's a stop sign coming up."

"I see it. Who's the guy?"

"His name is Joe Kanji. He's from Japan and he was hurt in a car wreck in Hawaii."

"Japan? Like China and Japan?"

"I'm not sure what that means unless you mean Asia. Watch the puddle."

Millie missed the puddle, twisted the big steering wheel around and turned the car in the direction of the ferry landing.

"Why are we taking him on my ride?"

"We're not taking him anywhere. Just a quick bite at his hotel."

Millie bit her lower lip, a habit she had when she was about to discuss any kind of funding. "Is he buying?"

"He invited us."

"And he's from Japan?"

"You'll like him. He's interesting."

The dining room on the Bergonian's second floor was filled with cloth covered tables arranged in regimental straight lines. Each table was set at an angle to its neighbor. The arrangement formed a chessboard of ivory squares on a dark red carpet laced with geometric patterns in blue. Joe Kanji chose his spot on the board with care. His square was on the far side of the sizable dining room next to a large window. The ivory handle of his cane was draped over the back of one of the empty chairs. The warm pool of sunlight coming through the window felt very good to him.

A child of six or seven in a pale yellow dress and very blond pigtails sat at the next table. She twisted around in her chair undoubtably finding Joe irresistible as he sat quietly at his table. Joe sipped his cup of atrocious American tea, then winked an eye. The child broke up in giggles, then turned around to whisper something in her mother's ear.

"I should have known I'd find you flirting with another female."

Joe rose stiffly to his feet and bowed slightly at the waist. "My dear Lucy. How splendid you look in the morning light."

Lucy nodded towards the little girl. "I saw that wink. Bet you told her the same thing."

"She seems fascinated by my presence. How do you do?" Joe asked, turning slightly to face the dark haired woman standing beside Lucy.

Millie clutched a small purse and looked around her at the brightly lit dining room. She had never been to the Bergonian before. "Hello."

"You are certainly Lucy's sister," Joe continued. "The resemblance is quite prominent."

"Joe," Lucy said formally, "my sister Miss Millie McAllister. Don't let her challenge you to a game of tennis. I hear she's quite good."

"You think we look alike?" Millie asked. She offered her hand, fingers pointing down and slightly curled.

Joe clasped her hand softly. "Absolutely."

"Most don't see much of a resemblance. Lucy favors our mother. I took after our father."

A waiter pulled two chairs away from his table. The women took their seats.

"More tea," Joe told the man. "I must disagree Miss, may I call you Millie?"

"Everyone does."

He pulled his chair closer to the table as he sat. "The hair is different, of course. But the face is quite the same. Anyone can see by the way you draw the attention of a room that you are both sisters from the same extraordinary lineage."

"Careful, Millie," Lucy warned her sister with a smile. "Joe's a charmer. Just ask the little one in the yellow dress."

Millie was smiling. No one had ever called her lineage extraordinary before.

It was a pleasant brunch. Millie spent most of the meal listening to Lucy and Joe talk about theirs and Donovan's days together at university and eating baked muffins that were the best she ever tasted. Her father never mentioned sending her off to university. Maybe the experiment with Lucy soured him on the idea. It hadn't really mattered to Millie, anyway. She had no interest in higher education. She also noticed that most of the conversation from Joe was directed at her sister. That wasn't so surprising. Men always noticed Lucy. What was surprising was the way Lucy seemed to be returning the interest.

"What time is it getting to be?" The waiter picked up their plates almost an hour ago and she had listened to all she could take about old classmates and hated professors.

Joe pulled a large gold watch from a vest pocket. "Half past noon."

"Is it?" Lucy asked. "Time flies."

"I believe I have captured your attention far longer than anticipated," Joe said as he slipped his watch back into his pocket.

"We really should be going." Lucy smiled sweetly at her sister. "I haven't finished paying my gambling debts."

Millie was on her feet in an instant. "It was swell meeting you, Mr. Kanji, and the breakfast was delicious."

Joe rose slowly. "As was the company," he replied, inclining his head towards the two women.

Millie led the way across the dining room. She was in a hurry and it showed as she quick marched through the straight rows of tablecloths. Half the day was gone and, although it was a pleasant morning with Lucy's friend, this was her day to drive. Lucy was wasting time sipping tea.

She flew down the wide staircase with hardly a glance in any direction. The lobby had a lot more people coming and going than when they came through earlier. She waited beside one of the divans for Lucy and the slower moving Joe to navigate the stairs.

Most people would describe Frankie Byrd as an unpleasant looking man, probably in his middle thirties with a generally unpleasant feel about him. It was hard to say for certain what was the source of bad feelings, but almost everyone who met him felt it. There was just something about him. Maybe it was the way he looked at you? Something in the set of his eyes that made the general public know he would never be a friend.

He wore a gray hat pulled low down over his forehead and a suit coat a couple of sizes too large for his frame. He had a seat in one of the two shoeshine chairs. Not because he needed a shine. He couldn't care less about his shoes. The chairs, sitting between the elevators and the hotel's newsstand, were perfectly situated to observe the comings and goings in the Bergonian's lobby. Big glass entry doors, elevators, front desk and hallway going towards the Pharmacy could all be watched from one of those chairs. It was a good place to sit if you were hunting someone and Frankie Byrd was hunting.

A good looking blonde in a cream colored blouse, small hat and dark skirt came down the staircase. There was something familiar about her. The blonde turned to say something to an Asian man beside her. He could tell it was a conversation between two people who knew each other well. Their mannerisms were familiar like they were old friends. The pair stopped every few steps because the man was having problems with the stairs. When they reached the lobby, the oriental tipped his hat to the blonde, then turned for the front desk.

The shoeshine boy finished buffing his shoes to as close to a mirror finish as the old leather was going to get.

The blonde headed for the front exit right as it came to him where he'd seen that head of hair before. It was a few years ago. Harry Watkins got out of a taxi one night with the dish inside. He'd seen her sitting in the seat. Same hair, same body in one of those slinky evening gowns with half her tits hanging out and looking good enough to eat. He'd tried to say something to her, but Watkins shut the taxi door before he got two words out.

Frankie Byrd folded the newspaper he was pretending to read in half and tucked it under his arm. She was leaving. He hopped out of the chair and walked quickly across the lobby.

"Hey," he shouted. The blonde was about to walk through the doors and out onto the street.

Lucy stopped and looked at the gray hat coming towards her.

"I know you, don't I?" Frankie said. He pushed his way past several of the hotel's guest. He needed to get closer.

She didn't recognize the man and there was something about him that didn't appeal to her. Something in the way he looked at her as he crossed the lobby.

"I don't think so," she said decisively. And never will, she thought to herself. Millie was on the sidewalk just outside the hotel's door. She pushed against the heavy steel and glass. "Ready?" she asked her sister.

Frankie picked up his pace. He was almost to the door when someone grabbed his arm. The shoeshine boy held on to the sleeve of his coat.

"Say, buddy."

"What do you want?" The blonde was getting away. He needed to catch her before she was lost in the crowd of pedestrians outside the hotel.

The boy stuck out a hand. His fingernails were stained black with shoe polish. "You owe me for the shine."

Reaching into his pocket, Frankie tossed the boy a dime. "I wasn't going to stiff you," he growled.

"Sure you weren't. I thought I would remind you before you forgot some more."

Frankie looked the boy in the eyes. "Beat it, kid."

"Sure," the boy said, unimpressed and unafraid of the man in the baggy suit. He dropped the coin into a pocket, then sauntered back to his chairs.

Frankie hurried out of the Bergonian's lobby and out to the front sidewalk. He went a short ways down the avenue looking for a light colored blouse and blonde hair, but didn't see anyone. Reversing his direction, he walked to the end of the block. Twisting his newspaper into a tight roll, he slapped it against his thigh several times in frustration. The woman had vanished. He turned and walked quickly back to the hotel.

The Asian, a cane clasped tightly in his left hand, was standing in front of the registry desk writing something on a pad. New suit, Frankie noticed. Expensive too, by the looks of it. The shoeshine boy lounged by his empty chairs. Frankie tossed his paper into the trash and approached the chairs.

The boy caught the eye of the man moving towards him and took a half step back. "Yeah?"

"See that guy over there talking to the front desk?" Frankie asked.

"I see him. So what?"

"You see him a lot?"

The boy spat into a small can of black polish cupped in his hand. He rubbed the spittle into the polish with the tip of a finger for a moment before answering. "What's a lot?"

"You seen him before?" Frankie asked again.

"Every day." The kid turned to his cans of polish and shoe brushes, giving his back to the guy who tried to cheat him out of his dime.

"What's his story?" Frankie asked.

The boy turned around, crossed his arms and looked the man in the eyes. If he had something to say, he wasn't saying it.

Frankie pulled a silver dollar out of his pocket and held it balanced between finger and thumb. "His story."

"His name's Kanji." The boy's eyes were glued to the bright, shiny dollar. "Got one of the big rooms up on eleven."

"What else is he?"

The boy pursed his lips and looked at the high arching ceiling of the hotel.

"Don't act wise, kid." Frankie Byrd placed the silver dollar on one of the chair's stirrups.

"They say he's got millions." The boy snatched the coin from its perch on the stirrup and flipped it in the air. "He's been here a few days spending money like he can't count it." He leaned closer to the man and said in a softer whisper. "The talk is he's a Chinese prince, son of the emperor himself. But that's just talk from the eleventh floor maids. He's got a whole load of opium on a freighter out in Elliot Bay and can't get it unloaded cause of the strike."

"He got friends?"

"Don't think so," the boy said. The boy looked at Joe Kanji writing on his pad at the front desk, then jerked a chin in Joe's direction. "Look, there he goes again with the telegrams. Sends one every day. Sometimes two."

Frankie and the boy watched the Asian man named Kanji take a seat by one of the big windows on the far side of the lobby.

"See ya, kid."

He was pretty good at arithmetic. He could count two and two and right now, his counting the blonde plus Harry Watkins equaled something profitable going on with the Chinese man sitting fifty feet away from him. He straightened his hat, squared his tie, and walked quietly towards the man named Kanji. Something was there. He could smell it.

The oriental sat in one of two high backed wing chairs reading the paper. Frankie took the other chair, crossed his legs, and studied the unknown man across from him. What would Harry Watkins be doing with someone like this? There had to be an angle. Only he didn't know what it was. Not yet.

"I saw you talking with Harry's woman," he said in an even tone.

Joe Kanji bent his paper and peered over the top of the pages. "I am sorry," he said in a polite tone. "Were you speaking to me?"

Frankie kept the surprise off his face. He expected some kind of pidgin English. Instead, the man's accent sounded smooth and well educated. He took his hat off and perched it on a knee. Running a hand through close cropped pale blonde hair, he said, "The piece you came down the stairs with."

"The piece?" Joe repeated. His dark eyebrows pinched into a tight line.

"Harry Watkins and me are partners from way back." Frankie sucked air through his front teeth. It was a habit of his; something he did when he was talking and thinking at the same time. "We work together."

"I do not believe I am following you," Joe said cautiously.

"Why don't we talk it over with Harry?"

"Talk what over?"

An old memory came to him. He was talking to Watkins about something when Harry mentioned some woman named Lucy. That was the name. Lucy something.

"Your angle. He can bring Lucy along."

Joe struggled to keep his face as blank and expressionless as he could. He laid the newspaper to one side. "What angle are you speaking of?"

"The angle you don't want the law to know about."

Joe suddenly felt a cold hand gripping his heart. How had he been found out? Who was this man with the uncomfortable demeanor sitting across from him, and what did he know? What was Lucy to this man?

Frankie had seen his share of faces. He'd learned a long time ago that a man's face could tell you things his voice never would. He was watching the Asian's face very closely. He saw everything he needed to see. This guy and Watkins had their fingers in something. He drew a deep breath through his nostrils as if he could smell the odor of money ready to be made. Pulling his makings out of a pocket, he rolled a cigarette while he considered his next question.

"You one of Chang Woo's boys?" he asked casually as he moistened the edge of the paper with his tongue.

"I am a businessman on holiday. I think you have made a mistake. Perhaps you should be on your way."

Frankie pulled a wooden match from his hatband and struck it with his thumbnail. "Opium. Is that it?" He inhaled deeply and exhaled a blue cloud over Joe's head. "Makes sense. Can't sell booze anymore. Or maybe it's tender little slant eyed girls from faraway lands?" He examined the bright glowing tip of his cigarette. "Watkins is running something." Frankie leaned forward in his chair balancing his elbows on his knees. "Running something is all that two bit nail bender knows how to do. What is it, Kanji? What's the game?"

"How do you know my name?"

Frankie examined the fresh gleam shining on the leather toes of his shoes. "I'm a guy who knows things."

Joe tried to regain his composure. Watkins was the name of the man Donovan had called a gangster. Now he understood. The man sitting across from him was also a gangster.

"I think you should leave now. I shall ask the manager to call for a policeman."

"You do that." Frankie leaned back in his chair and smoked. "Have him whistle up two or three. I'll tell them why I'm here. They're bound to arrest me and when they do, I'll tell them about you, Harry Watkins, and that fine looking woman you were with. Oh, and I'll mention Chang Woo for good measure. It won't matter how much money you've got then. They'll drag you out of this fancy hotel by the heels." Frankie sucked his teeth. "You'll talk to them whether you want to or not, Kanji." He looked into the dark, impassive eyes and waited to see if he had guessed correctly.

Joe Kanji didn't move.

"Didn't think so," he said after a moment. His lips twisted into his version of a smile. The corners of his mouth curled down and the top lip lifted to show his teeth. It gave his face a feral look.

"Who are you?" Joe said quietly. He could feel the hard outline of the automatic sitting in his hip pocket. Had the time come?

"Didn't I introduce myself? Frankie Byrd. Ask around. I'm known."

"And this Watkins fellow?"

"Don't act like you don't know him. I just saw you with his woman coming down the stairs practically arm in arm."

"The young lady is not anyone's woman. She comes from one of the better families and is a credit to her upbringing."

"Save the stories for Chang Woo's little girls. Harry's had his hands all over her for years. Everybody knows about him and Lucy." Frankie casually pointed a finger at the ceiling above and asked, "They still got that room on the sixth floor?"

Joe looked quickly at the carpet beneath his feet, unable to keep the surprise from his face. He remembered Lucy's sudden mood change after Watkins showed up in the bar.

"That is not true," he said. He needed a moment to think; to collect his thoughts. The palms of his hands were moist.

"You mean you didn't know?" Frankie asked. He blew another cloud of smoke over Joe's head.

"Mr. Byrd." Joe cleared his throat. "I met your man Watkins briefly last Friday night in the hotel's bar. I do not know him. I do not know this Woo you have referred to and I am as certain as I have ever been that the woman whose reputation you are carelessly slandering has no connection in your affairs at all."

The feral smile was on Frankie Byrd's face again. "Fuck what you think, Kanji. I know what I know and by sundown, I'm going to know everything about you. Where you're from. When you got here. Who you've been sending all those telegrams to. The questions you've asked and what's your angle. Whatever you and Watkins got cooked up, you just found yourself a new partner. It'll be like old times."

"I told you. I do not know this man. Miss McAllister and I are old acquaintances." Joe wiped the palms of his hands against the chair's armrests. Slowly rising from his chair, he stared at this unknown issue sitting before him. "Now, if you will excuse me? I must be going."

"Don't play poker, Kanji. You can't bluff worth a damn. You blew your chance to get rid of me when you didn't call a cop. I can tell you aren't used to having the bite put on you. That's okay. I'm reasonable. Ask anybody. They'll tell you Frankie Byrd is a reasonable hoodlum. All I want is a share." Frankie took a long drag on his smoke. "Consider it the cost of doing business in my neighborhood." He smoothed the crease running across the crown of his hat. "I'll need a retainer, of course."

"A what?"

"Think of it as a show of good faith in our new partnership. You can take it out of Harry's cut if it makes you feel better."

"You are asking me for money?"

"What made you think I was asking?" Frankie leaned closer to Joe's chair. "I never ask for nothing. It ain't my nature." He sucked air through his teeth before going on. "But like I said, I ain't unreasonable. Five hundred dollars will do for now."

"Will do what?"

"Will buy my silence for one thing. My protection, too. Working with me will keep the others away while we do our business."

"I do not need your protection. You are a criminal."

"And you ain't? See, there's the rub, Kanji. Criminals, being as they are always behaving in illegal ways can't call for help when somebody like me shows up."

Joe said nothing. The evil looking man sitting across from him wasn't part of his mission briefings. Staying undiscovered. That was in his mission briefings.

"Conundrum, ain't it?" Frankie smoothed the crease along the top of his hat again.

"A conundrum is a riddle of words," Joe told him. He pulled a wallet from his coat pocket, opened it and methodically counted out one hundred dollars in small bills.

Frankie Byrd's eyes counted with him.

"You are not a riddle," Joe told him.

Frankie stopped caressing the formed shape of his hat's brim.

"I congratulate you on learning what you have, even though most of it is idle gossip you have picked up here and there. I am willing to place you on a retainer. Keep your wild tales about me and about women you do not know to yourself. See that I am undisturbed by riffraff such as yourself while I am on my holiday and you can earn yourself a tidy sum." Joe laid the money on the armrest of his chair. "Silence is golden." He managed a smile. "You have heard this saying before, yes?"

Frankie stubbed his cigarette out in an ashtray. Standing, he straightened his tie, then hitched up his trousers with his thumbs. The stack of bills, he scooped off the armrest almost as fast as the shoeshine boy snatched the silver dollar from the stirrup. Folding the notes in half, he shoved them in a pocket.

"Do we have a deal?" Joe asked.

"Where's Harry these days?"

"The man was here Friday night. Other than that, I cannot help you."

"Kanji," Byrd growled.

"I cannot help you," Joe Kanji shouted.

At the sound of the shout, several heads turned towards the two men.

Frankie knew when he had pushed far enough. Kanji was getting his wits about him. It was time to go. "Don't try to give me the slip. If you switch hotels, I'll find you. My boys will be keeping an eye on you." Frankie settled his hat onto his head. "Tell Watkins we need to talk."

Joe kept to his chair as Frankie Byrd left. He didn't watch him leave. Instead, he returned to his paper, staring at the printed pages in front of him.

He wasn't reading.

Had he made a wise decision? Was it the correct thing to do, to pay the man off? If he had called for a policeman, would that have been a better choice? No, he didn't think so. Extortion was what the dictionary called it. Or insurance. He knew he would have to be careful from now on. Very careful or extortion would quickly graduate to blackmail.

Frankie felt pretty good about himself. He didn't have a clue what Kanji was doing, but once again, his nose pointed him in the right direction. It was the easiest hundred bucks he'd ever made. Either Kanji was a complete sap or he had something to hide, something he couldn't afford for the police to know. Frankie couldn't help but smile. He crossed the lobby, leaving Kanji to stew about what just happened to him. The kid who pointed him towards Kanji was standing by his chairs.

"Hey, kid," he called. He even said it cheerfully.

"Yeah," the boy said. "It's opium, like I said, isn't it?"

"What? No, you nosy little shit. It ain't opium." Frankie pulled the wad of bills out of his pocket.

The boy had never seen so much money in one hand in his life.

He drew a smooth, unwrinkled five dollar bill away from the rest, then stuck the wad of money back in his pocket. "You got something to write with?"

The kid rummaged inside one of the drawers under his chairs and produced a snapped in half pencil. The tip was rounded and dull but would do. He handed it to Frankie.

"You're a smart kid. I like the way you notice things. I want you to notice something for me." As he spoke, he wrote a phone number across the top of the five dollar bill. "If the Prince of China over there checks out suddenly or if he has visitors, if he does anything at all, you make it your business to know it." Frankie looked up from the five to catch the eye of the boy. "Did you get a good look at the blonde I was speaking to?" He cupped his hands in front of his chest. "The one with the melons."

The boy smiled. "Sure, I saw her."

"If you see her again or see anything else I need to know, you call this number right away."

The boy's eyes lit up when Frankie handed him the note. Then, very quickly, he tore the bill in half and handed the kid the end with the numbers on it.

"You call when you know something, and I'll give you the other half. Got it?"

"I got it," the boy said.

As he turned to leave, he said, "Ask for Frankie Byrd when you call. If I ain't there, ask for a guy named Squeaky."

Frankie went through the glass doors and into the beautifully bright sunshine outside. A hundred bucks for nothing and he was getting closer to finding Watkins. Her name was Lucy and Kanji said her last name was McAllister. Wherever she was, Harry wouldn't be far behind. He was getting closer. Time to go find Squeaky and do some celebrating.

Joe put his unread paper away, stood up slowly from his wing chair, found his cane and limped quietly towards the front desk. He had another telegram to send.

*****

"Do you know where you are?" Lucy asked her sister.

The questioned sister waved a hand over her shoulder. "Canada's that way," she said. Pointing past Lucy, she added, "Oregon's over there somewhere."

The gravel road went around a bend. A crossroads was coming up. "Turn right," Lucy said. "There's a road that follows the hills not too far away. We'll take it home."

"You know the way?"

127

"It's been a few years, but I remember where it goes. It's a nice road."

Lucy's road wound its way through the thickly forested hills and gradually increasing elevations as they edged closer to the mountains. It wasn't as nice of a drive as she remembered. The gravel gave way to muddy dirt after a few miles.

"Our definition of nice isn't the same," Millie said to her sister. "This looks like a logger's road."

"It used to be in better shape and there are flowers in the spring." The sound of mud being thrown against the fenders was almost constant now.

"Too early for flowers," Millie said.

The cream white paint of Lucy's motorcar had a healthy coating of some of Washington State's finest mud down both sides before long and its formerly gleaming wire spoke wheels were going to take some effort to clean. An hour later, the turnoff far behind them, the pair were running south through the steep hills and forests somewhere to the east of Lake Washington. They tore along in the rare winter sunshine, darting around sudden curves or splashing through shallow muddy ruts in the road. In those stretches where the limbs of the towering dark firs cast their shadows over the narrow lane, the sudden chill reminded both women that spring and its promise of flowers had not yet arrived in the northwest.

"I should make your Mr. Chandler wash my car when we get back."

"Clarence?" Clarence would scrub the car spotless if she asked him to but then he would be expecting certain rewards from her that were no longer in contemplation. "What?" She was lost in her thoughts, thinking about car washes, Clarence pulling at her buttons, and the possibilities of borrowing her sister's car next weekend. She had missed something.

"I said how was he?"

"Clarence?" She felt for the top button of her blouse.

"Harry." Lucy considered the risks of asking her sister this question all morning. She had never been able to tolerate being teased, even the good natured kind, and asking about Harry was an open invitation to Millie. "How was he?"

Millie thought about her options before she answered. If her sister went out with Harry next Saturday, she might not need her car. On the other hand, if Harry went out with Lucy, it would probably sink any chance she had of luring him away. Her finger tapped lightly on the Auburn's shifter. It was a very nice car. Elizabeth's family Ford didn't even compare.

"He vanished, you know. After you left. You ran away to New York and Harry fell through a crack and was gone. I couldn't believe it was really him last night." Millie glanced at her sister sitting next to her before going on. "You said you and Harry were finished for good."

"He didn't come to the train station. I was aggravated. That's all."

"You said you couldn't stand the sight of him anymore."

Lucy looked at the windshield and thought about her feelings for Harry Watkins. "That was a long time ago. We're old friends and we know a lot of the same people. It's complicated."

"Did he really sock Donny on the nose?" Millie had never seen a real, honest to Pete fight before except in the movies. She wondered if Clarence Chandler would have the nerve to punch Harry if the situation required it. Probably not, she guessed. Another reason why he wasn't right for her.

Lucy thought about that night. Why in the world had she agreed to meet Donny at the Pharmacy? Donny never went there. Not in those days. She knew how her brother felt about Harry, but thought their mutual animosity for each other would be put aside in the neutral territory of the speakeasy.

It hadn't. Not for very long.

Her brother had shown up with some of his friends from the Coast Guard station at Port Angeles. None of them were wearing their uniforms, not in an illegal nightclub. To the Pharmacy, they were just another group of men looking to blow off some steam and drink a little illegal hooch.

The evening began well enough. She didn't see the argument start or hear what caused it and didn't even know the man Roscoe hit. She hadn't really paid him any attention until then. He was one of her brother's friends from the station. Whoever he was, he grabbed Harry's arm. That was all it took for Roscoe. Those were the days when Roscoe could always be found standing behind Harry usually watching for anyone approaching from behind and always looking like someone who could deliver a swift verdict if he thought you were standing where you had no business to be standing. She had never seen him actually hit anyone before. Harry's bodyguard looked like someone who *could* be violent with his short, powerful build. He just never had been. Not in front of her.

Roscoe Harrison slammed the man's face into the bar's railing and looked ready to demolish anyone and everyone in sight and, just like that, the evening went to hell.

That was when Donny entered the picture, rushing up from somewhere and intending to beat Harry, Roscoe, or whoever else might get in his way to a pulp. She could still remember seeing her brother sitting on the barroom floor with a dazed look in his eyes as full scale war erupted in the Pharmacy.

"Yes," Lucy said to her sister. "He punched Donny in the nose. He had it coming." Thinking back on it now, at the time, she hadn't felt that way at all. "He was acting like a schoolboy on the playground and Harry decked him for it. It's getting chilly out. You want to stop and put the top up?" The conversation about Harry and Donny had gone as far as she wanted it to go.

"No, I like the way it feels, and the sun's still out. What did you do after he hit Donny?"

The Pharmacy's bouncers and a couple of the bartenders restored order in the bar. Donny and company were shown to the back exit while Roscoe walked escorted but untouched to the bar's half hidden front door and on into the Bergonian's lobby. Harry was asked to leave by someone she didn't know. Asked, she remembered. Not told. Her brother was tossed out the back, but Harry was asked to leave. Blood was thicker than water, she supposed, because it made her angry, angrier than it should have. But seeing Harry punch her brother lit something off in her; something that took a trip to New York and black silk lingerie to put out. The crowd separated her from Harry, but she caught up to him by the time he made it to the marble fireplace. The same one she reminisced about Friday evening. Her temper got the better of her and she called him names. She couldn't remember what names now, but they were some of her best.

"Sure you don't want to put the top up?" she asked her sister again.

"You're changing the subject." Millie twisted the automobile through a long S curve deep in the shadows of the ancient old fir trees lining the roadside.

"We got in a big fight. That's all that happened. Harry said I was a spoiled bitch. Can you believe that? I've never been called that by somebody not wearing a dress in my life." Thinking back on it now, the memory made her smile. All her life men bent over backwards trying to get her attentions. Not Harry.

Millie considered a response to her sister's statement about women wearing skirts and how she might interpret spoiled, but decided to let it go.

"If Pop was going to buy a car for me," she said, looking back over her shoulder, "I think I would have picked one with a back seat."

"I didn't pick it. It was a surprise. You don't like it now that you've hit every hole in the road there was for the last sixty miles?"

Millie rubbed her hand along the dash. "I love it. But I would want a backseat."

It was outside the little town of Renton that Millie's good luck with the powerful motorcar ran out. The Auburn Speedster, its engine revving high and hard, shot around a long curve in a road hugging blur of mud splattered cream paint. The canvas top was still down, despite the cooler temperatures. Millie's beret was threatening to give up the effort of hanging on and go sailing away in her wake.

"Now we're moving," Millie shouted.

The roadway had finally improved enough for Millie to run their speed up past fifty and the two women were flying through a long stretch of shaded, hard packed earth. Lucy had one hand braced against the dash and the other holding onto the passenger side door for support. With the wide turn disappearing behind them, Millie shifted into top gear and mashed the gas pedal hard. The next curve was a half mile ahead.

Lucy looked at the rows of telephone poles going past her door and shouted, "How fast are we going?"

The telephone poles answered her question with a whump, whump, whump sound as they passed by her vision in a faster and faster progression. Beyond the poles, the damp green trunks of fir trees clothed in dark shadows stood like huge witnesses to their speed. She was afraid to look at the speedometer and was just as afraid to take her eyes off the flying poles.

"Almost seventy and I bet I can go faster." Millie had the look of a jockey riding a thoroughbred hard for the finish line. Seventy. Locomotives could go that fast. So could the speedster.

"Not on this road, Millie. There are too many curves and it's too wet," Lucy shouted over the wind, "and if you don't slow down this minute, I'll never let you drive again."

Millie glanced at her passenger, saw a face that wasn't kidding, and reluctantly let the feeling of exquisite speed drift away until another day. The engine's howl came down several octaves as she pulled in the reins on her charging horse. She took the next curve at a sedate thirty miles an hour. Her sister was right. It was too wet although she was sure she could have hit eighty before having to slow down for the curve. She would have loved to feel what eighty was like.

"Do you think Papa will buy me one of these for my twenty-first?"

"That's still a month away. I wouldn't be in such a hurry if I were you." The telephone poles stopped talking to her outside her door and the feeling of sudden death approaching on a country road subsided. And her brother had accused her of driving too fast?

"Were you in a hurry when you were twenty?"

Lucy smiled, and both sisters laughed together.

"Are you kidding? I could hardly stand the wait."

The Auburn hit a rut in the road and they both bounced off the seat. Millie touched the brake and slowed the car down to a slightly slower pace. "What did you do on your big day?"

"Nothing special. Threw a big party. Donny got drunk on some homemade mash he took out of a runner's boat the night before. Papa gave me mother's diamonds. He'll give you grandmother's pearls. I guess he's saving the ring for Donny's wife." It might be a while before their father gave that ring away.

"I want one of these," Millie said, patting the seat's open leather between them. "And the pearls," she added.

A farm truck appeared ahead of them and she would have to go around it shortly. Passing other cars was something the Auburn's power plant did very well.

"I didn't get an automobile for turning twenty-one and you better not either." She reached across the seat to her sister and tucked a wayward brown curl out of her eyes.

"No, all you had to do was run away to New York to get yours."
Millie downshifted as the Auburn muscled its way up a steep
incline.

The truck was getting closer.

"You don't talk about New York much. Didn't you like it?"

"New York? New York was spectacular. It gets very fast
sometimes. Just when you think you have it all figured out, you find
out you don't." She didn't want to think about New York. She was
home, it was a gorgeous day, and her kid sister was finally driving
like a rational person.

They were almost to the top of the hill. Millie pulled over to the
left hand side of the road to shoot around the truck in front of them.

"Millie!"

An oncoming car cresting the far side of the hill let out a long
and loud blast from its horn. Millie, fear of a head on collision with
the automobile making her overreact, yanked the steering wheel too
far and too fast to the right. The passenger side wheels left the
smooth dirt of the road and dug into the soft, wet bank. She stomped
hard on the brakes as the Auburn lost traction. Both women felt the
car sliding on the wet road. Panicking, Millie turned the wheel away
from the oncoming car. The irate driver went past them shouting
curses never once letting off his horn until he was well clear.

Millie avoided the wreck, but her unpracticed driving skills were
showing. The county recently graded the road and there was a tall
wedge of dirt almost a foot high lining the edge of the roadway. The
Auburn, still sliding, plowed through it sending clods of damp mud
out in front of them. There was a clanging sound from somewhere
towards the front of the automobile. Both women lurched forward
as the automobile came to a sudden stop six feet from the trunk of a
massive tree.

"Did I hit something?"

"Felt like it." Lucy was straining her neck to see over the hood
of her car. She couldn't see anything. "Put it in reverse and see if
we can back up."

The car they nearly hit was vanishing down the road behind
them. Apparently, the driver didn't care whether they were stuck or
not. The farm truck Millie had been in the process of passing
crested the hill and went on about its business. Millie revved the
engine once, put it in reverse and eased out on the clutch. She'd

never backed a car up before, but didn't think now was a good time to mention it. The Auburn didn't seem to care because it pulled straight out and onto the dirt road without seeming to notice it ever left the freshly graded surface. Putting the car in first and driving slightly faster than a horse drawn wagon, Millie eased forward and straightened the automobile in the lane. Bringing the car to a stop, she put it in neutral and set the brake.

Lucy was out of the car and walking around to the front in an instant.

Millie sat behind the wheel not wanting to get out, too afraid of what her sister might discover. She knew she had run into something. So did her sister.

"Damn it, Millie." Lucy swore as she squatted to examine the shining steel bumper of her car. "You must have hit a rock," she shouted back over the hood of her car. Lucy ran a finger along the dent. The entire chrome front bumper of her car was covered in a layer of mud except for a freshly shining strip of bare metal below the radiator. Something hard wiped the mud clean and left a ripple in the steel. "I knew I shouldn't have let you drive." Her brand new car struck something a solid blow, who knew what, but a rock sounded good enough to her. It must have been lying just off the side of the road where winter killed weeds still standing between the road and the trees concealed it. Nervous energy made her angrier than what the dent was worth. The other automobile suddenly showing itself coming over the hill and the head on collision that almost happened rattled her much worse than bumping something on the side of the road.

"Damn it, Millie," she shouted again. "You and your tennis court pranks nearly got us both smashed to hell." Lucy pulled a scarf from around her neck with an angry yank. "Too bad your driving skills aren't half as good as your backhand." Lucy glared at her sister cowering behind the wheel with all the superiority of a passenger who wasn't driving when the accident happened.

Millie couldn't bear the withering look in those eyes. She stared at the steering wheel instead. She had wrecked her sister's car. A tear ran down her cheek. She knew she would be hearing about this day for a long time to come. She felt like a fool. Opening her door, she stepped out of the car and walked around the sweeping fenders to face her sister's anger and see how much damage she caused. She would certainly have to ask clumsy, groping Clarence to wash the car now. Plans for borrowing the automobile this Saturday went up in smoke. Probably gone forever.

"Stop crying," Lucy said. "It's only a dent. Come on," she said, putting an arm around her sister's shoulder. "You scared the hell out of me."

"I'm sorry, Lucy. Oh gosh, is it pushed in much?" Millie didn't want to look. "Papa's going to scream. He's just going to scream." Millie forced herself to look at the bumper's muddy coating and wasn't sure where she hit it.

"If you think I'm telling our father we've already wrecked this car you're dreaming."

"Can Donny fix it?"

"Donny?" Lucy smirked. "Our dear brother can fix a great martini, but I wouldn't let him near my car with any kind of tool except maybe a jack."

"Didn't we pass a station a few miles back? I'm sure they can whack it with a hammer and it would be fine."

Lucy looked down the hill and the long road winding its way through the forest as if she could see the distant station somewhere lost in the trees. There had been a gas station, she remembered, but it was closed. "Get in. I'll drive."

"Are you mad at me?" Millie's eyes were red, but the tears were stopped. "I never saw anything in the road and I've never hit anything before and you got to admit, I was doing fine until then."

"It's a small dent and I know someone who can fix it as good as new." She wasn't thinking about gas stations. They got back in the car.

"You're smiling, Lucy," Millie said as her sister released the car's brake.

"Was I?" She pulled a knob on the dash and the car's headlamps lit the darkening evening in front of them. Another half hour and it would be completely dark. She was trying to remember if she had brought her perfume.

*****

Harry noticed the smell immediately. It was a subtle smell, unobtrusive and coy, like a sledgehammer hitting a plate glass window. He first thought it was coming from the bilges. *Scarab* always had a slight odor coming up from below. You never really noticed it unless the boat was shut up for a prolonged period. But what he smelled now wasn't a bilge smell. Sitting at *Scarab's* galley table, motionless, his hands holding the old worn playing cards in an arc ready to be shuffled for the next deal, he sniffed the air around him. Fried bacon, his nose told him. That was from the dish with the remains of their dinner sitting by the sink. It wasn't that. He sniffed the air over his shoulder, back in the direction of the salon, but he didn't think it was coming from that part of the boat either. It was drifting through the tight spaced interior, something he couldn't identify exactly but one that reminded him of freshly sliced lemons mixed with a solvent of some kind. The door to *Scarab's* crew quarters opened and Roscoe stepped into the galley followed by invisible clouds of citrus vapors and something that he still couldn't quite put a name to. The cards in his hands fanned into a single stack as he completed the shuffle. He gave them a loud tap against the table, smoothing the well worn deck into a tight rectangle before dealing another hand of solitaire. He made a quick study of the rows of cards and smiled.

"Going to church, Roscoe?" he asked casually. The cards looked promising.

"What's that, Harry?" Roscoe had the look on his face of a man deeply involved in absolutely nothing out of the ordinary.

"Sunday evening and all and you putting on your finest, thought you were getting ready to get some religion in you."

His mechanic was a few feet away from him now, and Harry rubbed at an eye with a fingertip.

Roscoe paused to pick up the last piece of bacon. He had changed from his usual garb of coveralls and work shirt into his best set of clothes; a very dark colored double breasted suit that he swore was a deep blue in the daylight and turned black when it wasn't caught in sunlight. Everyone else swore it was black all the time, but Roscoe was a man fond of his notions. He bought it new six or seven years ago for a friend's wedding or funeral, he couldn't remember which anymore, and saved it for special occasions when a man needed to look respectable. He often wore it into the city on those nights when he and Harry were doing their business together. It wasn't the city that brought out his best suit this evening. Or religion. For tonight's business, he'd even shaved and made an attempt at smoothing down the bristles of his hair.

"You seen my hat, Boss?" he asked, disregarding the question about church.

Harry sat back against the bench seat and gave his mechanic a good natured appraisal then leaned forward and sniffed the air. "Are you wearing cologne?"

"It ain't cologne. It's aftershave and I often wear it. I'm surprised you haven't smelled it a hundred times before."

A gentleman's fragrance was how the man behind the drugstore counter phrased it. He picked up a pint bottle of the stuff in Bainbridge while Harry was settling his business with the sheriff. A cut on the inside of his little finger still sizzled like fire from where the liquid soaked into the skin. He thought the smell of his gentleman's fragrance matched well with the barbershop tonic he rubbed into his hair.

Harry was pretty certain he had never smelled his mechanic wearing any kind of manmade scent other than gasoline and motor oil, but kept his thoughts to himself. He wondered if the smell pouring off his mechanic would be flammable if he were to strike a match.

"That relic you call a hat was sitting on a chair in the salon last time I noticed it."

Roscoe, still eating the last of the bacon, headed for the steps to the boat's salon. "You should come with me, Harry. Do you good to get out for a little while and forget about things."

"Where are you going?" He played a red six on a seven of clubs. Evening was coming on and the light was beginning to fade in the *Scarab's* galley. He reached for the switch mounted behind him and turned on the little electric light above the table before dealing himself three more cards. The face card wouldn't play and he quickly slid it back into the deck.

Roscoe came back from the boat's main cabin with his newest old hat pushed back on the back of his head.

"Oh, you know. Just down the road a ways to Barefoot Nessie's." He paused next to the small table in the galley and looked over the rows of laid out cards. "Play the ten of hearts on the jack," he said, pointing a finger at the ten.

Harry moved the card without comment.

"C'mon Harry. There's no point in sitting here all night." Roscoe turned away from the cards and saw the small pile of dishes sitting where Harry left them.

"That's okay," Harry said. He moved the nine of diamonds one column of cards to the left onto a red king. It wasn't really cheating if you were playing by yourself. "I'm probably going to go see if I can get a line on Drake again, or I might just sit for a while and see if there's anything worth listening to on the radio. Depends."

Roscoe shrugged his shoulders and said, "Suit yourself, but a man needs his recreational activities to keep his health up."

Harry thought about the flavor of recreational activities offered by dives like Nessie's. "I thought the law closed her down last month?"

"You know how it goes," Roscoe said. "Sure, they closed her for a little while but it wasn't personal like. It ain't as if this is an election year." He sat the plate that held their bacon a few minutes earlier in the sink with the rest of the dishes.

Roscoe was officially the boat's mechanic but a more accurate title would have been mechanic, dishwasher, cook, and deckhand. A few months earlier, you could have added chauffeur and bodyguard to that list of titles. He put his boot on the short pedal sticking out at the base of the cabinet below the sink and pumped water over the pile of dirty dishes. He was careful not to mar the gleam on his freshly shined leather as the water squirted from the curved bronze tap and splashed over the cups and plates. He could see the cards from where he was standing and wanted to tell Harry to move the four of clubs over so he could play the queen, but knew Harry didn't like being helped. Still, it was hard for him not to give Harry advice. In another minute, he knew Harry would start shifting cards around whenever he thought nobody was paying attention. "You got any news on where Drake might be?"

Harry scooped the rows of cards on the table into a pile. He gathered them into a stack, then looked at his friend wrapped in his lemon and solvent scented aromas as he shuffled the deck for another try at beating the devil. "I know a lot of places where he isn't."

"What if he took off? What do we do then?"

Harry tossed his cards into a pile on the tabletop. He didn't feel like playing cards anymore. He left the cards sitting on the table as he stood.

"Well, if he really did leave, then I guess we'll have to put a for sale sign in the window of the old girl and see if there are any takers. Or maybe we could head down to California and see if we could find another buyer among those Hollywood types." He ran an appreciative hand over the mahogany trim running along the galley sink. He would hate to sell his boat and love to at the same time. "We're not broke, Roscoe. *Scarab's* worth a few pennies and she's paid for free and clear." He stepped out of the galley and up to the salon.

Roscoe followed him out, grabbing his coat along the way. Not broke, Roscoe thought, but upkeep on a boat like this one required a healthy bank account or things would go downhill pretty fast. "Tomorrow, I'll be taking the ferry over to Bainbridge," he told Harry. "Early. If I'm gone before you get up, you'll have to get your own breakfast together."

"My, whatever shall I do?" Harry asked with exaggerated sarcasm. He squatted in front of the radio. The knob turned with a click as he switched on the power.

"You're not still sore about me trying to buy your car, are you? If you want me to let it go, just say the word and they can keep it."

"I'm not mad about you buying my car, Roscoe. I'm mad at the circumstances."

"Well, it would come in handy on nights like this, don't you think? Having a car."

"Nights like this?"

"Nessie's ain't exactly across the street, Harry. I got a good few miles to make the Madison Park ferry."

"You could stay in."

"Not tonight I can't. I got a friend at Nessie's expecting me."

"Don't strike any matches while you're there."

Roscoe stooped slightly to look out the glass window of the boat's salon and the darkening sky. Clouds were forming again. Their sunny day was quickly becoming a memory. "Think I should take the umbrella?"

"I do not," Harry said as he waited for the radio to warm up. "A three year old Plymouth without a scratch and good rubber all the way round won't go for a bargain, Roscoe. Even at auction. It's worth four hundred easy."

"I figure more like two fifty times being what they are in Kitsap County. But even at three, maybe even three fifty, I can do it. If it was okay with you and if we was planning to stick around the area for any amount of time, I mean."

"It's not mine anymore, and I'd as soon see you driving it than some relative of the sheriff."

Roscoe stepped out onto the pier. "Last chance, Harry. The girls at Nessie's ain't half bad and they're all friendly."

"Maybe some other time," Harry told him.

"Suit yourself, Boss." Roscoe closed the mahogany door and made his way down the pier. Passing the boathouse, he knocked on the old weathered sides three times for luck.

CHAPTER 5

The proprietor of Barefoot Nessie's thought of her place as an establishment. She heard it described in other ways, none of them very flattering, but establishment was always how she referred to her business. Nessie, once an agreeable looking woman who had seen her forties come and go, hadn't been barefoot in a long time but the nickname stuck. She ran her affairs, her establishment, from the old unpainted two story for six winters now. The old house almost lost in the shadows of bare leafed maples mixed in with deep green firs, was far enough from the lights of Seattle to keep the preachers away and close enough to keep the customers coming.

She could usually be found either in her corner office tucked away in the dingier parts of the place or behind the bar keeping a watchful eye on her girls, her one eyed bartender or the drunk of a piano player who knew plenty of tunes but not how to play them.

Like most roadhouses in the county, there was no sign outside to advertise the business that went on behind her front door. Some things the community and the sheriff would tolerate. Some things they wouldn't. Places like hers were tolerated so long as they didn't get too much notice. Nevertheless, it was a popular spot on a quiet country road and the dirt drive in front of the old house with the long covered porch had a number of cars parked in it. It was a good crowd for a Sunday night.

She had eight permanent girls working for her ranging in ages from too young to too old and most of them were staying busy. Three were upstairs helping the customers help themselves in the little private rooms along the second floor hallway. The others were encouraging the drinking customers to keep their glasses filled. Nessie, sitting behind her roll top desk pushed up against the back wall, cocked her head to one side and listened. She could always tell when Jane was done with somebody. That particular girl's room was directly above the spot Nessie used as an office. The abrupt silence coming through the ceiling told her when things had finished as sure as the ring of a cash register told a dry goods clerk when money was changing hands. Picking up her pencil, she touched the tip to her tongue and made a note in a dog eared ledger sitting on her desk.

"You okay, sweetie?"

Roscoe finished lacing his boots. His girl Jane was standing by the foot of the old iron framed bed. She wasn't looking at him anymore, their business together being done, and the question was more her way of asking, "Will there be anything else before you leave?"

Most of the clientele who frequented Nessie's called her Two Dollar Jane either out of kindness or as an inside joke. Roscoe wasn't sure which and always made a point of just saying Jane. The springs squeaked beneath him as he shifted his weight and his attention back to his laces. He stood up accompanied by a loud squeak from the bed and started buttoning his shirt.

"Why sure, Jane," Roscoe said at last. "I'm right fine now." He caught a glimpse of himself grinning in Jane's cracked dresser mirror and decided he looked foolish with a smile like that on his face. Some men, he supposed, had a face built for smiling. He didn't. He quickly changed the unflattering grin to something he considered more dignified.

Jane pulled some kind of pink ruffled thing that passed for business lingerie in her trade up one leg and then the other. She was one of Nessie's girls for about three years now, and Roscoe was one of her regulars. She liked the old guy as much as she could like any of the men who paid for her time. At least he wasn't mean to her, didn't want anything out of the ordinary and never smelled like sawdust or fish bait. And he was quick. She hated it when they took their time to finish. With her pink ruffles coyly hiding her livelihood from casual glances, pink being her favorite color, Jane lifted a half empty bottle of *Old Crow* from the dresser and poured a generous shot into two glasses. She handed a glass to Roscoe.

"Old times," he said.

"Old times," Jane replied, then clinked her glass against his before tossing her whiskey back in one swallow.

Roscoe did the same, smacking his lips afterwards.

Jane took the empty glass from him and sat it next to the bottle. She usually didn't offer a drink on the house to the men in this room. Nothing in this room was ever supposed to be on the house, but Roscoe was a comfortable type and comfort wasn't something she got a lot of. It was worth a free drink. Most of the men, regulars or not, just put their pants on and walked out, especially the younger ones and first timers. Not Roscoe. Roscoe always appreciated a snort of free whiskey after they finished, or always wanted to help her with her robe while she fussed with his tie or helped him with a collar button. God knew she had seen worse out of her customers.

Jane picked up a brush, looked at her reflection in the same cracked mirror as Roscoe, then smoothed her permed, short, dark hair back into place. Her lipstick wasn't doing a lot for her appearance, so she reapplied a fresh coat of bright pink. Roscoe stepped behind her holding her robe ready. It was a knee length thing made from thin cotton. Just heavy enough to prevent her from freezing to death while sitting in the bar downstairs but thin enough to show the customers her wares. It was a garment that qualified as discreet when sitting in the public room at Barefoot Nessie's.

He helped her get her arms through the sleeves and pulled it over her shoulders without too much groping and wandering hands. "Coming down with me for a nightcap?"

"Sure, sweetie." She turned the key in her door. The lock was meant to reassure the shier gents who came to visit her. Uncomfortable interruptions were less likely behind locked doors.

Old Nick, Nessie's living, breathing insurance policy for good behavior from the house's paying customers, was sitting on his wooden stool at the end of the hall. The stool was out of the customer's way but visible enough when the men came upstairs.

One look at the Neanderthal sitting quietly against the wall was usually enough to ensure the lumberjacks, fishermen, and bored husbands who frequented Barefoot Nessie's stayed on their best behavior. Usually.

Nessie nearly ran him off a few months back for throwing a drummer down the stairs. One of the girls screamed behind her door and Old Nick used his pass key. The salesman was beating the girl with his belt while he held her pinned across his knees. Old Nick grabbed him by the neck, yanked him off the girl's bed and dragged him down the hall. Barefoot Nessie hadn't minded him dragging the belt swinging salesman down the hall. That was expected if you hit one of her girls. It was the pitch down the staircase that sent her into a blue fury.

Bethany Ann, her newest girl at the time and a fresh runaway from some farmhouse outside Spokane, was standing stark naked at the stair railing. She screamed filth at the drummer as Old Nick got ready to toss him down the flight. The salesman hit the floor square in the center of the public room about the same time as his clothes thrown after him by an indignant Bethany Ann still showing the red whelps across her rump.

Unfortunately for Barefoot Nessie's establishment, Nick broke the man's arm in two places. The belt swinging salesman went to the sheriff with a complaint. Business being business, as soon as the man's arm was taken care of, Nessie made the Spokane runaway apologize to Old Nick's victim. She made her apologies in a most professional way in the front seat of his DeSoto, indignant or not. The sheriff asked Nessie to close her doors for a while until things cooled off. She had, but only long enough until the law considered their request fully complied with and the incident settled.

Everybody pretty much decided things were even after that. The salesman left for the next town on his route and they hadn't had any more official business from the sheriff. Nessie warned Old Nick not to throw customers down the stairs and she was pretty sure he understood what she was saying. Sometimes with Nick, you were never quite certain what thought processes, if any, were going on behind those eyes. Violence was bad for business, especially in a respectable establishment like hers.

Nick had never said a word to Jane in all the time he'd been at the establishment. She wasn't even sure if he was capable of speech. He just sat there staring down the long hallway for hours. Sometimes he would be sitting motionless, looking at nothing. Sometimes he would be slowly twirling the pass key to the rooms around his fingers. Tonight, he just sat.

Roscoe and Jane walked past him as he slouched on his stool without much notice. Old Nick stared blankly at the far wall lost in his own internal conversations. If he noticed the half naked Jane walking by, no one could tell. The stairs led down one long wall that was papered in broad, faded red and white stripes. A large oil painting of a demur blonde reclining on a blue divan was the centerpiece of the establishment's interior decorating. Barefoot Nessie claimed the nude woman not entirely hidden by a spray of peacock feathers was a portrait of her in San Francisco when she was sixteen or nineteen. The age depended on which version of the story she was telling. Roscoe never failed to look at the painting and try to see the resemblance. It took some imagination.

Halfway down the stairs was the best spot for viewing the interior of the wide open first floor, if viewing was something you wanted to do. The main floor had an even half dozen tables with a varying assortment of chairs at each one. Three of the tables were occupied by the night's customers with different versions of Nessie's girls either sitting on their laps or sitting beside them. An old billiard table that needed new felt was on the far side of the room. The Spokane runaway was deep in a game of eight ball with one of her regulars.

One of Nessie's boys was building up the fire in an old iron stove that sat dead center in the middle of the public room. All the girls in the main room looked like they could do with some warmer clothes to Roscoe. It wasn't exactly balmy in the place. An upright piano sat empty against the near wall. Roscoe heard it being played once or twice when he was visiting the establishment by an unfriendly bald man whose skills were anything but impressive. Tonight, rather than piano music, the bar was listening to the sound of a Victrola wheezing out a scratchy waltz. One of Nessie's girls turned the crank on the phonograph with gusto. The waltz picked up the tempo as she spun the handle.

A handful of men leaned on the bar discussing something among themselves. Roscoe and Two Dollar Jane found a place not far from where they were standing.

"Beer," Roscoe said to the one eyed man serving the drinks, "and whatever Jane's having."

"Usual," Jane said as she appraised the three men leaning against the bar. None of the three seemed interested.

The barkeep pumped a heavy glass mug full of the house beer from his tap and slid it down the boards to Roscoe. He followed it with a shot glass of neat whiskey for Jane.

Roscoe laid a dollar on the bar. Leaning on his elbow, he looked at his girl Jane as she tossed her whiskey back in one well practiced movement. The other fellows at the bar were behind him. By the sounds they made, all were having a swell time. One of them shouted, "She's got a hell of a grip on that handle."

The girl cranking the Victrola said something back to the men at the bar making them all laugh. Roscoe only caught part of it. His hearing wasn't what it used to be. Too many years spent too close to screaming boat engines having taken its toll.

The clink of a fresh break came from the billiards table farther behind him. Roscoe thought of Harry and wished he had come out tonight. Harry fretted too much about unimportant things. Nessie's was a good place to go if you wanted to forget about troubles that were not worth thinking about.

Or at least he had thought so.

A door to one of the upstairs rooms opened. One of Nessie's younger girls came out of her room and leaned over the second floor railing. He had seen the girl a few times. It was hard to forget the head full of bright red hair. The redhead was wearing a dark green corset that was barely containing her breasts and a cotton shift almost identical to the one Jane had on. A man's fedora was sitting cockeyed on her head.

Two Dollar Jane, seeing the look in Roscoe's eyes, turned to see what he was staring at so intently. She smiled and pulled her best steady customer a little closer and said, "You want me to wear something like that next time?"

Roscoe didn't answer. Jane misunderstood. He wasn't looking at the girl in the skimpy underwear. He was looking at the man in the poorly fitting suit who followed the redhead out of the room. It was the last person he expected to see in Barefoot Nessie's.

"Frankie Byrd, in the flesh," he muttered. Roscoe tasted his beer without taking his eyes off of Frankie and the girl in the green corset. "That man up there with the redhead," he said to Jane. "He been coming here long?" He took another sip of his beer and sat the mug on the counter.

Jane looked over her shoulder at the second floor landing. "I've seen him a few times." She had seen Roscoe make a lot of different faces over the past few months, but she had never seen the determined attention he had in his eyes now. "Something wrong?"

"Not yet," Roscoe said slowly.

Jane leaned forward to whisper in Roscoe's ear. "We got a back door. It's around the far side of the bar if you need to slip out."

"Slip out?" he said in a surprised voice. "I don't need a backdoor. Besides," Roscoe tapped the dollar bill lying on the bar. "I ain't finished my beer." He quickly scanned the faces of the men in Barefoot Nessie's. He hadn't paid them a lot of attention until now. He was careful, looking at each one to see if he recognized any of them. But none of the men stirred any old memories.

"He one of your customers?"

Jane glanced over her shoulder again at the anemic redhead, one of Barefoot Nessie's more popular girls, standing beside the man Roscoe had suddenly developed an interest in. She couldn't abide customers who got jealous of other men.

"Me? No sweetie. I'm not his type. He only likes the young ones." Jane looked at her reflection in the mirror behind the bar. "The younger the better."

Frankie didn't look like he did the last time Roscoe saw him. He was paler, like he hadn't seen a lot of daylight and he'd lost weight. His straw colored hair, what there was of it, was shorn close to his head on the sides and up the back by someone who was probably more interested in speed than appearances. Roscoe was surprised Frankie Byrd hadn't noticed him yet, but Frankie wasn't paying a lot of attention to who was in the bar. He was drunk and the redhead had to help him down the stairs. The girl tried to put her bust away now that they were coming back down to the bar. Barefoot Nessie frowned on the girls giving the nonpaying customers too much of a free show. There was advertising. That was okay, but nothing was free inside the establishment for very long. Frankie amused himself by pulling her corset down every time she put her goods away. Each time she popped back out of the loose fitting top, he let out a scratchy baying sound that was supposed to be laughter. It sounded more like a dry gasp.

Roscoe kept his eyes on the pair the whole way down the stairs. He pivoted his body a few degrees in a clockwise traverse with each step as the couple crossed the room never once looking away from Frankie.

"Sweetie, you're going to be a good boy now, aren't you?"

The waltz finished and the girl at the phonograph selected a different record. Jane didn't like the look in Roscoe's eyes at all. She'd seen it in other men's eyes plenty of times. It was one of those things you learned working in a place like this.

"Sweetie?" she asked again.

Frankie and the redhead reached the long bar. "Whiskey and a beer chaser," he told the bartender. He didn't ask what the redhead was having. The bartender reached for a bottle sitting on a shelf behind him.

The redhead leaned against Frankie and whispered something in his ear. He made that dry, gasping laugh sound. When he noticed Roscoe standing beside Two Dollar Jane, the laugh died. A glazed, dead look came into his eyes as he focused on the older man. It was the look of someone who had done murder more than once in his life.

The redhead and Two Dollar Jane caught the mood change. After a silent communication between the two women, they each did their best to distract the two members of the male species zeroed in on each other. The redhead inhaled deeply and pulled her shoulders back making her best features bounce free from the corset. She did that same giggling laugh again, the one she used on the way down from the second floor.

Her companion didn't notice this time.

"Buy me another drink, sweetie?" came from Jane as she snuggled familiarly against Roscoe.

Roscoe didn't answer. All his attention was focused on Frankie Byrd.

Frankie blinked unfriendly eyes. He was surprised for a moment, seeing Roscoe Harrison standing at the bar, but only for a moment. Sucking air between his teeth, the corners of his mouth turned down in his face's version of a smile.

"Been wondering when I would run into you. I went over to Bainbridge looking around."

The bartender sat a shot glass filled with whiskey on the bar at Frankie's elbow. He followed it with a heavy glass mug filled with beer.

"But I guess I missed all the excitement," Frankie continued. Tucking a dull green tie inside his vest, he glanced quickly at the row of closed doors lining the upstairs hallway. "The place was chained up."

"You would know a thing or two about being chained up," Roscoe said with a smirk.

Frankie Byrd looked at the doors behind and above Roscoe again. "Don't think I've ever seen you in a roadhouse without your partner tagging along before."

"Harry's around," Roscoe told him. He thought about taking a sip of his beer but decided to keep his attention on the man standing a little more than an arm's length away.

Frankie pulled his hat off the head of the redhead, ran a finger along the brim then settled it on his own chopped hair.

"Hey Frankie," she said, trying one more time to distract him.

"Go sell it somewhere else, sister," Frankie replied and gave her a not very soft shove away from him.

The redhead looked at Two Dollar Jane and knew when to find another customer. She pulled the corset back into place.

"That wasn't very gentlemanly, you know. I don't need no bruises on my arm." She stepped away from Frankie and moved closer to the group of men standing at the bar. "Who's buying this round, boys?"

The girl standing by the Victrola made her selection. The sounds of Gershwin poured out of the brass horn sitting above the player.

Days can be sunny,
With never a sigh;
Don't need what money can buy.

"Has it been two years already?" Roscoe asked. "I thought for sure the Feds would want to keep you in McNeil Island for at least another six or eight months."

Frankie drank the shot glass full of whiskey in one swallow. Setting the empty glass onto the bar's top, he looked at Roscoe with the same flat, dead look in his eyes that Roscoe remembered so well.

"Don't think I've forgotten what you two did to land me there, Harrison. I had a long time to think about a lot of things."

Roscoe almost laughed. "What we did?"

Frankie's gaze drifted to the top of the stairs again and wondered what the hell was keeping that idiot Squeaky. "Harry in one of the cribs?" He said it almost casually, as if he were asking about the health of an old friend.

"I'll tell him you said hello," Roscoe answered. He was going to tell Harry a lot of things about tonight.

Frankie's right hand made a slow move toward the inside of his coat's lapel.

Roscoe's body tensed. He tightened his grip on the heavy glass mug resting on the bar. Frankie was too far away from him for a thrown glass to do much more than make him duck. If Frankie pulled a pistol from under his coat that might be the only chance he would have. It wasn't much of a chance.

Jane, still leaning against Roscoe, saw Frankie reaching under his coat. She felt Roscoe's muscles tense up. "Hey Butch," she said.

The bartender had moved farther down the bar.

"What?" He didn't particularly like Two Dollar.

"You got the correct time?" Jane asked, nodding her head sideways at the man Roscoe had taken such an interest in.

Butch exhaled noisily through his nostrils. Trouble at the bar was never good for tips, but he knew Nessie's rules. There was a button on the floor under the bar. If one of her girls asked the correct time, push the button. Whatever was eating the two fellows standing beside Two Dollar, it was about to get painful for someone. He put his shoe on the call button. In the upstairs hallway, a buzzer began an agitated squeal.

Old Nick's eyes began to focus more clearly on his surroundings. The quiet conversation he was having within himself ended as three hundred pounds of muscle and bone rose from the stool. As the bouncer got to his feet, the door to Number Four opened.

A tall, blond headed youngish man with hair slicked straight back over a bullet shaped skull and with a dim, pitiless look about him came out of the room. The man let out a loud whoop and with a grin from one side of his face to the other, fairly flew down the stairs. He jumped the last few steps and landed at the bottom of the landing with a loud thump. Seeing Frankie, he sauntered over towards him, hitching his trousers up with his thumbs as he approached.

Frankie, noticing Roscoe bunch up like a spring about to snap, smirked. "Relax, old man. I'm not packing." His other hand lifted his lapel. Slowly, he pulled his makings out of a vest pocket. He poured the tobacco into a rolling paper and twisted up his smoke with long, bony fingers. When he pulled a wooden match from his hatband, he struck it along the top of the bar.

Roscoe looked at the burning cigarette in Byrd's hand. His own hand scraped wishfully at the old scar over his lung. He saw another man, tall with a stupid grin on his face, coming his way, but he wasn't about to take his eyes off Byrd. His good times at Barefoot Nessie's had gone to hell in a hurry.

Frankie put his hands in his trouser pockets as Squeaky finally came down from upstairs. "It's about damned time you got here," he said angrily.

"She wanted it, Frankie. Told me so, too." Squeaky, too slow to make it far on his own, had always been quick to attach himself to people like Frankie Byrd. "Said she wanted it. Said it in my ear over and over." This made him burst out in laughter. He slapped Frankie on the back. He hadn't noticed Roscoe standing at the bar or Two Dollar holding her cotton robe closed across her front.

"Yeah, you and every other guy in the county." Frankie exhaled a lungful of blue smoke into the air. "How much money do you owe me, Squeaky?"

Squeaky's smile faltered for a moment, and he looked a little puzzled at the question. "You said I could borrow it, Frankie. You said I could pay you later."

"How much was it again?"

"It was eight dollars. I don't have it anymore." Squeaky had a worried look on his face. It was a face that looked close to turning mean.

Frankie's eyes went dead flat, lifeless and unmoving. "Put a bullet between the eyes of that old bastard standing right there and we'll call it even."

For a moment, Squeaky looked back and forth between Frankie and Roscoe, noticing him for the first time as he processed what he just heard.

Roscoe was caught between his desire to hit Frankie as hard as he could with his beer mug and trying to evaluate the tall kid who had suddenly walked up out of nowhere.

Gershwin played on.

"What about it, Squeaky? We got a deal?" Frankie asked.

Two Dollar Jane hadn't made it as far in life as she was now without learning when to get herself out of the line of fire. She backed away from Roscoe.

Squeaky didn't have to think about it long. Eight dollars was a lot of money. He went for his gun.

He almost reached it.

A fist not much softer than carved marble struck the side of his head with an impact that made Roscoe wince. The whole bar heard the sound as Old Nick's knuckles turned Squeaky's right ear into what professional fighters called cauliflower.

Squeaky, unconscious before he hit the floor, slid halfway to the front door. He came to rest near one of the bar's round tables, flat on his back and with his face turned away from the blow delivered by Old Nick. A regular of the establishment, sitting at the table with a member of Barefoot Nessie's plumper offerings on his lap, looked down at the young man lying motionless on the wooden boards. Turning to the woman on his lap, he whispered something in her ear. It must have been funny because it made her howl with laughter.

A dozen conversations ended all at once. The girl fooling with the phonograph spun around to see what she missed. The drinkers at the bar noticed for the first time trouble was happening an arm's reach away from them.

"Is he dead?" one of the men at the bar asked his neighbor.

"If he isn't he ought to be," his friend answered.

Old Nick took four slow, measured steps to where the unconscious Squeaky was stretched out on the floor, then put a boot on the man's head. The boot wasn't necessary. Squeaky wasn't getting up without help.

"What the Sam hell is going on in my establishment," screamed a shrill female voice from the backroom. Barefoot Nessie came out of her office with a baseball bat in her right hand and an ugly look on a face that never appeared very agreeable to begin with. She turned on Butch the bartender with a look that demanded answers.

For a moment, Butch thought she was going to hit him with the business end of her bat. Experience taught him to be prepared when Nessie came out of the office with a Louisville Slugger clearing the air in front of her.

"It wasn't me, Nessie," he said. He pointed a finger in Roscoe's general direction. "Two Dollar asked me the time so I stepped on the call button."

"Son of a bitch, Nick," she wailed. "Did you go and kill somebody now?"

Old Nick leaned forward, putting a considerable amount of weight on Squeaky's skull still penned under his boot, and flipped open the unconscious man's coat. The black handle of a revolver was sticking out of Squeaky's waistband. Nick pulled the short barreled pistol free from Squeaky's pants and stood up, taking the sole of his boot off the man's head in the process. The bouncer, ignoring Barefoot Nessie's question, looked at Two Dollar Jane with an expectant look.

"That one, Nick. The ugly one," she said, pointing at Frankie Byrd.

"Now, hang on," Frankie said pleadingly, holding both his hands up to the Goliath moving towards him.

"That's enough, Nick," Nessie shouted, waving her bat in a half circle.

The men standing at the bar moved farther away from the fast moving club.

Pointing her bat at the unconscious man lying on her floor, she said to Frankie, "He with you?"

Frankie nodded.

"Guess you can help your friend out the door, or should I let Nick do it?"

Frankie eased over to Squeaky still lying flat on the barroom floor. He walked a wide arc to make sure he stayed out of the range of Nessie's bat. Getting his hands under Squeaky's shoulders, he pulled him to a sitting position. Squeaky's ear was bleeding down his collar, and there was a large imprint of a boot sole on his cheek.

"Can we go now, Frankie?" he said groggily to the smaller man trying to stand him up.

"Get up, dummy," Frankie said through clenched teeth. "You damn near got us both beat to shit. Stand up."

Squeaky got to his feet with a lot of help from Frankie. His eye was swelling closed and there was a dull ringing inside his head. He had a vague recollection of shooting somebody but couldn't place which one of the people standing in front of him he just killed. He stumbled out the door with Frankie under one arm.

"Bye," the redhead in the green corset said low enough that no one but she could hear it. "Don't let the door hit you where the good lord split you."

It wasn't the exit either of the two men expected to make when they first entered the establishment. When the front door closed behind them, Barefoot Nessie turned a malevolent eye on Roscoe and took a double handed grip on her bat.

"This is a respectable establishment, you. You want to fight, do it somewhere else."

Old Nick took a step towards Roscoe.

"Nessie, I been standing in this same spot ever since I come downstairs. You can ask Jane." Roscoe took a quick glance at Old Nick. He didn't think a glass beer mug would have much effect, no matter how hard he threw it. "Those two no accounts came down here and started trouble. Not me," he added quickly.

"That's right, Nessie," piped in Jane. "Roscoe and me were minding our own business here at the bar, you know, having just finished upstairs."

"Shut up, Two Dollar," Nessie screamed. "You want to testify, find a revival. I don't need any opinions from a woman who makes her living on her back."

Nessie, feeling better about things now that she restored order to her establishment, lowered the bat and Old Nick stopped his slow advance on Roscoe.

"Finish your beer." She pushed a handful of grayish brown hair out of her eyes. "I don't want no more fighting in here, Roscoe."

"Yes, ma'am," Roscoe said, lifting his nearly empty mug to the bartender. "One more to settle my nerves, barkeep."

Barefoot Nessie laid her bat on the counter and put her hands out to Old Nick. "Let me see your hand, Nicky Boy. Does it hurt?" she asked, folding it in her own hands and pulling it to her breasts.

Nick shook his head from side to side.

"You run along to the kitchen and get Cookie to give you a big slice of that pie he baked yesterday." Barefoot Nessie shooed

Nick's bulk out of the public room of her bar while taking the pistol out of his hand as he passed.

"Roscoe," Jane said. "Who was that guy?"

Butch, the barkeep, set a fresh mug of beer in front of him.

"The little one's a bad sort who should never have been let out of McNeil." Roscoe blew the foam off the top of his mug, then took a long drink. He considered briefly whether he had it in him to ask Jane for her business one more time before he called it a night. There was something about nearly meeting one's maker that made a man crave the finer things in life. Two Dollar Jane's pink frock was open and he could see the shape of one smooth, pale breast. "He's only dangerous when he's behind you. The other one, the one that pet gorilla of Nessie's clocked, I've never seen before." He took a second long drink from his mug, finishing half the glass. "Remind me to buy that bouncer a beer, or bring him a slice of pie next time I'm here." He smiled as he remembered the sound of the tall kid hitting the floor. Wait 'til he told Harry what he saw tonight.

"Jane, why don't you and me step upstairs and—"

A set of very bright headlights lit up the windows of Barefoot Nessie's establishment as someone else pulled into the drive out front.

It was sure a lively night for a Sunday, Roscoe thought.

*****

"There, that's better," Lucy told the roof of her automobile. She pulled her skirt out of the way and slammed the Auburn's driver side door closed with a satisfied thump. She'd had all the convertible driving she could take for one evening and had stopped to put the top up and snap the windows in over the doors. The windows were the only feature about her car that she was not completely in love with. They kept most of the weather out, but the wind swirled past the gap between the door and the windshield, window or no window. Her papa bought her a beautiful and rare car, but it would never be described as warm in the winter. The sun set an hour ago and with its heat gone from the sky, the unusually warm day became a memory. She was cold and wishing she was wearing warmer clothes.

Millie rubbed her gloved hands together as her sister put the car in gear. It didn't help much. "We should have packed a blanket."

They had been driving around the back roads and lanes, trying to remember the right way back to civilization for a while now. The forest road had gone from ashen shades at dusk to dark shadows until now, fully dark, it was a twisting, unfamiliar path through the hills somewhere east of Seattle. Or maybe south. Lucy wasn't sure anymore. She turned on all six of the automobile's headlamps and a bright glow of electric light pierced deep into the darkness in front of them. What she needed was a road, a good road, pointing the way home. So far, she hadn't found one. Everything looked different in the dark and they had turned around twice already when the dirt road they were on suddenly narrowed to a muddy track to nowhere.

"We're lost, aren't we?" Millie was sure of it and wouldn't be surprised if they found the Oregon state line waiting for them over the next hill.

"I'm not lost. I just don't know exactly where I am right now."

"And there's a difference?"

"I took a wrong turn somewhere. That's all."

The path they were bouncing down for the last ten minutes intersected with a wider road and Lucy made a quick left turn. That was west, she thought, and west meant they would find the road going to Kirkland sooner or later. If it was west.

"Lucy?"

She looked at her sister in the glow of the dash lights. Millie looked very young in the near darkness.

"If we run out of gas going up and down these back roads, it will get really cold before somebody finds us." Millie watched the solid wall of trees going past her door much like her sister had the telephone poles when she was driving. "If they ever find our frozen bodies, I mean." Spending the night in a cold, damp forest filled with hundreds of unseen things didn't appeal to her at all.

"We aren't going to freeze. It isn't that cold." Lucy glanced at the fuel gauge hovering one mark above the E. "There's plenty of gas to make it to the ferry, kiddo. An eighth or a quarter of a tank. I never can remember which one the first line is." She wasn't worried about running out of gas. The road she turned onto wasn't nearly as good as some of the others, and it was very soft in places. Getting stuck would be easy. She was more worried about that than the amount of fuel in the car's tank.

Millie stretched her legs out in front of her and smoothed her skirt. The speedster's glass wind deflectors mounted on each side of the windshield weren't doing a lot to keep the cold blasts away from her legs.

"It's starting to get really cold. The wind is freezing my ears."

Lucy smiled in the dark interior of the car. "See what happens when you gamble? Even when you win, you lose. Let that be your lesson for the day."

"Next time you need a tennis lesson, let me know," Millie shot back.

Their car topped a short rise and Lucy stepped on her brakes coasting along the downward side of the slippery road. The car's powerful headlights showed the lane bending away to what she thought was east. East. They were still lost. East was not the direction she wanted to go. Once around the curve, they saw lights coming from a house's window snuggled in among the trees on the right. Lucy headed for it.

Civilization. It was the first sign of life they had seen since the sun went down and finally, she thought, she could find out where they were. As she got closer to the old home, her headlights swept past the metallic sides of several cars. There were at least half a dozen parked in front of the building in no particular order. She maneuvered the Auburn to an open spot to one side of a sedan.

It was an old, dark two story house with a big porch going across the front. It might have been painted once, white or maybe a light blue. Whatever color it had been, it was mostly gray wood now. Setting the car's handbrake, she shut off her lights and killed the engine. Immediately, both women heard the faint sound of a phonograph playing some unrecognized tune. There were no lights on at all outside. The only illumination in the dark night was the glow coming from the windows in the building's front and from a big opaque glass pane in the middle of the front door.

Lucy sighed. It wasn't a home after all. It was a saloon; a speakeasy still holding on to the old bootlegger's trade way out in the foothills of nowhere.

Millie leaned forward, closer to the windshield, and looked intently at the building in front of her. "I don't think this is a house."

"It's a saloon," Lucy said.

"Out here?"

"Popular, too. Look at all these cars." She had never been in a saloon unescorted and alone before and had no desire to do so now. But she really couldn't have her underage sister following her in, either. Millie was bound to tell their brother and Donny would spill it to their father the first chance he got. Weighing her options as she sat in the car, she made her decision. She needed to know which way was out and if playing Little Red Riding Hood would help her find the warmth of her own bed a little faster, that's what she would do.

"Stay here. I'm going to go ask somebody for directions." Lucy opened her door and got out of the car. Her heels sank in the soft dirt. She hated getting mud on her shoes. Glancing around at the dark cars, she couldn't see anyone outside the building. "I'll be right back."

Millie did a fast survey of the completely darkened and deserted front of the building and the looming trees all around. "Like hell," was her reply as she opened her own door. The wet soil didn't bother her near as much as the idea of sitting alone outside in the dark.

"You can't go in there, Millie. You aren't old enough."

"If you think I'm going to sit out here in the dark because of a few days on a calendar, you're nuts."

Lucy looked at the dilapidated old leftover from prohibition and felt her willpower deserting her. Papa would have to understand her explanation.

"Fine," she said at last. "Come with me then."

Both women walked up the steps and onto the porch. Someone was laughing inside and they could just see the movement of bodies through the cloudy glass of the front door.

"How's my hair look?" Lucy asked her sister.

"We're lost and freezing in the cold and you want to brush your hair?"

"Take that scarf off and we are not having anything to drink."

"Food?" Millie asked hopefully. "I'm kind of hungry."

"Nothing to eat, either. I'm going to ask directions and we'll be on our way. We can't be that far from the lake." Lucy reached for the door, then stopped. "Don't you dare embarrass me and if you tell our brother or Papa I let you come in a bar, so help me you'll never get away with sneaking into our home again."

Maybe her sister would keep the secret, but she doubted it. A male voice shouted something from inside. Lucy turned the doorknob and walked through the door.

Millie followed behind her. Finally at last, she thought to herself. Her sister was accepting the idea that she was a grown woman and not a kid anymore. Her sister was walking fast. She had to hurry to keep up. The lights were low and there was enough smoke in the room to make her wonder if the stove was drawing properly, but at least it was warm. That was the first thing she noticed. The warmth. She hadn't realized just how cold she was until she was inside and out of the night's chill. The phonograph's large brass horn sitting to her right sounded much louder now that they were in the saloon. Somebody with a pool cue in his hand was standing on the other side of the Victrola looking at her in a way she wasn't at all used to. She quickly looked away from the stranger. She almost smiled, though. It was a grown man to a grown woman kind of look. At least strangers weren't treating her like a kid anymore.

The front door closed with a loud bang. Everyone in the place looked at the two women marching in step across the main room of the bar. Lucy was vaguely aware of men standing to either side openly staring at her and her sister. That was familiar enough. Men always stared at her. She had long practice in looking straight ahead and not meeting anyone's gaze. The sound of her sister's heels followed behind her as she crossed the floor of the saloon.

"Lucy," Millie said. She wasn't so practiced as her sister at looking straight ahead and she was seeing plenty.

Oh Lord in Heaven, Lucy thought. Please don't let her tell Papa. The dent in the bumper was nothing compared to this.

There was a female standing behind the bar. She was a middle aged woman wearing a sack of a dress that shouldn't be seen in public. She kept her eyes fixed on the woman as she walked past several tables.

"Excuse me?" Lucy said, smiling as sweetly as she could.

Barefoot Nessie watched the two approach as soon as her front door closed. She couldn't quite make out the one behind, but the one in front was a walking gold mine. In her mind, she could already see the line of lumberjacks who would line up outside that one's door. "You're hired," Nessie told her.

"I beg your pardon?"

"Rooms are up the stairs to the right and down the hallway. Pick whichever one you want and I'll kick the girl out. Number Five is closest to the toilet." Barefoot Nessie looked around the very clean looking blonde with the tiny waist and money making tits to better see the small fry behind her. She was still a new one, probably untouched, or she would lick a spittoon clean. She found a fresh face wandering into her establishment every other year or so. They all started sometime.

"You together?" she asked the second one in her best business voice. These two were going to put her establishment on the map. No doubt about it.

"Lucy, that woman doesn't have all her clothes on," Millie whispered. "She's in her underwear." She wasn't sure if she had said it loud enough for her sister to hear or not. "Did you hear me?" Her friend Julie went into a saloon once, or so she claimed. She hadn't described anything like this.

Lucy's head did a slow ninety degree turn to the right. A woman about Millie's age, maybe a year or two younger and with a head of hair looking like it had been dipped in a bucket of Mercurochrome stepped clear of a group of four or five male patrons bunched up at the bar. To describe her as not having all her clothes on was a kindness. The girl was wearing a dark green corset and a wrap of some kind around her shoulders.

Lucy's face went white. All she could do was stand there, her mouth open in astonishment. The girl with the flame colored hair examined her with the look of a housewife trying to judge how fresh the market's fish was today. She placed her hands on her hips and ran her eyes over Lucy from her shoes to her blonde hair.

Lucy's head snapped back to the stocky woman behind the bar. The woman said something, but she wasn't listening. Reaching out, she used her fingertips to feel the surface of the bar. She wanted to laugh or cry or say something, but no sound came out of her mouth. Donny was going to mock her forever and her father was going to beat her. It would be in the papers. She could already see the headlines. Lucile McAllister takes Innocent Baby Sister to Brothel. She would have to move to Florida or some other godforsaken place if she was ever allowed out of her room again.

"Well?" the woman behind the bar asked. She had one hand

resting on her hip and used the other to wipe at her nose. "We doing business or not?"

Lucy laughed. Or tried to. A short chirp was the only sound she could manage.

"Lucy?" Millie had seen more and learned more in the last few minutes than she had ever seen or known before. A heavy woman in a lavender peignoir openly displayed herself to an old man not ten feet from where she stood.

"Lucy?" she said again, reaching to tug the back of her sister's blouse. "I don't think this is a saloon."

A glass dropped somewhere to their right striking the oak floor with a loud bang. Lucy didn't look in the direction of the sound. That was the direction of the Mercurochrome redhead, and she didn't want to ever look that way again. A hand grabbed her by the arm and swung her around. Someone, a man, pushed her towards the door. He was moving fast, so fast she stumbled over her own feet. The man holding on to her arm didn't slow down. She was vaguely aware of Millie having been grabbed by the man's other hand.

"Are those peacock feathers?" she heard Millie ask as she and her sister were pushed out the door.

The shock of hitting the much colder outside air brought her back from wondering what her father's reaction to his daughters' fall from polite society was going to be. The man who pushed and pulled her out of the house spoke.

"Miss Lucy. What in the," he began then stopped. "Why in the world would a nice woman like you come into Barefoot Nessie's?"

Roscoe looked at her with a face almost as astonished as Lucy's was at the site of the redhead. Her eyes adjusted to the dark night outside again, the interior of the bar not having been all that well lit to begin with. Roscoe Harrison, she thought. Roscoe's bulldog-looking face was standing in front of her. It seemed normal enough to her that someone she hadn't seen in ages would be in front of her now. After what she had just seen, nothing else could surprise her tonight.

"Why, of all places here?" Roscoe said.

"There was a dent in the bumper," Lucy stammered, "and," her voice trailed away as she realized there was no way she could explain how they had gone from hitting a rock to being offered a job in a whorehouse.

"There's a what?"

"Roscoe. It's a cathouse." Lucy nearly screamed. "I thought it was an old speak. I swear I did."

Millie snorted. "I tried to tell you."

"Where's your car, ladies? Let's get you out of a place like this."

Roscoe shuffled the women down the steps and out towards the parked cars. He moved with a quick urgency just in case some of the interior reputations behind that front door accidentally rubbed off on them. "You're Millie McAllister, aren't you?" he said to the little one. "Sure, you are. I almost didn't recognize you in this light."

"In the flesh," Millie said. She recognized the old guy dragging her across the parking lot easily enough, low light or not. "Did Harry tell you I came by his boat last night?"

She freed her arm from Roscoe's grasp. She wasn't nearly as stunned as her sister. It was the first time in her life she had ever seen Lucy so out of sorts, and it had made her whole day.

"It's that one," Lucy said, pointing at the Auburn's big shining front radiator. "I just remembered. I still don't know where I am." Lucy stopped in her tracks and turned around to look at the building she was just dragged out of.

For a moment, Roscoe thought she might actually go back inside and ask Nessie for directions. "I'll drive, Miss Lucy. You two can't be here. Not this place." He gave Lucy a gentle push towards the only white car in the parking lot. "Jesus Almighty," he muttered to himself. "Walked into a place like this like it was as normal as visiting the neighbor's."

The phonograph finished its song. The night was suddenly very quiet until they reached the car.

"Straight through the front door," Roscoe said, shaking his head.

Lucy still wasn't over the look on the redheaded strumpet's face as she stood there more naked than clothed while she sized her up. Because that's what the woman did. The woman in the corset did a visual comparison that was worse than anything any man ever did before.

"Scoot over," she said urgently as Millie slid into the passenger's seat. She shoved her sister into the middle and slammed the passenger side door closed. It was going to be a tight fit for three in the seat. She didn't care.

Roscoe ran an appreciative hand over the high curving front fender of the fancy automobile. It was a very similar touch to the one he gave Two Dollar Jane's high curving front fenders an hour or so earlier. He didn't know the make. A Duesenberg, maybe? His tracing fingers found a nameplate below a tall hood ornament. There was something embossed in steel, but there wasn't enough light coming from Nessie's for him to make out what it said. Looking up, he noticed both women sitting in the seat and waiting for him to get in. His fingers lingered on the steel trim around the little headlights mounted near the windshield as his eyes looked over the canvas top.

"This is some car," he said mostly for his own benefit. "Even with all this mud, this is some car." Bending down to look inside the driver's side window at the two women squeezed together, he said, "It's alright now, ladies. I have come to the rescue."

The driver's door opened from the front, its hinges being on the back edge, and Roscoe slid behind the wheel of the nicest automobile he had ever been in. He closed the door with a gentle tug. Harry's Plymouth wasn't even close to this. Lucy handed her ring of keys across to him and he started twelve cylinders with a smile. The switch for the lights was lost somewhere on the dashboard and he was having a hard time locating it in the dark when Millie grabbed a knob and pulled. The bright bulbs lit up the front of the house. It looked better in the dark, Roscoe thought as he put the transmission in reverse, released the brake, and backed away from the brothel.

He shook his head, still astonished by the night's events. Lucy McAllister in Barefoot Nessie's and nearly shot dead all in the same evening. He should have stayed home and played gin rummy with Harry. That's what he should have done. Roscoe pulled out onto the road, turning up the collar to his coat as he picked up speed. He would take the ladies back to the ferry landing and send them on their way. Harry was sure going to be surprised when he told him he ran in to Miss Lucy tonight. That wasn't something he would be expecting to hear. The two women were talking quietly to each other. He wasn't really listening. Something about keeping secrets, it sounded like.

"I'm glad you ladies happened along when you did. You saved

me a cold walk back to the ferry. Besides, I was a little concerned about running into an old acquaintance tonight." Acquaintance wasn't a very good word for a murdering bastard, but it would have to do.

"What?" Lucy asked. "Oh." She tried to think of something else to add but couldn't get the image of the woman behind the bar asking her which room she wanted out of her head.

"Are we a long way from the landing?" Millie asked him.

"Not far. A man can walk it easy enough."

"Do you have a ride waiting for you on the other side?" Lucy asked.

"It ain't so far back to the boat. I've walked it before several times."

Millie looked behind her at the cold darkness. "So, you're a regular customer, then?"

"What? No. I'm not, no."

The Auburn crested a hill and the far view showed tiny dots of lights glowing along the horizon.

"Look at that," Millie said. "Civilization."

"The ferry's just up the way," Roscoe added.

"We'll take you across. Millie and I don't mind."

"Now no point in doing that, Miss Lucy. That means you have to ride the ferry twice. And on a Sunday, too."

"Make you a deal," Lucy said. "We'll give you a lift home if you will take a look at a dent my precious sister put in my bumper."

Roscoe's heavy features smiled in the glow from the dashboard lights. "Is it a bad dent?" he asked the girl squeezed between him and Lucy.

"No," Millie said.

"Is there a *good* dent?" Lucy asked icily.

"Okay, I'll take that deal," Roscoe told them both. "It's Lake Union tonight for the three of us."

Millie was busily processing the things she saw inside the house that wasn't a house. "Was that mean looking woman behind the bar a madam?" She waited for either one of her fellow passengers to answer her question, but either they hadn't heard her or they preferred silence to saying anything. Roscoe looked like he was enjoying the feel of her sister's car far too much. She could tell he was living right now to be behind that wheel. Millie understood the feeling all too well having experienced it herself a few hours earlier.

"So that's what a brothel looks like," she continued with a satisfactory nod of her head. "It's a good thing Mr. Harrison just happened to be visiting that particular brothel tonight, huh Lucy?" Millie smiled sweetly and looked out the windshield and the circles of light on the road. Mr. Harrison, she noticed, wasn't enjoying her sister's car as much as he had a few moments earlier.

Lucy closed her eyes and swallowed something that didn't go down easily. She brought her innocent child sister, the girl she caught sneaking into their home last night, and accused of being with a boy to a whorehouse. She didn't open her eyes again for a long while.

"That's the ferry coming across the lake now," Roscoe told his fellow passengers. "You can see her lights. That's good. We won't have to wait long."

"Good," Lucy said. "I'm freezing."

"You ladies didn't wear your coats?"

"It was warm when we left," Millie told him. Like her sister was doing, she squeezed her arms tightly against her body doing her best to keep away the chill.

Roscoe drove down out of the hills and on towards Houghton, all the while thinking about old acquaintances turning up when you weren't expecting them to. There was more trouble in his and Harry's future. He was sure of it. That's what Harry needed, thought Roscoe. More trouble.

The Feds had sprung Frankie Byrd.

After the car pulled away from Barefoot Nessie's, Frankie Byrd stepped from behind a big overgrown rhododendron. He watched the red taillights driving away until they disappeared among the trees. A fancy rich man's car with a rich man's woman inside, he thought. Behind him, inside the house, he heard a whore's high pitched laugh. It sounded like the skinny redhead with the green corset. Somebody at the long bar was buying. He sucked air through his teeth and thought about what he'd learned today. The Asian guy with pockets full of cash was working something with Harry Watkins. That was his woman he saw being hauled out of Barefoot Nessie's. Maybe she came here looking to find Watkins doing what he shouldn't be doing? Maybe Roscoe pulled her out of the roadhouse before she caught her boyfriend with his hands full of the wrong woman? Whatever she was doing didn't really matter. He still didn't know all the answers, but he was getting closer.

Fortunately for him, he was out of the way of the car's headlamps when Roscoe hit the switch. Harrison almost saw him crouching in the bushes when the night disappeared in their bright glow. He was hoping to catch him coming out of the roadhouse too drunk to be paying much attention to his surroundings. He almost had, too. If he hadn't been playing nursemaid to a punch drunk Squeaky on the far end of the porch, he could have had Harry Watkins' woman too. That would have made his night. Every time Watkins got between those legs, he would know he, Frankie Byrd had been there.

He didn't get a good look at the dark haired woman and didn't really care who she was. The blonde was the key and he'd almost gotten to her twice in the same day. Sooner or later, he'd have a private word or two with her.

Frankie cleared his throat and spat in the mud at his feet. "Hey Squeaky," he yelled down the porch's length. "You finished puking? It's time to head back." Frankie bent over and used the sharp steel blade of his knife to scrape some of the mud off his shoe. "Unless you feel like going back in and telling that bouncer to give you back your pistol?" He smirked and shook his head in the darkness. He would never have let himself be disarmed by some backwoods ape like Squeaky had. He should have known what was walking up on him. Frankie ran his fingers down the ice cold blade, closed the knife and slipped it soundlessly into a pocket.

Squeaky, crouched over and unnoticed on the far end of the darkened porch with his head between his knees, hadn't seen Roscoe, the women or their departure. His ear stopped bleeding, but his eye was in a bad way. It was swollen closed and his head was aching. He was trying to remember what exactly happened inside. He remembered coming down the stairs clear enough, but the rest was sketchy after that.

"Yeah, Frankie, I'm ready. But I don't want to drive no more."

CHAPTER 6

Inga Swenson pushed the predictably amorous Donny McAllister away from her. "Your hands are giving me frostbite," she said, pulling her favorite sweater back where it belonged. "It's too cold tonight." She sat up straight in the front seat of the car. "I can see my breath."

Donovan wasn't looking at her breath. "C'mon baby," he told her. "We've done it in colder." Ignoring the pair of hands pressing into his chest, he tried to pull Inga closer to him.

"Don't be crude." Inga said, deftly intercepting a set of icy fingers and holding them away from their objectives. "You know I don't like that kind of talk."

Donovan sighed, his intentions frustrated by a chilly night, and exhaled a thin fog of cold air towards the windshield. She was right, he supposed. It was getting uncomfortably cold. "Didn't you say your mom was working the night shift this week?"

"From now on, probably. Why? Are you hungry? They got a new cook."

Starved, he thought to himself, and his nourishment was sitting right beside him. "Already ate." He slid his index finger along Inga's cheekbone. "I was thinking, your house is empty. We could have the place to ourselves." Donovan placed his hand on the front of her sweater and gave her breast a soft squeeze. "It's warm in your house," he whispered. He tried to kiss her, but she pulled away from him then pushed his hand off her sweater.

"I've got neighbors," she told him. "My mom and everybody on my street would know I had a man over before you killed the engine." Inga crossed her arms, turned her body in the car's seat and looked out her window. "That's all you're looking for, isn't it?"

Yes, Donovan told himself. "Of course not, baby. I was thinking out loud."

"Don't think, lover." Inga looked at the night sky outside her window. "It gets you in trouble."

"Ha, ha," Donovan said. He was getting tired of Inga and would end things between them pretty soon. He thought about the hatcheck girl at the hotel, the one who gave him her number when he went to visit Joe with his sister. He hadn't called her yet.

"Donny," Inga said, twisting back around from examining the night sky through her window. "Couldn't we go sit for a while at your house?" She slid her arm through his and leaned against him. "Sit in that big room downstairs and snuggle. Maybe build a fire and listen to the radio for a while." Her chilly nose nuzzled the skin behind his ear and traced a short, invisible line up and down. "Your hands wouldn't be so cold," she whispered.

"Wouldn't that be fun. Just you, me, my old man and two gawking sisters. Sunday evening at the McAllister house." Donovan thought about his father and his opinion of the women he spent time with. "You at the house would go over swell with the old man."

The familiar touch of Inga sitting very close to him changed from feminine seductiveness to frozen distance. Inga pulled away, removing her arm from his.

Donovan caught her mood change clear enough. He began his damage control. "They wouldn't let us be at all." He gave her the best innocent look he had. "My sisters would be right there the whole time."

"Yeah, like you said. It would go over just swell if you brought somebody like me home."

"That's not what I meant," he said, smiling. "It came out wrong. What I meant was—"

"What you said was your family doesn't want a woman like me

in their home, but what you meant was, neither do you."

So much for damage control. The hatcheck girl might be hearing from him very soon. Inga had gone almost as cold as the air outside. He could drive her back to Beacon Hill and drop her off then see if anything was doing downtown, but he didn't really feel like it. Sunday nights were always a bust in town, anyway.

"Start the car," Inga said in a flat voice. "I would like to go home now."

"What's wrong? I didn't do anything."

"I told you not to think, didn't I?" Inga said. She slid as far across her seat as she could and rested her head against the window's glass.

"Look," Donovan tried again.

"I said start the car."

She told herself this one was different; that he would want to come home and meet her mom. He would show up in his uniform with his white hat under his arm and with flowers, maybe? But he wasn't different. It was just a replay of all the ones who were there before him.

Donovan put on his best winning smile, the one that almost always changed their minds and said, "Honest baby, I didn't mean for it to come out like that." His hand gave the tip of her breast a playful pinch. The forward approach usually worked best with Inga. It always brought her attitude around and put her in the right mood. Tonight, it brought her around very suddenly.

She was fast. He had to give her that. The slap blistered his best seduction smile off his face before he even saw it coming.

"I said start the damned car," she yelled at him in a voice probably heard by passing boats out on the Sound. It was a voice she didn't know she had in her until just then. It was a voice the future *Mister* Inga Swenson would one day hear often.

Donovan touched his cheek and looked at her in a way like none of the other men had ever looked at her before. She wondered if maybe she shouldn't have slapped him and instead pushed him away. They were parked at the end of a dirt road out by West Seattle with a view looking towards the southern end of Elliott Bay. She came here with Donny before and a few times during the day. They liked it here because there was no one anywhere near that might disturb them. Now, looking at Donny touching his cheek where she smacked him, she was wishing there were houses around. Lots of houses.

Donovan's hand stopped rubbing his cheek. He grabbed angrily for the white tipped knob of his old Buick's choke and pulled the handle out without a word. The thin metal rod squeaking as he pulled it was the only sound in the cold interior of the car. His fingers, as cold as before but no longer trying to find their way beneath Inga's sweater, turned the key in the dash. He pushed the starter button down with the toe of his shoe. His best innocent face and best smile were long gone. They were replaced by an angry scowl. The engine turned over but didn't catch. He stomped the gas pedal several times, but the Buick still wouldn't kick over.

"You're going to flood it," Inga said, looking out her window.

"I'm not going to flood it," he said angrily.

The engine started with an unhealthy sounding slow idle as its mechanical parts tried to make up their mind if they were going to run or die.

"C'mon, baby," Donovan grumbled as he moved the choke lever in and out.

"Humph," Inga told her reflection in the side window's glass. "I've heard that line before."

The engine didn't die and Donovan revved it hard. He twisted in his seat to look out the back window and the half seen lane behind him. The Buick tore down the brush lined road recklessly fast, the reverse gear whirring in protest and the steering wheel swinging back and forth as he followed the bends in the muddy track.

Slapped, he thought. After sitting in a freezing damned car for almost an hour, all he had gotten for his trouble was slapped. She never slapped him before. He doubted Inga Swenson had ever slapped anyone. Inga Swenson, of all people, had suddenly discovered morals.

Donovan twisted the steering wheel hard to the left as they backed out onto the main road.

"Turn your lights on," Inga said. "You can't see."

"I've seen plenty," Donovan said, giving Inga a long, appraising glance in the seat next to him before turning on the headlights. He could still feel the sting from her slap on his cheek.

The gears ground in protest as he tried to shift out of reverse and into first before the car came to a stop. The Buick's engine coughed and nearly died.

He hated his car and he hated the cold night that wrecked his plans for the evening. His sister ran off to New York to screw around with some stockbroker for a year, and what does his father do when she comes home? Gives her a brand new automobile she couldn't even drive properly. The Buick was worn out, he thought to himself as he waited for the engine to go fast enough to shift into second. He had to make do with a five year old hand me down with a screwed up carburetor and a girl who suddenly discovered how to say no.

Donovan gave the Buick more gas and felt the engine begin to falter. He crushed the clutch against the floorboard and revved the engine. The Buick jerked when he popped the clutch, coughed, then picked up speed. His car was a lot like Inga. They both demanded attention he didn't feel like giving and right now, he was stuck with the pair of them.

"I thought you were special," Inga said.

Donovan weighed his options before replying. He would take Inga home, give her a day to cool off, maybe two, and see if she would come around. Maybe he would drive her out to Port Angeles and show her the station. That would probably be the ticket. If the hatcheck girl didn't work out, that is. The little scrap of paper she wrote her number on was still in his coat pocket.

"I thought *you* were special, Inga. I really did." She would like hearing that. No sense in burning bridges if you didn't have to.

"Really?"

The Buick made it into top gear.

"How special?" she asked him. "What does special mean to you?" Inga sat with her back against the door and put her left leg on the seat between them. She bent her knee, making her wool skirt rise up past her calf. Leaving her shoe on the floorboard, she rested her bare foot on the cloth of the car's seat.

Donovan caught the not-so-subtle change in Inga's attitude. Automobiles and women. It was all in the way you handled them. Tell her she's special and she opens up like a rosebud in the springtime. He glanced at the shadow covered skin of her leg on the seat. His eyes traced the line of shadow and the deeper darkness beneath the hem of her dress.

"Baby, why are you mad at me?" This was more like the Inga he knew so well, he thought as he cautiously put his hand on her knee. She didn't push it away.

The Buick swayed from side to side as he negotiated it around a muddy puddle in the middle of the road. Inga's knee swayed wider with the motion of the car.

"You know we can't go back to my home tonight. How would I get you back to Beacon Hill? The ferry doesn't run all night." He gave her knee a squeeze and tried the smile on her once more. The sting was gone from his cheek.

"I wasn't thinking about ferries." Inga lifted her foot and stretched out her leg, placing her bare foot in Donovan's lap. The Buick swayed again. Inga put a hand on the car's dashboard and steadied herself better in the seat. She also pressed her foot more firmly into Donovan's crotch. "You didn't answer me."

"What? I was trying not to think so much." Donovan smiled. "Like you told me," he said as he moved his hips into a more comfortable alignment with her foot.

"How special am I?"

"I'm surprised you even have to ask me that."

Donovan grabbed her foot as Inga rubbed her heel against the bulge in his crotch.

The night might not be a total loss after all, Donovan thought. He could turn the car around. His favorite spot at the end of the muddy lane wasn't going anywhere. Pushing against the long hem of Inga's dress, he slowly slid it farther up her leg. His hands, still cold, touched the smooth, stockings cover skin of her thigh. Maybe he could buy her another pair and not need to deal with the hassle of taking her all the way to the station in Port Angeles?

"You know I love you, even when you're mean to me." The smile was on his face again.

Inga sighed with relief and looked at the upholstered roof of the Buick. "Oh, Donny. I'm so glad to hear you say that." She moved her leg a little more, letting her knee open wider. Donovan McAllister, her dashing lieutenant, slid his hand farther up her thigh. She pressed her foot hard into his crotch. "Because I'm five weeks late," she said with a sigh as his fingers touched the clasp to her garter.

Donovan's attention left the close examination of Inga's splayed leg and a skirt pushed over her bent knee. He saw a cold and unfamiliar reptilian stare in her eyes. They gleamed like a pair of black diamonds in the darkened interior of the Buick.

Inga didn't blink.

Donovan's smile melted away. He couldn't speak. A soul freezing feeling of dread wrapped its icy hands around his throat and squeezed the voice out of him.

"I love you too, Donny," Inga purred. "I'm hoping we have a boy."

Donovan froze. All his awareness was focused on the face of the woman half reclined on the seat beside him.

"What?" he said.

"Donny," Ingrid screamed as the car's motion changed as it left the road.

The old Buick with its bad carburetor slammed head on into the four foot thick trunk of the elm tree. The impact demolished the front in an explosion of escaping steam and bending metal. The windshield's glass shattered as the automobile ran headlong into something unmoving. Donovan's chest slammed hard against the steering wheel when the Buick came to a sudden, unmoving stop. Inga was crying. She didn't stop. She didn't stop for a very long time.

*****

Lucy jabbed her elbow into her sister's side. It wasn't hard to do. The Auburn's small front seat had Millie practically sitting in her lap.

"Told you so. There's the sawmill."

Millie craned her neck to look past Roscoe as they drove around the same gate Elizabeth had driven around the night before. The brighter lights from their car illuminated the stacked trunks of trees piled high in long rows beyond the closed gate. To Millie, it reminded her of a giant toy train set tossed to one side and forgotten. "That's a lot of trees."

"Used to be a lot more." Roscoe said, hardly giving the trunks of trees stacked a dozen high a second glance. He was wondering if Harry was on the boat. He said he was thinking about going to look for Drake again. If he missed seeing Miss Lucy, Roscoe wondered who would be the more disappointed, him or Lucy?

The women hadn't done a lot of talking since leaving Barefoot

Nessie's except for one "now I know where I am" from Lucy once they hit the main road. Roscoe was glad they were quiet. He didn't want to answer any questions about what he was doing back at the house, especially any questions from the little one. He had an uncomfortable certainty in his gut he wouldn't like the questions she asked.

The Auburn rolled down the gravel road and along the curve to the small clearing. Roscoe could see the lights shining in *Scarab's* main cabin. Harry hadn't gone hunting Drake after all.

Harry was about to give up on finding a clear signal. Kneeling in front of the General Electric radio, he gently twisted the tuning knob in an attempt to coax something from the speaker. The atmosphere wasn't cooperating tonight because nothing much was coming through except static. He gave up and switched the power off. In the silence, he could hear a car's engine coming down the hill. It was probably Roscoe coming home early, he thought. Someone gave him a lift back to the boat. The engine shut off and Harry glanced at his wristwatch. Twenty minutes past ten as outside, he heard the double thump of two car doors closing.

"It's right there," Lucy said.

Roscoe ran a calloused finger along the Auburn's bumper trying to see the dent in the reflection of the boathouse's overhead light.

"Are you sure it was dented?" he asked both women. He could see a ripple in the reflection of the light on the shining metal, but it wasn't something he would call a dent. If Lucy hadn't pointed it out, he would never have noticed it.

"Can you fix it, Mr. Harrison?" Millie didn't really care if he could fix it or not anymore. The events of this evening had completely eclipsed any concerns she had about her father finding out she hit something with her sister's new car. She was looking in the direction of the big white boat and the glow of lights coming from the interior. She could see her sister out of the corner of her eye. Lucy wasn't looking at the dent, either. There was a shadowed movement behind a curtained window.

Both sisters smiled.

Roscoe straightened from his examination of the patient. "Sure, it won't take a second. Let me get a hammer out of the shed and something to soften the blow with. A wood block will work fine and it'll be as good as new in two taps."

Leaving the muddy front grill of the Auburn and its unseen dent, he crunched heavily across the gravel. The shed's door was a few steps away from where they parked the car.

Both women followed.

When he stopped at the door to the shed, the women kept walking, stepping onto the pier without a pause and heading towards the boat tied up at the end. Roscoe leaned one hand on the side of the weather beaten building, the other resting on his hip as he watched them walk silently towards *Scarab*. They were almost to the end when he muttered, "Why don't you both go on down to the boat where it's warm while I fix your pretend dent."

The shed's door swung open on rusty hinges. "Good luck, Harry," he said to the dark interior.

The squeal of rusted hinges was a familiar enough sound to Harry. Someone was going into his boathouse, most likely Roscoe, but it wouldn't hurt to make sure. He slipped on his leather jacket with its fur collar turned up against the night's cold and opened the boat's door.

At least this time, it didn't feel like he was seeing a ghost. He expected to see Roscoe. He hadn't expected to see Lucy with a smiling Millie trailing close behind coming down his pier.

"Hi Harry," Millie said, stepping around Lucy and opening the hinged gangway to the boat as if she had done it a hundred times before. She stepped across the gap between the pier and the boat's deck then pecked him on the cheek. "Miss me?"

He gave her a hug with one arm and said, "Sure, kid."

"You'll never guess where we've been tonight," Millie said. "Lucy got lost and had to stop and ask for directions. Guess where?"

Lucy sighed. "What happened to our deal?" she asked her sister. She knew there was no chance her father wasn't going to find out about tonight. Millie told the first person she saw.

"That didn't include Harry," Millie said. "Mr. Harrison would have told him, anyway."

Roscoe came out of the boathouse slamming the heavy wooden door behind him. He had a hammer in one hand and a short piece of wood in the other. He waved the hammer in the air and shouted, "Look who I bumped in to, Harry. They had a little driving issue and I'm going to give their bumper a few taps." Roscoe crunched his way across the gravel again and squatted in front of the bumper. "You and this bumper got a lot in common tonight, Harry, but I bet you'll never know it," Roscoe said. He tried a soft tap with the block of wood upon the steel. "Yes sir, Mr. Watkins, I bet you didn't even feel the dent, did you?"

Millie, one arm hooked through Harry's and looking back at Roscoe said very loud and very clear, "Yeah, Mr. Harrison just happened to be visiting the same cathouse as we were this evening."

Cathouse. She liked that word and was pretty certain that was the first time she'd ever used it in a conversation. She couldn't wait to tell Julie and Elizabeth all about it.

"Millie," Lucy said. "Your language."

Roscoe never looked back. The second blow of the hammer was louder.

"Cathouse?" Harry asked with a raised eyebrow.

"Wait until you hear the story," Millie told him, pulling at his arm with excitement. "It was the most fun I've had in years. There was this girl in her unmentionables and I think she was afraid Lucy was going to get her room after the madam offered Lucy a job."

"Millie." Lucy yelled it this time. "Please," she added in a quieter tone.

"Where are your coats?" Harry asked the two women.

"It wasn't cold when we left the house," Lucy said.

"Not the cathouse," Millie piped. "Our house. The one we live in."

Lucy exhaled slowly through her nostrils.

"I didn't want him to misunderstand which house you were talking about."

Lucy took a step closer to the edge of the pier. "Are you going to stand there watching me shiver or invite me in?"

Harry looked at the night sky. The stars had gone into hiding and a cold fog was forming out over the water. The nice weather they had enjoyed all day was coming to an end, and tomorrow was sure to be cold and damp. There would be ice by morning. They might even get a little snow.

"Come inside. Let's get you warmed up."

A dull thump came from Roscoe's hammer as he gave the car's bumper another tap.

Lucy stepped across the gap almost, but not quite as nimbly as her sister. She didn't kiss Harry's cheek.

Harry had to untangle Millie from his arm then turn his body sideways to let Millie pass inside. As Lucy followed, her hand strayed briefly on the open front of his leather coat. She used his body to steady herself against the slowly rocking motion of the boat. She glanced around her at the varnished exterior. Looking briefly into Harry's eyes as if he were just another part of the boat, she said, "Nice."

Her hand left his chest as she followed Millie into the boat's interior. Both sisters went straight to the steel heater mounted on the far bulkhead. The warmth from the heater felt like heaven as they held out their hands to the low flames. Millie was mewing like a kitten as the heat thawed frozen fingers.

Lucy turned around to warm her other side at the heater. "We didn't plan on being out after sundown, but it was such a beautiful day for a drive. I guess we should have planned better." The cabin was empty except for her sister. "Harry?" she said questioningly.

"I'm here," Harry answered. He had gone to his quarters for something warm for his visitors to wear and came back into the main cabin with a heavy coat in his arms.

"I think Papa should have bought you a warmer car," Millie turned around as well to warm her backside. "Thank heavens," she said, seeing the coat. It swallowed her in folds of wool, making her look very small.

"You get to experience the thrill of driving better when you are halfway in the elements." Lucy rubbed her arms up and down the sleeves of her blouse. "But it could be a little warmer." She touched the back of her hand to her nose. It felt like ice. "Is my nose red?"

"A little," Harry told her.

"It's a meat freezer if you ask me." Millie held out her sleeves to the heat again.

Harry took off his leather jacket and offered it to a still shivering Lucy.

"Aren't you going to be cold?"

"I haven't been touring the countryside in a meat freezer. Put it on," he said, holding out his coat.

Instead of taking the leather from him, Lucy turned around and held out both her arms pointed down and slightly behind her. It was a posture recognizable to every man born since Adam. Harry helped her slide first her left and then her right arm into his coat. As he settled the garment around her shoulders, Lucy turned her face to one side so that her cheek touched his hand.

"I remember you doing this once before," she said.

Harry let his hand linger on the collar of his jacket for a long moment. More than once, he thought. "Your cheek feels like ice."

The moment passed and Lucy pulled the jacket closer around her. "I'm sorry to just show up like this." She wasn't, but thought she should say so for appearance's sake.

"A meat freezer," Millie repeated.

"It hasn't been until tonight." Lucy looked around her at the cabin's interior. "Some boat you've got for yourself. I like all the windows."

Lucy stepped away from the warmth of the heater and ran her fingernails across the paneling. "Very nice," she said as she looked up the steps to the darkened wheelhouse. "Very, very nice," she said again.

"We built her to order." Harry thought of the dead buyer in Hollywood.

"So, she's sold?"

"The buyer died before we could deliver her to Long Beach."

"Oh, how terrible."

For the first time, Harry was thinking it wasn't so terrible. If Hollywood hadn't died, he and Roscoe would probably be drinking tequila in Old Mexico right now and he would never have known Lucy had come home. "Just one of those things."

The door opened and closed again almost as quickly. "Whew," Roscoe said, stepping into the cabin. "It is chilling down fast out there." He slapped his hands together and rubbed them back and forth. "I tell you Harry, it was sure a good thing I went down to the roadhouse to see Tom Jackson about that five dollars he owed me."

"Tom Jackson?" Harry had a questioning look on his face. "I thought he was in Olympia driving a lumber truck?"

"Yeah," interrupted Roscoe. "Sure was fortunate. These nice ladies were needing assistance and there I was collecting on my debt from Tom." Roscoe smiled his most convincing smile at Millie.

"Roscoe, can I borrow a handkerchief?" Luc asked.

"Why sure, Miss Lucy. I never go anywhere without a handkerchief," he said, digging a light blue checkered piece of cloth out of a back pocket.

Lucy took the handkerchief from his hand and stepped close to him. "Let me help you. Tom Jackson left her lipstick all over your cheek."

"Harry?" Roscoe said with a beseeching look at his friend.

"You old buzzard. A man of your years still having carnal desires," Lucy told him as she wiped strongly at a pink smear at the corner of his mouth. "You're almost as old as my father."

"Cathouses," Millie said from somewhere within her woolen cocoon.

Roscoe could feel the tips of his ears burning. He decided a change of subject was the best he could hope for right now. "The bumper's fixed good as new, Miss Lucy. Not a ripple in it anywhere."

She handed him his handkerchief. "I'm forever in your debt and you might want to wash that," she added, pointing at the checkered cloth. "I'd hate to hear you had *caught* something." Turning to Harry, she said, "We might have gone around in circles for hours if we hadn't bumped into Roscoe."

"He comes in useful from time to time," Harry said.

Lucy looked intently at the creased face of Roscoe Harrison who was making a great effort to tuck his handkerchief back into a hip pocket. "It's time to go, Millie. Better give Harry back his bearskin."

"We can stay awhile," Millie said. She lifted a sleeve longer than her arm and pointed it in Harry's direction. "Harry won't mind me being here at all, will you, Harry?"

"Papa will be worried. Besides, Roscoe looks worn out."

"I ain't worn out," Roscoe said, moving towards the galley. "Anybody like some hot coffee, or maybe you ladies prefer tea? I think we got a bag or two somewhere."

"You old buzzard," Lucy said again as he walked by. "You ought to be."

"We got sugar," he said.

Lucy smiled. "Some other time. It's been a long day."

Millie let Harry's heavy overcoat slide off her shoulders.

"Keep the coats," Harry told them. "I can't have you catching pneumonia on the ride home."

"How will we get them back to you?" Lucy asked. She hadn't offered to take off Harry's leather jacket.

"We aren't going anywhere anytime soon."

"We aren't?" Roscoe said from the galley.

"I still have business with Drake."

"Uh huh," Roscoe said, hardly loud enough to have actually said it out loud. "Thought so. There's a dent in your bumper, too."

"Do you still keep a room in the Bergonian?" Lucy ran a hand down the leather sleeve. "I can drop them off if that's okay?" She was thinking about the ring of keys dangling from the ignition of her automobile. She was also thinking about his old room on the sixth floor.

"You have a room in the Bergonian? We had brunch there this morning," Millie said.

"I've kept a room there for a long time, but I'll probably let it go pretty soon. I used to have business in the city, but I don't use it anymore."

"Would have come in handy last night," Roscoe called from the boat's galley. The kettle boiled making its whistle screech with hot steam. He took it off the stove's burner.

"I'll pick them up next time I stop by," Harry said. "The desk clerk knows me." He opened the door to the boat's exterior deck and Millie, still cocooned in his coat, stepped by him.

"Bye, Harry. Two nights in a row. I think it's a sign."

Lucy came next wearing his brown leather jacket. "Walk us to the car?"

The door shut behind him.

The pier was wide enough for two people to go side by side. Lucy put her arm through his. She didn't think he would mind. No argument lasted forever.

Harry didn't mind.

"Nice meat freezer you have there," he said when the three reached the end of the dock. "Did you manage to miss any mud holes with it today?"

"Millie was practicing her racing skills."

The passenger side door opened and closed as Millie got in. If she made any reply, neither of them heard it.

"Thanks for the warm clothes," Lucy told him. "I guess it's my night to play damsel in distress."

Harry put his hands in his trouser pockets and hunched his shoulders against the bite in the air. "Never thought of Roscoe as a knight in shining armor before. Probably a good thing he felt the need to go collect a debt tonight."

Lucy smiled in the darkness. "I'll tell you all about the debt collecting sometime."

He could see her breath in the cold air. A tiny snowflake drifted down on the wind and he lost it somewhere in her curls. She had her hands in the jacket's pockets and was looking at him again. She did that a lot, Harry remembered; just looked at him as if she could hear his thoughts. He pulled the collar closer around her neck.

"Millie beat you to the warmer coat tonight," he said to her.

"I'm not cold."

"You're not doing forty down the road yet, either."

Her hands came out of her pockets and Harry pulled the collar and its blonde contents towards him.

The Auburn's horn gave one long and very loud blast as Millie pushed the button.

"Let's go, Lucy," she said in a not very friendly voice. "It's starting to snow and I want to get home." There was no damn way she was going to sit here in the cold and watch Harry kiss her sister if she could help it. If she wasn't so cold, she would have thrown her borrowed coat out the window.

Harry let go of Lucy's collar and opened the car door. Lucy got behind the wheel and hit the starter. She was smiling as she reversed the long automobile around in a half circle. He could see Millie sitting in the passenger seat as the muddy white car pulled away. She wasn't smiling.

CHAPTER 7

"What is the girl's name?" a stern faced middle aged nurse asked Donovan.

"Inga." He swallowed. "Inga Swenson."

The nurse reached for his sleeve.

"It's not my blood," he told her. "It's hers."

She let go of his sleeve. "The washroom is around that corner. You can wash your hands in there."

Donovan's demeanor told the emergency room nurse all she needed to know. She had seen young men like him in her waiting room far too many times. She saw young women like the one who came in with him almost as often. "When you are finished cleaning yourself, come back here. I shall require some information from you."

Donovan washed his hands, his face, his hands again, and walked meekly back to the waiting room. The nurse handed him a clipboard and pencil. He did his best to fill in the details, but didn't know the answers to half the questions. After he handed the clipboard back to the nurse, he used the telephone sitting on a corner of the gray desk to make a call. Then he sat in a silent, indifferent slump on one of the hard wooden chairs. The chair was one of many in a long row arranged like pews in a church and equally as uncomfortable. On this particular Sunday night, his was a church pew with a single practitioner.

The hospital's emergency room entrance was sterile, poorly heated, and seemed designed to enhance Donovan's misery. The nurse sat behind her gray metal desk. She quietly arranged clipboards filled with the paperwork of the sick and hurt and hadn't uttered a single word for the better part of an hour while Donovan waited.

The nurse was perfectly aware of Donovan's general discomfort, but she was not about to offer any sympathy, verbal or nonverbal. Her whole demeanor was one of disapproval. The young man sitting in the chair arrived in the same ambulance as the injured woman only he walked in, unhurt and whole. The woman was carried in on a stretcher by two attendants, hardly conscious and bleeding from a gash in her scalp.

Rubbing his forehead with one hand, Donovan examined the floor between his feet. It would be hard to recognize him as the same pleasantly entertaining lieutenant from the Bergonian's bar two nights ago.

The sudden opening of the emergency room's door caused a very cold wind to chill the unfriendly room even more. Donovan lifted his face to see if his father had arrived.

He had.

He stood slowly as his father came storming into the hospital's lobby. Cold air advanced towards him with each step his father took. One glance and he knew it was a mistake to call home. He'd hoped one of his sisters would answer his call, but it was his father's voice on the line. Seeing his father's determined approach moving purposely towards him, he wished now he'd hung up. A taxi and an explanation of the wreck after a night's sleep would have been a far better idea.

No matter how hard he tried to think of a plausible explanation to give to his father, there really wasn't one. His father never wrecked a car before and he damn sure never put a woman of doubtful morals in the hospital.

"Papa," he began. His father cut him off with a raised hand.

"Are you drunk?" Archie McAllister demanded. He already knew the answer, but he asked it, anyway.

Donovan braced himself for the inquisition that was to come. "No. I'm sober."

"Don't lie to me, Donovan. I can smell liquor on you from here." The elder McAllister dumped his overcoat and hat onto one of the chairs in the row next to his son. "Do not take me for a fool." He said words far louder than he should have. "I knew the minute I heard your voice on the phone you were drinking again."

The night nurse sitting behind her desk cleared her throat and showed the pair her of disapproval without needing to use words.

Archie McAllister glanced at the woman and was about to make some comment, but whatever it was, he chose not to voice it. Instead, he continued in a lower, but just as angry tone to his son. "Well? Tell me not to believe the evidence standing in front of me. Tell me," Archie McAllister said with a sneer in his voice.

"I had a drink after. From my flask. I'm not drunk."

"After? After what, Donovan? After noon? After sundown?" He looked his son up and down and scowled. Sunday night. On a Sunday night when decent people were supposed to be, if not in bed at least in their homes. "Your sisters are not home, either. I came out of my study and there was no one in the house. Where are they at this hour?" He clasped his hands behind his back and waited, every inch of him expecting an answer to come from his son.

"I don't know, Pop. Lucy said they were going for a drive." It was like his sister not to be where he needed her to be. Had she been home, his father would not be standing in front of him now. He sat down in the chair and rubbed his forehead again. He wasn't drunk, but it would do no good to argue with him. His father had all the moral high ground tonight and he would have to endure it.

"I've told you countless times not to call me pop, have I not?"

"Yes, you've told me countless times." He stopped rubbing his forehead, crossed his arms over his chest, and looked at the tiled floor. It was checkered like a chessboard and he had played this game too many times with the old man. It was the white king's move. Checkmate wasn't far away.

"The middle of a Sunday night in a hospital waiting room is not a good time to mock me, Donovan."

"There was ice. We slid off the road and I hit a tree."

"Who is this girl you said was hurt?" Archie walked past his son to look down the corridor as if the answers were waiting for him there. Another nurse sat behind a desk at the far end of the hallway. No one else was in sight, not at this hour and not on a Sunday. He wished someone would walk into the corridor, bring him the answers to his questions, or ask him what they could do for him. Archibald McAllister didn't want to look at his son right now.

"Inga. Her name's Inga Swenson. You met her last night at the party. I brought her up to your study."

Archie had a vague recollection of the girl. It was the same woman he used as an excuse to get his son out of his office so he could settle things with Kanji. He hadn't paid her much attention. Donovan always had some member of the female sex hanging about him. The faces changed often.

"Swenson. Do I know her parents?"

Donovan sighed. "I don't even know her parents. Her dad is on a tuna boat I think she said. Somewhere off Mexico or hell, I don't know. Her mom works nights at a diner over by the train station."

"The Peterson's girl came by the other day to say hello to Lucy. She asked kindly after you." I don't know why, Archie thought to himself.

"Judith Peterson? Papa, she's so." Donovan tried to think of an adjective that wouldn't anger his father even more. Judith Peterson was one of those females who were taught to close their eyes and think of England whenever a man was showing interest of the amorous type. "She's boring. Not the kind of woman I'm interested in."

"No, she wouldn't be. The Petersons are an excellent family and you could do far worse." Archie looked at his son and wished he knew how to change his proclivities. A fisherman's daughter out in the middle of the night with his son and a mother not at home. Waitresses and shop girls. The usual fare. "How badly injured was this young lady you were with?"

Donovan looked up from his study of the tile floor to look through the door his father came through. His father was standing in front of him with his hands behind his back. It was the same posture he used when questioning him ever since he was a child.

"I think her head broke the windshield. It happened so quick. She was unconscious some of the time and I couldn't wake her up. Her head was bleeding pretty bad." Donovan stood from his chair again and flexed his wrist. He guessed he wrenched it against the steering wheel when he hit the tree. "Real bad," he said again.

For the first time, Archie noticed the red stains on the front of his son's coat. "Have you spoken with the girl's doctor?" he asked in a more reasonable voice.

"Inga. Her name is Inga and no, I haven't. I rode in with her in the ambulance and they took her straight back right away. Nobody's come out since. I called you right after I washed the blood off my hands." Donovan's eyes darted towards the stern faced nurse sitting behind her desk. She wasn't looking at him.

A black police cruiser pulled up to the entry doors and stopped with a squeal of brakes on the asphalt drive. A heavier, older version of Inga Swenson still wearing her waitress' apron came quickly into the hospital lobby clutching her purse and looking as if her world had met a disaster. Donovan thought for a moment of stopping her as she hurried by. He thought he should try to explain or reassure her, but her questions would probably be harder to answer than his father's. The woman hadn't even known her daughter was spending her evenings with him.

The nurse, no longer looking like the disapproving matron, spoke quietly with the woman, then walked her down the hallway.

Donovan exhaled slowly, the chance to speak to Inga's mother gone. "I think that was Mrs. Swenson."

Archibald looked at his son as if he had just told him snow was made of water.

The two men could not hear the conversation as the nurse, Inga's mother and the second nurse at her station farther down the hall spoke quietly together. Both men watched as Mrs. Swenson disappeared around a bend in the corridor escorted by the other nurse. The unforgiving matron returned to her post at the night entrance desk not bothering to look at either of the McAllister men who watched expectantly.

Archibald turned to look at the police car sitting on the street outside the emergency room's doors. The officer driving hadn't got out yet. "Can you drive?" he asked his son.

"I don't even know where my car is. Besides, the radiator's done in."

"I said, can you drive?"

"Yeah," he answered, noticing the black patrol car. He would have to tell the police what happened. He wondered if the policeman would clasp his hands behind his back when he asked his questions like his father had.

Archibald reached into his pocket and pulled out a small ring of keys. "Take these," he said, handing them to his son. "My automobile is in the lot. Take them now, Donovan, and walk straight out."

"I'm going to stay until the doc comes out."

"Do as I say. Exactly as I say. Do you hear me?"

Donovan took the keys from his father and looked at the glass door again. It wasn't his fault, he told the quiet voice far back in his mind. It wasn't his fault at all. Inga shouldn't have distracted him.

"Donovan." Archie put his hand on his son's sleeve. "Did you hear what I said? Go to my car and drive home. I'll speak to you in the morning."

"What about the cops?" He pointed with a nudge of his chin. "They will want to do a report or something, won't they?"

"Take my car and go home this instant. I'll call for a taxi after I have spoken with Mrs. Swenson, and we know something about the girl." Archibald looked out the glass doors at the police officer. He was still sitting behind the steering wheel and looked to be writing something on a pad. He walked his son towards the door with an insistent hand in the middle of his back. "Straight home, Donovan. Do you hear me? Straight home."

Archie didn't follow his son through the double doors of the hospital's emergency entrance. Instead, he waited in the dead center of the room and watched his son walk out into the night and past the front of the patrol car. The officer never looked up as Donovan went by the black painted cruiser. His son turned to the right, disappearing from his view as he went around the corner. He waited until he saw his automobile go by before turning around.

The officer sitting behind the wheel opened his door.

McAllister walked across the lobby without a backward glance, scooping up his hat and coat from the row of hard wooden chairs as he passed. When he reached the nurse's desk, he heard the emergency room doors opening behind him as the policeman entered the room. Archie felt the same cold blast of air his son felt earlier. He didn't stop as he reached the desk, nor did he slow his step.

"Sir?" The nurse looked surprised as Archie McAllister walked past her. No one ever walked past her. "Sir?" she tried again.

"Not now," he said with an upturned hand. Inga, he repeated to himself. He wasn't good with names and was afraid he would forget it. Inga. Inga Swenson.

"Sir," he heard repeated behind him.

Another voice, the policeman's no doubt, said something to the nurse. He kept walking down the hallway and around the turn to the left in the direction he saw Mrs. Swenson go. He wasn't sure where he was going after that. He nudged a pair of double doors open and looked inside. It was some kind of examination room; its central feature a waist high gurney ready for its next victim. There was no victim tonight. The door swung closed and he moved on. He came to the end of the hallway and turned right. The passage was lined with rows of closed doors each one neatly numbered with a small black plaque on the side. As he neared the end of the hallway, a door on his right opened and the nurse he saw in the corridor earlier came out of the room. She seemed surprised to see him.

"Is that Inga's room?" he asked, assuming an air of what he hoped the woman would think of as fatherly.

"Are you family?" the nurse asked. "Mrs. Swenson is with her daughter now."

"I came as soon as I was called." Archie opened the door, stepped through, and left the nurse standing silently in the hallway.

*****

"That's what he said, Harry. Just like that, 'Don't think I've forgotten what you two did.'" Roscoe said the words in a parody of Byrd's scratchy voice.

Harry leaned his body forward in the chair, resting his elbows on his knees and clasping his hands together. What started out as another one of Roscoe's tales of nightly adventures in the local roadhouse had become a very serious conversation. "That's all?"

"Pretty much. It wasn't long after that when that tall kid came down the stairs." Roscoe's hand scratched at the old scar on his chest. "Then Frankie told him to shoot me for an eight dollar debt."

Harry reached for his glass with the *Black & White* in it. The scotch was warm as it went down. "We could try the cops?" he said, more thinking out loud than expecting an answer.

Roscoe snorted. They both knew how far that would get them.

Every badge in the county knew what they did for the last half dozen years.

"He's got it in his head it's our fault he got sent up." Roscoe didn't understand it, but there was never much understanding what went on inside Frankie Byrd's skull. "Now he's looking to settle up on old scores."

"Frankie always had a strange way of looking at things." Harry emptied his glass and thought about having another. He motioned with the empty crystal at Roscoe. "One more?"

Roscoe shook his head no and sat his own glass on top of the liquor cabinet. He scratched at the short cropped hair sticking up on the back of his head.

"I didn't push him that night. The evil little bastard didn't have enough sense to grab onto something solid and it's our fault? Hell, we all almost got picked up that night." Roscoe never had much use for Frankie, not even when he, Harry, Frankie, and Drake were in business together. He pulled the cloth hat from his head and gave it an underhand toss across *Scarab's* salon. "I tell you, Harry, I thought I had tasted my last beer this side of the pearly gates." Roscoe grasped both armrests of his chair and prepared to stand up. There was something about remembering the look on the tall stranger's face when he went for his gun that made him want to be on his feet. "When I heard Frankie tell that idiot to shoot me, I thought I was a dead man for certain."

"He wouldn't have done it," Harry said. "Not like that. Not in front of a room full of witnesses."

Roscoe paused from lifting himself out of his chair. "He was going to do it." His voice dropped to a low grumble inside *Scarab's* salon. "He had the look in his eyes. Like murder wasn't a problem to do at all. That kid would have pulled the trigger then remembered there were people standing around after the smoke cleared."

"Frankie Byrd." Harry sighed, not sure what else he should say. He put his glass next to Roscoe's. "That's a name full of good news, isn't it?"

Their old acquaintance was trouble on two legs. He always was and he always would be.

"Frankie told you he went to Bainbridge trying to find us. He said that?" Harry looked at the closed door on the boat's port side as if he half expected Byrd's gun pulling killer to step through at any minute. "That's kind of direct for someone of Frankie's temperaments."

He doubted if Frankie went to his grandfather's old boatyard. More likely, he snooped around or asked some of the locals what they knew. That was more his style. If Frankie was looking to settle a score, deserved or not, he wouldn't do it face to face. Not Frankie.

Roscoe's chair groaned under him as he finished heaving himself to his feet. "That's what he said. He must have just missed us." Leaning forward, he used a finger to ease the curtain over a window to one side. He peered intently into the night for a moment, looking at nothing in particular. Except for the single, dim light shining by the boathouse, all he saw was inky blackness. The bulb glowed in a cloud of lightly falling snow. The trees lining the shoreline were shadows in the dark. He let the curtain fall back into place, stuffed his hands in his pockets, and walked to the far side of the cabin. "It wasn't nobody's fault. That was the business. We all knew the risks."

"Men like Frankie always think somebody else is responsible for their own bad luck," Harry told him. "Frankie was never lucky and doing what we did, you needed luck."

Roscoe recrossed the cabin, eased back the curtain on the window once more and looked out into the darkness beyond.

"It might not be a good idea for you to be frequenting Nessie's again," Harry said. "Not for a while, anyway. Till things play out some more."

"I like Nessie's." Roscoe thought of Two Dollar Jane standing beside him at the long bar. "I got friends there. People I like to call on socially. Frankie won't show his face back there again. He missed his chance. I think he knows it. Besides, even if he did, so what?"

The night outside the boat's window was still empty. None of the shadows were moving. Roscoe let the curtain close over the glass. He moved towards the chair again, stopped, then drew himself up very straight in front of Harry. "It's him that might want to think about taking his business somewhere else. I go where I please."

Roscoe spun on his heel, crossed the small cabin in three steps then returned to the lakeside window with its closed curtain.

"I need my recreation," he muttered as he edged the curtain open with a finger like he had on the opposite window. The lake was dark with a few twinkling specks of light showing on the far hillsides.

"You can recreate up and down the coast if you want to. I'm just saying, maybe you should pick a different location?"

"Frankie isn't the kind of sniveling shit I ever felt the need to change my accustomed ways for." He was thinking about Jane and the curve of her fenders. No one would ever call her beautiful, but she was spirited in ways he appreciated and she knew his ways. He didn't see any reason to find somebody else to like because a bad influence was roaming the neighborhood.

"I wasn't saying anything like that. Frankie will be gone in a few weeks. You can't run around trying to kill somebody in a whorehouse and not expect to stay out of the pen for very long. My money says Frankie's back in McNeil before Easter. I'm just saying a little prudence might be called for. He's traveling with company and whatever Frankie does or doesn't do, it won't be a fair contest. You know that."

"No, fair and Frankie aren't two words often heard in the same sentence." Roscoe let the curtain fall and put his hands back in his pockets. "Old Nick sent that dumb hayseed he had with him sliding across the floor. I wish you could'a seen it." Roscoe smiled at the memory. "He won't be coming around no more. Not at Nessie's anyway. Nick took his heater and put a knot on his head that won't be going away soon." Roscoe shook his head. "I wish you could'a seen it," he repeated, slapping his fist into his palm. "Whack, and a slidin' across the floor he went. Out like a burned out bulb. I never seen a man hit so hard in all my life."

"You say you didn't know him at all, the one the bouncer hit? What about that bunch of no accounts from Vancouver? Burke had somebody loading on his dock the last time we made a run to his place. He was tall and kind of stupid looking. Maybe we should head up to Vancouver and ask around?"

"Nah, I'd remember if I'd seen him before. I knew all of Burke's cutthroats. I didn't know this guy."

"There weren't any headlights behind you when you left Nessie's, were there?" Harry asked cautiously.

"I seem to recall it was me who taught you how to drive with one eye looking forward and the other looking behind."

Harry smiled. "Yeah, I learned all my best habits from you. Don't go getting offended. I wasn't suggesting you don't know how to look after yourself in a tight spot. Just thought you might have been distracted by the company you were chauffeuring."

Roscoe laughed. "I've had a hell of a night, didn't I? Got my whistle wet, damn near shot dead in a whorehouse and rescued a pair of good looking women straight from the jaws of perdition. That ain't something a man gets to do very often."

"I really would like to have been there when Lucy realized where she was," Harry said laughing. "Millie's going to tell everyone she knows. I wouldn't be surprised if she writes letters to out of state relatives and tell them too."

"Yeah, Harry, but if you would have been there, what would you have told Miss Lucy when she caught you with a couple of Nessie's finest under each arm?"

"I would have said I was doing the same thing you were. Collecting an old debt."

Roscoe grinned. "They didn't buy that story, did they?"

"The lipstick kind of killed it," Harry said, "but it was a nice try."

Roscoe's grin spread wider across his face, turned into a yawn then vanished into a sea of wrinkles and a lifetime of experiences. He looked at the curtained window one last time before turning for the stairs leading down to his quarters. "I'm calling it a night. My bones are tired."

"See you in the morning, Roscoe."

Harry turned the knob on the lamp and darkness filled the cabin. He didn't need light to find his way to his own quarters in the opposite end of the boat. Walking down the short passageway, he ducked his head from long practice in the darkened interior and opened the door to his cabin. Built into the stern, the owner's cabin ran the full width of the boat from one side to the other. It was just high enough to stand upright in without stooping. He liked the cabin, even if the bunk was a little wider than he would have preferred. It took up too much of the available space. If he had designed it to his own taste, he would have made it narrower, but the extra width on the mattress had advantages from time to time. Watkins Yacht Building's best carpenter finished the small room with storage cabinets on three sides and a built in set of drawers under the bed. He opened the louvered wooden door to a locker mounted forward of his bunk, moved a pile of dirty linen to one side and pulled a shoebox out from beneath the pile of clothes. He sat the shoebox on the bed and tossed the lid on top of his blankets.

Pistols were something he thought he'd left in his past. Like Frankie Byrd and his type; things left in his past. For a moment, he thought about putting the lid back on the box and shoving it all back under his laundry. But it wouldn't do.

The leather straps were wound tightly around the shoulder holster and were hiding most of the gun from view, but the smooth elephant ivory handles, dead white in the cardboard box, could still be seen even in the dim light coming through the cabin's porthole. Harry lifted the holster out of the box and pulled the pistol free from the soft leather. He hadn't had it out of its cardboard container in a while, but he had always known where it was.

Just in case the past turned up again.

The shiny blue metallic coating on the .45 had a thin film of oil on its surface. Using a dirty sock from his pile of laundry, he wiped the automatic down, then pushed the round stud in front of the trigger guard. The clip dropped into his hand. The shiny bullet sitting in the top of the flat metal tube glowed in the semidarkness; one bullet held by the steel clip with six more like it underneath. Harry worked the slide back and forth in a familiar motion and sighted down the barrel with the pistol at arm's length.

Everything still worked the way it should.

He slammed the clip back inside the grip of the gun, pushed the release with his thumb making the slide of the heavy pistol clang home. The .45 meant business now, with a round in the barrel and the hammer cocked. He looked at the automatic in his hand and thought about all Roscoe told him.

His thumb eased the pistol's hammer back down from the firing position, but he didn't put it back in its holster or return it to the shoebox. Instead, he slipped it under his pillow and tossed the holster back into the bottom of the locker.

Frankie Byrd was out and looking for him. His past had returned to his present.

He didn't think Frankie knew about their dock at the old sawmill, but there were others who did. If Byrd asked enough questions from enough people, he wouldn't be too hard to find, but he didn't really think Frankie would come calling. Like he told Roscoe, that wasn't the man's style. The other guy, however, the one that was willing to shoot Roscoe for eight dollars, he was an unknown factor. He would just have to see how things played out.

And be ready.

Stooping slightly to peer out the small round porthole, he looked at the night covered lake. The weather couldn't make up its mind. The twinkling lights Roscoe saw earlier were gone. There were no lights at all showing on the water now. How many times had they ghosted along out there in the dark, engines barely turning, not daring to show a light and keeping sharp eyes out for revenuers, Coast Guard cutters and rivals? Cutthroats, Roscoe called them, and cutthroats they were. It was a night just like this one that was Frankie Byrd's downfall. He remembered that night well.

"You're late," Frankie had shouted two years ago from where he stood on the barely seen wooden dock. "I was about to pack up and go home."

"We got delayed," Roscoe shouted back, far louder than Harry would have liked.

Byrd stepped out of the darkness between the stacked cases of Canadian whiskey, gin or something that would pass for gin in the speaks, and a few scattered cases of French champagne. He had the collar of his slicker turned up to the drizzle, his hat's brim making his face a dark shadow. The glowing stub of a cigarette between his lips was the closest thing to a facial feature that could be seen.

Both men could barely make him out in the dark with the soft rain falling as Harry maneuvered their boat alongside the wharf.

They were on *Minotaur* in those days, *Scarab* still just a laid keel in the boatyard. *Minotaur* was an altogether different boat. The boat was half as long as *Scarab* would be and built for fast runs to Canada or offshore rendezvous with the ships sitting outside the Line. The Line was the three mile line. It was where Prohibition ended and it was where the old schooners and tramp steamers, some barely seaworthy enough to stay afloat, anchored and waited for their customers, each ready to do business with anyone who had cash on hand.

Minotaur had no enclosed wheelhouse like the future *Scarab* would have. All she offered for protection from the weather was a glass windshield and the combing around the cockpit and as Harry stood behind the wheel easing the boat alongside the pier, the drizzle and chill of winter was freezing cold.

Harry throttled the engines back and shifted the twin levers into neutral. Roscoe, standing on the boat's long bow, tossed a line onto the pier. The fire axe was close by, Harry saw. If the exchange turned bad or somebody got stupid, there would be no time for untying lines. The axe was insurance.

"Where's Drake?" Harry expected to see him waiting at the landing. Leaving the engines idling in neutral, he moved to the stern to toss another line onto the pier. An unknown man in a plaid woolen coat picked up the rope and dropped a loop over a thick pylon driven into the deep water below them.

"I thought he was with you?" Frankie answered.

"He didn't show." Harry swiped a hand over his face to remove a cold layer of rainwater. The weather was getting worse.

Frankie flicked the stub of his smoke into the water. "Doesn't matter to me. You have my money?"

Roscoe, coming aft down the boat's side, paused by the entrance to the cockpit. "We thought we heard engines a little while ago, Byrd." He couldn't see Harry well enough from the bow and Frankie, standing between him and a stack of whiskey cases was half hidden from view. "You see anything of the patrols?"

Harry was trying to look beyond the stacks of liquor at the forest beyond. There was a truck of some kind parked behind the small wharf. It looked like someone was standing on the running board, but he couldn't be sure. He moved back to *Minotaur's* cockpit and killed his engines. Things became very quiet. The night was unbroken silence until the half seen man on the running board rattled out a deep, prolonged cough.

"You're the nervous type, Harrison. I wouldn't have unloaded the truck if there were revenuers around. The Coast Guard's off looking for some place warm and dry tonight." Frankie glanced at Harry standing next to his ever present watchdog. "The money," he said again. "You have it?"

Roscoe stepped past Harry to the closed hatch mounted dead center on the boat's deck. The boat wasn't that large but below, her insides were nothing but open space able to hold over a hundred cases if you packed carefully.

"We shouldn't be here," he said. "It don't feel right. Where's Drake?"

When did it ever feel right, Harry asked himself. Feel right or not, this is what they did. "We'll load fast." Nudging his chin in the direction of the boat's flush mounted loading hatch, he said, "Open her up. Let's get this over with."

This was always the tricky part, Harry knew. Cash changing hands made some people get ideas and Frankie wasn't far from the bad idea type. He had that feel about him. Everyone in this business did.

Roscoe kicked the latching dogs away from the heavy lid of the hatch and pulled it open. The opening door masked his hand reaching behind him to the revolver tucked in his belt. Drake was their go between, or was supposed to be. Frankie provided the goods, him and Harry transported and Drake paid. That was the deal. Something didn't feel right. He scratched at the old scar over his lung and kept one eye on the stranger in the plaid coat for signs of a double cross as he lifted the heavy hatch. If it was going to be a shootout, this was the moment it would begin while he was distracted with the hatch and not watching the bums on the pier.

Nothing happened and the plaid coated stranger wasn't paying much attention to anything. Roscoe relaxed a little.

Harry looked at the canvas bag sitting on the deck beside *Minotaur's* wheel. The bag held three thousand dollars cash that he was supposed to hand to Drake, not Frankie Byrd.

Everyone on the patrol boat heard the smuggler kill his engines.

"That was our fish alright, Mr. McAllister," whispered the man standing next to him.

Donovan lowered his binoculars and looked into the mist surrounding the boat. Somewhere to his east a smuggler motored by, running quiet, blacked out and very near the shore.

Right where he was told they would be.

He hunched his shoulders inside his heavy uniform coat and wished the drizzle would stop, but knew it wasn't likely. Drops of water fell steadily from the brim of his cap as he tapped one finger against the binoculars hanging around his neck. He would have to make a decision soon.

They shut their engines down a half hour earlier and drifted southward, pushed by the tide and a biting north wind, all the while listening for the sound of someone else's engines on the quiet water. There was a roll on the sea and his boat, rising and falling with the swell, was beginning to twist clockwise. If they kept turning away from the shore, the six pounder mounted in the bows would be masked from their target and unable to fire if he needed it.

Lieutenant Junior Grade Donovan McAllister was planning on needing it. The gun was going to end a lot of his problems tonight.

Ten minutes more, he thought. Give them another ten minutes. If he timed it right, he could catch them loading and roll up the whole gang all at once.

"How far off the rocks do you think we are, Chief?" he whispered to the man next to him on the bridge.

The Chief, almost twenty years Donovan's senior, pushed a black watch cap farther back on his head and peered into the gloom. He had a rasping voice, molded and sculpted by his trade to send fear down the backs of the enlisted seamen under his control.

"Hard to say in this soup," he whispered, "but judging by the sound of those engines, I'd say not far. Three hundred yards at the most." The Coast Guard chief looked at the glowing binnacle beside him as if the compass could give him a better estimate of the distance. "We might be a little closer."

"Who's that on the mount?" Donovan asked, looking at a shadowy figure standing in the bows. The patrol boat's deck gun was trained to port, its barrel pointing in the same direction as the sound of the unseen and now silent engines.

"Parsons," the chief answered.

Donovan looked aft down the side of his boat. His boarding party was on deck, armed and staring into the dark mist towards the shore. Some were smiling, knowing they found a runner.

"I've got the money. Three grand, as agreed." Harry lifted the canvas bag at his feet and held it in his left hand, keeping his right free. His coat was unbuttoned and the weight of the .45 under his arm was reassuring.

"Toss it over, then." Frankie held his hands out like a kid playing catch in the backyard.

"I'm not throwing three thousand dollars anywhere. Besides, we need help loading all that." Harry waved the canvas sack at the stacks of alcohol sitting on the wharf. "When we're loaded, then you get paid. That's the deal."

"Fine." Frankie put one foot over the side of the pier and stepped onto the deck of *Minotaur*. The boat rocked slightly as he came aboard. "Start loading," he said to the plaid coated man standing behind him.

"Go below," Roscoe said. "I'll hand the cases down to you," he told Frankie as he came aboard.

"Tote your own product, Harrison. I don't do the heavy lifting."

The man in the plaid coat picked up the first crate of liquor and handed it across to Roscoe standing by the boat's hatch. "Here," he said, holding the wooden crate out in front of him. "Stack 'em on deck and we'll put 'em in the hold."

"I'll see what's in that bag, Watkins. Before they start packing." Frankie jerked a thumb at the man in the plaid coat. "Him and Harrison can keep loading while I count."

An unnatural metallic clang coming from somewhere out on the water behind them made everyone's eyes snap towards the direction of the sound. No one moved and all four men stood very still looking out at the dark water beyond them. Roscoe, holding a crate of whiskey in his arms, didn't breathe.

"Harry," he whispered.

"Son of a bitch," the chief swore. He grabbed the seaman standing an arm's reach away from him by his coat's collar. The seaman's Springfield rifle had fallen from his hands and tumbled down three steps, nearly going over the side, before someone below grabbed it. "Why don't you ring a fuckin' bell while you're at it," the chief snarled in his face.

"I didn't mean to, Chief. I was putting on my gloves and it slipped."

"Son of a bitch," the chief swore again as he bodily slammed the eighteen year old's back into the deckhouse. "I'll drown your miserable ass over the side, sonny boy, and write your momma a real sad letter if our fish gets away because of you." The chief turned to face Donovan. "They heard us for sure." The collar of the young seaman's pea coat was a twisted knot in the old chief's fist.

Donovan slapped the surface of the superstructure in front of him twice with an open palm. The sound boomed like a gunshot on the quiet bridge. "Engine room," he yelled as loud as he could into the brass speaking tube. "Light 'em off. Helm, hard a'port as soon as she'll answer and all ahead full." Donovan turned his face to the sky behind him, up to the patrol boat's short mast ignoring the confirmation of his orders coming from the helmsman. The lookout standing by the spotlight was ready. He jabbed a finger towards the shore.

"Lookout," he screamed. "Find that boat." Instantly, a brilliant white beam of light shot across the water illuminating a rocky shoreline packed with trees. The chief's guess about the distance was a pretty good one. The shore was two hundred yards away. That would make it difficult, Donovan knew. Two hundred yards was a good head start if the smuggler sitting quiet just across the way had a fast boat. They usually did.

Roscoe dropped the case of whiskey, bursting the wooden box and scattering broken glass and bootleg alcohol at his feet. A searchlight, incredibly brilliant in the misty darkness, was tracing along the shore north of them.

And it was close. Too damn close.

Harry hit the starter to his engines as he watched the searchlight sweep north along the shore. "Roscoe, cut us lose," he yelled as *Minotaur's* twin engines came alive beneath him.

Just one light, he told himself. One light meant one boat. They had a chance. At least he wasn't ringed in by them and trapped against the shore. The distance wasn't good, but *Minotaur* was a flyer in any sea and the Coast Guard sitting between him and the way home would be hard pressed to keep up with him once he got past. If he got past.

Harry couldn't take his eyes off the searchlight, even when he heard the chunk of Roscoe's axe biting into his boat's deck. High above him, a flare burst in the sky brighter than anything ever seen on the Fourth of July. The burning chemical light cast a greenish-white pool of illumination all around his part of the world. The searchlight's beam was pointing like a milk colored dagger from a single boat sitting like a vulture on the black water. It was one of the Coast Guard's six bitters. His mouth went dry. The man in the plaid coat was gone. He hadn't seen him leave. The wharf was empty of everything but crates of illegal alcohol destined for a thirsty America.

Frankie was wrong. Revenuers knew they were here.

Harry shoved both of his throttles all the way forward. Roscoe came running into the boat's cockpit from the bow still holding his axe in one hand as the searchlight lit them up in a blinding glare. He shouted something, but Harry couldn't hear him. Both of *Minotaur's* engines were screaming in a mechanized roar of gasoline and horsepower. The prop wash coming from the double screws sent an icy spray of cold, drenching water over the stacked cases of alcohol on the pier. *Minotaur* was leaving.

Straining in the darkness, Donovan could see the form of someone at the controls of his target. Two men moving, he thought, and maybe another farther forward. It was hard to tell through the mist and the jagged background caused by the stacks of liquor behind the boat. His heart raced as he unconsciously squeezed the binoculars in his hand. He couldn't identify the speedboat lying a touch too far away from him. It was just another one of the very fast boats built from the ground up to run the gauntlet of patrols between Canada and the U.S. borders. Everyone on the patrol boat heard the sudden scream of powerful engines on the smuggler's boat.

"Chief, get a BAR ready," he shouted. "They're going to run for it." Donovan leaned over the railing of the boat's small bridge. "Gun mount. Put a hole through that boat."

The explosive blast from the muzzle of the bow gun went off like a giant flashbulb beneath him. The sound of the gun echoed back from the trees lining the shore a split second after the shot. Donovan's night vision was gone, replaced by a bright spot seared into the center of his eyes. He could still see the dock and the runner's boat in front of it caught in his searchlight's powerful beam, but that was all. Standing on his small bridge, he blinked his eyes as he heard the gun crew clearing the spent round. They missed. The target hadn't erupted in a blast of flying wood splinters. Instead, one of the trees standing beyond the landing took the round with its trunk blown in half. Nobody noticed its slow, majestic fall along the shoreline. The hull beneath his feet vibrated as his boat's engines came to life beneath him. The engine telegraph next to the helm clanged as its bells sent his speed commands to the engine room.

Donovan's fist beat a rapid drumbeat on the steel rail in front of him. "Let's go," he shouted. "Before they get away. Let's go. Let's go."

The explosive shell fired from the patrol boat's deck gun ripped through the air just missing them. Both Harry and Roscoe hit the deck by pure reflex after the round shrieked by.

"He missed us," Roscoe shouted to Harry as they crouched on the deck.

Roscoe stood up to look in the direction of the patrol boat when *Minotaur* jerked hard to a very sudden stop. Unbalanced, he lost his footing and slammed into the boat's wheel. Byrd, standing on the open bow with nothing to stop his motion, pitched over the side and into the water.

"The aft line, Roscoe," Harry screamed. "We're still tied to the pier."

Minotaur's wake with both engines running flat out, was throwing water completely over the wooden wharf behind them. The line, acting like a pivot point was causing their boat to twist to the props' torque. It was pulling them around until they were pointing due west and almost directly at the patrol boat waiting for them offshore. Roscoe, his axe raised high above his head, raced aft.

"Help me," someone yelled.

Frankie was in the water beside the boat, arms flailing as he tried to keep from going under. "Help me," he shouted again.

Roscoe paused long enough to look at Byrd thrashing in the water. Then he looked at the taut rope straining to hold the boat anchored to the wharf. There wasn't enough time. He ignored Frankie and headed for the mooring line.

Frankie swam to the side of the boat. "Throw me a rope," he

shouted.

Harry twisted around in the boat's cockpit. Frankie had a hand in the air with his fingers spread like he was grasping at a line that wasn't there.

Roscoe's axe struck the deck fitting with all the strength he had. He split the cleat in half and sunk the steel head on the end of the wood handle six inches into the deck. The line parted instantly right as the second mushroom of bright light lit up the bow of the patrol boat. *Minotaur*, freed from her tether, took off like a race horse at the starting gate. Caught off balance by the sudden forward lurch, Roscoe nearly fell headlong down the sloping transom as the boat's screws tore the water behind them. If not for the hard stuck axe handle, he would have joined Frankie Byrd in the churning wake behind the boat.

The second shot fired by Donovan's gunner was aimed at the exact spot *Minotaur* had just left. Instead of blowing a sizeable hole in the side of the boat, the gunner scored a direct hit straight into the packed crates of bootleg gin lined up on the wharf. The alcohol exploded in an eye hurting blast of light. The wooden dock was swallowed in flames as liquid fire ran hissing into the sea beneath the pier.

Minotaur, engines screaming at full throttle, ran directly towards the Coast Guard blocking the path between them and the open sea. Harry found himself looking straight into the unblinking eye of the patrol's searchlight with its light blindingly bright in front of him. He had to turn, and turn quickly before the deck gun found the range and sent him to the bottom. Tiny dots of light like fireflies on a summer evening and barely seen because of the searchlight in his eyes went off in front of him as half a dozen men fired their rifles. *Minotaur* healed far over momentarily showing her bottom to the patrol boat as Harry spun his wheel and pointed his boat south. The windshield in front of him shattered as bullets punched through it. The wood foredeck splintered and cracked as the firing guns found something solid to hit. He yanked his wheel to the opposite side as *Minotaur* heeled far over again turning due west and ran. Ran for all she was worth.

Behind him, he could hear the rapid firing of the machinegun that ruined his foredeck and had so narrowly missed him. He gritted his teeth as the gun, firing a long burst, slammed unseen bullets into his boat. Harry spun his wheel again as he tried to get distance between him and the patrol boat and spoil the aim of the shooter behind him. The searchlight stayed locked on his boat. There was very little room to maneuver, the rocky shore being so close and the patrol blocking his exit out to sea.

A geyser of water and foam exploded just past and in front of him as the deck gun fired again. If a round found them, Harry knew, he, Roscoe and *Minotaur* would be turned to driftwood in an instant.

Glancing behind him, the glow of the searchlight lost its blinding force as the distance between them widened with every second. A row of splashes from the machinegun traced a line across his wake as *Minotaur* turned again running south and directly away from the Coast Guard boat. He was trying to remember how far down the coast he could go before he had to turn back to the west, towards open waters and, he prayed, not towards any other waiting patrol that might be lurking to cut him off. There was a line of rock somewhere out there pointing an unforgiving finger across his path, one he did not want to hit. However far it was, he wasn't going to turn west until *Minotaur* put more distance between them and the patrol boat's guns. If he put them on the rocks, then he would put them on the rocks. If they survived the impact, maybe they could swim or crawl to shore and disappear in the forest.

The Coast Guard was behind and to the right of them now. *Minotaur*, her engines screaming defiance with both throttles pressed as far forward as they could go, ran a half loop around the patrol boat. They were almost free from the trap. The searchlight, still holding his boat in its beam, was a fading glow in the mist filled night.

They might have the guns, but Harry knew he had the speed.

Roscoe, grabbing for handholds where he could find them along the way, pulled himself into the cockpit beside Harry.

"You bleeding?" Harry screamed. The sound of *Minotaur's* engines running at maximum speed were all but impossible to talk over.

"I think I singed my eyebrows when all that hooch went up."

Roscoe was watching the brightly burning dock still visible through the drizzle. He ducked again as another bloom of flame came from the deck gun. "Good gun crew. They're getting a round off every ten seconds. They might want to work on their aim a bit.

That warning shot almost hit us."

"Well, maybe we should buy them all a beer sometime and tell them how much we appreciate their skills," Harry shouted back. He spun the wheel hard over again, turning to the west and hoping he had enough distance between him and that fast firing gun to make it to open water.

Roscoe smiled wide as he hung on to a rail. The feel of the boat beneath them changed abruptly. They left the sheltered waters of the cove and made it into the Straights. *Minotaur* bounced hard over the wave tops.

"Think Frankie made it?" Roscoe shouted as the glowing spot on the coastline that was almost their undoing disappeared behind them.

Harry forgot all about Frankie Byrd. The boat hit a wave hard enough to make the hull jump free of the water. She came crashing down on the other side as both men took the impact with bent knees. He needed to get his bearings. Victoria wasn't far away. Any minute now, he should be able to see lights in the gloom ahead of him. The canvas bag with the three thousand dollars bounced around between his feet. It was too rough to bend over and pick it up so he stepped on it instead penning it to the deck. "Don't know," he said. "I saw him go past us when you cut the stern line."

"Wasn't time to fish him out of the drink," Roscoe added. "Tough luck for him."

"Almost tough luck for all of us," Harry said.

"Wonder which boat it was found us?" Roscoe asked. His voice was as calm as if they were taking one of Watkins Yacht's out for a sea trial.

Harry didn't answer.

The searchlight still pointed in their direction making a long cone of light across the water, but the light no longer covered them in its bright grip. As Harry turned the boat again, the light lost them in the mist continuing to shine where they had been instead of where they were.

The deck gun flashed once more. No one ducked this time. They had pulled too far away from their pursuers.

"We're going to make it, Harry. We're too fast for 'em to keep up."

"If they'd caught us loaded down with all those crates," Harry jerked a thumb over his shoulder at the glow from the burning alcohol now far behind them, "they would have had us easy."

But they weren't loaded and *Minotaur* wasn't in a mood to be caught. Not that night. They lost their cargo and their boat was damaged but that was the chance you took. Nothing was ever guaranteed in their business. Luck sometimes rode with you and sometimes she didn't. She wasn't riding with Frankie Byrd that night. It was McNeil Island for him and its penitentiary.

Harry turned his back on the view of the lake through *Scarab's* porthole. It was a perfect night for rumrunners, but those days were over now. Everything had changed. Except for the old associations. *Minotaur* was long gone and the comfortable quarters of his cabin was his world now. Not frozen nights out on the Sound risking prison or death. He undressed and climbed into his bunk, listening to the creaks and groans of his floating home. Lying on his back, his hands behind his head, he put thoughts of criminals and past deeds out of his mind. Closing his eyes on his day, he thought instead of Lucy.

There were other women in his life since she left, but none of them lasted long. He had almost forgotten how having Lucy so close made him feel and now she was back from wherever she disappeared to. Still as beautiful and desirable as the day she left.

He almost kissed her, would have kissed her if not for Millie and her horn. Harry smiled in the darkness of his cabin. All around him were the sounds of his boat and the lake, sounds he was very used to and hardly noticed anymore. The wind was picking up outside pushing against the boat. He could feel the motion of the lake beneath him. The water softly nudged *Scarab's* hull, sloshing along the waterline playing an old, familiar song.

Scarab rubbed against the pier and Harry's half awake, half dreaming mind remembered the feel of Lucy's sister as she rubbed against him in the car not at all feeling like a kid anymore. The wooden hull of his boat groaned in the quiet of the night as the lake leaned against her timbers. Harry dreamed and remembered similar groans from Lucy.

She was back, his dream whispered.

CHAPTER 8

The drizzle coming out of the night sky turned into a heavy wet snow right as Lucy and Millie drove off the Houghton ferry. When they made the last turn onto their street, it fell harder. Fast falling wet flakes were all around them in the darkness. The parallel rows of tall, silent alder trees in front of their home were a welcome sight to Millie. What was supposed to have been a few hours' drive around the city turned into a long day and a good part of a night. It was an interesting day and a long one. She was tired, cold enough to think she might never get warm again and was glad to be almost in her bed. Their father added a curving horseshoe drive in front of their house right after Donovan learned to drive. When their brother was in town, it was his favorite parking space. The curved drive was empty.

"Donny's out late," Millie said.

"I wouldn't call us early." Lucy yawned sleepily. "It's going on two."

Turning into their driveway, she eased past the horseshoe and rolled slowly towards the garage behind their home. She was thankful her father's bedroom was on the opposite side of the house. There was a good chance he would sleep through their late night arrival. He usually did. Her father slept through a lot. Sleeping, she supposed, was easier than trying to deal with a daughter who had taken up with a whiskey smuggler or a son who drank too much of the smuggled whiskey.

The car idled down the driveway, rolling quietly towards the closed doors of the garage. The second floor's row of bedroom windows were dark as Millie got out of the car and swung open the wide wooden door. Lucy pulled the Auburn inside, easing into the spot next to their father's Packard. She killed the engine and got slowly out from behind her wheel. "Well, that was a pleasant afternoon drive."

Millie pushed the heavy door closed. "Wasn't it just," she said. "I can't believe how cold it's got after being so nice all day."

In the darkness, Lucy closed her door with a soft shove and ran her hand along the canvas top.

"I want to go to bed," Millie said, "and sleep until noon like Donny."

"Where do you suppose our brother is?" Lucy asked, as the pair went through the side door and out into the backyard.

"Howling at the moon, probably. Maybe he's gone to Mr. Harrison's cathouse."

"If Papa hears you using words like that, he'll have you eating soap." Lucy spoke with the wisdom of experience in her words. "Besides, you promised, remember?" Before Millie could open their home's back door, she placed her hand over her sister's, stopping her from turning the knob.

"If Papa asks, we missed a turn somewhere. I had to stop and ask for directions. If anyone asks anything more, the place we stopped was an out of the way saloon somewhere out in the sticks. We got directions from a waitress." She leaned closer to her sister. "A waitress, and remember, volunteer nothing and keep your secrets to yourself." She let go of her sister's hand. "Say the word cathouse, or god forbid something worse, and Papa will be dragging you down the hall to the bathroom before you know what's happened. He might even drag me after you for good measure."

The backdoor opened with hardly a sound and both women tiptoed into the dark and silent kitchen. Lucy stopped in the middle of the room and took off her shoes motioning for Millie to do the same. She needn't have bothered. Millie already had one shoe off and was working on the second.

"Learn from your big sister's past mistakes. Don't touch the second step on the stairs. It squeaks."

"I know about the damn squeaks." Millie went up the back staircase to the bedrooms above as quietly as a silent movie.

Lucy watched the backside of her sister disappear into the gloom at the top of the stairs. "She goes into a house of ill repute by accident," she said to the refrigerator beside her, "and now every other word out of her mouth is profane." Their father was sure to notice a difference in his baby girl and want to know why. Millie would be sorry she ever thought of herself as an adult the first time she cursed in front of him.

As she followed her sister up the stairs, she heard a noise coming from somewhere in one of the front rooms. It sounded like a chair sliding across the floor. Instead of taking the stairs, she turned and walked quietly through the swinging doors of the kitchen and into the hallway. A lamp was turned on in the seldom used second sitting room. Her brother was sitting on the divan. "Donny?"

Donovan finished his swallow from the cut crystal glass in his hand before answering. "I thought that was you pulling into the garage. I was wondering if you two still lived here anymore."

"Lower your voice," Lucy said in a whisper. "You'll wake Papa. Why are you sitting in here?"

"Pop's not here, and the shortest distance to the decanter is a straight line." Donovan sighted down one finger at the glass container sitting on the bureau across from him. "Straight line," he added.

"He's not here? It's two in the morning." She waited for an answer but didn't get one. Her brother stared at the glass decanter. He looked drunk. "What do you mean, Papa's not here and where's your car? I didn't see it when we came in."

"My car? I wouldn't worry about my car too much. I put it out of its miserable misery. Smashed it." Donovan looked into his empty glass. "Miserable misery," he said again. "Now we know which is more powerful, the bumper or the mighty tree." He saluted the elms of the world with his glass.

Lucy took a seat beside her brother. The single lamp burning in the room wasn't bright enough for her to see him well. "Are you hurt?"

"Why Lucy, thank you for enquiring about my health. More than the old man did." He mumbled something under his breath that she didn't catch. "I am fit for duty," he added as he tried to take another drink from his empty glass. "Pour me another, would you? My legs seem to have betrayed me all of a sudden. Old war wound."

Lucy took the glass from his hand and set it aside. "You don't have an old war wound and I think you've had your limit if you can't stand."

"I wasn't drunk. The old man said I was drunk, but I wasn't. So, I got drunk to prove him right." Donovan belched and patted his chest with his fist. "You know how he likes to prove he's right. Thought I'd help him along."

"Donny, where's Papa?"

"A tree." Donovan ran a hand through his hair. His gaze went to the decanter. "It was an accident. We had a, we hit a tree. She was bleeding bad." He looked at his sister sitting beside him, noticing the dark brown leather jacket for the first time. "Whose coat is that? You look like Amelia Earhart."

"Who was bleeding?" She put her hand on her brother's face and looked directly at him. "Did you run over someone?"

"Inga. She told me I got her in trouble, then we hit the tree."

"In trouble?" Lucy said softly. "In trouble," she said again much louder. "You mean she was out too late," Lucy swallowed, "and got in trouble. Is that what you mean?"

"The windshield." Donovan twirled a finger in front of his forehead. "She hit the windshield pretty damn hard." He made a halfhearted attempt to reach for his glass, but Lucy sat it beyond his reach. "In trouble like *in trouble*," he said. "She says she wants a boy."

Lucy stood slowly from the divan. "Oh," she groaned. It was the only sound she could make right then.

Donovan found his legs at last. He crawled his way up from the divan and grabbed the glass decanter from the bureau. "Maybe we can call him Archibald. The old man would love that. Where's my glass?" he asked, looking around him.

Lucy stared at the rug for a moment before going on. "Did you take her home after you hit the tree?" She didn't know whether to scream or kick her brother, and she was afraid of the answer that was about to come out of his mouth.

"I didn't tell the old man that part yet. It wasn't exactly," Donovan burped, "exactly the right circumstances, not with that nurse looking down her nose at me." He found his glass and splashed a healthy shot of bourbon into it.

"Papa's with her at Swedish, if that bitch nurse hasn't thrown him out already. Her head was bleeding a lot. From the windshield. She smashed into it pretty hard."

"Hospital?"

"Papa made me leave the waiting room. The cops showed up and," Donovan shrugged his shoulders, "you know." He rubbed his face with his hands and looked for his sister. "Where are you going?"

Lucy's bare feet echoed hollowly as she stomped across the wood floor of their home. "I'm going to the hospital you stupid fuck. Where do you think I'm going?" The words came out in a shrill scream.

Millie was standing in the short hallway between the kitchen and the second parlor. When Lucy hadn't followed her upstairs, she came back down to see where she went. "I'll go with you."

"Help him find his bed," Lucy said without a pause. "I'll be back later."

*****

Darkness. That's all he could see. Harry blinked his eyes in the dim light of the cabin. The boat moved softly below him, her wooden frames groaning in the quiet of the night. His grandfather was telling him something, but he stopped suddenly in mid-sentence. The old man looked past his shoulder.

"Did you hear that?" his grandfather asked him.

Rolling over on his side, the dream already forgotten, Harry tucked a hand under his head and drifted off to sleep again.

His eyes snapped open.

This time the sound was unfiltered by whispered conversations with dead men. A noise. Something outside the normal sounds. Something that wasn't a wave pushing against the hull, the boat bumping against the pier or a mooring line chafing against a chock. The .45 was in his hand before his feet touched the chilled wood of the deck. He stood crouching in his cabin as wide awake as he had ever been in his life and wondering if he was imagining things going bump in the night. If Frankie Byrd thought he wouldn't blow great big holes in him, then Frankie was a very bad judge of character.

Grabbing his trousers from the foot of his bed and pulling them on as quickly as he could, he tiptoed down the passageway forward to the steps leading to *Scarab's* main cabin.

He froze in the middle of climbing the stairs and cocked his head to one side, listening. No, he wasn't imagining things. There really was a monster in the closet. He recognized the sound of someone trying to work the latch on the boat's life rail.

The pistol in his hand clicked as his thumb cocked the hammer. It was a simple latch if you knew how to do it and you could see what you were doing. Whoever was trying to open the railing rattled the clasp. If he hadn't known the sounds of his boat so well, he might not even have heard it. It was just a soft rattle easily missed in the normal background noise, especially if you were asleep.

He advanced up the remaining steps into the main cabin, the barrel of the Colt leading the way in the dark interior. He could barely make out the glow of the faraway light coming from the boathouse. The dim light was backlighting the cabin's curtains enough for him to see something was there.

Someone was on the pier.

The shadow was indistinct but definitely standing on the other side of the gate. Pointing his pistol, Harry sighted down the barrel at the silhouette.

The latch rattled again. Softly. Barely heard.

His hand tightened its hold on the elephant tusk grips of the gun. He could shout a warning at Byrd, fire a killing blast through his windows or grab the door and open it.

And do what? Ask him in to have a drink and talk about his misplaced desire for revenge?

"Oh hell," he heard the ghostly figure on the pier say as the latch rattled again, louder this time, but still refusing to open.

Harry lowered his Colt, grabbed the door handle, and pushed the door open with a hard shove. Icy air blew in from the cold night outside.

Lucy jumped in surprise. "Mother of God." Her hand went to her chest as if her blouse had suddenly fallen open.

"Don't swear," Harry said.

"You scared the hell out of me. I almost peed my pants." Lucy noticed the pistol in his hand. She lifted both her arms in the air.

"Don't shoot," she crooned. "I surrender and call my daddy's lawyers."

"I hope they are better lawyers than you are a burglar." Harry eased the hammer closed on the automatic. "I nearly shot you. Hell, I still might."

She gave Harry a long look. "I didn't wake you, did I?" she said nonchalantly.

No, his grandfather had. It snowed while he was sleeping, he noticed. A heavy dusting coated all the trees surrounding the gravel path to his boathouse. He looked from Lucy to the white forested background behind her and noticed something was missing. "Where's your automobile?"

"Can I put my arms down? Or do you still want me to reach for the sky as they say in the westerns?"

"No, keep 'em up. I haven't decided if I'm going to shoot you yet or not." Harry scratched a spot in front of his ear with the barrel of the pistol. There was something about seeing Lucy with her hands up in the universal posture of surrender that appealed to him. "Where's your car?" he asked again.

Lucy half lowered her arms. She turned and pointed back up the hill.

"Hands up," Harry said. "I've still got the drop on you."

Lucy raised her hands again, palms towards him. "Look, I refuse to stand here, held at gunpoint with my hands up by a man with his pants unzipped." She looked at the front of Harry's trousers. "If you're going to shoot me, the least you can do is preserve my reputation first." She wiggled a finger at the front of his trousers. "Besides, I do believe you're glad to see me."

Harry did a quick about face while he fooled with his zipper. Thinking it was better to be safe than sorry, he tucked the heavy Colt under one armpit before ensuring Lucy's reputation remained intact.

"Bang, cowboy. You're dead. Some gunslinger you'd make." Lucy lowered her arms and put her hands into the pockets of her borrowed leather jacket. "I was going to knock, you know? Your damn swinging gate thing is stuck."

Harry retrieved his pistol from under his arm, reached over and flicked the latch open then lifted the bar out of the way. "It's easy when you know how." He rubbed his hand up and down his arm a few times trying to generate some warmth. His undershirt wasn't doing much against the cold. It felt like frost was sinking into his bones. "You still haven't answered my question. Where's your car?"

Lucy waved an arm in the direction of the gravel lane twisting away up the snow covered hill. "Up there on the blacktop. Moby Dick ran out of gas right before the turnoff."

"Not exactly your neighborhood."

"It's been a day for strange neighborhoods. If you only knew."

"Haven't seen any murderers lurking in the bushes, have you?" he asked, as he examined the wall of snow dusted trees just beyond his boathouse.

"Murderers?" She followed Harry's eyes and looked over her shoulder at the wall of trees.

"Never mind. Inside joke. Come in. I'm freezing standing out here."

"You mean I'm not going to be shot for breaking and entering?"

"Not this time." Harry took her hand to help her onto the boat's deck. Lucy went past him quickly and on into the dark interior of the boat. He flipped on the lights as he followed her inside.

"I'm sorry to show up like this. I really am. I didn't know where else to go except here or back home and I wasn't ready to go back there yet." Lucy sat on the sofa. "I see you're still a light sleeper. Where's that carousing lady's man that's always hanging around? Did I wake him, too?"

Harry snorted. "Not unless you went in the galley screaming fire and banged two pots together. I don't think he would have budged if I really had shot you."

"Speaking of, since when do you come to the door with a pistol?"

Harry sat the .45 beside the liquor cabinet. "That's complicated."

"You're not doing the old business again?"

"There is no old business anymore. Those days are over."

"So why the gun?" Lucy slipped her shoes off and pulled her feet up onto the couch.

Harry sat beside her. "Roscoe sort of ran into some bad history. The kind with a score to settle."

"Bad history, meaning you need a gun?"

"Exactly that kind of history." Harry told her about Frankie and Roscoe's run in earlier in the evening, or last night since he doubted he'd be going back to sleep. The sun would be up in a little while. Sunday was over.

"I don't remember meeting anyone named Byrd."

"You never met him. I kept you away from his kind. Frankie was a sort of provider. He provided what we delivered."

Lucy put her hand on Harry's arm. "Go to the police. Tell them what you told me."

"That would probably work if I was Harry Watkins of Watkins Yachts but I'm not. Haven't been for a long time. The cops know how I made my living. If I went to them for help, they'd probably use it as an excuse to hold me as a material witness or tell me to take my troubles to some other neighborhood."

"They might surprise you."

"Kitsap County didn't surprise me. The sheriff foreclosed on my granddad's business."

"Foreclosed?"

"It's all gone." Harry spread his arms out in front of him. "What you see in front of you is all that's left. Didn't your brother tell you?"

"No," Lucy said softly. "My brother pretends I don't know you and I pretend I care what he thinks. I'm sorry, Harry. I really am." Lucy leaned over and kissed his cheek.

He put his arm around her shoulder and she curled her body closer against his.

"What did you mean when you said you didn't know where else to go?"

"If I went home, Donny and I were going to have a huge fight. I might need to borrow that pistol." Especially after the conversation she had with Inga Swenson's mother an hour earlier. She knew it was bad of her to think such thoughts, but she wished her brother had put a different woman in the hospital. She could think of something else of Donny's she wished he had put in a different woman as well. "Are we still fighting?"

"I didn't shoot you. Isn't that a good start?"

Lucy dug an elbow into his ribs. "I was so mad at you." She whispered the words as if they were sitting on a park bench and didn't want the couple next to them to hear. "I waited for you at the station. You were supposed to come and tell me you couldn't live without me. You didn't show, and I knew it was over between us."

"I didn't know you were at the train station."

"Yes, you did. Millie told you."

"No, she didn't."

Lucy sat up straight beside him. "She damn well better have. She told me she did."

Harry shook his head. "I haven't heard a word about you, where you were or where you went since the fight at the Pharmacy. Someone told Roscoe you went east."

Lucy had an incredulous look on her face, her blue eyes wide open. Then she laughed. "My baby sister. I guess she had an unbelievable backhand even then." She leaned against the sofa's back and crossed her arms. "You don't know what I'm talking about, do you?"

Harry shook his head. "Not really."

"Never mind. I'm having sister issues."

Harry remembered the way Millie pressed the length of her body against him in the backseat of that girl's automobile. Sister issues. That was a good way of describing it.

Lucy nuzzled her nose against his neck. "Tell me you missed me," she whispered.

"I just saw you a few hours ago. What's to miss?"

Lucy bit his ear.

"Ouch," he said, pulling away from her.

She stood slowly from the sofa, straddled both his legs then settled down onto his lap. "Tell me you missed me."

"Are you going to bite me again if I don't?"

"I'll bite something."

He kissed her. Not a peck on the cheek this time. "I missed you," he said. "Every day." His eyes watched the tight fabric of her blouse as she moved her arms out of his coat. Lucy slid the leather jacket off and let it fall behind her. "But I won't apologize for punching your brother," he added. It was Donovan's boat out there that tried to sink him. Her brother bragged about nearly killing him and warned him about being seen with his sister. That's what Lucy hadn't heard the night of the fight. Harry's only regret was he hadn't hit him harder.

"Next time I'll hold him for you." Lucy sighed. "My brother," she whispered. "My brother has put a silly idiot of a girl in the hospital. He hit a tree in his car and she was hurt." She slid out of

Harry's lap and stretched out beside him. "I'm so tired."

How long had it been since she laid her head on his lap? He couldn't remember.

"He told me he's gotten her pregnant."

"How bad?"

"She's not showing yet."

"I meant, how bad is she hurt?"

"Oh. I don't know exactly. I spoke to her mother. She said they put a few stitches in her scalp. I wish they had sewn something else up." Lucy yawned sleepily. "Her mom said they told her she had a concussion." Thinking about Inga made her want to cry, but she was determined to keep the tears from coming. She couldn't abide thinking of Inga as a sister-in-law. She just couldn't.

"Mrs. Swenson said Papa talked to her and Inga earlier about things after the doctors were finished with her daughter, and everything would be okay. That's what she said, 'everything will be okay.' I thought that was an odd thing to tell me."

"Your father? He knows?" Harry tried not to smile. He almost felt sorry for Donovan McAlister.

"Donny called him from the hospital."

"And the baby?"

"Inga's mom didn't mention it when I talked to her and it wasn't like I could ask her in front of the nurse." Lucy yawned again and snuggled closer to Harry. "I don't think she knows. Donny said he didn't tell Papa about that yet." Lucy's voice was getting drowsy. "Wait till our father finds out Donny has gotten Inga Swenson pregnant."

"What will your father say?" Harry waited for an answer and didn't get one. "Lucy?"

She was asleep.

Harry stood up gently sliding her head out of his lap, then reached for a cushion. The room wasn't very warm. He went to one of the empty cabins for a blanket. On his way, he took his pistol back to his own cabin, grabbed a warmer shirt, and found his shoes. Lucy didn't move when he tucked the blanket around her.

Four pairs of faint dings came from the galley's clock. Eight bells. Four AM. He picked his jacket up from where Lucy dropped it and laid it across the armrest of the sofa. Far forward in the small double bunked cabin occupied by his hard sleeping mechanic, an alarm clock began the slow process of waking Roscoe Harrison. Harry went into the galley to light a fire in the stove and put the coffee pot on a burner. As the water boiled, Roscoe came out of his quarters pulling suspenders over his shirt.

"You're up mighty early this morning," he said sleepily. He pulled a chipped coffee mug free from a hook over the sink.

"I didn't get much of a choice. We had prowlers last night." Harry motioned up the steps to the salon with a nod of his head.

Roscoe stepped to the passageway so he could see into the boat's main cabin. "That's Miss Lucy," he said with surprise. "She's sleeping on the settee."

"And people say you're not very sharp in the mornings."

"She been here long? I don't mean to be indelicate or nothing."

"No, not long. God forbid you get a reputation for indelicateness. What would they think down at Barefoot Nessie's place? Her car ran out of gas up on the road and she hoofed it down here." Harry smiled to himself and muttered Moby Dick half out loud.

"Is that little one with her?"

"Not this trip."

"That's good. How far back did she say?"

"Up by the turnoff."

Harry wrapped his hand in a thick cloth, then lifted the percolator off the burner. Roscoe pulled a second mug from a hook and Harry filled the cups with the hot, dark liquid.

"Well, I better get my coat on and see about things pretty quick." Roscoe added a fourth spoonful of sugar to his coffee before he and his cup disappeared back into his cabin.

"We got a gas can anywhere around?" Harry put a small spoonful of sugar in his mug and stirred it with a spoon.

"There's one out in the shed."

"Boathouse," Harry corrected.

"Sure, Boss. Boathouse."

Roscoe drank half his mug of steaming coffee apparently without burning his tongue clean out of his mouth. "I may have to siphon some gas."

"You mind taking care of it? I'd help you, but I gave all my warm clothes to the orphanage last night."

"I won't need no help, Harry." He ducked in and out of his

quarters to grab an ancient wool pea coat. "Besides, I get to drive it if I go get it."

"Why are you rolling out of your bunk so early? Four's hardly a human hour," Harry said as he took a cautious sip from his cup.

"It's Monday. I need to be over to Bainbridge by seven." He scratched at the whiskers on his cheeks and reminded himself he needed to shave before he left this morning. "The auction is today, you know?"

"No, I didn't know." He didn't want to think about foreclosures and seizures this morning.

Roscoe finished off the rest of his coffee and poured himself another cup. Harry left the galley and his mechanic's ritual of liquefying half a pound of sugar in his caffeine and went back to the settee with its sleeping blonde burglar.

"Lucy?" he said, touching her shoulder.

"Mmmm." She pulled the blanket up closer around her neck and stretched out her legs.

"Where are your keys, sweetheart?"

"My jacket," she murmured without opening her eyes.

"Roscoe's going to get your car, okay?"

"Mm hmm."

Harry reached for his jacket, her jacket, and pulled a hard gray roll of twine about the size of a golf ball out of the side pocket. It was a monkey's fist, a miniaturized version of what seamen used to throw heaving lines from ship to shore or vice versa. The decorative knot, made by wrapping coils of line around a center weight to form a hard ball, was attached to a steel ring of keys. He made it for her years ago. There were six or seven keys on the ring, including the one to her automobile. One other key, slightly larger than the others, caught his attention. The number 618 was stamped into the brass. Harry remembered the monkey's fist. He had forgotten about the room key.

Turning his back on his sleeping burglar, he discovered a grinning Roscoe standing close behind him. He held the ring of jangling keys and its monkey fist out to him.

"Thanks, sweetheart," Roscoe said, as he snatched the keys out of his hand. He hurried out the door before Harry could make any replies.

Harry could hear Roscoe laughing as he stomped his way down

the wooden pier.

CHAPTER 9

"This is far enough, Miss Lucy. No point in you taking me all the way across," Roscoe said.

"I really don't mind. What's another hour now?" The nighttime cloud cover was slowly changing from coal black darkness to leaden gray. The beginnings of sunrise were starting to appear in the east. Out all night. Her father was going to have a screaming fit.

Roscoe wasn't paying attention to the sky. He was trying to make out the unseen running lights of the ferry somewhere out in the darkness.

The Auburn parked to the side of the Bainbridge ferry landing. A few automobiles were lined up, their bumpers almost touching, waiting their turn for the ride across Elliott Bay even at this predawn hour. On the other side of the line of cars, a cluster of pedestrians, workers mostly by the looks of them, stood quietly in the crisp, cold morning air.

A ride all the way to the old boatyard was tempting but Lucy hadn't killed the engine and Roscoe knew her offer to take him across to Bainbridge was made out of politeness.

"The old boatyard ain't that far from the ferry dock," he said. "Besides, you've got your own boat to catch back to Kirkland."

Lucy thought of her father again. If she left now, she would probably be home right about the time he was leaving for the field.

He was sure to throw a fit about her coming in at the crack of dawn. Even her brother didn't do that. No, she wasn't going to Kirkland. Not this morning. But there was no need to tell Roscoe that. "Are you sure? It's pretty cold out there."

Roscoe opened the car door. It was cold, but at least it was dry. The front that brought the overnight snow passed through and was now somewhere beyond the Cascades. The snow would be slush in a few hours and gone before the day was over. "I'm sure. Besides, I'm used to chilly mornings."

It was hard for him to hide his disappointment when they left Harry and the *Scarab's* warm interior almost an hour earlier. After the half awake, half asleep Lucy offered to give him a lift to the ferry, he expected her to hand him the keys to her car and let him play chauffeur again. But she hadn't. Still, a ride all the way to the landing saved him a fair amount of time, and he was well ahead of schedule now. The fast trip into town was better than standing outside and waiting for a streetcar to rattle its way over the hill. Even if he didn't get to drive. Thanks to Lucy, he would likely be the first person to show up for the auction.

The boatyard itself wasn't going on the block until next month. Today's auction was pretty much tools, parts, fixtures and building supplies and one shiny red Plymouth. Roscoe had a pretty fat roll of bills stuffed in his front pocket. Unless things went really wrong, he didn't plan on walking home.

It wasn't that he really needed a vehicle. He made it all these many years without one. There was a principal involved. The Kitsap County sheriff chased him and Harry for years and never once came close to catching them doing anything. Today's auction was the fat old bastard's way of getting even. Roscoe heard the talk. The sheriff planned to buy Harry's car himself. A trophy. Something to show the folks around Bainbridge. Proof he was the one who put Harry out of business in the end. The bulging wad of bills in Roscoe's front pocket wasn't going to let that happen.

"Thanks for getting me going again last night," Lucy said. "First time I've ever run out of gas." Before Roscoe could get out of her car, she leaned over and kissed him on the cheek. "You saved me twice in one night."

"Anytime you need saving." Roscoe pulled himself up and out of the car's leather covered seat. He had to stoop to see under the convertible's top. "You let me know and I'll be there in a flash."

"Got your handkerchief?" Lucy touched her finger to her cheek. "You might want to wipe off my lipstick. I wouldn't want to make anyone jealous."

"I might just leave it there, Miss Lucy. I don't get kissed by somebody as pretty as you every day."

Lucy smiled. "You old buzzard. Good luck with the auction. I hope you win."

Roscoe shifted his leg and felt the tight roll of bills. "With my good luck? How could I lose?" He closed the Auburn's door.

"See you next time," she said with a wave of her hand. The Auburn pulled quickly away from the curb as she accelerated through first and shifted into second. She was glad Roscoe turned down her offer to take him all the way to Bainbridge. She was exhausted. What she needed was a few hours undisturbed sleep free from a troubling brother with paternity problems or an angry father who was certain to lecture her about the ruined reputations of women who stayed out all night. Looking at the ring of keys dangling from the car's dashboard ignition, she saw the old brass key. It was mixed in among three or four others whose locks were lost or forgotten somewhere in her past. But she remembered that particular key. The one with six one eight stamped into the brass head.

Harry wouldn't care.

By now, her father would be awake and asking Millie for his breakfast. Millie would tell him she went to the hospital to see about Inga. Lucy touched the key dangling from the ignition. Why had she kept it all this time? A key that didn't fit any of her locks. But it did fit one lock and deep down, she had never really wanted to throw it away.

She would tell her father she stayed in town for the night. Donovan did it often when he was out carousing with his buddies and missed the last boat back to Kirkland. The family had bigger things to worry about. No one would care where she had been all night. Hopefully.

By the time she made it to Fourth Avenue, she no longer needed her headlights to drive. Sunrise was a dreary low blanket of cold winter gray. Harry's borrowed jacket felt warm and snug. The old leather was soft as a glove and smelled faintly of after shave and sweat.

The Bergonian wasn't far away.

The avenue in front of the hotel was lined with automobiles and no matter how aggressively she tried to swerve in and out of traffic this time, there were no parking spaces available. She parked her car around the corner and did a fast walk down the sidewalk to the front door clutching Harry's jacket tightly closed against the bitter cold. A different doorman opened the heavy metal and glass for her. She hurried past him, the early morning cold making her move quickly. The monkey fist keychain was in her hand.

The elevator was to the right of the front desk past the closed coat check. A sleepy looking boy was unpacking a box filled with waxes and brushes beside one of the shoeshine chairs. He stopped sorting his cans of polish as Lucy walked past. A ferret-like smile formed on his face. The torn in half five dollar bill was in his pocket and he just saw his payday walk by.

The boy, wide awake now, headed for the payphone in its wooden booth. Call if he ever saw the blonde again. That's what the owner of the other half of the five dollar bill told him to do. Call if he saw the pretty lady.

Next to the elevators, half way to the front desk, a newsstand filled with the headlines of the day was open for business. Lucy stopped and caught her breath. Her brother, Donny, stepped out into the lobby from behind the newsstand. He had a folded paper in his hand and was walking towards the front desk. He hadn't seen her and Lucy had no intention of letting him see her if she could help it.

Joe, of course, she thought. He was coming to see Joe. Still, it was a surprise to see him here. Millie was supposed to have put him in his bed and he should have been sleeping it off. But there he was standing in the Bergonian's lobby. A drunken scene with her brother was something she would avoid if she could. Besides, what would she say when Donny asked her what she was doing here? Tell him she had a key? She looked the other way, not wanting to make accidental eye contact with him, and followed a woman about her own age and a small boy of four or five into the waiting elevator.

"What floor?" the elevator operator asked.

"Nine for me," the unknown woman said. She gave Lucy's leather jacket, soiled shoes and wrinkled skirt an unapproving stare.

"Out all night with a former bootlegger," Lucy said to the

woman. "You?"

"I beg your pardon."

"Six," Lucy told the small framed man standing by his control lever.

The man pulled the elevator's cage door closed. Lucy could see her brother standing with his back to her at the front desk. He was talking to the desk clerk. She made it unseen.

"I'm staying with my husband. He's in real estate," the woman with the child said.

Lucy watched the dial above the door as it slowly marked their upward progress. The elevator slowed to a stop at six. The operator reached past her to slide the cage open.

"Everybody's married," she said as she stepped off the elevator. "Me, I've got an old key."

Back in the lobby, the shoeshine boy watched the dial above the elevator doors. He expected it to stop at eleven, Kanji's floor. But it didn't. The arrow-shaped dial stopped at six and then at nine before beginning its descent back to the ground floor. Six or nine, he thought. The blonde with the leather jacket got off on one or the other.

He dropped his nickel into the payphone's slot and started dialing the numbers written on the torn five dollar bill. The phone rang a long time before someone answered.

"You've got a Yoshiro Kanji staying here," Donovan told the man standing behind the polished wooden counter. He was talking too loud for the room and for the hour.

The Bergonian's clerk wasn't sure if he was being asked a question or told a fact he already knew. "The Japanese gentleman," he said. "Yes."

"I'm his wake up call."

The clerk smiled. "Of course. I'll have the hotel operator ring his room."

"I'd rather you didn't," Donovan said. "I prefer the surprise attack."

The clerk caught a strong whiff of liquor coming from the tall, lanky man standing across from him. "Why don't we ring the gentleman's room and see if he is in?"

Donovan took his money clip out of his trouser pocket, pulled a five dollar bill free from the metal clasp then slid the note across the counter. "Let's not."

*****

Like Harry Watkins had earlier, Joe awakened with a start. It wasn't a barely heard noise or the usual nightmare that jerked him from a sound sleep. It was the door. Someone was pounding on his door loud enough to wake everyone on the floor.

Joe forced his brain fully awake and glared at the ticking clock on his bedside not quite making out the time. Too dark. If the sun was up, he couldn't tell. The curtains were pulled closed over the windows and the hotel room was surrounded in darkness. "Coming," he said groggily. "I'm coming."

Whoever was at his door knocked again. Four booming thumps as if the hotel room's door was in a different wing of a palatial home.

"I said I'm coming," Joe shouted. There was nothing groggy in his voice now. After a night's sleep, getting his joints working again took a moment. He swung his legs over the edge of the bed with a groan. His fingers fumbled for the little metal chain hanging on the bedside lamp. The bright electric bulb made him squint as he saw the time on the clock. The big hand was pointing straight up, little hand straight down. The door to his hotel room boomed again under the attack of powerful fists.

"Joe Kanji," someone yelled on the other side. "You awake?"

He pulled on his robe, self-consciously holding the neck closed with one hand to hide the scarring as he limped slowly towards the door. His cane was on the opposite side of the bed, and as always, his first steps made him wince as the familiar sharp pain reminded him of his damaged hip. He had to steady himself for a moment, holding on to the edge of the room's table before taking the last few steps towards the door. He closed the bedroom door behind him, touched the light switch mounted on the wall, and crossed the sitting room. The papers were still stacked in their neat piles on the table's black enameled top. Everything was as he had left it.

"Joe," a voice yelled from the outside hallway.

A dozen slow steps and he was at the door. Clearing his throat, he turned the key in the lock and twisted the knob. The door swung open.

"It's about damn time. What if the joint was on fire? You'd have cooked."

Joe tightened the grip on the front of his robe. "Donovan," he said, as he tried to look past his visitor to see if anyone else was in the hall. "It is very early."

"Yeah, I noticed. I ordered breakfast from the kitchen. Hope you're hungry. Can you believe that skinny little prick on the front desk said I couldn't go up without being announced first?"

Donovan pushed past him as he stood in the doorway and walked into the room. Joe caught the strong odor of alcohol as he squeezed by in the narrow passageway.

"Won't you come in?" Joe asked. He closed the door with a thump.

"Announced. Prick. I told him I didn't need to be announced." Donovan collapsed heavily into one of the room's chairs.

"Are you intoxicated? The sun is not even up yet."

"You mean the sun's still down. Everybody asks the same question. I didn't realize I had such a reputation." He belched. "I was sober at the time," he said in a quieter tone. "You know, Joe, there's nothing like a two hour walk in fresh morning snow to either freeze your nuts off or fortify the soul." He moved his feet out of the way as Joe walked slowly past him.

"I must use the facility, Donovan. Excuse me." Joe went into the bedroom and crossed to the bathroom.

"I'm pretty fortified right now," he heard Donovan say from the front room.

"You walked all the way from your home?" Joe said from behind the bathroom door.

"Not all the way. I got a taxi after a while."

"What?" Joe called from the bathroom.

"Not all the way," Donovan shouted. "I didn't have a choice." He picked up one of the pages sitting on the table and gave the Japanese characters a glance. He sat the white page packed with unintelligible figures back onto the stack as Joe came out of the bathroom in gray trousers and a long sleeved white shirt buttoned to the neck.

"What do you mean, you didn't have a choice?" Joe sat slowly on the other chair and looked at his early morning visitor. "You did not drive?"

Donovan sighed. "Well, that's an interesting, ah…" Donovan turned at the sound of knocking at the door. "There's breakfast," he continued. "I'm half starved. You?" He sprang for the door before Joe could answer. "I hope you like omelets."

"How very thoughtful of you," he murmured. Omelets. He would rather have sent Donovan away and gone back to bed.

A young man in the hotel's uniform pushed a cart draped with a long white tablecloth topped with two domed metal dishes into the room. A pot of coffee sat dead center of the cart between the domes. A small pitcher of orange juice and two glasses finished the ensemble. The man busied himself about the dining table, arranging the food and pouring two cups of coffee before standing back with a white cloth draped over one arm.

Joe approached the table slowly, still not fully awake. Omelets, toast, orange juice from California and coffee and Donovan. His Monday had started off with a bang.

Donovan gave the young man some coins out of his pocket and closed the door behind him. "Breakfast. There's nothing like a good breakfast, Joe, to make you forget all your troubles and cares."

"I did not have cares. I was having a dream."

"Sorry about that. I waited until six." Donovan pulled a chair out for himself and dropped heavily into it. "Dig in. I'm in a talking mood," he said as he carved up his omelet.

Joe took the opposite seat, shook out his napkin, picked up his fork, and sampled his omelet. He sat the fork on the edge of his plate. Eggs weren't his usual breakfast fare. He preferred pancakes. American pancakes with maple syrup, but he ate the toast and drank the hotel's coffee while Donovan devoured an omelet right down to the crumbs. They didn't speak as Joe waited for him to finish his meal. Apparently, Donovan's talkative mood could be postponed by a hot breakfast laid out in front of him.

When his early morning guest sat back from his empty plate and his napkin tossed into the middle of the dish, Joe said, "Why did you walk all the way over here so early? I cannot see you doing it for your health."

"Me first. I've been thinking about things. I've had a good night for thinking. I'm thinking you used me to get to my old man so you could add your business card to his collection." Donovan drummed his fingers along the top of the table. "You told me and Lucy you were here recuperating from a car wreck."

"I am," Joe said.

"From Hawaii to Seattle. In winter?"

"It is complicated, Donovan."

"Uncomplicate it. Did you or did you not use our friendship to make a sales pitch to my old man?"

"I came to Seattle because my employer wanted me to come here. That part was business. Getting to see old friends from my college days was a fortunate coincidence."

"And coming to my home? Did your employer tell you to do that, too?"

"I did not ask to come to your home." Joe's hand reached for the comfort of his cane. "You invited me. I planned to go to Boeing Field to see your father." He stood slowly from his chair at the table. "What was I supposed to do? Not introduce myself to Archibald McAllister after my employer sent me here to meet him? I saw it as an opportunity to kill two birds with one stone." Joe crossed the room to the windows on the far wall. He used the tip of his cane to slide the drapes open. It was getting light outside and Seattle's workday was beginning. Already, a few of the concrete monoliths had lights showing from their windows.

"You could have told me what you were here for."

"Told you?" Joe turned away from the predawn sights of downtown outside his window. "Did your father speak to you about me?"

"My old man talks to me when he needs somebody to pass the butter dish at dinner." Donovan reached for his crumpled napkin, squeezed it in his fist for a moment then flung it back onto his plate. "You've changed somehow, Joe. Something is different about you."

Joe smiled and held his arms out away from his sides. "I am older, wiser, and slower. That is all."

"You're right on at least two points." Donovan looked around him for a moment. "Nice room."

"It suffices."

"When are you leaving?"

Joe glanced at the valise sitting beside their breakfast table. "In a few days."

"Back to Japan?"

"San Francisco first. Then a steamer home." He wasn't going to San Francisco and his eyes looked at the valise again. "Why did you come here, Donovan?"

"I like the eggs." Donovan reached for his empty cup, looked inside as if he might have somehow missed some of the brew, then placed it back on the table. "And I had to get out of the house for a little while. I wrecked my car last night."

"An accident? That is unfortunate," Joe told him. "Can it be repaired?"

"Well now, Joe, I think that depends on which accident you are referring to."

"You had more than one accident? In one night?"

"I'm thinking about canceling the rest of my leave and going back to Port Angeles."

"Port Angeles is?" Joe asked.

"My duty station. Or it might still be my duty station." Donovan rubbed his forehead with his hand. "The old man and I had a fight last night. A bad one."

"About my coming to your home?"

"What?" Donovan looked at Joe with a puzzled look. "Coming to the house? No, not that. About the girl I put in the hospital."

Once Donovan began to tell the story, it all came out. Inga Swenson, the wreck and the ride to the hospital and the fight with his father. Joe listened in silence wondering how someone as advantaged and well situated in life as Donovan McAllister could get himself in such a situation. These things were dealt with much differently in his country.

"My father says he spoke with Inga and her mother. Can you believe that? I've never even met her mother and they have it all arranged."

"What was that?" Joe missed something Donovan said.

"He bought her off. Money fixes everything. That's my father's philosophy about life. Not that I disagree. I just hate it when he makes me feel like a simpleton." Donovan picked up the coffee pot, swirled it around a few times to confirm it was still empty, then sat it back on the table with a yawn. "Twenty thousand dollars. Hard cash. That's what he said Inga told him it would cost for her to go away. Twenty grand. Can you believe that? Twenty grand or she shows her growing belly to the whole world." Donovan lifted the little China lid to the pot then dropped it back into place. The lid vibrated and rattled around the rim for a moment making a chiming noise. "I was going to tell him she was pregnant when he got home. Inga beat me to it."

"Forgive me, Donovan. I do not wish to be out of place, but even for a man of your father's means, is not an amount like that going to be hard for him to come by?"

Donovan stopped fooling with the coffee pot's lid and sat back in his chair. "Indelicate isn't exactly the words my father used. Hell, if I keep screwing fisherman's daughters, Lucy may have to get a job." He tried to laugh at his joke and failed. "Then there's the Governor."

"The Governor?"

"Pop says he has a spot for me. State politics. Apparently, it's all arranged. Or almost all arranged. Except Inga Swenson is in the hospital and I've pollinated the wrong apple orchard."

"Does your father not want grandchildren?"

"Sure, I suppose. Just not those kinds of grandchildren."

"You could not marry the girl? Do the right thing by her?"

"Inga Swenson?" Donovan smiled slyly. "Afraid not."

Then it's the money, Joe thought. Archibald McAllister will have to buy the woman off.

"Damn I'm sleepy," Donovan said, emphasizing his words with a long stretch and yawn. "I've been up all night."

"Perhaps the hotel can call you a cab?"

Donovan stood, grabbing his hat and coat. "I don't suppose you know what time that coat check girl in the lobby comes on, do you?"

"No. I have not noticed."

Donovan looked at the gold watch on his wrist. Seven thirty-five. His father would have left for the office by now. "I think I'll see about that cab ride. I'm all done in. Bet I could sleep for a week."

"The girl?" Joe asked. "Will she be in the hospital long?"

"Hell if I know."

"Visiting hours will start in another hour or so, will they not?"

"Yes." Donovan considered his options for a moment. "I'll go by a little later and see how she is. Maybe have Lucy drive me over."

Joe followed Donovan to the door.

"Get some sleep, Donovan. Wash up and sober up then go to the hospital. You might want to change your coat. There is blood on the sleeve."

Donovan looked at the dried brown stain running along his coat's right sleeve.

"I forgot about that." He ran his hands down the stain, remembering the sight of Inga's bleeding head. "I won't be seeing you again, Joe, and you should have told me you had business with my father. My pop said you used me to get to him." Donovan opened the door. "I came here thinking, no, that wasn't so. You were on vacation." He looked into the dark, unblinking eyes of his former friend. "But now, I don't think you're on vacation anymore."

"Goodbye, Donovan."

He put his hat on his head. "Good luck with that leg."

Joe Kanji closed the hotel room's door.

CHAPTER 10

She broke one of the yokes. A yellow smear of liquid ran along the side of the plate mixing with the grease from the bacon, bacon that was fried crisp just like her father liked. It was too bad about the yolk. She liked her presentations to be perfect and rehearsed like a school play. The egg yolk was a performer who had forgotten its lines. Millie sat the plate of eggs, one perfect, one not so perfect, two slices of crisp bacon and buttered toast on the kitchen table. She slid the morning's copy of the Sun Times out of the way. "Eat it while it's hot, Papa."

Paper on the table, McAllister thought. His youngest was running short of funds again. When her purse was full, his morning paper was waiting for him to fetch it from the front steps. Archibald pulled a gold watch from the charcoal colored pocket of his vest. Eight o'clock on the first day of the workweek and he hadn't even had his breakfast yet. He was behaving like his son, who also hadn't made it to the breakfast table.

"Call your brother down," he told his daughter.

"Donny's not here." Millie slid the paper a touch closer to her father's plate.

McAllister sighed. Maybe it was best he didn't speak to his son so soon after last night's misfortunes. "What time did he leave?" he asked the watch's open face.

"Right after the fight, I think. Last night."

So, he was gone all night. He put his watch away and said, "I'm sorry you had to hear that, Millicent. I would rather you not know about these sorts of things. Your brother has not lived up to the standards of good society. I fear he has placed his future in doubt."

"Donny's not perfect, Papa, but he has good qualities."

"They are sorely overshadowed by the bad ones."

Millie opened the tap at the sink and started washing the iron skillet. "Can he still work for the Governor?"

Archie tucked his napkin under his chin. He was unaccustomed to having these sorts of conversations with his daughter. "I suppose you heard a lot last night?" he asked after a moment's pause.

"I think the neighbors might have heard some of it." Millie turned off the tap over the sink and dried her hands on a dishtowel.

"What else did you hear?"

"It's okay, Papa. I like Inga. It's Lucy that can't stand her. Those two have never gotten along."

"You know this Swanson woman?"

"Swenson. Yes, Papa. Everybody knows Inga."

No doubt of that, Archie told himself. He belched gas and felt the scorching burn begin in his chest. There had never been an illegitimate McAllister before. "You're not to mention this Swenson business to anyone, Millicent. Especially that young rooster I've seen you making eyes at, Mrs. Chandler's boy. Fine family the Chandlers." His knife and fork sliced through the eggs on his plate. Millie's broken yoke disappeared among the strips of bacon. Archie dug his fork into his breakfast, picked up his paper, then read the headlines above the fold as he ate. The longshoreman's strike was still the big news. He half expected to see a picture of his son staggering out of some waterfront bar with floozies under each arm.

"I haven't been making eyes, and Clarence and I are on hiatus."

"Hiatus." Archie smiled. "A woman with a good vocabulary will go far, Millicent." He flipped his paper over.

"What about the Governor, Papa?"

"Never you mind about the Governor. You heard far more than was good for you already."

Last night, after he returned home from the hospital and found his son waiting in the parlor, drunk and looking like the greatest

233

disappointment in his life, the yelling that couldn't happen in the hospital's waiting room began in earnest. He'd forgotten himself and he regretted that; forgotten that his daughters were upstairs and he and Donovan were not alone in the house. He hadn't told Donovan about the Governor's offer to come work for him until last night. He hadn't told anyone. There was no reason to. Not yet. Besides, the offer wasn't exactly an offer to Donovan. It was an offer to him to take care of his son. The Governor hinted, hinted strongly about putting Donovan's feet on the path to a career in state politics. Who knew where that could lead? But his disappointment of a son got a woman from a family no one knew with child. A woman who probably wouldn't know what hiatus meant. Archie pushed his half eaten meal away. Standing, he tucked the morning paper under one arm.

"You didn't finish your breakfast."

"I need to make a phone call."

"Donny can have the bacon when he comes in. He likes it when I make him breakfast," Millie said, with a touch of protest in her voice.

"Millicent," Archie said, reaching for his daughter's arm. "I meant what I said. You heard more than you should have and you aren't to repeat any of it. Do you understand? This Swenson business, if it became known." Archie McAllister paused and pursed his lips. "If it became known," he repeated with deliberate slowness, "it would ruin your brother's prospects."

"Yes, Papa. I understand."

McAllister released his daughter's arm and, turning towards the kitchen stairs shouted, "Lucille? Millicent's made breakfast. Rise and shine. It's past eight already."

"Papa," Millie said. "Lucy went to the hospital last night. After Donny came back. She went to see about Inga. We're the only ones here."

"All night?" Archie's eyes fastened on the hallway at the top of the stairs as if he could somehow will his daughter to be there. "She hasn't been home all night?"

"Sunday night, Papa. The ferry stopped running before she could get back."

He'd caught the last ferry across the lake last night himself. His taxi from the hospital refused to carry him across, knowing he would be stuck on the other side until morning and he was forced to walk from Houghton to Kirkland. An unpleasant walk on a cold night to cap an even more unpleasant evening. It was that long, cold walk that caused him to lose his patience with his son, he was sure.

"I can call the hospital. See if she's there?"

"What?" he said, startled by the whole idea of his daughter calling the hospital where his son's trollop plotted her extortion. "You will do no such thing. No one from this family is to go near that woman's room." Archie's voice went up in a roar almost as loud as it was last night when he was bellowing at his son. "I thought I made myself clear to you."

Millie shrank against the kitchen sink clutching her apron in one fist. "Yes, Papa," she said quietly. "I was just trying to help."

"Why didn't you tell me your sister went to see that woman?" He exhaled heavily through his nostrils, the wind from his lungs coming out in a hiss.

Millie thought of her difficult financial position before answering. She'd badly botched her morning presentation. The broken yoke was an omen. "You're right, Papa," she said, shaking her head. "Lucy should have known better."

The kitchen telephone was mounted on the wall next to the entrance to the downstairs hallway. It only took a few minutes for him to get the hospital on the line. It wasn't visiting hours yet, the voice on the other end told him. No, there was no one in the lobby at all; no young woman with blond hair. Yes, there had been someone there earlier, long before sunrise. No, the voice didn't know who she was and was asking who wanted to know.

Archie hung the phone back on its hook.

"Whoremongering sons and daughters out all night," he muttered to himself. Turning to his youngest child standing across the room from him, he said, "Where would your sister go if she missed the last ferry?"

Millie thought of Harry's boat. It was on the far side of Lake Washington. She could have gone there. She felt her cheeks redden at the idea of Lucy spending the night in Harry's arms. "I don't know," Millie said quietly. "She said she was going to the hospital to check on Inga." Millie swallowed. "Maybe she spent the night at the landing. She only had to wait a couple of hours before the morning shift started."

"God above, I will gain control of the children living under my roof," McAllister said with a scowl.

"I'm not a child." Millie stood away from the kitchen sink. "I've come of age, you know."

"Be quiet. I've known how old you are and how old you aren't since the night you were born."

"I know Papa, but I'm still not a child anymore." Millie turned to the kitchen sink, lifted the heavy iron frying pan and set it on the stove's burner to dry. "You're going to be late. I put your coat by the door." Better now to wait until his workday was over before she asked for the advance on her salary. She would try again before dinner.

"I'm not going in today."

"You aren't?" Millie was surprised. Her father seldom missed a day at the field.

"No. I have things to take care of. I'll be in my study."

McAllister stomped slowly up the kitchen stairs. "I'll see your sister when she comes in on the morning ferry and your brother, too when he shows himself back under my roof."

"I'll bring your coffee up right away, Papa." Maybe she wouldn't have to wait for her advance all day after all.

"Do that," McAllister muttered. Coffee brought to his office. Yes, his daughter was very short in her financials this week.

His study was soundless and filled with a still, cold morning air. He looked at the pile of ashes in the fireplace with last night's half burned logs. Bertie would be in soon to carry out the ash. The room needed a fire. He always liked this room when there was a fire burning. A fire roaring away in the old hearth would distract his mood from the call he was about to make. Crossing the room to his desk, he thumbed through the stack of business cards leaning against the bronze golfer. Finding the card he wanted, he reached for the telephone sitting on his desk. Archie put the phone next to his ear and jiggled the hook with his thumb. The phone, like his study, felt chilled and cold.

"Operator," a voice said in his ear.

"Get me the Bergonian Hotel on Fourth." McAllister waited impatiently for his call to go through. He considered his options since the very early hours of the morning, whether to make this call or not. This wasn't at all like '28. He knew that. This was beyond what was done six years ago. This was dangerous. It could cost him everything if it went wrong.

The phone rang twice before the Bergonian's operator answered. "Good Morning, the Bergonian. How may I direct your call?"

Another woman's voice. Crisp, clean and impersonal. He almost hung up. The little white business card was in his hand. "Papa?"

He hadn't heard the door to his study open. His youngest was standing at the threshold holding a saucer and cup in both hands. Come of age, she told him. She looked almost childlike now.

"Just a moment," Archie told the woman on the phone before waving his daughter in with one hand.

Millie walked slowly across the room. She was doing her best not to spill the contents of the cup.

"Thank you," McAllister said around the phone's receiver.

"I can clean your study for an advance on my salary." She had her best starving look in her eyes. Not too starved. Just starved enough.

"This is the Bergonian," the voice in the phone repeated.

Archie put his hand over the mouthpiece. His chin motioned towards the fireplace. "Bring the bucket up and clean those ashes out, would you?"

"I can bring up some more logs?"

He peered into the doe-like eyes of his baby girl. "How broke are you?"

Just starved enough. Millie smiled and gave her father a hug. "Flat busted," she said, her cheek pressed to his chest.

"Well, I see your spending tendencies aren't on hiatus." He spun his daughter towards the door. "Now out with you. This is an important call."

"But my advance?"

"After my call. Now leave."

Millie walked slowly and reluctantly out of her father's study pulling the door shut behind her. She wanted to stay in the room and hear the conversation. The Bergonian, she heard her father say right as she walked in with his coffee.

Archie waited for the door to his office to close before he turned his attention back to the telephone. He suddenly felt like a little boy caught looking at a classmate's exam as his voice lost its usual force.

"Mr. Yoshiro Kanji's room, please." Tossing the business card to the feet of the golfer, he closed his eyes and exhaled slowly. He crossed his own personal Rubicon. The burn in his chest was getting worse.

Millie glanced behind her and down the empty hallway. Aunt Bertie would be arriving any moment now. The Bergonian only meant one thing. Harry. Last night, he said he kept a room there. Her father asked her where Lucy might have spent the night and now, he was calling the Bergonian. How could her father have found out about Harry so quickly? Millie glanced behind her again before she placed her ear against the solid oak door of her father's study. If Aunt Bertie found her eavesdropping, there would be hell to pay in the McAllister household. Her father's voice was muffled, but she could make the words out well enough if she closed her eyes and concentrated.

Joe was breathing hard as he opened his hotel room door. He pushed himself almost beyond his limit for his morning walk and his limp was the worst it had been in months, but he made it farther than ever before. He may pay for it later, but victory was his for now.

It snowed in the night and there were small, wet drifts in the corners of buildings and in the gutters of the streets. Despite the snow and slippery footing, he walked all the way down Olive to Belleview and from there, north into an area of Seattle he had never seen before. Stopping when he came to Franklin Avenue, he considered walking the one block west of where he was and giving the Lake Union Line his business for the ride back to his hotel. A nickel was the price to avoid the pain he knew was coming. He decided to keep his fortunes in his pants and walk. He would ride streetcars again when he could touch his toes with his fingers. Now as he twisted the white porcelain handled faucet to his tub and waited for the gushing water to heat, he wasn't sure if he made the correct decision or not. Standing naked in his washroom, the wreck that had been a healthy body two years ago still seemed like a stranger's skin to him. Stepping gingerly over the high edge of his bath and into the soothing heat, he stood for a moment in shin deep hot water before painfully and thankfully sitting down in the tub.

Sighing as if he just left the arms of his lover, Joe leaned against the sloping back of the smooth porcelain and eased his injured hip into a more comfortable position. The water was up to his neck now. With his undamaged leg's toe, he opened the cold water tap a slight turn and quickly twisted it closed again. The water was scalding hot and felt like a small piece of heaven. Joe closed his eyes.

The telephone started ringing.

Opening his eyes, he focused on the wood paneled wall of the bathroom. "Of course, it rings now," he told the wall. The bath lost its womb-like feel as he heaved himself up and on to the edge of his bathtub. The phone rang four more times before he could complete the slow process of lifting his damaged leg over the tub's edge. Water dripped off his torso and pooled on the cold tiles beneath his feet. It might be the front desk calling to inform him about some hotel service or it could be Donovan again, but he doubted it. Joe could think of only one other person who would be calling his room.

The telephone was on its eighth ring by the time he reached it. Naked, dripping water and feeling the chilled air in the room, he lifted the receiver from its hook.

McAllister drummed his fingers on the top of his desk. Kanji wasn't in. Just as well. Maybe even a good thing.

There was a click on the line.

"Joe Kanji speaking," said the voice on the other end.

"I was about to hang up."

"Who is this?"

"I think you know," McAllister said tersely. "And I want to be very clear about things with you." His voice was low and edgy. "Lucille has a tendency to feed stray cats."

"Ah, so it is you," Joe said. The room was getting cold. He had to stretch to reach the bathrobe lying across the foot of his bed. "How good of you to call."

"Once you feed an animal like that," McAllister said with the same edgy tone in his voice, "a stray. It expects to be fed forever."

Joe thought about Lucy's diamond necklace the night of her party and the way the stones sparkled as they sat deep in the cleavage between her breasts. The cat food analogy somehow fit quite well.

McAllister continued, not waiting for an answer from Joe. "I don't want to see or hear of my daughter in your company ever again."

"Oh hell," Millie whispered very softly. Her father called Harry's hotel looking for Lucy. Her sister was going to have a lot of explaining to do.

"I do not believe you rang my room to discuss cats and daughters, did you?"

Archie turned to face the pair of tall windows behind his desk putting his back to the room's oak door and the eavesdropper on the other side. The drive in front of his home was empty. No Buick was parked in its usual place when his son was home from his station. If he bought that unfortunate girl off, made her disappear, Donovan might still find a place with the Governor. Bertie, wrapped in a calf length coat, dark brown hat and stooped slightly against the early morning cold walked quickly down the sidewalk. A shopping bag was in the crook of one arm.

"No, I did not," McAllister said into the telephone's mouthpiece. He hadn't planned to mention Lucille at all. It just came out. Bertie disappeared from his view as she moved down the driveway towards the kitchen's door.

And so it has begun, thought Joe. The world would never know his mission was a success because a friend from his long ago days at a California university seduced the wrong woman and drove his car into a tree. It didn't matter. The fish was tempted by his bait regardless of the motivation. Joe put the speaking tube of the phone against his chest for a moment before continuing. "When my business here has reached its conclusion, I shall return to Japan. Would that satisfy your paternal worries?"

"Are you mocking me?" McAllister growled into the phone.

Absolutely, Joe said to himself.

Outside the door, Millie struggled to hear. Her father's voice was more muffled and she couldn't make out the conversation as well as she had moments earlier.

"That goes for her brother as well. You keep away from my family. If Donovan saw you looking at Lucile the way I did Saturday night, he would kill you."

"Donny," Millie said. She heard her brother's name clearly and something about what her father had seen. The words "kill you" had been very easy to hear.

"You are jumping to conclusions. Donovan and I are old friends. As are Lucy and I."

"I doubt that," McAllister said. "You're just another one of her strays she's heard scratching at the back door."

Joe closed his eyes and pictured Lucy in her green dress again. Was that what he was doing? Scratching for attention at a beautiful woman's door?

"When I have what I came for, what you yourself can easily provide, I can assure you, Donovan and Lucy will be far from my world. You yourself need never hear from me or my associates again."

McAllister looked at the bundled rolls of blueprints sitting on his desk.

Downstairs, Millie heard the kitchen door opening. Aunt Bertie. She tiptoed down the hallway to peer down the back stairs. Their housekeeper put some packages down and began cleaning up what was left of her morning's bribe.

"I told you. I can't provide what you are looking for," McAllister said into the phone.

"We believe you can. We believe you can easily provide what we require. It is a win-win situation, is it not? You become wealthy when all those around you are becoming poorer and poorer in these troubling times. Your son can go on to a promising career with the Governor's patronage once his woman is paid off and your daughter will not be seen feeding stray cats ever again."

Archie McAllister felt his heart grow chill. "Who told you about that?"

Millie, peering down the staircase, could see the top of Aunt Bertie's head as she messed about in the kitchen. It didn't look like she was coming upstairs. Not yet anyway. She turned away from the stairs and looked down the long hallway towards her father's door. If Aunt Bertie decided to come up, she would surely hear her heavy shoes clomping on the stairs in time to get away from the door.

"The Governor's offer? Donovan himself told me. We had a long chat this morning over breakfast. Old friend to old friend. There is no reason for anyone to know about your son's unfortunate," Joe paused, changing the word he was going to use.

"Unfortunate luck," he said instead. "I am certain you will be successful in keeping it out of the papers."

There was a long pause on the phone. Joe could hear the deep, measured breathing of Archibald McAllister on the other end. It was a dangerous game he was playing. Too much pressure on Donovan's father and his quarry would go defensive. That would accomplish nothing.

Millie was taking a high risk now. Aunt Bertie was only a few steps away, but the temptation was great. She decided she needed to know what her father was telling Harry. She had to risk it. Hurrying back down the hallway, Millie resumed her post outside her father's door. Her ear pressed soundlessly against the oak.

"So now you are blackmailing me? Is that it?" Archie McAllister said into the phone.

"Blackmail? Hardly. I am offering you absolution."

"The authorities might see things differently."

Millie stood back from her father's door. Blackmail? She forgot all about Aunt Bertie puttering around downstairs and placed her ear solidly against the door.

"Foolish threats gain nothing," Joe said persuasively. "We both know you cannot do that. You forfeited that option in 1928."

"You're a bastard," McAllister said with a voice filled with venom.

"Once again, I am not here to bring harm to you or your family. I offer a straightforward business arrangement. Give me what I seek and I will give you the means to solve all your son's problems. It is just business. Just like in twenty-eight."

It was nothing like twenty-eight and McAllister knew it. "If I give you what you want, this is the last time we do this. Is that understood?"

Joe considered for a moment before going on. It didn't really matter how he answered the question. The future would take care of the future. "That is understood, Mr. McAllister. Give me the P-26 and I will give you your children's future assured."

"Don't talk about my children, Kanji. They are none of your concern. I'll give you the plans for the P-26 but it won't come cheap."

Millie, her ear against the door, listened to the conversation going on in her father's room with something between uncomprehending confusion and profound disbelief. It wasn't Harry her father called. It was Donny's friend, Joe Kanji, and it wasn't Lucy's troubles she was overhearing. It was something far different. She placed her hand against the door, as if she were trying to feel the room's heartbeat.

Joe exhaled slowly. McAllister said it. He would give him the new American fighter.

"I am listening," Joe said slowly.

"How do I know this is the last time you people bother me?"

"In my way, Mr. McAllister, I am trying to help you deal with your son's circumstances. Once that is dealt with, there will be no legitimate reason for me to return. It is a straightforward transaction." Legitimate. It was a good word to use. His heart was beating strongly in his chest. McAllister wanted to negotiate.

"I want fifty thousand dollars up front. Consider it proof of your company's commitment to deliver the goods and my insurance against you calling the papers. Fifty thousand, and I'll give you the best airborne killing machine in the world."

Joe moved his arm and felt the scar tissue running across his chest tighten and pull with the motion. Fifty thousand. Donovan said the girl's family demanded twenty. McAllister was looking to make a profit in his treason.

"That is an unreasonable expectation from any company." He balanced delicately on one foot and tried to slowly rotate his left ankle. Yes, it had gotten easier to move. "However," he continued, "in light of our past associations, I believe it is possible to provide five thousand relatively fast."

"I, that is, I…" McAllister's voice trailed off into silence. Five thousand dollars all at once was more than most men would see in their lifetime.

Joe said nothing.

"Five thousand is insufficient. I'm the one taking all the risks and five thousand isn't worth the effort. You're thinking too small, Kanji. I can go to jail for doing this. We both can. I don't do business with people who think small."

Jail. Millie heard her father say jail as clearly as if she was standing beside him. Her hand touched the knob on the door.

"Millie?"

It was Aunt Bertie. She was calling to her from the kitchen.

Millie let go of the knob and looked behind her. She heard the first heavy footfall on the staircase. Hurrying away from the door, she said, "I'm coming, Aunt Bertie."

Archie McAllister, oblivious to the sounds outside his study heard only the voice coming through the telephone's wires.

"Tell me what you have to sell and I will tell you what it is worth to my company," Kanji said calmly.

McAllister's eyes looked at the large roll of design drawings bundled on his desk. It was all there. The P-26 from start to finish laid out in mechanical precision. Every rivet detailed. Every measurement exact. He placed his hand on the stack of documents like a witness about to be sworn in.

"I can get you a sketch of the flying prototype without any trouble." He felt a tremor in his voice and he put his hand over the phone and cleared his throat.

"Who is thinking small now?" Joe asked.

"It's a very good sketch."

"I am not in the market for artwork to hang on the office wall. I told you Saturday night what we were looking to buy. I want the whole package. Now, I will ask you again. What do you have to offer my company? How many blueprints do you have now, right now, in your possession?"

McAllister looked at the tight roll of papers sitting on his desk. Did anyone know he had them? Was there anything on them to directly connect them to his possession if they were discovered? Annotations, notes, anything in his handwriting?

No, they were unmarked.

"I have one hundred and sixty-three drawings with me right now. A complete set. Numbered and dated." He sighed deeply. "It is everything you need. Everything to build your own airframe."

If his hip was still hurting, Joe didn't notice it anymore. The bank account had over one hundred thousand dollars in it. The itinerary's codes, still sitting in his valise, told him what to do when he was ready to leave. Once he had what he came to get from this cold, rainy mountainous end of the American continent, he was to leave the reach of America's military and police as fast as the Imperial Japanese Navy could arrange.

"Ten thousand today. Ten thousand tomorrow. After I have had time to examine what you have. I would not want to buy rejected ideas and past mistakes on behalf of my employer."

"They're dated drawings not two months old," McAllister said. "Rejected ideas. To hell with you, Kanji. First you think small and now you think stupid. Fifty. Up front."

"You cannot expect me to give you that kind of money without first examining what it is you have to offer."

"Fair enough. How long will it take for you to satisfy yourself they are what I say they are?"

"That many drawings?" Joe considered for a moment. "At least an hour."

"I'll give you half an hour to make up your mind. The decision is yours. Fifty thousand in cash or get the hell out of my city. Strictly business." There, he said it.

"I am not sure I can confirm the validity of what you are selling in so short a time."

"Then your masters sent the wrong man for the job."

Joe considered the risks. Would Donovan's father try to deceive him with phony plans? He didn't think so. "Alright, McAllister. We will conclude our business together rather quickly then."

"Pick some place where we won't be seen, but not where we'll be alone. I don't trust you."

"Are you familiar with the Bergonian's lobby?"

"Never set foot in the place."

"At two o'clock this afternoon, come to my hotel. Enter the main doors and turn left. At the far end of the room, there is a sitting area. You will see a pair of large columns. I will be sitting in one of the wing chairs behind those columns. I sit there every day with the paper. No one will notice anything out of the ordinary about seeing me there today. I will examine what you have and we will conclude our business together." Joe waited. There was no answer coming from the phone pressed against his ear.

"I will be at your hotel at two o'clock this afternoon," McAllister said at last. "I will not ask for you nor are you to tell the hotel you are expecting me."

"Of course," Joe said. It was done, he told himself. Nakajima would get their plans and his father would pin a medal on his chest. "Today. Two o'clock. Behind the columns."

Archie McAllister pulled his watch out of his vest pocket. "But I warn you now, Kanji. I will not bargain with you like a gypsy arguing over some peddler's trinkets. Fifty thousand. That's what it cost. Cash." He snapped the gold cover of the watch closed and slipped it back into his pocket. His hand was shaking. McAllister made a fist to squeeze the nervousness out of his fingers. He put the phone back in its cradle, not bothering to wait for Joe Kanji's reply. The conversation was over.

McAllister looked at the dead telephone and thought about what he had done. He didn't have twenty thousand dollars to give to that woman, Swenson. Not without breaking himself, and there were his daughters to think about. Lucile would be expecting a society wedding one day, probably sooner than later, and Millicent wouldn't be far behind her. He wished now he hadn't bought such an expensive automobile for Lucille but, he was so pleased to see her home after so long away. The gift was to make her stay this time.

"Two o'clock sharp," Joe said into the dead receiver. "I will be the stray cat in the gray suit." He hung up the phone. His sore limbs would have to wait for their daily soak. There were more important things to do now.

*****

The desk clerk at the Bergonian tilted back his head in order to bring the bootlegger's face into alignment with his glasses. "No one's asked for you that I know of." He turned to inspect the empty boxed rectangles behind him. "And no messages, either," he added.

"His name's Byrd," Harry said. "About this high." He held out his hand nose high. "If he asks for me, do me a favor and tell him I've left. No forwarding address. In fact, if anybody asks, you haven't seen me."

"Absolutely, Mr. Watkins." The clerk pocketed the bills the bootlegger slid across his counter. "The Bergonian's staff has always been the soul of discretion."

"I might have left a few things upstairs."

"Not a problem," the clerk told him. "You may drop the key off on your way out."

Harry nodded. It was done. He had a feeling he was going to

miss calling this spot in downtown Seattle home more than the clerk was going to miss him. Even so, he liked having a room here. Maid service was something that was easy to get used to. Drake kept a room here for a while, but Drake never stayed long in one place. He often advised Harry to move his location. Keep on the move. Prudence. Insurance caused by the business they were in. He never really saw the reason to do that. The room was registered to Watkins Yacht Building on the pretense that out of town clients with large sums of money to spend on his boats would need a place to stay. Getting rid of the room was his last connection to the old business, both the legitimate one and the after hours one. If Drake needed to find him, this is where he would look and with no boatyard in Bainbridge, no rooms at the hotel and no street address, even if Drake was looking for him, he wouldn't be easy to find.

"Shoeshine, Mr. Watkins?"

"Not today, kid." Walking past the stand, he headed for the elevators. He didn't think he left anything in his room, but it wouldn't hurt to check. The elevator operator didn't ask him his floor.

"Morning, Harry. Haven't seen you in a while."

"Morning, Sam."

"The Tigers are looking good this year. I like that catcher they got, Cochrane."

"Thought you were a Yankees fan?"

The elevator stopped on the sixth floor. It was an old joke. Harry knew the operator hated the Yankees. The brass cage slid open.

"Yankees," Sam said. He made the word sound like he was discussing a case of the shingles with his doctor. "We'll see who's still playing and whose watching come October."

Words to live by, Harry thought. Walking the short way down the hallway, he stopped in front of his door. He put his key in the lock, turned the knob and opened the door, the same one he had been opening for three years. The room wasn't exactly a home, but it was the closest thing he had to a permanent address. In a few more minutes, it wouldn't even be that anymore. It served a purpose once, back when the business was still the business and he and Roscoe needed to be near their customers. Roscoe had never taken a room at the hotel himself. He didn't think a highbrow joint like the Bergonian was the kind of place he wanted to keep a room in. It didn't suit his nature. Nature or not, it didn't stop him from sleeping on the couch when the need arose.

Harry folded his raincoat across the back of the dinette's nearest chair. The room had a sitting area and small table with a door separating the bedroom from the rest of the space. He moved into the dim room with practiced familiarity, dropped his key onto the table and reached for the pull cord for the drapes. Cloudy light filled the room. Turning from the window, he saw his leather jacket neatly folded across the armrest of a chair. Lucy left his boat before the sun was up with Roscoe. She was still wearing the jacket when she left. The door separating the sitting room from the bedroom was closed. He reached for the knob.

She had closed the curtain over the bedroom's window. A small opening between the drapes allowed soft, gray daylight filtered by heavy rain clouds to slice across the bed in a long diagonal. He could see the outline of her legs beneath the hotel's linens. She was on her side, her back to him, facing the dappled light coming through the opening in the drapes. Her clothes and some white silky undergarment he wasn't sure the name of hung in the closet. Her shoes, dried mud covering one toe, were sitting neatly side by side on the floor in front of the closet. The bed's heavy spread covered her to her chin. He couldn't see her face. Just a mess of blonde curls and two hands clasped in front of her prayer like. The room was quiet except for the very low sound of her breathing.

He sat on the bed. Lucy stirred, wrinkled her nose for a moment, realized someone was in the room and jerked awake.

"Oh, Harry. You scared me. I didn't hear you come in."

The mattress moved as he adjusted his position. "Well, Goldilocks," Harry said as he pulled the sheets away from her face, "the bear's come home and somebody's still sleeping in his bed."

Lucy rolled onto her back and peered over the edge of the covers. "I think I overslept."

The fuzzy light from the partially opened curtain gave her features a pastel glow.

"You were up all night."

She yawned, stretching both arms out to each side. "What time is it?"

"Close to ten. You said you were going home."

"Changed my mind. Woman's prerogative. Didn't I teach you

anything?"

"You used your key?"

"Mm hmm."

"I thought you would have tossed it away by now." He knew she'd kept the key. He saw it hanging below the monkey's fist when Roscoe went to fetch her car. He touched the tip of a finger to the spot where Lucy's toes would be. She jerked her foot.

"Stop that. You know I can't bear to be tickled."

"Why did you keep the key?"

"Souvenir," she said nonchalantly. "Something to show the grandchildren when they ask me what I did during Prohibition." She pulled the covers up to her chin.

"I'm surprised they let you come up. I was a little behind on the bill."

"I didn't ask if I could go up." She pulled one arm free from the covers. "I never ask hotel people what I can do. I don't believe in setting dangerous precedents."

"You snuck in?"

She pulled a platinum strand of curls away from her face in a way he had seen her do a thousand times before.

"I'm good at sneaking in. It's an old family secret passed down by all the McAllister women." She quit fooling with her hair. "Who are you calling Goldilocks, anyway? I never eat porridge."

"You reminded me of the fairytale. Goldilocks fooling with the bears."

"I don't think that's what it's called," she said smiling.

"I've forgotten my fairytale titles. You'll have to refresh my memory."

Lucy pointed one long, slender arm at the hotel's dresser. "You used to keep pajamas in the dresser drawer. There's nothing there now. I looked." She dropped her arm, letting it lie next to his hand on the bed's covers.

"I don't keep things here anymore. I hardly even use the place."

Somehow, hearing him say that made her feel good. It wasn't that long ago when the two of them used this room often. "Poor planning on your part, lover. I didn't have a thing to sleep in." She sat up in the bed using one hand to keep the sheets from falling away from her breasts. Twisting sideways, she puffed the pillows behind her. He could see the smooth nakedness of her back and shoulders as she rearranged her pillows. Turning back to face him again, the cotton sheet slid down far enough to reveal the milk white rise of her breasts.

"I wonder," he asked, "if the Bergonian approves of young women sneaking into the rooms of paying customers?" Lucy's body moved under the covers. He could feel her legs stretching out. "And helping themselves to forty winks," he continued.

She shrugged her shoulders. The sheets slipped downwards a fraction more. "Probably not, but you won't tell on me."

"I might."

"No, you won't."

Lucy dropped her hand from the cotton sheet covering her front. The edge of the cloth dimpled and creased along the soft folds of the fabric's hem. The subtle shadows playing along the tops of her breasts drew Harry's eyes like a magnet. She pulled the sheet higher, embarrassed at herself for allowing him to see so much of her. He leaned forward and kissed her. Lucy kissed him back and the sheet, caught between their bodies, pushed lower. It was a long kiss, a kiss between lovers who had not been with each other in a very long time. When it ended, Harry drew away from her. Once again, the sheet was very low. Lucy reached for it to pull it back to her neck.

"Don't," he said.

She turned her face away. "You're going to make me blush if you keep looking at me like that. I'm not wearing anything underneath these covers."

In the room's dim light, he could see the outline of her body beneath the bed's linens. He couldn't pull his eyes away from her. She was still the most beautiful woman he had ever seen. Reaching for the white cotton sheet, he tugged it away from her body. Lucy resisted, holding the thin fabric tight against her. Harry pulled harder. Slowly, one small inch at a time, she allowed the sheet to be pulled away. Feeling herself very exposed, she crossed her arms across her bare chest. He kept pulling the sheet away from her until it was bunched around her waist. In the semidarkness, he could see the outline of her ribs, the smooth softness of her stomach and the shadow that was her navel.

Lucy rolled onto her side. She kept her arms crossed across her chest. "I feel like Little Red Riding Hood only the wolf's at my bed instead of the other way around."

"Goldilocks didn't know Little Red Riding Hood, did she?" He ran his finger down the line of her backbone from her shoulders to the rise of her rump. "And I don't see you wearing anything red unless you've got it under here." He lifted the bunched up sheet where it was pushed against the small of her back. Lucy slammed the bedclothes down with an arm, then quickly covered her exposed breast again.

"Those girls should have compared notes," she said. There was an edge to her voice that surprised her. She sounded nervous. Men never made her nervous. She cleared her throat. "Because you sure remind me of a wolf I used to know."

He placed his hand on her side and slid it across her waist to the smooth tautness of her stomach. He pulled. Lucy rolled back towards him, still trying to use her arms to preserve some level of modesty. He touched her forearm with his hand. "Move your arms."

"A demanding wolf, too," she said smiling. She thought about the party last Saturday night and the forbidding figure of Mrs. Chandler and her concerns for her morals. What would the old woman think if she could see her now? She couldn't care less. She wasn't going to be a frumpy old woman sipping tea and disliking everything around her. Slowly, her arms uncrossed. "I'm not afraid of the big bad wolf."

Lying in the bed with the sheets crumpled around her waist, he thought she looked like a Michelangelo sculpture come to life.

Lucy laughed softly. "Why grandma, what great big eyes you have," then blushed scarlet at the brazenness of her behavior. She crossed her arms over her chest again.

"Now I know why all those princes were willing to slay dragons for distressed damsels," Harry said, "and you can't see my eyes in here. It's too dark. Besides, you're mixing up the fairytales."

"I do that sometimes." Her breathing changed. It was deeper now and her chest was rising and falling as she breathed deeply in and out. She would never admit it, but she liked it when he looked at her the way he was looking now. Slowly, seductively, cupped her hands beneath her breasts. Holding herself like some maiden offering forbidden delights to a pagan god, she said, "I think you still like them." She was certain Mrs. Chandler never said that to a man before.

Harry stared at her with a look that was half fascination and half animal hunger. Her wolf had arrived and was ready to devour.

He touched her with his hand. She sighed. "You are the only fairytale I've ever wanted. I like still them."

"Well then," she said softly. "Come closer and I'll tell you my version of Jack and the Beanstalk. It's got a great ending."

*****

Millie was having a screaming debate with herself. Twice she started down the upstairs hallway of her home, intending to have it out with her father, and twice her resolve melted away. She couldn't even bring herself to go ask for her advance on her salary. She desperately wanted to know what Joe Kanji had on her father and even more than that, she wanted to know what she could do about it. There was no one she could ask for advice. Lucy still wasn't back from wherever she disappeared to, and her brother left the house hours ago.

Millie walked out of her bedroom and came down the kitchen stairs, still debating with herself what she should or shouldn't do with the information she overheard. Bertie saw the look on her face.

"Something wrong, dear?"

Aunt Bertie had never been a confident, not like Lucy or her brother. Millie bit her lip, trying to decide what she should or shouldn't say.

"Bertie!" Archie McAllister was on the first floor, haven taken the same stairs Joe Kanji struggled to navigate the night of the party. Their housekeeper left the kitchen to see what he wanted.

Now or never, Millie thought. Ask him now before it was too late. She heard the front door closing followed quickly by the sound of his automobile. Her father left. Never it is then, she said to herself. She sighed, then took the kitchen stairs back to her bedroom. Walking down the long hallway, she saw her father's study door wasn't all the way closed. Pausing at her own door, she looked behind her at the back stairs. Jail. She heard the word clear enough spoken by her own father.

And blackmail.

And plans.

Where was her damn brother? If Donny was here, he would know what to do. Even Lucy might know. Her palm pressed against the door.

"Alright then," she whispered.

Feeling horribly guilty, Millie looked around the empty study. He had gone to his closet, she saw, and dug out his bag. It was the big brown one; the one he packed his things in when he was going away on one of his business trips. The valise was sitting center stage on his desk and it was crammed full of rolled up blueprints. It wasn't hard to figure out what plans her father was talking about.

What should she do? She didn't know. Her father was being blackmailed by Donny's friend, Joe Kanji, and she didn't know why. She pulled one of the rolls from the case, slipped off the band holding it closed and spread the large curling paper across her father's desk. It was a large drawing and exactly like hundreds of others she'd seen spread across this same desk countless times before. It was an airplane drawn like a skeleton. It was all lines and wires without the skin. She rolled it up and shoved it in among the others in the valise. Biting her lip, she breathed slowly through her nose. Something about these drawings was putting her father in jeopardy. Snapping the bag closed, Millie slipped the leather carrying strap over her shoulder.

She never stole anything in her life, especially from her own father and there was no way to hide it. He was going to know. Even worse, he was going to know who did it.

It was heavier than she expected, and she had to adjust the thin leather strap as she hurried down the hallway to her room. It only took her a second to pull on her coat and grab Harry's much larger, much heavier coat from her closet. Harry would know what to do. He was like her brother. He always knew what to do.

Millie moved fast even with the extra weight of the valise and Harry's coat. If Aunt Bertie called after her, asked her to go to the market or wanted to know where she was going, she knew her face would be covered in guilt. Bertie was in the living room and didn't see her hurrying down the stairs. The umbrella was beside the back door. She grabbed it as she ran to the street. Skipping over a puddle in the walk, she tilted her umbrella to a better angle against the cold rain. The trolley stop was two blocks away and if she didn't have to wait too long, she could be at the ferry in Houghton in time to catch the ten o'clock boat.

Her timing was just right. She reached the stop minutes before the next car arrived. It was a full car this morning filled with matronly women heading into town to do their shopping and a few men. Millie had to stand in the middle aisle holding onto one of the leather loops in the ceiling for support. Her father's bag sat on the floor between her feet covered by Harry's coat. The trolley lurched as it crossed an uneven part in the track. She chewed her lip and tried to think. It didn't make sense. Not a bit of it. Joe Kanji was Donny's friend from college. What could he be threatening her father with? Fifty thousand dollars and the drawings in the case between her feet. That's what Kanji demanded. That, or her father could go to jail.

And now her father had left.

No doubt to get the money. Did they have that kind of cash? Their father never talked about how much money they had, at least not in hard numbers. They were doing okay. That's all she knew. But fifty thousand? Did they really have that much?

The trolley stopped at the Houghton landing right as the ferry was coming in. It was her morning for great timing. At least she wouldn't have to wait long. Madison Park was minutes away. She was off the trolley before it came to a complete stop and ran for the boat. The rain stopped and there was no reason to run except for running's sake.

Only a couple of cars were on the inbound ferry. No big white convertible and no Lucy, either. What would her father make of that? She didn't care anymore. Her father was in trouble and she had decided to go to Harry. Harry would have an answer.

The ferry took forever to make the short crossing and by the time the captain blew the whistle announcing their arrival at the landing, she was already standing by the forward rail. Followed by a small group of pedestrians, she headed towards the Madison trolley stop. There was no direct connection to the Eastlake Line. She would have to ride the trolley into town and transfer to the Capital Hill Line and ride for a short while before she could transfer again. Eastlake would take her all the way to Harry's boat.

When the first trolley finally arrived, she was lucky. There was a spot open on one of the wooden benches. Harry's wool coat felt good draped like a rug around her legs.

The second trolley was full. She had to stand in the aisle again. The turnoff to the sawmill on Lake Union looked different in the daylight. She almost missed her stop, not recognizing the road that disappeared past the old mill. The gravel lane going down to the water curved around behind the trees. The sawmill vanished behind her and for a moment, she looked like a girl lost in a forest before the lake opened up before her. The white painted hull of Harry's boat came into view tied up on the far end of the T shaped pier.

Harry was going to be surprised to see her. Maybe a little put out by her showing up like this, but she had his coat and he wouldn't be cross for very long. He would know what to do about Mr. Joe Kanji. She was sure of that. She might even make him a late breakfast.

The leather strap from her father's valise felt like it was carving a groove into her shoulder by the time she reached the end of the gravel road. She passed the dilapidated old shed at the beginning of the pier and walked slowly towards the boat.

"Hey Harry," Millie shouted in a loud sing song voice. Slipping the valise off her shoulder, she carried it by the handle the last few feet down the dock. The boat's curtains were closed. So was the folding life rail. Reaching the side of the boat, she dropped the heavy bag onto the wooden boards of the pier.

"Harry," she tried again. "You aren't asleep, are you?" No answer came from the boat. She tried the closed rail, found the latch to open it easy enough, and swung the teak railing out of the way. The boat moved slightly as she came aboard. Millie knocked softly on the door. The sound carried throughout the boat, but nothing moved. She hit the wooden door with her fist. She even placed her ear against the cold wood and listened for any sounds coming from the seemingly dead interior. All was silent.

"Shoot," Millie said. "No breakfast for you, Mr. Harry Watkins."

The rain started falling again in soft, chilling splatters of small drops. Millie opened her umbrella. The top and sides of her father's valise was spotted with dark brown freckles. She dropped the teak railing back into place, picked up the heavy bag, and walked slowly to the shore. Where would Harry be on a Monday morning if not at his boat? He could be anywhere, she knew. On an impulse, she scanned the edges of the small clearing to see if her sister's automobile might be parked out of view. It wasn't, she was glad to see. There was really no place for it, anyway. Harry wasn't at his boat, her brother was who knew where, and Lucy hadn't come home on the morning ferry.

She was beside the old boathouse's door now. There was an iron knob with a skeleton key slot below it. Millie tried the knob. It wasn't locked, and the door opened on rusty hinges. Inside, there was dingy light coming through a small window in the far wall. The shed was filled with boat junk. There were coils of rope hanging from the rafters, dusty old trunks, a sawhorse, some tools sitting on a shelf and stacks of one gallon paint cans and old brushes along one wall. She sat the valise in a corner and pulled a canvas tarp over it. Her shoulder felt bruised from carrying it all the way out here, and she didn't relish the idea of hauling it back into town. She thought about leaving Harry's coat in the shed, but decided to bring it with her. She would rather give it to him in person.

Pulling the old shed's door closed, she raised her umbrella to the rain. The gravel path was easier to manage now that she wasn't lugging a heavy case on her shoulder. The rain stopped before she reached Eastlake, but she kept the umbrella opened, anyway. It rested on one shoulder as she thought about what she was going to do as she headed for the Eastlake trolley stop. She would go to the Bergonian and drop off the borrowed coat, maybe Harry was headed that way to see if his coat was waiting for him, then they would go tell Joe Kanji they knew what he was up to and tell him to leave. Leave or she would what? Millie didn't know. That was the part in her plan that Harry was supposed to fill in. It didn't matter. Once they told Kanji her father didn't have the drawings anymore, what could he do? Go to the police and tell them he'd been caught trying to blackmail her father?

The trolley arrived, and Millie stepped aboard and dropped in her nickel. There were plenty of seats this time. She took a spot on the front bench.

*****

"You want me to come in with you, Frankie?"

"No," he said emphatically.

Squeaky looked disappointed. "I ain't never been inside the

Perkonian before."

"Bergonian," Frankie said. He opened the door to the Ford. "Find a parking spot close by and watch the front. If you see me come running out, bring the car quick."

"You going to rob the place?" Squeaky asked. He couldn't help but smile. He had never got up the nerve to stick up anything bigger than a country gas station, but Frankie was smart. Frankie could rob the big places.

"Fuck no," Frankie said. "I told you. The kid I paid to watch for that big tittied blonde called me. I got business with her." It didn't do any good to give Squeaky too many details. "Just park where you can see the front and wait for me to come out." Frankie slammed the door to the Ford, pulled his hat down lower over his eyes and walked quickly towards the entrance to the hotel. The doorman pulled the door open and Frankie ducked inside, grateful to be out of the rain. He shook his coat sleeves and slapped his hat against his thigh to get the rain off. The boy, wearing the same cloth cap, pullover sweater and knee length pants he had on the last time he was here was putting the finishing buff on a customer's shoes. Frankie strolled over to the newsstand and picked up a paper then handed the clerk a coin from his pocket. The boy's customer got out of the chair, paid for his shine, and disappeared among the crowds milling about inside the lobby.

"You took your time," the boy said when Frankie sat in his chair. "Got my money?"

"Shine my shoes," Frankie told him. He opened the paper and scanned the headlines.

"Sure," the boy said, smearing chocolate colored wax onto Frankie's shoes. "She came in right after I got here."

"Who was she with?"

"Nobody." The boy used his brush to push the polish around the well worn leather. "She walked through the lobby like she knew where she was going." The boy buffed the polish with his cloth. "Headed straight for the elevator."

"What room?"

The buffing stopped.

"Room? You didn't ask me to find out what room. You said I get the other half if I tell you when she comes to the hotel."

"What about the King of China?"

The boy began buffing Frankie's shoes again. "The millionaire? He goes somewhere every morning. A walk I think."

"It's raining outside. What kind of a dope goes for walks in the rain?"

"Rich ones do, I guess."

"Is he back yet?"

"He's back. He's got a room on the eleventh floor."

Frankie turned the page to his paper. "You know Harry Watkins?"

"Mr. Watkins, like the Pharmacy's Mr. Watkins?" He said it quietly, like he didn't want strangers to know about the hotel's private backroom or who was connected with it.

"That would be the one."

"He's lived here a long time," the boy said.

"You seen Harry lately?"

The boy glanced up from his polishing and looked with apprehension at the newspaper hiding the face of the man named Frankie Byrd. Yeah, he'd seen Harry Watkins lately. He'd seen him a few hours ago. Even though the Pharmacy wasn't an illegal speakeasy anymore, old habits die hard. He wasn't supposed to talk to strangers about those kinds of things. The cloth changed its rhythmic movement. "Not in a while," he said as smoothly as he could.

Frankie folded his newspaper in his lap and leaned forward in his chair. Something about the boy's answer sounded different. "Look, don't try to lie to me, kid. If you..." Frankie stopped talking and concentrated on hearing a conversation that was just close enough to make out. He tapped the kid on the shoulder with his shoe. "Turn around and look at the brunette standing at the front desk."

The boy did as he was told. "So?"

"You know her?"

She was a pretty girl with short brown hair in a wool overcoat that came halfway down her calves. She looked frustrated by something the desk clerk told her. As she twisted her body towards the elevators, he could see she was a trim package. Like someone who was used to swimming laps in a pool. The brunette tapped a light blue umbrella on the floor several times before turning back to the desk clerk.

"Don't know her," the kid said.

Frankie didn't know her either, but he was pretty sure he just heard her ask if Harry Watkins was in.

"I'm finished with the shine," the boy said.

"Do them again." Frankie pulled the torn five dollar bill out of his pocket and handed it to the kid. The boy's polish-stained fingers snatched his fortune from Frankie's hand and shoved the five into a pocket. He stuck his rag into his can of polish without another word and smeared the wax on Frankie's shoes. Pushing the wax around Byrd's shoes, the kid started whistling some happy melody.

Frankie settled the newspaper in front of his face and tried to listen to what the pretty brunette was saying. He couldn't quite hear the conversation. "Stop whistling," he told the boy.

The desk clerk had to tilt his head back so he could peer through the glasses sitting on the end of his nose. "Mr. Watkins?" The bootlegger again, he said to himself. "He used to be one of our guests, but the gentleman has checked out."

Millie twisted away and tapped her umbrella on the marble floor in frustration. What was she supposed to do now? She lifted Harry's overcoat above the counter and showed it to the clerk. "You see, I'm trying to return his coat. He told me to leave it here, that everyone knew him."

"You can leave the coat with the hatcheck there in the corner and we can hold the ticket for him here. If the gentleman should return, I'll see he gets his property."

That would help her with the coat, she thought, but it wouldn't help her with her problem. What was she supposed to do now? She could go back to Harry's boat, but there was nowhere to wait for him there and who knew when he would get back? She could go home, but if she did that, she would have to answer to her father. She still had no idea where her brother or her sister were. She was beginning to realize her decision to take her father's valise and hide it might not have been one of her better plans. Millie chewed her lip.

"Is Mr. Joe Kanji in?" she asked at last.

The clerk turned to consult his rack of room keys lying in the rectangle boxes behind him. He didn't need to check which room their most eccentric guest was staying in. Everyone at the front desk knew his room number. The brass key was not in its slot. "Was Mr. Kanji expecting you?"

"Tell him Miss McAllister is here and would he please come down." Millie opened her purse, took out a small round compact makeup case, and looked at her reflection in the mirror. Touching up the powder on her cheeks, she said, "He knows my family well."

"I'll have the operator ring his room."

Millie looked around the large lobby. She needed some place private, but not too private. There was a small settee in front of the fireplace. "I'll be over there," she told the clerk.

She didn't have to wait long.

"Miss McAllister," Joe said, tipping his gray hat and trying to keep the surprise off his face. "How unexpected," he added. He was anticipating a different sister waiting in the lobby. The girl looked upset, or perhaps unhappy. "Is something wrong?"

Millie adjusted the folds of Harry's coat and looked into the eyes of her adversary. "Do sit down, Mr. Kanji."

"On any other day, I would like to, but I am afraid I have pressing business this morning. Can I help you with something?"

"I'll come straight to the point, Joe Kanji. I know your scheme and you are not going to get away with it," Millie said. She kept her face frozen in a stern mask.

"My scheme?"

"You're not going to hurt my father. I know all about it."

Joe sat slowly onto a soft chair opposite the settee. "I do not think I follow, Millie." His head was swimming. He could not imagine Archibald McAllister involving this girl in what they were doing. Donovan perhaps, but not his daughter.

"He doesn't have the drawings anymore, Mr. Kanji. Your scheme has fallen apart and I think it is time for you to go back to wherever you came from." Millie smoothed the wool of Harry's coat with her hand. "I know someone who will not like hearing my story when I tell him. He's a dangerous man and will do what I ask him to do."

"Is that so? Perhaps we should call your father and straighten this out. There seems to be some tremendous misunderstanding," Joe said, his hands spreading wide to either side as he spoke. "I am afraid you have me at a disadvantage."

"What I have is a suitcase full of airplane drawings and you aren't getting them. I've hidden them and I'm the only one who knows where. So, you see, Mr. Joe Kanji, you can't blackmail him for something he doesn't have and when I tell Harry what I know about you," Millie jumped to her feet, "it isn't going to be a friendly conversation anymore."

"Could I buy you a cup of coffee, Millie?" Joe asked politely. He was thinking hard and fast about what he should do.

"I don't want coffee. I want you to leave Seattle. Today."

"Millie. I certainly am not blackmailing your father. I hardly know him."

"I heard you on the phone. I have the drawings and whatever it is you are trying to pull, it isn't going to work."

"Where are the drawings now?"

Millie smirked. "I notice you didn't ask what drawings. It's none of your business where they are."

"Does your father know what you are doing?"

"No," Millie said, "and leave my father out of this. I want you to stay away from him."

"I see. Are you not a little young to be fooling around in your father's affairs?"

"I'm a grown woman and I know what I am doing."

Joe rose slowly from the soft prison of his chair. "Do you? You have my drawings, Millie. You have made a very grave mistake by meddling in the business of your father's employer and mine. I want my property. I would like it now."

Millie's resolve faltered. She hadn't considered the implications of her father's employers. What if she was wrong? What if it was a business deal? Had she stuck her nose squarely where it didn't belong? No, she didn't think so.

"Since when does a company threaten to send my father to jail? I heard Papa say it on the phone. Jail and blackmail. I'm not stupid. I have the drawings. Your so called property. They are hidden where you will never find them and now, I think I shall call the police and tell them all about you, Mr. Joe Kanji."

Police. The police were the one thing he feared. A thousand conversations argued with themselves inside his head. He closed his eyes the better to silence the inner screaming.

"That is an unfortunate decision, and I am truly sorry for it. You will kindly take me to where the plans for the P-26 are hidden."

"I will not." She gasped as soon as the words were out of her mouth. Almost casually, and with his hand close to his body, Joe Kanji slid a shiny automatic from his pocket. He was holding the pistol close to his side so that the wingback chair blocked most of the lobby's view of the gun.

"Do not make a sound, Millie. Do not scream or flail your arms about. If you do, you will leave me no choice but to shoot you, and I truly do not wish to do that. Have you ever seen someone shot before?"

Millie's face went pale. She shook her head slowly from side to side.

"I saw someone shot once. I watched a soldier shoot a Chinese man in a picturesque little village outside Shanghai. It was nothing like what you see in the moving pictures. The bullet makes two holes. One where it goes in and one where it comes out. There is a great deal of blood. The pain makes the victim scream and thrash while the body slowly bleeds out. It can take a long time to die. A long, painful time. Do you understand, Millie?"

"Why did you come here?" she asked, her voice sounding surprisingly calm.

"I was never given a choice." He reached and took the overcoat from her hands. Millie didn't try to stop him. Joe draped the coat over his arm hiding the pistol from anyone who might look their way. "I am truly sorry for the actions your statements have forced upon me. You will take me to where you have hidden my property at once or," Joe paused, "I am afraid I shall put a bullet through your heart."

Millie felt a cold knot in her stomach. "You won't get away with it. They will catch you and put you in prison."

"Probably, but if you were to go to the police and tell them what you know, I would certainly be arrested. Either way, the outcome is the same for me, but you will still be dead."

"You were my brother's friend."

"As strange as it sounds, I like to think I am still your brother's friend."

Millie almost laughed. "You won't shoot an unarmed woman." She heard a clicking sound coming from somewhere under Harry's coat. Her forehead wrinkled for a moment, then she realized what made the sound. She heard it in the movies often enough. Joe Kanji cocked his gun.

"We are leaving now and you are going to take me to those drawings." He grasped Millie's arm and pulled her to her feet. The heavy overcoat completely hid the pistol. He spun her around and gave her the slightest of pushes. "Walk normally and do not scream," Joe said quietly into her ear. "Please, Millie, do not force me to kill you."

"Ain't that something," Frankie said to the boy finishing up the second polishing of his shoes.

"What's something?" the kid asked.

"Nothing. I was thinking out loud." Kanji and the pretty brunette walked towards the exit. The brunette looked close to panicking. Her face was frozen and unmoving, with her eyes darting from side to side. She was clutching her umbrella and looked scared to death. Kanji moved pretty smoothly. If he hadn't been looking straight at him, he wouldn't have seen him pull the pistol. Frankie waited until the couple had their backs to him before he jumped from the shoeshine chair.

"You want me to call you when the blonde comes down?" the boy asked.

Frankie paid no attention to the kid. He was moving towards the door with his unread paper tucked under one arm. The glass doors swung open as he pushed quickly through them. Kanji and the girl were heading for a parking lot down the street. The pair mixed in among the pedestrians holding umbrellas against the drizzle. Frankie went to the curb and waved his paper in the air. The old Ford with Squeaky behind the wheel pulled suddenly out into the traffic from half a block away. He stood on his tiptoes to try and see where Kanji and the girl went. He caught a glimpse of him opening the door to a dark colored sedan.

Squeaky pulled to a stop in front of him.

Frankie went to the driver's side. "Slide over."

Squeaky slid across the seat. "Did you rob the place?"

"You're about as sharp as an old dog I had once when I was a kid," Frankie told him.

Squeaky's face clouded. "Don't say things like that."

"Relax. Something's happening." He looked for an opening in the traffic. "I'm not sure what, but I smell it." A green Dodge with

Kanji behind the wheel and his passenger beside him pulled out onto the street. The Ford followed.

"We going to rob somebody?" Squeaky asked.

"You never know," Frankie said.

*****

By the time Joe Kanji's rented Dodge turned off Eastlake and onto the gravel road leading to the boat, Millie had quit crying. Things had gone terribly wrong with her half thought out plan.

"Is this the place?" Joe asked. His question was met with silence. "Millie?"

Millie was looking at Harry's boat. They were still too far away for her to be certain, but it appeared the curtains were still drawn and the railing was closed. Harry hadn't come home. Her spirits fell. "Over there. The shed," Millie said despondently.

Joe eased his automobile slowly down the sloping drive towards the wooden building sitting beside the pier.

"What are you going to do to me?" Her chin trembled when she spoke. "Murder me?"

"I am not a murderer. I do not know what I am going to do with you just now." He pressed on the brake and stopped the car beside the shed. "I will have to leave very quickly," he said, looking out his window at the large yacht sitting quietly at its moorings. "After I have my property and my plans are in motion, you can take the car and go home." Joe opened his door. "Now, take me to the drawings." He stepped one leg outside the cab of the car and reached for his cane. "And please do not run. I am a poor runner, but an excellent shot."

Millie opened her door and, dragging Harry's coat after her like a child's security blanket, walked slowly around the front of the car. Joe followed. His cane made tapping sounds on the wooden planks of the pier.

"In the boathouse," Millie said, gesturing towards the unlocked door with her chin.

"After you," Joe told her. He waited as Millie walked past him and into the shed. The pistol was still in his pocket.

Frankie Byrd eased the rusted grill of the Ford into the damp ferns and dead brush growing beside the road.

"Where we at?" Squeaky asked.

They were beside an old mill with a gravel road running along one side of it.

"The lake's down there," Frankie said, "and this sawmill must have a dock on it. Dock's mean boats and I think I figured out who that little brunette is. She was one of the girls Roscoe hauled out of Barefoot Nessie's last night. "

"So?" Squeaky said.

"Harry's always got a boat." Frankie pushed his hat back on his head. "Do the math, Squeaky. That cripple on the cane is up to something and that brunette and Harry are hooked up in it." Frankie killed his engine. "I'm about to find out how."

Squeaky looked puzzled. "We going to rob a sawmill?"

Frankie sighed. "We walk from here. Quietly. Which means no questions from you."

Squeaky had to reach through the window to open the Ford's door. The inside latch didn't work. "Okay, Frankie."

Millie stood inside the dimly lit shed and chewed her lip. She folded Harry's coat and sat it on top of an old steamer trunk. "If you're going to shoot me," she said at last, "I don't want to suffer. Make it quick."

"Do not be so dramatic, Millie. Kindly give me the plans. I have a lot to do before the day is out."

She pulled the canvas tarp to one side. Her father's valise was still there. "Why are you doing this?"

"Because of something that happened two years ago." Joe lifted the heavy leather bag from the floor and balanced it on a sawhorse. "I was sent here because of my former association with your family." He opened the brass clasps on the case and pulled the top open. The interior was stuffed full of blueprints. He took the top one out and unrolled it. Joe Kanji forgot about Millie and what he was going to do about her as he pulled several more sheets of paper from the valise. Millie stepped a half step closer to the shed's door.

"Be still." Joe rolled up the drawing he was examining and pulled another from the valise. Was this the P-26? He needed more time to be certain, but time was something he didn't have anymore. The mission was over. He was found out. It was time to go home.

"Check the boat, Squeaky. See if Harry's home."

Joe spun around almost falling when his hip shot electric jolts of pain up his side. The paper drawing crumpled in his fist. "You." He couldn't keep the astonishment out of his voice.

"You're a sloppy criminal, Kanji. Always check to see if you're alone before you pull a job." Frankie leaned against the shed's doorjamb. He took his makings out of a pocket and leisurely twisted the tobacco into a cigarette.

"What are you doing here, Mr. Byrd?" Joe tried to think fast.

"What are *you* doing here, Mr. Kanji?" Frankie said mockingly. His eyes surveyed the small shed, pausing when they came to Millie. "Saw you back in the hotel."

"I've been kidnapped by that man." Millie stabbed a finger at Joe.

"Kidnapping?" Frankie said gravely. He licked the paper of his cigarette. "That's a serious crime, Kanji."

"What I am doing is no concern of yours."

"He's stealing, that's what he's doing," Millie shouted, "and he's got a gun in his pocket."

Joe, one hand holding the crumpled drawing and the other balancing the valise on the sawhorse looked at the criminal Frankie Byrd. "Be silent, Millie," he hissed between his teeth.

An old boathook that was broken in half leaned against one wall of the shed. Frankie picked it up and balanced the four foot length of wood in his hand. The bronze fitting on the end was pointing at Joe.

"Nobody's on the boat, Frankie," Squeaky said as he came up behind him.

"Got a light, Kanji?" Frankie asked.

"I do not."

"Those drawings aren't his," Millie said. "They belong to my father and he was trying to make him pay fifty thousand dollars for them."

Frankie's body stiffened. His eyes went to the valise and the dark blue rolls of paper bulging from the opened top.

"See, Kanji. I told you I knew you were up to something, didn't I?" Frankie slapped the wooden haft of the boathook in his hands.

"I can always smell it when somebody's up to doing wrong."

"I hid them from him," Millie went on. "I was going to give them to Harry for safekeeping, but he wasn't home." She shifted her weight from one foot to the other. Her hands were balled into fists.

"That would be Harry Watkins, right?" Frankie asked.

"You know Harry?"

"We go back."

"Harry's sweet on me and I was going to bring the drawings to him to keep them away from that man, but he forced me to come back here and—"

Frankie interrupted her. "Where's the fifty grand?" He stepped to one side and allowed the dimwitted Squeaky into the close confines of the shed. Squeaky was slow, but he had good instincts for anything criminal. His instincts told him to step inside.

Joe Kanji was an arm's length away.

"Be quiet, Millie," Joe said again. "You are misunderstanding the situation."

"Harry has the fifty grand. He was going to give it to you for what's in the case?" Frankie asked.

"No, not like that," Millie said. "Harry doesn't know about the money. I came here earlier to tell him, but he wasn't here. I put them under that tarp and went to his hotel."

Frankie stepped closer to Millie. "Harry sent Kanji down to talk to you." His hand touched the fabric of her dress. She was even prettier up close.

Millie pushed his hand away. "Please don't do that," she said. "I need some air. It's stuffy in here." She tried to move towards the door, but Frankie's raised hand stopped her.

"Let's go through this again." Frankie lifted the valise from the sawhorse, pulled the loose blueprint from Joe's hands, shoved it inside the case then walked towards the cloudy sunlight coming through the door. He rummaged around inside the valise before closing the lid and tossing it onto the pier. "You," he said, pointing at Millie, "belong to Harry you say. You," he said, looking at Joe, "stole that satchel back there on the pier."

"I have stolen nothing," Joe said.

"You know, I once said those same words to a judge. He didn't believe me. Did he believe you, Squeaky?"

Squeaky laughed. This was a game he understood.

"I want to leave now," Millie said. "My father will be wondering where I am."

"Where's Harry Watkins these days, Millie?" Frankie asked. "It is Millie, isn't it?" he said, looking questioningly at Joe.

"He'll be here any minute," she replied.

"Boat's locked up and there are no cars around." Frankie's fingers felt the fabric of Millie's dress again. "You wouldn't have gone all the way into town if you thought Harry was coming back here."

Millie tried to get distance between herself and the unpleasant man who kept touching her dress. "Please don't touch me," she said again, pushing Frankie's hand away. She grabbed the lapels of her coat and quickly buttoned it around her.

The hand came back as soon as she pushed it away. This time, he didn't just feel the fabric. He pressed harder, feeling the swell of her breasts beneath the coat.

Millie took a step backwards. No one, not anyone had ever touched her like that before. It frightened her. "Do not do that again."

"No? Harry owes me three thousand dollars. He never paid for my last shipment and even worse, when the deal went sour, he left me to take the fall. If I was trying to find Harry, where do you think I should be looking?" He stepped closer towards her. This time, his hand rubbed her thigh.

Millie moved farther away from Frankie Byrd's touch. Frankie moved with her.

"I said don't do that."

"Thanks to Harry, I spent seven hundred and thirty-nine nights in McNeil Island. Do you have any idea what kind of hell goes on in the nighttime in a place like that?"

"No, I don't," Millie said. She was trembling now. She'd heard of McNeil Island. It was a penitentiary.

"I hate Harry Watkins," Frankie growled. "I can make my money back, but what do I do about my hate?" He put his hand on Millie's waist and squeezed. Her body was very firm. Frankie could feel the smooth silkiness even through her coat. He thought about a swimmer doing laps in a pool. She would look good in a bathing suit.

Millie twisted away from him again. "Will you please keep your hands to yourself?"

"This Watkins you are asking about," Joe said quickly. The gangster's hand touched the girl's clothing. She would move away from him and he would reach for her again. "He is not the one with the money. I am."

Frankie turned slowly away from the girl. His attention focused on Joe. "You have it?"

"Let the girl go. She is just a kid sticking her nose into the affairs of others. I will make you the same offer I made her father."

"Offer away, Kanji. You've got my full attention."

"That bag out there on the pier, I came here to buy it." Joe paused for a moment to look into the uncomprehending eyes of the man standing beside him.

Squeaky blinked.

"I still will. Fifty thousand dollars. You give me the bag and the young lady, and we can all go our separate ways."

"Where's the money?" Frankie asked. "I seem to be asking that question a lot today."

"In my hotel's safe." He drew the money from the bank earlier and left it at the Bergonian expecting to give it to Archibald McAllister this very afternoon. "I can get it easily enough. All we have to do is go."

Joe moved for the door. Frankie's chin nodded at Squeaky. The message was passed. Squeaky's palm shoved squarely into Joe's chest. The blow tripped him and he tumbled onto the shed's wooden floor.

"Careful, Squeaky. The man's got a limp." Frankie turned back to Millie. "Now, where were we? Oh yes, we were talking about Harry Watkins."

"I don't know where he is." Get up Joe, she was thinking. Pull your gun and shoot somebody.

"I figured that out already." Frankie tugged at one of her coat's silver buttons. "You don't look like one of Nessie's girls."

"I don't know what you are talking about," Millie said.

"Last night at the whorehouse. You were there with Harry's woman. I saw you coming out with Roscoe."

Millie stiffened. "Lucy's not his woman." She put her hands behind her back and leaned against the shed's wooden wall. "We didn't mean to go in that place. It was an accident. Harry's not going to like you being here when he's away."

Frankie tugged at the front of her coat until it pulled open again. He pinched the fabric of her dress between his finger and thumb, then pulled the dress up a couple of inches and smiled appreciatively at her legs.

Millie shoved his hands away, then straightened her dress. "Stop touching me," she said as firmly as she could. The man was frightening her. She saw Joe looking at her. "Mr. Kanji," she said haltingly.

Joe struggled to his feet. He had never been knocked down before. "Byrd. Do we have a bargain?"

"You mean a deal." Frankie's eyes went up and down Millie. "Yeah, I think we'll do business. As soon as I finish explaining my needs to Harry's doxy." He touched the short brown curls of Millie's hair. "Squeaky, take our new partner outside for a minute. Watch him. He's got a shiny little cap gun stuck in a pocket." Frankie handed the broken boathook to his partner. Squeaky had that same grin on his face he had right before Nessie's bouncer punched him. "Hit him with this if he doesn't play nice."

"Okay, Frankie." Squeaky took the club and slapped it in the palm of his hand. Grabbing Joe by his collar, he pulled him out of the boathouse.

"Now, where was I?" Frankie said to Millie. "Oh yes, we were talking about whorehouses and I was about to explain how much I hate your boyfriend."

Millie could see the leer in Frankie Byrd's eyes. She didn't like the look. Frankie leaned against her. She smelled old tobacco and sweat mixed in with damp clothing. She tried to move away from him, but there was no place left to go. The wall pressed solidly against her back.

"Are you a swimmer?" Frankie said in her ear.

"Please don't," she said as she tried to push the vulgar man away from her. He didn't move.

Frankie hooked a finger through the front of Millie's dress and pulled the fabric towards him. "Does Harry take you out in that boat and let you swim around?"

"Let go of my dress." Millie pushed his hand away. "I'm leaving now."

Catching her around the waist, Frankie shoved her back against the shed's wall. Taking off his hat, he sat it on the corner of the sawhorse, then scratched at his chopped hair.

"Mr. Byrd, we have no time for this. You and your partner here can make a tremendous amount of money right now," Joe said from the doorway.

"You can lay your coat on the floor if you want," Frankie told Millie. "It's up to you. Wouldn't want you to get any splinters."

Millie's eyes went wide. Her voice broke as she said, "I'll scream. I swear I will."

"You do that. Scream real loud."

Millie shoved both hands hard into Frankie's chest. She was stronger than she looked and the push, catching him by surprise, knocked him off balance. Millie shot off the shed's wall with all her might. As she flew past Frankie, he grabbed for her coat's collar. She left him holding it as she ran for the doorway.

Squeaky caught her in his arms. With a stupid laugh, he shoved her back towards Frankie. Millie spun around and brought her hands up. Fingernails connected with Frankie's face as she scratched the skin on his cheek. Frankie yelled, then grabbed the front of her dress. He yanked hard, ripping a long tear down the front and sending buttons rolling across the wooden planks. Millie twisted around, trying to hold her dress closed and get away from him at the same time. Grabbing her around the waist, Frankie slung her to the floor.

The impact hurt, but she didn't really feel it. Millie screamed. She screamed as loud as she could.

Blood ran down Frankie's cheek as he grabbed the bottom of her dress. "What do we do about my hatred? What are we going to do about that?"

Millie rolled over and tried to crawl away. Frankie grabbed her by an ankle. He pulled her leg into the air, then reached beneath the dress. She screamed again as she felt his hand grabbing at her underthings. Twisting around, she pulled her knee towards her, then kicked out with all her might. It was a hard kick and the muscles in her legs were strong for a woman of her size. It hit Frankie squarely in the place where she knew it would hurt the most. Pain exploded in his groin. Doubling over, he fell to his knees.

Squeaky watching from the doorway, one hand holding Joe

271

Kanji and the other holding the boathook, howled with laughter.

"You little bitch," Frankie groaned as he crawled his way on top of her then pushed his body between her legs.

"Don't," she said. "Please stop."

Roscoe was feeling pretty good. He was whistling as he drove the shining red Plymouth up Eastlake. Their Plymouth. His and Harry's. No more walking or waiting in the rain for a trolley. Harry was right. The car went for more than it was worth, but that was okay. The important part was he had won it and the Kitsap County sheriff could go to hell. Harry's grandfather would be proud of him. He made a promise to the old man's coffin long ago that he would always be there to see after his grandson.

And he always had.

A promise was a promise. He had taken care of Harry once again.

Roscoe passed the rusty Ford sitting off to the side of the road next to the sawmill's entrance. He didn't pay it much attention, thinking it was somebody doing business with the mill. As he rounded the bend, he saw the other car. A Dodge was parked not far from the pier.

They had company.

He didn't recognize the automobile, nor did he recognize the two men standing on the pier. The pair were standing at the open door to Harry's shed looking inside. Roscoe stepped on the gas and gunned the Plymouth down the gravel road. It was a dangerous move since there wasn't a lot of stopping room at the bottom. The Plymouth slid to a halt beside the Dodge. Roscoe was out the door as soon as he could set the brake meaning to ask for a proper explanation as to why two strangers thought it was their business to go poking around inside his shed.

The woman's scream from the boathouse stopped him in his tracks. It was a pitiful, shrieking wail that was like nothing he ever heard before. The two men standing half hidden by the boathouse's door heard the same sound, but their reactions were different. One of the men turned away as if something upset him. The other man straightened from a hunched over position and let out a loud, braying laugh. His hand slapped the side of the wooden door with a broken boathook. He laughed again.

The door swung wide and Squeaky noticed the red Plymouth for the first time. He also noticed Roscoe coming quickly towards him.

"You," Roscoe shouted.

"Frankie. It's him. He's here," Squeaky yelled into the shed's interior. He raised the broken boathook in his hands.

Joe Kanji grabbed the bronze end in his hand and held on.

It all happened very fast. Roscoe's powerfully built body hit the tall skinny man in front of him like a bowling ball slamming into the pins. He recognized the man as the killer from Barefoot Nessie's and he wasn't about to give him time to pull another gun or yank the boathook out the other man's grasp. The force of the collision knocked the boathook out of the unknown man's hand as Roscoe and Squeaky tumbled through the narrow doorway. Both men tripped over the sprawled form of Frankie Byrd.

In an instant, all was total confusion. Frankie, his pants around his knees, tried to stand while Squeaky tried to pull Roscoe's hands away from his windpipe. Under them all, a half naked Millie McAllister did her best to get away from the desperate fight breaking out inside the boathouse.

Roscoe hit the skinny killer once under the chin, then twice more in the face before Frankie Byrd had him around the neck. Frankie tightened his grip and Roscoe fought for his wind. Pulling himself up from the floor with Frankie clinging to his back like a spider, Roscoe tried to ram Frankie into the wall behind him but the woman trying to crawl her way to the shed's door tangled his feet. The lunging force he wanted to hit the wall with turned into a staggered stumble.

Frankie held on, and Roscoe still couldn't breathe.

Squeaky got up from the floor. Blood poured out of his nose and the swollen eye from Sunday night's beating at Barefoot Nessie's was starting to close again. Roscoe tried to break the death grip that Frankie Byrd had on his neck. The female, clutching the ripped remains of her dress in front of her, got to her feet and made a run for the door.

That was the moment when Roscoe recognized who she was. A black rage boiled up inside of him.

Squeaky, seeing the girl was about to get away made his fatal mistake. He went for her instead of the man being strangled by

Frankie. Catching her arm, he wrenched her violently back into the boathouse. Her body flew into the sawhorse and sprawled across the dirty floor of the shack.

Roscoe's hands went around Squeaky's neck in a grip strengthened by a lifetime of pulling mooring lines. Ignoring Byrd's attempt to choke the life out of him, he pulled the violently thrashing Squeaky through the doorway. The three of them, Roscoe in a screaming rage to hurt someone, Squeaky with one eye closed and Byrd hanging onto Roscoe's back ran into Joe Kanji.

Joe, seeing his chance to end the uneven fight, pulled the automatic free from his pocket. In all the kicking and punching and three sided struggle, the gun was knocked from his hand. The four men fell onto the wooden planks of the pier as the gun went sliding along the boards until it vanished among the dead weeds lining the lakeshore.

Roscoe had his hands around Squeaky's throat and was doing his best to rip the killer's head free of his neck. Frankie still clung to his back and was trying to break the bigger man's grip on Squeaky. Lurching to his feet, Roscoe lifted the smaller Byrd as if he were a hiker's half filled backpack. Still holding the dead eyed killer from Nessie's by the neck, he hauled the man to his feet. The killer's face was turning blue.

Joe used his good leg to push himself away from the other men. Where had the pistol gone? It was right there, then it wasn't. Right as he managed to get to his feet, the newcomer struck the man named Squeaky fully in the face.

Squeaky's head snapped backwards. Two of his front teeth fell from lips split open. His vision went out of focus. Yelling something, he spun away from the fight spitting blood as he fell.

Roscoe grabbed Joe by the front of his shirt and pulled him up within range. His fist made a knot of his necktie as he cocked back his arm. Frankie, still hanging on to his back, grabbed that arm. Roscoe twisted, spun and flailed his arms about as he tried to hit both men at the same time. An elbow made hard contact with Frankie's face. When he tried to tighten his grip on Roscoe's neck, the elbow hit him a second, harder blow. He fell away from Roscoe then hit the hard wood of the pier with a solid thud. Both hands grabbed at his nose that wasn't as straight as it was before the double tap from Roscoe's elbow. Squeaky struggled to his feet. He was swaying and unsteady and breathing hard. The man who hit him stood in front of him looking more like a hairless gorilla than a human.

"Frankie?" he burbled through his ruined mouth. "Grab him."

Frankie wasn't in any shape to grab anyone. Not right then. He rolled onto his hands and knees with one hand still holding his nose. Squeaky lowered his head and charged meaning to knock the gorilla off his feet and onto the boards.

Roscoe lost his grip on the necktie. The murderer's momentum slammed him into the side of the boathouse as something crashed to the ground on the inside. No one paid it any attention. Roaring with primordial energy, he wrapped his arm around the murder's neck then swung the man's body into the hard wooden corner.

Squeaky grunted from the pain of a rib cracking. His knees buckled as he lifted an arm in the air. "No more," he mumbled through the ruined mess of his mouth. "I give. You win."

Roscoe didn't hear him. He was beyond hearing anything. "I know that girl," he growled at the broken man in front of him. Grabbing the blonde killer by the throat and crotch, he lifted him shoulder high before pitching him into the cold deep water of the lake. The murder's body landed with a loud splash.

Roscoe, breathing hard, pointed a hand at the man. "Yeah," he yelled. "I win."

Squeaky slapped at the surrounding water. It was too deep. His feet couldn't touch the bottom. He went under for a moment, then struggled back to the surface. No one ever taught him how to swim.

Roscoe didn't care. Still breathing heavily from a fight with three men and in a wrestler's half crouch, he turned towards the other two men. Byrd was half a second faster. Squeaky lost his fight, but the beating gave Frankie time to get out his knife. He leapt at the older man's back with the razor sharp steel gripped tightly in his hand.

Roscoe gasped. A horrible killing pain was in his back. With a grunt that sounded almost pleasurable, Byrd sank four inches of steel into the small of Roscoe's back. He tried to reach behind himself. Grab on to something. Pull Byrd around in front so he could hit him.

Frankie had the back of Roscoe's collar in his hand in much the same way as he had Millie's collar.

"Hello, Roscoe," he sneered. "I've dreamed about doing this. You should have thrown me that rope when the Coast Guard jumped us."

The two men did a macabre dance on the planks of the pier. Roscoe waving his arms in the air trying to grab Frankie while the smaller man stayed behind him keeping Roscoe stuck tight on his knife. He wrenched the blade from side to side as the blood poured out of Roscoe's back. The big man sagged to his knees as his strength bled out of him. Frankie pulled his knife out slowly relishing the feel as the blade cut its way through the flesh. Roscoe moaned in pain still trying feebly to hit something with his fists.

"Fight's over, old man," Frankie told him. He wiped the blood off of his knife on the fallen man's back.

Blood darkened the wooden planks as Roscoe collapsed onto his side. He tried to say something, but all that came out was a low groan twisted with pain.

Frankie looked for Squeaky.

His partner in crime was losing his battle with the icy water.

"The bank," he shouted. "Swim to the bank, idiot. It's right there."

Frankie watched until the man's arms stopped beating at the cold water. The body slipped under the surface one last time. Only the ripples on the surface remained.

"Guess that's it for you," Frankie told the dead man. "Done. That's twice in two days you let somebody get the drop on you. Serves you right, idiot."

Joe found his cane and used it to get to his feet. The valise filled with the plans for the P-26 was still sitting on the pier. He moved towards it.

Frankie nudged it away from him with the tip of his shoe. "Don't think so, partner. We made a deal, remember?"

"You are a criminal and a rapist," Joe spat. He was looking around him. Where was the pistol? It was right there and then it wasn't.

Frankie smirked. "You're half right, Kanji." He felt his nose then lifted his face to the sky. "Does it look broke to you? If it isn't, it aught to be. Hurts like I was kicked by a horse." He hawked and spat into the water then, one hand examining his nose and the other holding his crotch, limped towards the open shed door. "Don't know why you kicked me like that, girl. Damn near ruptured something. I wasn't going to do nothing Harry goddamned Watkins doesn't do to you every week." He looked at Kanji, then spat again. "You can take a turn if you want. I ain't in the mood anymore. I need an ice pack and a drink." He slid up the sleeve of his jacket and looked at the deep blue bite mark above his wrist. "Scratching and biting bitch. Wasn't any call for that," he shouted at her. "None at all."

Roscoe groaned and rolled onto his stomach. He made an effort to stand, but couldn't get farther than his hands and knees. Frankie kicked him in the ribs.

"You couldn't have waited five more minutes?" Byrd asked. "She was right there under me with those pretty legs of hers spread nice and wide then here comes good old boy Roscoe to the rescue. Now look what you done. Squeaky is trying to explain things to Jesus, Kanji looks like he ate a plate full of bad oysters and I think my nose is broke."

Roscoe groaned again. He pulled his arms under him, but he couldn't find the strength to rise from the boards. Frankie knelt beside him.

"You don't look so good, old man. Anything I can do?" Frankie smiled. "End your suffering, maybe?" The knife went under Roscoe's throat. "Sure. I can do that."

"Byrd," Joe shouted.

"What now, Kanji? You never seen a man's throat cut before?"

"Think about what you are doing. You were looking for someone named Watkins, no? That man probably knows where he is. If you murder him, the information dies with him."

Frankie held the knife against Roscoe's throat. "Fuck it," he said. "Go on and die nice and slow." He removed his knife, then shoved Roscoe's head toward the wooden pier.

Roscoe collapsed with a moan.

"Let me think a minute," Byrd said. "Things are happening too fast. I need to consider."

Roscoe tried to reach for him, but Frankie pushed his hand away.

He put his mouth close to Roscoe's ear. "Old man," he said calmly. "If I let you live a little longer, can you tell Harry something for me? Can you do that?" Frankie pulled the injured man's head away from the rough planks. "I just had a brilliant idea, but you have to live long enough to tell Harry." He grabbed the short bristles on top of Roscoe's head and forced the older man to look at him. "Tell Harry I got his girl." He nodded towards the boathouse. "The sweet little piece is still in one piece, more or less, but I can't confirm how long that condition will continue. You understand my meaning?"

"Going to kill you," Roscoe moaned.

"You tried that already. In case you haven't noticed, you're the one bleeding all over the boards. Not me. Now, this is the important part. You tell Harry he can come and get his little brunette at the old spot, the one where you and him left me in the water. Tell him to come quick cause I won't wait long." He looked at Kanji. "I got pressing business in up Canada way." Frankie grabbed Roscoe's jowls, then forced his mouth into a mirthless smile. "Can you tell him that before you bleed out? Me and the girl will be waiting for him at the place where he didn't wait for me." He released Roscoe with a final shove that forced the older man to roll over onto his back with a groan.

Frankie folded his knife and dropped it into a pocket. Taking out a handkerchief, he used it to blot his cheek. Four raw claw marks cut crimson streaks down one side of his jaw.

Adjusting the fit of his coat on his shoulders, he looked at Kanji. "Do I look presentable? I'm a man particular about my appearance." He turned in a slow circle. "No rips or tears in my suit?"

"You are an ass," Kanji said.

"At least I'm not a cripple."

Joe glared at the man but didn't say anything.

"Lost your pistol, didn't you?" Byrd asked. "Thought so. That must really be aggravating." Picking up the valise, he walked through the door to the shed. Millie was holding the torn fabric of her dress closed in front of her.

"Get yourself straightened up and stop that bawling." He picked up her coat where it laid soiled and stomped on and threw it at her. "Put it on or don't. I like a half naked woman as much as the next man. If you freeze, don't go blaming me."

Someone stepped on his hat in the fight. Picking it up, he worked on the creases. Satisfied, he placed it on his head and pulled the brim down over his eyes. Leather valise in hand, he rejoined Joe on the pier. "Not exactly how I planned for my Monday to go, know what I mean?"

"This was all unnecessary," Joe said angrily.

"Yeah, but it was a hell of a lot of fun except for my nose and I won't need to split my fortune with poor Squeaky. Speaking of, what about our business together?" He twirled the valise by its handle.

"The girl is sure to go to the authorities."

"Only if I let her."

"What are you planning to do with her?"

Roscoe groaned again.

Frankie snapped his fingers several times beside Joe's head. "Concentrate Kanji. You look more rattled than the girl. What was her name again? Julie? Millie? I can never remember their names for very long. What you need to be considering is I'm selling this fancy bag and wondering if you are buying? If you don't want it anymore, that's fine. I can dump it in the drink and we can all go home."

Frankie held McAllister's valise filled with the P-26's secrets over the dark waters of Lake Union.

Joe smoothed the front of his shirt where the stabbed man twisted it into a knot. He needed a moment to think about what just happened. There had to be another way, but he could not think of one.

"No," he said after a moment. "My offer to buy what you have in your hand stands."

"That's what I figured." Frankie lowered the bag.

"I have to go to my hotel."

"Then you go to your hotel. You give me the fifty grand," Frankie shook the leather bag, "and I give you this."

"You will give me the girl as well."

"Can't do that, Kanji. She's a wild one. That gal would claw your eyes out as soon as I handed her over, then run straight to the cops."

Joe started to object, but Byrd cut him off. "Not negotiable, Kanji."

"What about that man?" Joe said, pointing at Roscoe. "He needs medical attention."

"I bet he does." Frankie kicked the door to the boathouse farther open. Millie screamed at the sudden noise. She wore her coat again, but had to use her hands to keep it closed. He grabbed her by the wrist and pulled her outside.

"Mr. Kanji," she said in a very small voice.

"Leave the girl, Byrd."

"Not a subject open to discussion," Frankie said. "You mind your business and I'll mind mine."

"She has no part in our business."

"She sure as hell had a part in it earlier when you pulled that little pistol on her back in the hotel."

Joe's face was a frozen mask. He would forever regret doing that. He looked along the edge of the pier again. The pistol must have slid into the lake. It was easy to picture Byrd with a bullet hole in his forehead. "None of this was necessary," was all he could say.

Frankie pushed a stumbling Millie onto the gravel road. The Plymouth was still parked beside Joe Kanji's Dodge. It was a pretty car and he was tempted to take it, but if he was caught driving it, it would connect him to the pier and that could put a noose around his neck if things went bad. Better Squeaky's beat up Model A. He opened the rear door of the Dodge, tossed the valise onto the floorboard then pushed Millie into the back seat. "Let's go, Kanji. My car's at the top of the hill and I don't feel like walking."

Joe knelt slowly and painfully beside the bleeding man.

Roscoe was on his side. "I need sewing up," he said weakly.

"I am sorry. I meant for none of this to happen."

"The car," Roscoe said with a low groan. "Get me to my car."

"I am sorry. I cannot." Joe stood, leaving the bleeding man lying on the pier. Byrd and Millie were sitting in the backseat of the Dodge. Millie was crying. Byrd was holding his nose and grimacing as he felt the cartilage. How, he wondered, had things gone so bad so fast?

CHAPTER 11

Lucy whipped her automobile onto the gravel road and pointed the long white hood towards the boat dock. The sawmill, its stacked rows of fallen timbers forming a solid wall, blocked most of the mill from her view. There wasn't much to see even if the long row of felled timber hadn't been there.

"Used to get noisy during the week," Harry said, seeing Lucy looking at the almost deserted mill. "Not so loud anymore."

"Lucky you."

"Lucky me. I feel sorry for the hands that worked there."

Looking at her passenger and what part of her blouse he seemed so fascinated by, she said, "Eyes up here, Mister." She used a lacquered nail to touch her cheek just in case Harry didn't understand her instructions.

Harry brought his gaze a little higher. "That's not what you told me this morning."

"What I may or may not have told you this morning."

"Or what you—"

"No, sir," she said before Harry could finish his sentence. "We aren't going to mention what I might or might not have done this morning. Gentlemen keep such details to themselves."

"It was just you and me. It's not like I'm telling everyone at the trolly stop."

"To themselves," she repeated. "Else there will never be a repeat. Understood?"

Harry nodded. "Understood. Silence is golden."

Lucy pressed on the Auburn's brake, making Moby Dick stop where it was.

In the distance, sitting silently on the water sat *Scarab*.

"By the way, I meant to ask the other night. When did you start building battleships?"

"Something, isn't she?" Harry asked as they both stared at Watkins Yacht Building's last example of the boatbuilder's art lying tied to its pier.

"Yeah," she agreed. "Something."

"She's really too big for just me and Roscoe to handle by ourselves."

"Uh huh," she replied as her foot came off the brake and the car began to slowly roll down the hill.

She shifted into a lower gear and pressed a high heeled shoe against the brake as the Auburn picked up speed. Harry touched the soft skin along the back of her neck. It felt smooth and warm. His fingers traveled to the curve of her ear. She twisted her head away from his touch.

"Stop that. You'll give me the giggles and I might put us in the lake."

"You could try slowing down?"

"You could try keeping your hands in your lap." Sliding into the lake seemed like a real possibility to her. She didn't like the way the lane ended so quickly and so close to the water.

For the second time, the Auburn ground to a halt still on the sloping part of the road.

"He did it," Lucy said, bouncing a fist off the Auburn's steering wheel for emphasis. "Good for Roscoe."

Harry stopped playing with the lobe of her ear and glanced down the gravel road toward his boat. Sitting right in front of the boathouse was his bright red roadster. His car. "Good for Roscoe." He didn't sound very excited.

"Don't be like that. It wasn't yours anymore." The Auburn rolled the rest of the way down the lane accompanied by the sounds of gravel crunching under its tires. When she killed the motor, they both heard the low rumbling of the Plymouth's engine. The car was idling in neutral.

"Hey, Roscoe," Lucy called in a strong voice. "I want to go for a ride in your new car." Opening her door, she hopped out of the Auburn. Harry did the same on his side. "Roscoe?" she called again when there was no answer.

Harry put one hand on the Auburn's spare tire where it was mounted on the long front fender. "Hell," he muttered. His car only it wasn't anymore.

Lucy practically bounced with excitement as she went around the back of the shiny red roadster. When she reached the far side, she froze.

"Harry," she screamed. The excitement she was feeling vanished.

Harry hurried towards her. "What?"

What he saw almost made him scream as well. Roscoe had crawled and dragged himself all the way from the boathouse to the roadster. He was collapsed on his back with his head resting on the car's running board.

Harry dropped down beside the crumpled body. There was a dark red pool of blood staining the ground under Roscoe. Cradling his head in the crook of one arm, Harry felt for a pulse along the jugular. There was a quiet, slow rhythmic throbbing on the artery. He was alive. The eyes fluttered for a moment, stared vacantly into space then found their focus.

"Bleeding," Roscoe mumbled. "Hurt real bad."

"Don't move," Harry said.

"I forgot and let 'em..."

The voice was weak and strained as it trailed off into silence.

"What happened, Roscoe?" Harry asked. The old weathered face was pale and the skin too cold.

Lucy knelt beside the two of them. "There's blood on the ground."

"I know that." His voice was harsher than he intended. His anger at finding the man like this made him want to scream at somebody. "Was it Frankie, Roscoe?"

The eyes found their focus again. Roscoe coughed. "Forgot and let 'em get behind me."

"We've got to get him to a hospital," Harry said.

Lucy, looking horrified at the sight of Roscoe pale, frozen and bleeding asked in a half whisper, "Can we lift him? Get him to the car?"

Harry rolled the partially conscious Roscoe onto one side. "He's been stabbed." Pulling his handkerchief from his coat pocket and dragging the blood soaked coat out of the way, he stuffed the white cotton into the wound. The cloth quickly went from white to bright crimson.

"Oh, Harry. He's bleeding bad." Her voice was quavering, and she sounded desperate. She'd never seen bleeding like that before.

"I got to get him in the car." The sound of his own voice surprised him. Harry could hear the fear he was feeling. He tried to lift Roscoe. The old man groaned with the pain of movement.

The boathouse's door swung open by a breeze coming off the water. Lucy's foot crunched on something. She looked down and saw a button the size of a walnut under her shoe.

Harry moved Roscoe into a better position.

Lucy saw a bundled pile of something inside the shadow of the boathouse door. It was a dark colored coat. She went to get it, then handed it to Harry. "Here, cover him with this. He's shivering."

Harry took the coat and draped it over Roscoe's body. "This is mine." He turned to look inside the shadowed interior of the boathouse. "It's the coat I gave Millie last night."

Roscoe lifted a hand and pulled Harry closer to him. "Frankie," he said in a gravelly whisper. "They got to the little one. Millie. Tell Miss Lucy I, tell her I…" The eyes lost their focus again and the old man struggled to get enough breath to continue.

Lucy's face went white. She'd heard the half whispered words. "What was that about my sister?"

Harry didn't answer. Something inside of him turned cold. Frankie did this and Millie was here when it happened.

"Harry." Lucy's voice quavered. "It's the coat you gave to Millie." Her chin trembled with fear, a fear like she had never felt before. The button was on the ground between her feet. It was a big silver thing shaped like an acorn. Just like the ones on her little sister's coat. "My sister was here." Lucy knelt beside Roscoe. "Roscoe? Roscoe, my sister?"

The old man's lips moved, but no words came out.

"Where's Millie?" she asked. She held the silver button in front of his face like some kind of talisman. "What happened to my sister?" Lucy faced the trees then yelled Millie's name with all her might.

Nobody replied.

"Help me get him in the car," Harry said again. Lucy was crying and on the verge of panic. "You have to help me," Harry said as patiently as he could. "You have to."

Lucy looked like she was about to go running into the woods to look for her sister. She had never been in this kind of situation before.

"My sister," she demanded. "What about Millie?"

"He's going to die if we don't do something."

Roscoe groaned. "I was too late." The voice could barely be heard. "I got one of them but Frankie, he stuck me."

"Lucy and I are here now. We got you." Harry moved an arm around Roscoe and pulled him to a sitting position.

"Miss Lucy." He coughed and his face twisted in pain.

"What happened to Millie?" Lucy asked again. She pulled the coat tighter around him. "Can you tell me?"

"Frankie said he'd be waiting at the old load dock." Roscoe winced when Harry moved him. "The one that burnt down when…" The voice trailed away. "The one where the Feds caught 'em. He'll be there. With the little one." Roscoe opened his fist and dropped something into Harry's hand. "Other one. Don't know who he was." He coughed and tried to breathe deeply then screwed his eyes closed from the effort. He mumbled something Harry couldn't catch. It sounded like ornamental or accidental.

Harry looked at the thing Roscoe dropped in his hand. It was some kind of jewelry. A big red ruby set on a tie pin. "What's this? I didn't understand what you said."

Lucy saw the ruby in Harry's hand with its intricate array of red bars radiating around it. A ruby like that one was stuck in the center of Joe Kanji's tie the night of her party. "He said Oriental." The words came out in a whisper. "Oriental," she repeated, shocked by her own words.

Harry closed his fist around the stone and pulled Roscoe's arm around his shoulder. Lucy took the other arm. He groaned as they both hauled him to his feet. Taking most of his weight, Harry half carried the wounded man to the other side of the roadster. The blood ran out of his back as Harry wedged the semiconscious Roscoe into the passenger seat.

"What about my sister?" Lucy asked as Harry jumped behind the wheel of the Plymouth. He stepped on the clutch and put the car in gear. There was hardly enough room for him to get around Lucy's car without scraping against a tree.

"Harry, I know him. That ruby belongs to Joe." The Plymouth rolled forward. Lucy grabbed for the top of the door. "Stop the damned car."

He stopped.

"Joe Kanji," Lucy said.

"Who?"

"Joe Kanji. Millie and I had breakfast with him yesterday morning. He's a friend of Donny's."

Harry kept his foot on the brake. He was trying to think. Donovan was responsible for Byrd's going to prison. He looked at the red stone still clutched in his fist. Roscoe groaned and leaned against the passenger door.

"Go home," he said. "I'll meet you there as soon as I can."

"Do you know where Millie is?"

"I know where he's taking her. He couldn't have got there yet."

"Will he hurt her?" Lucy's chin trembled as she said the words.

Harry glanced at Roscoe slumped against the door. He had to go now or his friend was going to die.

"Whoever this Joe is," he told her, "he didn't come out here by accident. There has to be something between him and Frankie. Donovan arrested Byrd and he knows this Joe person. Maybe that's the connection."

"You think my brother is involved?"

"I don't know. If he is, then we know Millie's safe. If he isn't, then I know what I have to do." Harry held the ruby pin in front of her. "Find out what you can about the owner of this." He gunned the engine of the roadster. "I'll meet you at your home as soon as I can." Lucy nodded her head and released her death grip on the roadster's door.

Harry's car disappeared around the bend throwing gravel from the rear wheels. She had to go. The acorn shaped silver button fell from her hand. She gasped as if she dropped some magic link to Millie. Dropping to her hands and knees, Lucy rummaged through the weeds. She found the button and something else. A small, shiny nickel plated automatic. The tears started again as she dropped the button and the gun into the pocket of her coat. "Oh Millie, what's happened? Where are you?"

The mud splattered Auburn Speedster followed the tracks left by Harry's roadster. At the top of the hill, she turned in the opposite direction as she headed for the ferry.

*****

Joe filled the bathroom basin full of water and splashed double handfuls onto his face. This was what running felt like. He was nervous and felt cornered. The face looking back at him in the mirror was filled with guilt. That poor girl. Running a hand through his hair, he tried to think of what to do next. The criminal Byrd had upset everything. Was Byrd going to kill Lucy's sister? He felt sick to his stomach. If he convinced him to let her go, the girl would run to her father and McAllister would, would what? He didn't know. The one thing he did know was it was time for him to flee. Just as soon as he had what he came for.

He couldn't pack. The longer the hotel thought he was still a guest, the longer his head start. He changed quickly into his black suit. The fabric was thicker than the gray one and Byrd said it would be cold where they were going. Where they were going? What did that mean?

It was while he was changing his shirt that he noticed the rising sun stickpin was gone. He didn't have time to worry about it. Pulling on his heavy overcoat, he stuffed his gloves in one pocket and his papers in another. Was he forgetting anything, anything essential? He opened a dresser drawer and took out a long white silk scarf and quickly stuffed it into the overcoat's pocket. The specially made black suitcase was the last thing he took. Would it look suspicious, he wondered? Him walking out of the hotel carrying two bags.? He didn't know. It didn't matter. He was fleeing. That was what mattered. He had to move fast now. Move fast and stay one step ahead of the American authorities and one step ahead of Frankie Byrd. A few more hours and his mission would be over. One way or another.

The Bergonian's lobby was full of eyes. Everyone looked at him as he made his way to the front desk. He could feel their stares on his back. The police would be bursting through the front doors at any moment. His heart began to race.

No one looked at him.

The clerk turned around slowly to see who banged on the top of his counter. He was busy putting message envelopes in the rectangular slots behind the front desk when he heard the loud slaps.

Joe was flushed, anxious and for the first time since coming to this country, he was disheveled. He had never slapped his cane on anything before.

"Mr. Kanji," the clerk said. His voice was smooth velvet. He was used to patrons behaving rudely. It was something of a surprise coming from a guest like Kanji. The man was always the epitome of politeness. He gave the cane a disapproving stare before going on. "May I help you?"

"I left something in the hotel's safe this morning." Sliding a blue colored claim check across the counter, Joe said, "I would like to retrieve it now."

The clerk waved at one of the bell hops idling in the lobby. A short, chubby boy in the hotel's purple uniform with more gold braid than an army general jumped for the desk. He'd noticed the hotel's only resident millionaire as soon as he stepped out of the elevator. The Japanese man was known to tip well.

"Yes sir," he piped in a boy's not yet broken voice.

The desk clerk handed him the claim check. "Have Peterson open the safe and bring Mr. Kanji's property."

Ignoring the boy, Joe said, "I would like to send a telegram."

"To Nippon Heavy Industries again?" the clerk asked with the same velvety voice. Their eleventh floor guest sent at least one telegram a day to Japan. This would be his second one today. He pulled a yellow Western Union pad from under the counter along with a pencil and slid both towards the millionaire.

Joe touched the tip of the pencil to his tongue before starting to write.

NO CHOICE OPTION FOUR WAIT FOR BOX

Option Four. Joe managed a smile. That would get their attention. Option Four would tell them he was discovered and was running to Victoria. Wheels would be set in motion in his faraway home. The box was the small suitcase he carried down from his room. He hadn't wanted to bring the box with him when they sent him here. It was the one thing in his possession he could not explain if he was questioned. Now, thanks to that maniac Byrd, it might be the only thing that could save him from a prison cell.

The boy returned with a black leather briefcase. Fifty thousand dollars in cash was inside.

"Please have one of your boys take this to Western Union immediately." He tore the message from the yellow pad and handed it to the desk clerk, along with a crisp, new twenty dollar bill.

"Thank you, Mr. Kanji."

Joe spun away from the counter and reached for the case in the bellhop's hand. Rather than surrender the black case, the boy reached for Joe's other bag.

"Still got the Dodge?" he asked cheerfully.

Joe nodded as the boy pulled his other bag out of his hand and led him towards the double glass doors of the hotel. Joe followed, fifty thousand dollars and his future a few steps in front of him.

The doorman helped him with the heavy glass doors. Joe's steps were slow and measured, but inside, he was running as fast as he could. The bellhop followed him down the broad concrete sidewalk towards the lot where guests parked their cars. It was cold outside. That didn't stop tiny beads of sweat from forming on his brow. The boy set the leather case filled with a fortune in American money on the ground, then opened the car's door. Joe reached into his trousers' pocket, pulled some coins out to give to his impromptu porter, and slid behind the wheel. The bag containing the money went in the floorboard. The slim black suitcase was on the seat beside him. Pulling out of the parking lot, he watched the Bergonian's facade slowly shrink in the rearview mirror. There were no sirens. No police. Not yet. This was what running felt like. Option Four.

*****

Frankie took his time. The last thing he needed was to attract the attention of a traffic cop. He drove slowly, making sure he stopped at every stop sign and kept his speed to a sedate crawl as they crossed Seattle and drove north. He wasn't in a hurry. Kanji needed time to get the money. Fine with him. For fifty grand, he could take all day.

He gave Kanji perfect directions before they left the lake. If the sap didn't get lost, he should catch up to them right about sundown. "Wish you could run away, don't you?"

Millie, sitting as far away from him as she could in the front seat of the Ford didn't answer.

"I understand," Frankie said. "I wanted to run away too when they pitched me into McNeil."

He didn't speak again for hours.

*****

Archie McAllister hung up the phone, resting his hand on the instrument for a moment. It was his seventh phone call and was of no more use to him than the six before it. "They haven't seen her," he said at last. He couldn't think of anywhere else to call.

"Papa," Lucy began again. "Something has happened to Millie. She isn't at a friend's home. Believe me, I wish she was."

"We don't know that." McAllister rolled the silver acorn shaped button across his desk. He could vaguely remember seeing his daughter wearing a coat with silver buttons. Lucille said it was Millicent's. "You are jumping to a lot of ugly conclusions based upon a button."

Lucy leaned forward in the red leather chair in front of her father's desk. "The hell I am."

McAllister gave his daughter an icy stare. He did not tolerate cursing from his daughters, but this time, he didn't have the will to correct her.

"For one thing," he said, "why would Millicent go to Harry Watkins' boat? It makes no sense." Archie ran his eyes across the top of his desk, trying again to find an explanation for how his valise and its contents had suddenly vanished from its polished top. Bertie said no one had been here while he was gone. Only Millicent was in the house and now there was this story of Lucille's, of bleeding men and ruby stickpins.

"Harry said—"

"Harry," Archie cut in. "Harry Watkins. A man you promised

me in this very room you would never see again."

"Harry said," she began again, her voice slow and measured. "Roscoe was stabbed by someone named Frankie. That man was arrested by Donny some time back. He's a convict. The ruby in Roscoe's hand was the same one Joe Kanji had in his tie. Trust me, that stone isn't something a woman would forget." She cleared her throat. "Roscoe said they have Millie." Lucy leaned back in the red leather chair. "We need to call the police. We should have already called them."

McAllister put a hand to his forehead and closed his eyes. "Millicent wasn't here the night of the party. How would she even know Kanji?"

"I had brunch with Joe yesterday morning. She was there, too."

Archie drummed a finger along the top of his desk. He was beginning to understand what had happened now. His daughter must have overheard his conversation with Kanji after she brought his coffee upstairs. That was the only thing that made sense. She took his valise for reasons known only to her and gone to some location on Lake Union to where Harry Watkins was keeping a boat. Kanji had an accomplice. A man named Frank who had at some point been arrested by Donovan.

"You're acting very strange," Lucy said.

"I most certainly am not. You have this moment told me a horrific tale of bloodshed and possible murder. My youngest daughter is out of pocket and my oldest daughter has confessed to seeing the one man in all the state who I have forbidden her to see. I think I am acting quite calmly given those precedents."

Lucy reached for the telephone sitting on her father's desk. "I'm calling the police. I think Joe is involved with whoever this Byrd person is, and I think Millie is with them. They can at least go talk to Joe and get his side of the story."

Archie pulled the phone away from his daughter. "We are not calling the police about this, and we certainly aren't going to mention anything about Yoshiro Kanji to anyone. I forbid you to see that bootlegger again. You are to stay away from him."

"Stay away from who?" Donovan asked from the doorway of the study.

Lucy jumped out of the red chair and ran to her brother. Wrapping both arms around his waist, she hugged him close against her. Donovan was surprised. He couldn't remember the last time she did that. "What's all this?"

"Donovan, where have you been?" Archibald asked his son. "Something has happened."

Lucy took her brother's hand and led him to the chair in front of her father's desk. "Millie's missing," she said, her voice flat.

Donovan was smiling. In fact, he was beaming from ear to ear.

"Did you hear what I said?" Lucy asked.

"In a minute," Donovan replied. "Pop, I was at the hospital. I had a long talk with Inga."

Archie McAllister's face clouded.

"Just hang on," he added. "You'll be glad I went." He leaned forward placing his hands flat on his father's desk. "She's not pregnant," he said, his voice barely over a whisper, as if he was discussing state secrets. "Said she made the whole thing up." Donovan laughed, then sat down in the chair next to his sister. "Made it up," he said again. This time, he said it in full voice.

"Nobody cares about Inga Swenson. Something's happened to Millie," Lucy shouted.

"Made it up?" Archie said, nearly choking on the words. "Do you know what I, what's happened?"

Donovan looked genuinely surprised. "I thought you'd be happy. Hell, I thought you'd be thrilled."

"What about my sister?" Lucy asked again.

"Where's the brat gone to now?" Donovan said, slumping into the upholstery. There was no pleasing his father. "I'm not waiting dinner on her. Bertie's made a roast. I can smell it."

Lucy began her story all over again. The same one she told her father.

"Harry Watkins," Donovan said. "That didn't take you long, did it?"

"Shut up and listen to what I am telling you. Do you know a man named Byrd?"

"Hell no I don't."

"Harry said you arrested him a few years ago. Think. His first name's Frank or Frankie."

Donovan regarded his sister like something unclean. "Oh, yeah," he said after a moment. "One of Harry's bootlegger friends. We fished him out of the drink after he fell off Harry's boat. Damn DA said there wasn't enough evidence to arrest Watkins. His pal got sent up the river."

"Does he know Joe?"

"Joe who? Joe Kanji?"

"Lucille," Archie said. "Would you leave us alone for a moment? I need to discuss some things with your brother."

"Excuse me?"

"Wait in your room. I'll call for you if I have any questions."

Lucy was stunned silent. Her father rose from his desk and pulled her to her feet. "Go to your room or go help Bertie in the kitchen."

"I'm not going to my room or the kitchen."

Archie, a father's authority in his movements, gently moved his daughter towards the study's door. "You are." Opening the door, he forced her into the hallway. "Watkins," he said. "I told you, never again." Archie closed the door then turned to his son. "Donovan, I have to explain some things to you. After you have heard me out, we will decide what actions to take next."

Lucy stood there for a moment staring at the heavy oak panels before turning on her heel and marching to her room. She didn't close her own door as quietly as her father had. She slammed it hard enough to rattle the painting on the opposite wall.

*****

Millie clutched her coat more tightly about her. She tried the door to the Ford as soon as the man driving the car killed the engine. It wouldn't open. She wished she'd paid more attention to what roads they went down. She remembered going over the Aurora Avenue Bridge, but that was about all. There was a gas station a little way behind them. That's where she planned to run to before she found out the door wouldn't open. The man, her captor, what had Mr. Kanji called him, Byrd? Yes, that was the name. Byrd was sitting behind the wheel of the Ford cleaning his nails with a knife. She shivered. Partly from the cold and partly from the memories of what this man tried to do to her.

"You scream," Frankie said slowly, "and I'll do you the same way I did Roscoe." He tapped the shiny steel blade against the steering wheel. It made a dull clinking sound as it struck the hard surface of the wheel.

A farm truck passed them on the road going north. She watched the cab slowly disappear over a hill.

"Tell me about Harry," Frankie said casually.

"Did you kill Mr. Harrison?" It was the first thing she'd said since he shoved her into the front seat of the Ford.

"Mister Harrison," Frankie said, his voice full of derision. "He was alive when I left him." He grinned. "That's what I'll tell the judge if this deal turns sour." Frankie went back to cleaning his fingernails before continuing. "It was only fair. Hell, he drowned poor old Squeaky."

"I want to go home." Her voice was very low. "If you let me go, I won't tell anyone. I swear I won't."

"What happens to you is up to Harry Watkins."

"I," she began.

Frankie interrupted her. "Right on the button," he said, his eyes on the rearview mirror. Joe Kanji's Dodge pulled up behind him. Frankie waved his hand out the window motioning Kanji to follow. The fun was about to get better.

Cranking Squeaky's Model A, he eased the car onto the dirt road and pulled away from the Dodge. Kanji followed close behind. Sucking air through his teeth as he watched the car behind him in the Ford's rearview mirror, he muttered, "You sap."

Turning to the girl cowering in the seat beside him, he said, "I used to run these roads back when me and Harry were partners." The light was fading, so he pulled the knob for the headlights. "I bet I hauled a million gallons of gin down this very road." The Ford hit a bump and bounced hard. "Might have broken a bottle or two doing it." His joke seemed very funny to him and he laughed long and hard. "You're a looker, I'll give you that, but I wouldn't trade you for fifty thousand bucks and a bag full of paper. Know why? Because I'm not a sap. Kanji, he's a sap, and so is Harry Watkins."

The road got worse and Millie was forced to brace herself in the seat to keep from being flung against Frankie as the car slewed around a sharp turn. "Where are we going?"

"I'm going wherever I want. Harry and Kanji are going where I want, too. You, you're along for the ride."

The two cars bumped and swerved down the deeply rutted road for what seemed like ages to Millie. The spruce trees grew bigger and closer to the sides of the automobile as the sky grew darker. Finally, as the sun was about to drop beyond the mountains to the west, the brakes on the Ford squealed as Frankie Byrd stopped the car with a jolt.

"Far as we can go by road."

The Dodge pulled to a stop behind him. Frankie opened his door and stood in the double glow of Joe's headlights. His hands were in his pockets and he had the same twisted smile on his face as he had when he cut Joe Kanji loose by the sawmill.

Kanji did exactly as he was told.

How many times did a man get to make fifty thousand dollars?

"Get out, Kanji."

Joe killed his engine and suddenly, all was extremely quiet. He left the lights burning as he slowly opened his door. For the second time, he imagined what Frankie Byrd would look like with a bullet hole in his forehead. "How is the girl?"

Frankie ducked lower so he could see inside the interior of Squeaky's Ford. "My business, not yours, Kanji. Did you bring my money?"

"Where are we?"

Frankie jerked a thumb over his shoulder. "The Sound's right over there."

"Why did you bring me out here?" Joe asked.

"It's on the way to where I'm going." Frankie spat into the mud at his feet. "You're an amateur crook, Kanji. That was pretty obvious back on the dock. You wanted me to let the piece run off and that would have put us all in the jug. As it is, if I turned you loose in the city, they'd a caught you before the sun went down." Frankie waved an arm at the dark woods surrounding them. "This is my backyard. Out here, maybe even you can make it to sunrise without being caught by the law."

"My drawings. I want to see them."

Frankie hauled the valise from the backseat. "Got 'em right here." Reaching inside the car again, he grabbed Millie by the arm and pulled her out of the car. "That way," he said roughly as he shoved her towards the trees. "C'mon Kanji. We're almost home." Catching Millie's arm, Frankie pulled the struggling girl towards a small opening in the trees. A path cut through the rocks and brush twisting its way down the steep hillside. "Grab the rope and hang on. It gets steep fast."

The rope was on her right. An inch thick length of hemp knotted every few feet and tied from trunk to trunk between the trees.

"Byrd," Joe called as he and Millie disappeared down the path.

"Follow me down, Kanji," Frankie called back. "We ain't going far."

"What is not far?" Joe turned off the headlights to his car making the surrounding trees feel much closer in the forest gloom.

"Our boat to Canada."

Frankie Byrd and the struggling Millie disappeared into the darkness of the hillside. Already, his voice sounded far away.

It was the shortest, hardest walk of Joe's life. When he left the dirt road, it was like being swallowed by a cave. There was no moon and even if there was, the solid cloud cover above him would have made it invisible. The ground fell away as small pebbles rolled under his feet and threatened to send him tumbling down a steep hillside. His hands found a rain soaked rope running alongside an unseen trail but trying to hold on to it, his cane and to his two suitcases proved to be an ordeal. His hat was knocked off by a low hanging branch and disappeared into the darkness. Gripping the rope so tightly the knuckles on his hand hurt, he made it to level ground. He fell three times before he got there. Gasping for breath, he strained his eyes to see where he was. There wasn't much to see without a light. The trail ended at a small gravel filled clearing. He heard the water as waves not much larger than strong ripples washed against the shore. The receding seawater made a slithering, sucking sound as it crawled across the stones. He finally made out Byrd and Millie waiting for him near the water's edge.

The gangster who stole his drawings cut a piece of the rope from the path and tied Millie's hands in front of her. The man was leading her around the small clearing as if she was an unruly puppy discovering what a leash was for the first time. Joe could see he appeared to be enjoying it.

"Finally," Frankie said when Joe emerged from the steep trail. "I thought you might'a got lost on the way down."

Joe was determined not to show Frankie Byrd how much the climb down the hillside had taken out of him. "Byrd," he said, steadying his voice as best he could. "We need to talk."

"No we don't, Kanji. Follow me." He headed down the narrow

strip of sand and gravel pulling Millie along behind him.

For the first time, Joe noticed the glow of a light coming from somewhere up ahead. Swatting at a buzzing mosquito trying to make a meal out of his ear, he trudged after the criminal and his captive. It was a short walk.

At the far end of the clearing, perched next to the tree line, was a wood framed cabin set on pylons higher than a man could reach. A narrow set of stairs led to a single, unpainted door. The light was coming from a pair of small windows on either side of the door. Seeing the stairs made him sigh. His hip was sending piercing jabs of pain into his bones with every step.

Frankie stopped a few paces from the stairs. "Hey Blue," he called in a loud voice. "Not a good idea to surprise Blue," Frankie said in a much quieter tone to Joe. "Blue, you home?" he yelled again.

The door to the cabin opened a few inches. A large man silhouetted in the door called out in an unfriendly, gruff voice, "Who's there?"

"It's Frankie Byrd."

The door opened a few inches more. The long barrel of a shotgun nosed its way through the crack. "I thought you were locked up?"

"Not tonight."

"Who's that with you?"

"Something to keep the blankets warm." Frankie jerked the rope, pulling Millie in front of him, "and a friend."

The man in the doorway couldn't quite make out the shadowy figure standing behind Frankie Byrd, but he could see the girl clear enough. "Ain't that a sight."

"Come on," Frankie said to Joe.

The door opened wider. The cabin's owner was a bearded man in a black and red checked flannel shirt. A kerosene lamp was in one hand. The shotgun was in the other.

"I'll be damned," he said when he could finally identify Frankie Byrd coming up his steps. "It is you. Who's the lollypop?"

"Long story," Frankie said.

"Why's she tied up?" Blue asked as Frankie pulled Millie into the small cabin.

"She bites."

Millie was half dragged into the cabin as Frankie pulled on the rope tied to her wrists. As she went by the man named Blue, it was easy to see where he got his name. His face was scorched black by something.

"Gunpowder," Blue said when he saw Millie staring at his face. "Makes me pretty, don't it?"

Joe was the last to arrive. The steps going up to the cabin were almost impossible for him to manage. He wanted to set the case down, but he was determined to keep it with him.

Blue raised the lantern higher as Joe made his way slowly up the steps. "You're not white."

"No," Joe answered. "I am Japanese."

Blue stood in the doorway blocking Joe's entrance into his cabin. His back was to the room more concerned about Joe standing on his steps than what was behind him.

"What is this shit, Frankie?" He turned to look behind him. The woman Frankie dragged into his cabin screamed.

Byrd swung the split log with all his might. It hit the much larger Blue somewhere above the right eye. The shotgun fell from his hands as Blue made a head first roll down the wooden stairs. One arm, flailing through the air struck Joe in the chest and nearly sent him crashing down the steps after him. The kerosene lantern struck the wooden steps. It bounced twice before hitting the rocky ground. The glass globe shattered. The cloudy yellow light extinguished in a damp hiss. The only remaining light came from the open doorway and the dimly lit room inside.

Blue mumbled something unintelligible as he began to stand. Blood was pouring from his scalp and his legs were unsteady. "You little bastard," he growled. The sound of the pump shotgun being cocked silenced anything else he was going to say.

Byrd spat into the darkness as he raised the gun to his shoulder.

Blue raised his hands. "Now wait a damn minute."

To Joe, standing close to the hapless Blue, the blast sounded like the end of the world. His ears rang with the explosion of sound. Blue's ears never rang again. The buckshot caught him in the middle of his chest as the hard punch of the lead shot drove him into the ground. He was dead before his back hit the mud and rocks.

Frankie worked the slide tossing an empty red casing from the shotgun and chambering the next round. "Inside," he said to Joe.

"Why did you kill that man?" Joe asked as he walked slowly into the poorly lit cabin. The barrel of the shotgun touched the base of his spine.

"Spur of the moment thing," Frankie said. "Blue was a man of rash decisions. Fifty thousand dollars and a pretty thing like her might have put ideas in his head that I didn't feel like dealing with."

"You are not concerned by casual murder?" Joe asked.

"Casual murder. I don't believe I've ever heard it called that before. When he got so interested in you, I took it as a sign from above."

Frankie quickly ran his hands through Joe's clothing patting his chest and emptying his pockets. The papers Joe grabbed in his hotel room fell to the floor. He pulled Joe's passport from an inside coat pocket, thumbed through it briefly, then tossed it onto the floor with the other papers. "Where's your pistol?"

He wished he knew. "It was knocked out of my hand during the fight at the boat. It fell into the lake."

"You remind me of Squeaky," Frankie said disgustedly as he walked into the center of the room. The shotgun was cradled under one arm. An iron stove crackled with warmth and he held a hand out to it. A second kerosene lantern, its globe half blackened with soot, hung from a hook in the ceiling. "Now, let's see the money."

CHAPTER 12

The Imperial Japanese Navy's heavy cruiser *Takao* pushed southward through rough seas. Rain, hard and cold, followed the ship all the way from the Gulf of Alaska and down the long coast of British Columbia. Ichiro Daishi, captain of the *Takao*, stared southward into the night's darkness. This whole mission, he felt sure, was a waste of fuel oil. No one at the ministry asked his opinion.

A messenger brought him his position report. He was approximately ninety-eight kilometers due west of the entrance of the Strait of Juan de Fuca steaming at seventeen knots on a course of two five zero degrees. The navigation beacon at Estevan Point, British Columbia was due north of him. Area Twelve, his orders called it.

Daishi, standing exposed on the ship's weather bridge, seemed immune to the night's discomforts. Not so the young ensign shivering silently behind him. With one gloved hand holding fast to a steel life rail, Daishi watched the rhythm of his ship as ten thousand tons of steel rose and fell to the movement of the sea. The long Pacific swells, exploding in a frothy white spray across his bows, reached all the way to the second gun turret before returning to the ocean. If the youngster standing quietly at attention behind him failed, he might well have to use those twenty centimeter guns pointing silently into the night. It was a foolish risk they were taking.

"It will not be easy," Captain Daishi told the wet night around him.

The ensign thought he should answer this statement but remained silent when his captain continued speaking.

Without turning around, he said, "Do you know what is the most important aspect of your orders?"

"To bring honor to the ship," the ensign said without hesitation, "and succeed where others would fail." The ensign squared his shoulders as he spoke and wished again he thought to grab his foul weather gear before answering the summons to the bridge.

Daishi turned, his winter slicker glistening, and looked the ensign up and down. "The most important part is that no one knows you did it." The captain nodded towards the unseen eastern mainland. "Especially the Americans. Rumors we can ignore. Evidence we cannot. If you leave evidence, we might well have to fight our way home."

The ensign cleared his throat. "I will leave no evidence behind, sir."

Daishi raised Zeiss binoculars to his eyes and scanned the dark waters around him. The visibility was too poor to see or be seen by anything. "After twenty-four hours," he said, "if we have not received word, the mission will be aborted. Until then, you will remain ready."

The ensign said nothing. He'd already been told there were two choices in the matter. He could either be passionate about his orders or be very passionate. "For twenty-four hours, I shall remain prepared to do my duty." Passionately, or very passionately as necessary, he added to himself.

"If the weather clears, you will abort immediately."

The ensign, shoulders hunched against the biting wind, said, "I shall hope for unremitting clouds and fog."

Daishi grunted. "That will be all."

The ensign bowed quickly and hurried to the heavy steel hatch and the warm shelter of the ship's interior. He spun the wheel on the hatch and disappeared inside. The heavy steel door clanged shut behind him.

Daishi let the position report flutter away in the hard blowing wind. "A fool's errand," he told the night.

*****

Harry rolled the roadster to a stop behind Lucy's car. He idled the Plymouth for a moment looking at the imposing two story façade of the McAllister home before killing the engine. He wasn't welcome here. He hadn't been for a very long time, but he promised Lucy he would come as soon as he got Roscoe to the hospital. He almost broke that promise. Roscoe might not live through the night and he wanted more than anything to stay there with him.

But there was Millie.

Roscoe said Frankie had her and would be waiting for him. He hadn't said how long he would wait.

Harry expected to see a police cruiser or maybe sympathetic neighbors come to commiserate with the family, but the house was mostly dark. The long double windows on the second floor, the windows he remembered as belonging to Archibald McAllister's second floor office, glowed with light. The first floor looked like a house asleep. Getting out of his car, he closed the door with not too loud of a bang and began walking up the drive. Halfway to the front door, he changed his mind and continued down the driveway towards the rear of the house. A bright glow of light was coming from the kitchen windows. As he approached the back door, he could see a gray haired woman sitting at the kitchen table. She didn't seem all that surprised to see him looking in through the glass panes of the kitchen entrance.

Harry tried the knob. It wasn't locked. He stomped his feet on the concrete steps before entering her kitchen. He hadn't forgotten her rules. Not even after all these years.

"Do you remember," Bertie said, her voice sounding older than ever before, "that old swing in the elm tree?" She looked through the kitchen window as if it was full daylight outside. The tree was lost somewhere beyond the glow coming from the kitchen lights. "She would laugh and laugh as you and Donny swung her on that old rope swing. Do you remember, Harry?"

"I remember, Aunt Bertie." He bent and kissed the gray hair.

Bertie reached for his arm and hugged it against her. "Lucy told me. I am sorry about your friend. Is he alright?"

"Roscoe's fighting. He's a tough old bird."

"I heard some of what they said upstairs. My Millie's in trouble, isn't she Harry?"

Harry's heart sank. He was hoping they heard from Millie and she was safe. Bertie's words meant Frankie still had her. "I'll do everything I can. I swear I will."

The old woman nodded.

A sound caught his attention. Lucy was standing on the kitchen stairs. She changed her dress for chestnut colored woolen slacks and a dark red sweater over a thick cotton blouse. A cloth hat was tugged down tight over her hair. The closest thing she owned to boots, low heeled closed toed shoes, were on her feet. She pulled her arms through the sleeves of the borrowed leather coat. The zipper growled as she pulled it halfway closed. Her eyes were red and puffy. "Roscoe?"

Harry cleared his throat. "I don't know."

Lucy came the rest of the way down the stairs. She went straight to him and kissed him.

"You told your father?"

"I told him. He thinks I'm making too much out of a button."

"Then he's a fool. I better talk to him." Harry started for the kitchen stairs but stopped. An argument started in the far upstairs corner of the McAllister home. Everyone could hear the shouting.

"Donny and Papa are plotting strategies."

Harry thought about going up the stairs anyway and telling them what he knew about Frankie Byrd. Instead, he asked Lucy, "Did you ask your brother about the owner of that fancy stickpin?"

"Joe Kanji? I didn't get a chance. I was asked to wait in my room."

She didn't sound happy about that to Harry. "Why aren't the police here?"

The shouting upstairs was getting worse.

"I'll tell you in the car."

"I can't bring you where I'm going, Lucy. I only came by to see if there was any news."

"We haven't heard anything." She bent to hug Bertie and said something in her ear that Harry couldn't hear. "This place Roscoe talked about. The place he said Byrd would be waiting. How do we get there?"

"It's a half forgotten spot on the charts that someone would never find unless they knew it was there. Only way there is by water."

Lucy kissed Bertie's cheek before straightening. "Good thing we've got a boat, then. I dressed warm."

"Lucy, this is for me to do."

"It's for the police to do, but my father has forbidden it."

Harry opened his mouth to say something but closed it again. "Aunt Bertie. Tell her she can't go."

Bertie rose from the kitchen table, crossed to the stove and pulled open the oven door. His stomach turned over, the delicious smells suddenly pouring out of the oven reminding him he hadn't eaten anything in hours.

"Are there plates on this boat?"

"It has a full galley," Harry said.

Bertie pulled a large cast iron pot out of a cabinet and, using a fork as long as his forearm, placed the roast inside the pot. She used a spoon to scoop out potatoes and sliced carrots and added them as well. Covering it all with a heavy lid, she held the iron pot out to him. "Millie hasn't eaten. She'll need to put something in her stomach."

"Lucy shouldn't be going."

"Harry," Lucy began.

"No, she shouldn't," Bertie agreed, "but she tells me she is, so there you are."

He took the pot from Bertie's hands.

"Bring my little girl back, Harry. You bring her back."

Lucy looked at him with that defiant look she got when somebody was trying to talk her out of something. "All right," he said. "You can come."

She pulled the monkey's fist keychain out of her coat pocket. "Let's go. Before my brother comes downstairs." She opened the kitchen door and held it open.

"Quick now," Bertie told him. "Before Mr. McAllister hears voices and wants to know who is here."

Harry followed Lucy down the driveway with the heavy iron pot swaying beside his leg. He shouldn't be bringing her, he knew, but it would be hard to operate the boat by himself. He needed a second person and right now, Lucy was all the second he had.

"Tell me how he's doing," Lucy said when they reached the

street.

"The doctor said it looked bad. He lost a lot of blood. That's about all they would tell me since I'm not next of kin."

"Don't give up hope, Harry."

"I wished I could have stayed with him."

She placed her cheek against his shoulder. "Why did they take Millie?"

"I don't know. Frankie's been looking for me and Roscoe because of something that happened a while back. I don't know how Millie got involved." A dog barked somewhere in the night. "I can take you to the police if you want. Tell them what we know and let them deal with it."

Lucy turned to look at the front of her home. The double windows of her father's study still glowed with light. A shadow moved behind the curtain. She imagined her father standing behind his desk as he argued with her brother. "You ever get a feeling, Harry?"

"Now and then."

"When I told Papa about Joe Kanji and that ruby, he," she paused before going on, "he showed something for a moment. In his face. I can't really describe it."

"And you got a feeling?"

They made it to the cars right as the downstairs windows in the house blazed with brightness. The front door flew open as Donovan McAllister stormed outside.

"Lucy," he yelled. "Get back in the house." He began rolling up his shirt sleeves as he marched across the lawn.

Harry sat Bertie's iron pot on the ground. Donovan was coming fast.

Lucy stepped in front of Harry. "That's right, Donny. Let's all have a fistfight in the middle of the street while Millie is missing."

Her brother made a sweeping movement with his arm. It shoved Lucy out of the way and nearly sent her sprawling on the wet grass.

"Get in the house," he screamed. Spinning around to continue his advance on Harry, he was about to say something else. The words never made it past his intentions. Harry's fist hit him square on the nose. It was a hard punch. Donovan, the would be pugilist, staggered backwards. He hit the wet ground with a grunt.

Lucy hurried to get in between the two men. "Harry, stop."

"Wanted to do that for a long time," Harry said.

"You sucker punched me," Donovan mumbled as he struggled onto all fours.

Harry looked at Lucy. "You okay?"

"I'm fine. He just shoved me."

Donovan got to his feet. A neighbor's dog sounded the alarm as lights came on in houses up and down the street.

Harry grabbed the collar of Donovan's shirt and yanked him off balance. Dizzy from the punch, he slumped back onto all fours. Harry held his hand out to Donovan. The ruby stickpin was in his hand.

"Recognize this? It's kind of distinctive. The owner might have helped murder my best friend tonight." Harry shook Donovan by his collar. "Look at it."

Donovan shook off Harry's fist, then slowly got to his feet. Harry cocked back his arm.

"Harry," Lucy warned. "He is still my brother. Don't punch him again. Unless it is necessary," she added. "Is it necessary, Donny?"

Harry wanted to hit him again. He could feel the rage deep down inside telling him to hit Donovan over and over. But he didn't. Donovan rose to his full height, then raised his fists in some parody of a nineteenth century prizefighter.

"No sucker punches now," he said over clenched fists. "I'm going to beat you into the mud."

Neighbors were coming out of their houses.

"Donny, we don't have time for this."

"Shut up, Lucy. He knocked me down in my own front yard. He's going to take *his* licks now."

Harry held the ruby between his thumb and finger. Ignoring the threat of Donovan's fists, he asked, "Frankie Byrd, you remember him? You should. You're the one that sent him up the river. He's out of prison now. I think he's working with an Asian man." Harry glanced at Lucy.

"Joe Kanji," she said.

"You know him, too," Harry continued. "Today, Byrd and this Kanji fellow tried to kill Roscoe Harrison.

"We think they took Millie," Lucy said.

Donovan wiped at the blood leaking from his nose. "I know all that." He glared at Harry. "What I don't know is what was Millie doing out on some boat dock with a coat that belonged to you? Don't tell me Millie is spreading her legs for you, too?"

"Hit him again, Harry. A hard one this time."

"Our mother is rolling over in her grave," Donovan said. "Both her daughters whoring with a bootlegger."

"Donny," Lucy said. Her voice was as smooth as butter left out on a kitchen table. "Spread *your* legs."

"What?"

Lucy's leather shoe slammed into his crotch. Donovan grabbed at his manly pride, then sagged onto his knees. "Mother fuck," he groaned before toppling onto his side on the wet ground.

"You learn to do that in New York?" Harry asked.

Lucy leaned over her somewhat incapacitated brother and said, "Inga sends her love by the way."

For the second time that night, her brother struggled to get to his feet. He kept a hand covering his damaged parts. "If you were a man and did that." He swallowed. "We're done, you and me. For good."

"We've been done a long time," Lucy said. "Go climb back in a whiskey bottle. It's the one thing you know how to do with perfection."

"Donovan." Harry twirled the ruby between his fingers. "What do Frankie Byrd and Joe Kanji have in common? I know one of them, but I never heard of the other one."

"Go to hell, Watkins."

"I'm not asking for me. I'm asking for Millie. I think she's in trouble."

Donovan glanced over his shoulder towards the second floor windows of his home. He spat in the dirt before saying anything. "Pop says Kanji was blackmailing him. Something about a new airplane. He thinks Millie somehow got her nose in it and Joe took her hostage to keep him quiet while he makes his getaway."

"What?" Lucy said. "If you are making that up, I swear I'll do worse to your boys than kick them."

"That's why he can't call the police," Donovan said.

"Blackmailing him about what?" Harry asked.

"Why don't you go back inside," Donovan shouted at a neighbor across the street. "Nosy bastard," he said in a lower tone. "Blackmailing him about me and a woman I told Joe about."

"Oh god," Lucy groaned. "You're talking about Inga, aren't you?"

"Donovan." The shout came from the front door of the McAlister home. Archie stood on the front step with both hands behind his back. "Bring your sister and come inside," he said with his voice pitched loud enough to carry to the street.

Harry ignored Archie McAllister. "When did Joe Kanji find out about this woman?"

Archibald McAllister came down the front steps of his home. "Did you hear what I said?"

"I told him this morning," Donovan answered.

Harry looked at Lucy. "Roscoe ran into Frankie Byrd on Sunday night. He had problems with him. That's the night before you told Joe Kanji about your problems with…"

"Inga Swenson," she finished. The words came out of her mouth like she was spitting out poison.

"Inga Swenson," Harry continued. "It doesn't work. Byrd and Kanji were working something before he knew anything about this girl."

"Leave my property, Harry Watkins," Archie McAllister said. "Lucille, I have forbidden you to see this man and yet here he stands in my very own front yard." Archie surveyed the condition of his son who was still standing in a half crouch with one hand between his legs. "And brawling. Why am I not surprised?"

"Pop."

"Do not call me Pop," he yelled.

"You think it is blackmail?" Harry cut in.

Archibald's face turned crimson. "You will kindly stay out of my family's affairs. When Millicent comes home, I shall have a satisfactory answer from her as to why she has been associating with the likes of you, Watkins."

Harry put his hands in his pockets. "You think she is going to come waltzing in at any moment? Is that it?"

"Millicent is unharmed. I am certain of it."

"I've got a friend fighting for his life who is certain she isn't." Harry looked at Donovan. "Can you find Joe Kanji?"

"I know where he's staying."

"Since your father is unwilling to call the cops, maybe you could pay him a visit and see if he knows anything."

"You will do no such thing, Donovan." Archie McAllister reached for his daughter's arm. "Come, Lucille."

"I haven't got a car," Donovan said. "Joe's in the city."

Lucy, pulling her arm out of her father's grasp, tossed the keychain with the monkey's fist towards her brother. He caught it with the hand not pressed against the front of his pants.

"Try not to hit any trees with this one. Remember, it's just a loan," she added.

"What about you? Where are you going?" Donovan asked.

Harry lifted the heavy iron pot containing Bertie's roast and turned for his roadster. "I've got a dinner to deliver." Opening the passenger door, he sat the pot on the floorboard.

"*We've* got a dinner to deliver you meant to say." Lucy hopped onto the car's seat, then closed the door with authority.

Donovan pointed a finger at Harry. "We aren't done with this. You sucker punched me."

Lucy smiled. "I didn't."

"You're no lady," Donovan spat. "Not anymore."

Harry got in his car and stepped on the starter. "Don't be an idiot, Donovan. Millie could be in trouble. Your father's lying through his teeth about something and you want to practice your boxing techniques."

"How dare you call me a liar," Archie McAllister hissed. "You, a common criminal."

Harry shrugged his shoulders. "I got a feeling." He put the transmission in gear. "Go find your pal, Donovan. Joe Kanji. Ask him how he knows Frankie Byrd."

Archie, understanding his daughter was about to defy his wishes, moved to grab the roadster's doorhandle. Harry let out the clutch. The car pulled away from the curb.

"Lucille," Archibald McAllister yelled.

Lucy bit her lip, then looked at Harry. "Are we doing the right thing?"

"My gut says so."

"Mine too. How far is this place where we're going?"

"The Haro Straits."

Lucy thought for a moment. "Isn't that in Canada?"

"On one side, yes."

"How long before we can get there?"

"It's going to be a long night and cold."

Lucy tipped up the fur collar of her coat. "Like I said before, I dressed warm."

*****

"Once again," Joe said, "you have done something unnecessary." He threw the case with the fifty thousand dollars across the room. It landed with a dull thud at Byrd's feet.

"We still talking about Blue? He's killed three men I know of which means he's probably killed twice that many I don't know about. Ain't nobody seen his wife this decade. Word is nobody ever will if you get my meaning. My conscience won't be bothered by his unexpected and sudden demise."

Frankie opened the top and turned the case upside down. Bundles of twenties, still in their paper bank wrappings, tumbled onto the wooden floor. The empty black leather case fell from his hands. It was the biggest pile of money he had ever seen. "So this is what retirement feels like," he said, smiling at the pile of money before him.

"My blueprints," Joe said.

"My father's blueprints," Millie countered as she sat against a wall with her hands still bound by the rope.

"Her father?" Frankie asked. He slid the case containing the drawings across the floor with his foot.

"Yes," Joe said as he retrieved the bag from where Byrd pushed it. The pain in his hip felt like a bayonet stabbing into the joint. Sinking onto a wooden cane-backed chair by the cabin's door, Joe opened McAllister's valise, then selected one of the drawings. "Millie was trying to protect her father from people like you and me. Unfortunately, the man she went to for help was not where she expected."

"Watkins," Frankie said. "So that's why you went to the lake."

"Where were you, Harry?" Millie asked. She said it low enough that neither of the men paid her any attention.

"I believe that is his name, yes," Joe answered. He unrolled the drawing.

"I knew she wasn't Watkins' type of whore."

"She is the only one of us here who has done the proper thing and has paid the worst price for doing it."

"Spare me the sermon, Kanji."

Frankie eased a step closer to the shotgun. It was time to end this. He had a meeting with Harry Watkins to get to, and he didn't want to be late. "This is as far as you go."

Joe Kanji didn't blink as Frankie Byrd slowly swiveled the shotgun towards him. Millie's father accused him of thinking small. "You need to think larger."

"Talk fast, Kanji. Me and the lollypop got a long night in front of us."

"If fifty thousand dollars represents retirement to you, what does one hundred thousand represent?" he asked calmly. The shotgun was pointing straight at his chest. "I'll pay you another fifty thousand dollars cash to take me, the girl," Joe tapped the leather case sitting on his lap, "and these to Victoria."

Frankie sucked air through his teeth for a moment while he considered things. His laugh filled the cabin.

"I almost like you, Kanji. I swear I do. I don't know if I believe you, but I believe you enough to keep you breathing for a little while longer." He leaned the shotgun against the wall. "You're finally starting to think like a crook." He slid a chair across the floor and sat in front of his fortune. Bundle after bundle, he started counting. "I'm listening." Money always made him listen. One by one, Frankie dropped the wrapped bundles of twenties into Joe Kanji's black case.

"How many more people are you planning to murder?" Joe asked.

Frankie paused in his counting. "I told you. I had to do that. Once Blue knew I had this," Frankie waved one of the bundles, "he'd a slit all our throats. Yours last," he added with a look at Millie. Dropping a thousand dollars' worth of twenties into the case, he continued with his counting. "For a thief, Kanji, you don't seem to understand the criminal mind very well."

"I am not a thief."

"What are you then?"

"Someone with access to large amounts of cash."

"Which explains why you haven't joined poor old Blue out there in the mud." He was at twenty thousand and still there were more bundles of cash waiting to be counted. "But that don't mean you still might not join him if you aren't careful." Frankie looked at Millie. "If looks could kill."

"If only," Millie replied,

Before he started counting, he tied the end of her leash to a peg set in the wall. Blue used it for a coat rack. Millie sat on the floor with her knees pulled up. Her bound hands were above her head.

"You are going to Canada, no?" Joe asked.

"As soon as I'm done with my business with Harry." There were no more bundles of cash on the floor. Fifty thousand, just like Kanji said.

Joe sat Archie McAllister's valise on the floor next to his feet. The blueprints told him what he needed to know. The dim light from the room's single kerosene lantern made it hard to see everything clearly, but there was no doubt. He had the P-26.

"How will you get to Canada?"

"Didn't you see the boat?"

He was too busy trying to walk up the steps without falling to look for boats. "I did not."

"You should notice things more. It's my boat now. I bought it with a load of buckshot from a twelve gauge." Frankie pointed the barrel of the shotgun at the second suitcase Joe hauled down the side of the hill. "What's in there? I might want to do some more buying."

Joe lifted the case from the floor, flipped the clasps, and pulled the top open. Frankie sauntered over and gave the contents a brief examination. He looked disappointed.

"A radio? Didn't take you for a music lover. I thought maybe you had more cash on you."

Joe closed the lid, snapped the clasps back into place, and sat the case beside his feet. The papers Frankie tossed on the cabin floor when he searched his pockets earlier were lying next to the radio. Using his shoe, he moved the pile around until he saw the page he was looking for. It was the bank statement.

"Take me to Victoria in your newly purchased boat, give me the girl, and I will give you all the money in this account." Joe handed the statement to Byrd.

Frankie took the paper from Joe's hand. "What's this?" He tilted the balance sheet towards the lantern and quickly scanned the page. "You can't have this much money." There was something like unbelieving wonder in his voice.

"Are you wanted in Victoria?" Joe asked.

"Only by those types that can't call the Mounties."

"There is nothing stopping me from walking into my bank and transferring those deposits into hard cash." Joe paused a moment before going on. "All you have to do is turn Millie loose and take me to Victoria. You go your way, and we shall disappear."

"Why are you so concerned about the girl? She mean something special to you?"

"I am responsible for her being here and I like to think that if her brother was in my place, and it was my sister tied to a wall, he would do the same for her as I am trying to do for Millie."

"You're one of those noble thieves?"

"I have told you. I am not a thief."

Frankie used the barrel of the twelve gauge to tap the black case sitting beside Joe. "No, too dim for a thief and too noble to be a criminal." He sucked his teeth. "What are you, Kanji, if you're not a thief or a criminal and if you tell me a lie, I'll blow you right off that chair." Frankie's thumb cocked the hammer on the shotgun. The click was very loud in the small, quiet cabin.

Joe stared at the gun's barrel pointing unwaveringly at his chest. He had no doubt this man would pull the trigger as easily as if he were swatting away a fly.

"My name is Lieutenant Yoshiro Kanji. Imperial Japanese Navy. I was sent here to acquire by any means possible the plans to an aircraft built by the Boeing Corporation." He pointed to the valise sitting on the floor. "That aircraft. Archibald McAllister, the girl's father, was in charge of the project that produced the final airframe." Joe paused before going on. The barrel of the shotgun didn't move. "He was helpful to my country in the past."

Frankie lowered the barrel of the gun.

"My mission was to make contact with McAllister and see if he was willing to be helpful again. He was."

"That's a lie," Millie hissed. "You were blackmailing him. I heard you on the phone."

"No, Millie, I was not. You misunderstood. Your father was to meet me at my hotel with these plans at which time I would have given him the cash this man has now."

"I don't believe you. You're a liar."

"I don't know, lollypop. I think he's telling the truth." Frankie eased the hammer of the shotgun out of its cocked position. "Now it all makes sense to me, Kanji. You're not a thief. You're a spy." His laughter bounced off the cabin's four walls. "The girl screwed Watkins, her proud papa, and you." He laughed again. Looking at Millie, he gestured with his thumb at Kanji. "He's a spy and all this time I thought he was just a really bad crook."

"Time is wasting sitting here, Byrd. We could be halfway across the Strait by now and could be at my bank when it opens. You get your money, and the girl and I go our separate ways."

"Me having that girl is eating at you, ain't it?"

"You did not have to bring her into this."

"You're the one who pulled a pistol on her back at that hotel. I didn't bring her into it. You did."

Joe's face reddened. He could feel Millie's eyes on him, waiting for him to say something, something to refute the truth they both heard from the killer standing in front of him. Joe couldn't look at her.

Byrd pushed his hat a little farther back on his head. "Not that I'm complaining," he continued, with a leering look at Millie. "What I don't understand is, how come the girl had those plans you want so bad in the first place?"

"I do not know why she had them."

"Because I wasn't going to let you get them," Millie suddenly screamed. "Harry's going to know what's happened." Millie jerked at the knot tying her hands. "He's going to find you, Lieutenant whatever you said and you to, Byrd." Her eyes were thin slits boring into Frankie's soul. "He'll come for me. You'll see. He'll come."

"Do you see it now, Kanji?" Frankie said with a smile. "The reason I brought the girl along? Harry's bound to follow. Sure as the sun's going to come up in the morning, he's coming." Suddenly, he grabbed Millie's hands by the knot and hauled her to her feet. His knife, the same one he stabbed Roscoe with, sliced through the cord. "Cook something," he told her. "I'm hungry."

"I'd rather watch you starve," Millie spat back at him.

Frankie smiled then lunged, pinning Millie against the wall. His body pressed into hers. Millie turned her face away.

"I like a spirited woman, but don't make the mistake of making me notice you. Either you feed me," Frankie ground his hips into

Millie's loins, "or you feed me. My nose don't hurt that bad and I ain't forgetting the sight of you with that dress opened up. Understand?" He released his hold on her and shoved her towards an enameled sink at the far end of the cabin. "And don't be trying to palm any of those butcher knives," he told her. Folding his knife, he dropped it into his pocket.

The cabin's owner had tacked a piece of burlap cloth across a row of cabinets. Millie pulled the sacking aside and grabbed the first can she saw. There was a hand crank can opener screwed onto the wooden counter. She sat the can under the opener and slammed the handle down.

Frankie stuck his hands out to the warmth coming off the iron stove. "What are we having?" he asked cheerfully. The shotgun was cradled in the crook of his arm.

"Hash," Millie answered. She finished opening the can and dumped the contents into a mostly clean iron skillet.

"My favorite. You hungry, Joe? Nothing like home cooking."

"No, I am not." Joe retrieved the rest of the papers Byrd dumped on the floor when he searched him and put them in his pocket.

Millie placed the skillet on top of the iron stove, making sure to keep out of the reach of Frankie. She pulled her coat closer about her and slowly sank into the far corner of the room while hugging her legs and looking at the floor.

"Tell me, Kanji," Frankie began. "If I hadn't suddenly upset your apple cart, how did you plan to get away with your heist? I mean, your *espionage*?"

"There was nothing to get away with. No one was chasing me."

Frankie shrugged. "That's a point, I guess, but even so, you had to have a getaway plan of some sorts. Canada is still a long way from Japan."

Joe preferred silence to answers.

"Do I have to cock this thing again?" He dropped the shotgun from its tuck under his arm and deftly caught it in his hand.

"You are not going to shoot me, Byrd. I am worth far more to you alive than dead."

"Don't be so certain about things. I'm a little impulsive. Ask my good friend Blue." Frankie moved the twelve gauge from one hand to the other. "But I've been watching you, Kanji." A fork was on the counter beside the sink. Picking it up, Frankie wiped it against his pants leg, then started mashing the hash inside the frying pan. The corned beef sizzled. "You're not worried enough. Like you already know what's going to happen next. Like you think you're one step ahead of me. So, I'll ask you again. How did you plan to get away?" Frankie leveled the barrel of the shotgun straight at Joe. "And Kanji, don't make the mistake of telling me you didn't have a plan." He spooned a forkful of the half raw hash into his mouth and chewed with gusto.

Joe tapped the end of his cane against the suitcase containing his radio. "With that," he said at last.

"Keep talking," Frankie said.   Another forkful of hash disappeared into his mouth.

*****

"You don't really know it was Donny's boat that shot at you," Lucy said.

"I couldn't see him," Harry said, "if that's what you're asking. But it was him. He made it clear enough when we argued that night in the Pharmacy."

"But it could have been a different patrol boat and not Donny's at all."

They were standing in the wheelhouse of *Scarab*. He just finished getting the boat ready for sea. All but two of his mooring lines were untied, the fuel lines to the engines were open, and he had given the boat a quick walk through to make sure there were no problems. Harry pressed the starter switch to number one. The engine whirred but didn't start. He tried the switch again and the big motor roared to life. He let it run at high idle for a moment before easing off the choke. Number two started almost as easily.

"It could have been, but it wasn't," he said, answering Lucy. Harry left *Scarab's* wheelhouse to duck into his cabin. The boat's engines were making the yacht vibrate as he took off his slicker in the small master's cabin and tossed it on the bunk. The .45's holster was still lying in the bottom of the locker. It only took a second to slip the leather over his shoulder. The Colt slid into its familiar place under his arm as if he had never put such things away.

"Just like the old days," Lucy said. He hadn't heard her enter the small cabin over the sound of the twin engine's noise.

"Something like that." In the old days, he wore the gun for protection from the men he did business with. It wasn't protection he was thinking about now. "I need to untie us."

"I can do it." She scooped up Harry's slicker and left the cabin. Light rain was falling as she slipped the mooring lines from the pier's cleats, then tossed them along the deck. The wind caught the boat and she had to jump from the pier to the boat's deck as *Scarab* slowly drifted away from her mooring. Lucy watched the pier for a moment before turning for the interior. "That wasn't so hard," she said to herself. Harry was in the wheelhouse. "What time is it?"

"Near midnight, I think. We'll be there about sunup." Harry gave the wheel a clockwise turn, pushed the double levers forward to engage the transmissions, then eased his throttles forward. The throb of *Scarab's* motors increased in tempo as he straightened his boat out from the turn, then scanned the surface of Lake Union. A small red light was coming down from the north probably headed for the Ballard Locks. He planned to beat whatever boat it was to those locks. *Scarab* shot around the anchored hulks, lifeless memories from the Great War that sat in the middle of the lake for years, and ripped across the water.

Lucy grabbed a brass handrail in front of her.

"We're coming, Millie," she said. No one heard her over the roar of the twin engines. Harry opened her up giving the powerful motors full throttle.

*****

Frankie had the collar of Blue's flannel shirt and was dragging him down the slippery wooden dock. He had already stopped twice to catch his breath. Blue was heavier than he looked. "You could help," he said reproachfully to Joe.

"I did not murder him." Joe stood beside the fishing boat. It was a good sized boat; longer than twenty feet with a partially enclosed cabin in the bow. Like its late owner's home, it was filthy, damp, and in need of paint. A mast was mounted behind the cabin with a long boom extending aft. Small rigging lines running the length of the mast slapped against the wooden pole as the boat rocked from side to side. The sound made an endless noise in the close, dark night. Millie cowered in a corner of the forward cabin. She found a spot out of the way and was sitting on something that looked like an old fishing net. Byrd retied her hands with a fresh piece of rope he found onboard. The boom rocked back and forth on a rusty hinge where it joined the mast. Its slight grinding sound competed with Frankie's grunting as he dragged his victim down the pier.

"Goddam," he said at last as he reached the end of the short wharf. "Probably should have waited till I got him down here before I wrapped that chain around him. Why didn't you suggest that, Kanji?" Byrd rested the butt of the shotgun on the pier as he removed his hat, then wiped a handkerchief across his brow. He had taken Blue's slicker from the cabin and put on a pair of knee high rubber boots. Shoving his hat back on his head and balancing the shotgun in his other hand, he said, "Grab his feet."

"I did not murder him," Joe said again.

"Get his damn feet or I'll murder you."

Grabbing the cold, damp chain, Joe asked, "You knew this man well?"

"Well enough," Frankie answered. He tried sliding the corpse closer to the edge. "Just another rumrunner." The body teetered on the edge of the boards. "Like Harry Watkins."

Millie looked away as the dead man began to roll towards the water.

"Once upon a time, he was useful." The body splashed into the black water. "Sorry about that, Blue," Frankie told the corpse. "Nothing personal, but I thought it was prudent on my part to kill you before you killed me."

It wasn't much of a eulogy.

"You are going to kill this man, Watkins?"

"I am." Frankie spat into the dark water.

"Why not wait for him where you stabbed that other man and shoot him like this one?"

"Because Kanji, Harry Watkins ain't like this one. Blue was skilled, but he was also stupid. I mean, c'mon, knowing me like you do now, would you let me behind you?"

"No."

"Neither would Harry." Frankie smiled his twisted grin. "He ain't stupid. When he's thinking, that is. Do you know when men stop thinking?" He slapped the top of the small wheelhouse. Millie jumped. "When they start thinking about the smooth inner thighs of a sweet little thing like I've got right here. He'll get stupid and that's when I'll kill him."

The ripples in the water caused by the corpse's splash were dying out.

"Is that what you are going to do with me?" Millie asked from the corner of the small cabin. "Wrap a rusty chain around me and throw me in the water?"

"No, Millie, he will not." Joe wiped his hand that held the chain against his thigh. "He knows if he does that, he will not get the financial windfall that awaits him in Victoria." Joe stepped closer to Frankie Byrd. "Not one dollar."

"Ain't you the brave one," Frankie said. "Get in the boat, Sir Galahad, before I decide fifty grand is enough and call it a day." Frankie balanced the pump shotgun on his shoulder.

Joe, his message delivered, stepped slowly across the space between pier and boat. The rusty hinge attached to the boom squeaked as the angle of the deck canted with the new weight. Using the handle of his cane, he hooked the grips of each of his two cases and lifted them one by one into the boat. First came his drawings and then the radio.

Frankie jumped into the middle of the fishing boat. He pushed the valise under the small wooden wheel inside the cabin. "Know anything about boats, Kanji?"

"I am a flyer."

"Is that so? A flying spy. Well, trust me to partner up with someone who has no kind of skill I can use." Frankie turned switches on the small helm in front of him. Lights came on at the tall mast, then went out again. Green and red navigation lights clicked on in the bow. "Kanji," he yelled. "Find the fuel tank and see how much gas we got."

Joe looked about the boat for something that resembled a tank. A metal cap was screwed into the deck of the boat flush with the old peeling paint. He unscrewed the cap and smelled the vapors coming out of the pipe.

"Look for a stick," Frankie said from the boat's cabin. "Poke it down the pipe to see how much's in the tank."

He found a wooden rod about as big around as his little finger in the stern of the boat. The murdered man cut notches along the length. The rod went down the fuel pipe. When he pulled it out, the fuel mark was almost to the topmost notch. "It's almost full."

"Our lucky night." Frankie reached underneath the wheel for the boat's wiring. "Ever steal a car before?"

"No."

"Of course not," Frankie said. He used his knife to strip the insulation back from a handful of wires. "Ever bought a car?"

"Several."

"Not me. What about you?" he asked Millie. "You got a car?"

Millie didn't move in the near darkness.

"You don't talk much," he told her as he touched two wires together. Sparks jumped in his hand as the starter on the boat growled. He touched the wires again and suddenly the engine was running with a loud staggered knocking sound. "Untie us," he said in Joe's direction.

Joe did as he was told, slipping the old cordage from around a post. "How long before we reach this place you told your enemy about?" The boat started rolling on the swell making Joe reach for the mast to steady himself.

Frankie gave the boat more throttle. Their speed increased as chilled salt spray came over the bow making Joe step under the shelter of the small cabin. There was just enough room for the three of them.

"This old tub doesn't look like much but she's got legs and back a few years ago, Blue could make the run from my pier to his in five hours, six if it's rough out on the Sound. That puts us there a little before sunrise."

"You can find this place?" Joe asked. "In the dark of night?"

Frankie touched the compass screwed to the wood in front of the wheel. "I can find it."

An old tattered chart was stuffed into a corner of the small overhanging shelter of the cabin's roof. Joe unfolded it and held it under the small light coming from the glow of the binnacle.

"Where are we?" he asked Byrd.

Frankie took the chart from him, flipped it over, and ran a finger along the coast. "There."

Joe examined the chart. It had been folded and refolded so many times the paper had ripped down the crease. He needed to know where they were to get his bearings.

"That's Canada over there," Frankie said over the roar of the engine's exhaust. He touched the northwest corner of the map. "That's another fifty grand. Victoria, I mean."

Joe wasn't looking at Canada or Victoria. He was looking at the larger printed words west of the spot where they dropped a corpse into the sea.

Strait of Juan de Fuca, he read. So close. "Where are we going?"

"There," Byrd answered, touching a finger to a spot on the chart.

Joe had to look closely to see the small printed name written on the old paper. The words Haro Strait were printed on the chart's surface where the criminal Byrd placed his finger. Another name in smaller print was barely legible in the dim light.

Mosquito Pass.

CHAPTER 13

"Is that it?" Joe shouted. Standing in the bows of the fishing boat, he tried to peer into the eye stinging mist in front of him. The weather turned steadily worse the farther away they got from Blue's dock. Water sloshed in the bottom of the boat, soaking his shoes and making his feet feel like they were surrounded in ice. Far ahead, he could see a light making a slow sweep across the water.

"That's the Lime Kiln light," Frankie told him. The square glass window was smeared by the rain and the occasional spray from waves coming over the bow. Joe Kanji looked half frozen, standing as he was exposed to the weather. Frankie adjusted his course a little farther north. "We're almost there."

Joe, teeth chattering, ducked back under the protecting overhead of the wheelhouse. "We could be in Victoria in minutes," Joe suggested. "Get out of this weather and dry off."

"You're the one who's wet." Frankie ran his hand down the front of his murder victim's slicker. "I'm dry." He was smiling in the darkened wheelhouse. "Besides, Watkins isn't going to Victoria." Frankie's voice took on a harder edge. "He's going to my old wharf, and so are we. Ain't that right, lollypop?"

Millie didn't answer. Next to Joe, she was the coldest person on the boat. Her back was aching from sitting so long in the cramped space without moving. She could stretch out a little farther and ease the kink in her spine, but that would mean being another inch closer to Frankie Byrd. She preferred the cramp.

"How long before he gets to this wharf?" Joe asked.

"Beats me. Depends on circumstances. This weather is going to slow him down some. He won't want to put that pretty boat of his on the rocks."

"How long are you going to wait before we go to Canada?"

"You got instincts, Kanji?"

"What?"

"Instincts." Frankie checked his course again with the boat's compass, measuring the angle against the watery beam of light from the lighthouse. "That feeling you get when you know a woman you've been chasing is finally going to let you play with her titties or when to look and see what's coming up behind you."

Joe remembered the sudden terror in Shanghai when his A2N's instrument panel exploded into wooden splinters. Did he have instincts?

"What is this to do with anything?"

"Because Kanji, I live and die on my instincts and my instincts tell me that sorry fuck Roscoe delivered my message and my old partner Harry is on his way right now. In fact, I'm so certain of it," he put his foot on Millie's thigh and shoved, "I'm willing to bet her life on it."

Joe stepped a little closer to Byrd, putting himself between Millie and the killer standing behind the boat's wheel. "She is not his woman."

The lighthouse was behind them now and Byrd idled down the boat's engine. He shrugged in the close confines of the cabin. "She's something to him. Maybe not his woman, but close enough."

Neither man spoke for a long time after that. The rain stopped and Joe went forward. He could think better without the killer standing beside him, and he desperately needed to think clearly. His mission was the P-26. It was why he was sent here. Not a girl who managed to wreck his plans and throw herself squarely into mortal danger. What would he do if it became necessary to choose between Millie McAllister and the P-26?

"Kanji," Byrd called, interrupting his thoughts.

Joe turned to look through the glass window. Byrd was a shadowy presence on the other side of the rain spotted glass. In the east, the sky was starting to lighten.

"What is it?" They were close to shore; maybe a hundred meters or so away from the forested shoreline and running a little northeast. The waves were smaller now; more subdued. In the almost total darkness of the night, Frankie Byrd brought them deftly into an unseen cove. The killer pointed at something across the water.

Joe turned to look where Byrd was pointing. He could see some kind of structure on the near shore. Pylons, it looked like, and maybe something like a building behind that. The boat's engine idled down to a very low growl as Byrd steered their stolen boat closer to the pier. Joe could see it better now. It was a wharf, or what was left of one. A giant of a tree had fallen beside it and its long dead trunk stuck out into the waters of the cove. The boards nearest the water had fallen in, leaving the large pylons sticking up like misaligned teeth. Almost everything was charred black.

"It's been burned," Joe called back over his shoulder.

"Not all of it," Frankie said.

Byrd reversed his engine a little too late and the fishing boat struck one of the empty pylons with a glancing blow. "Get useful, Kanji. Throw a rope around something before we bounce out of reach."

Joe wrapped a line around a fitting on the fishing boat's rail and tied a loose knot around the closest piece of solid wood he saw. He could just touch the edge of the remaining wharf with the tips of his fingers.

Frankie Byrd killed the engine. It got very quiet in the isolated cove.

"Move," Frankie said to Joe. He had a boathook in his hand and used it to pull their boat alongside the sloping boards of the wharf. "Hold us," he told Joe, giving him the boathook. He went aft and grabbed a stern line. Taking the shotgun from where he left it next to the wheel, he quickly scrambled over the side and onto the wharf pulling the line with him. He wrapped the rope around one of the half burned pylons sticking out of the water.

"Untie our passenger, Kanji. This is her stop."

The boathook clattered on the deck as Joe tossed it out of the way. Millie was still crouched on her fishing net inside the small cabin. The rope was wet and the knot was tight. It took him a moment to free her from the rope.

"I am sorry you got involved in this," he said quietly to Millie.

Millie rubbed her hands together before pulling the ruined coat tight across her chest. Her fingers were numb from the cold and her legs were too cramped to stand on her own. Joe helped her to her feet.

"I hope they hang you when they catch you. Both of you," she said loud enough for Frankie Byrd to hear. She stumbled as she made her way to the side. Joe caught her by the elbow, but she shook his hand away. "I can do it," she hissed at him. "Don't touch me."

Frankie moved quickly and, reaching over, grabbed her by the arm as she came over the side. "No foolishness out of you, woman. Do you hear me? You're alive as long as you're useful, but if you get stupid, you can join Blue." Frankie violently shook Millie's arm. "I'll sink you and let the crabs make a meal of you. You understand me? Say you understand."

"I understand."

"Toss me the money, Kanji, then get out of the boat and bring that rope with you."

The boards of the wharf were higher than the deck of the boat, and Joe wasn't sure if he would be able to climb the side or not. He sat the case filled with the cash on the boards. Frankie pushed it farther along with his foot. It was easier than he expected to make it onto the pier. For once, his hip cooperated, and he was able to crawl up the side without falling back into the boat that brought him to this half burned piece of nothing in the middle of nowhere.

"Pathetic," Frankie said once Joe made it onto the wharf. "Give me the rope."

Joe handed the length of line to him and leaned on his cane to catch his breath. He left McAllister's valise and the radio in the boat.

"I won't run," Millie said. "You don't have to tie me again."

"This is an island, lollypop. There's nowhere for you to run anymore. But that's not why I'm tying you." Frankie pulled Millie down the half fallen in wharf to one of the pylons that stuck out of the water higher than any of the others. An iron ring was driven into it for some forgotten reason. "That's convenient," Frankie said when he noticed the ring. He wrapped the rope around her wrists and quickly bound them together. "Hand's up," he told her as he pushed her against the high post.

"Please let me go." Millie's chin quivered.

He fed the end of the rope through the ring and drew Millie's hands over her head then tied the rope to the ring. When he finished, he gave it a hard yank. She wasn't going anywhere. "Ever notice those road signs that say home cooking two miles ahead or some such thing?" He stepped back to examine his work. "Well lollypop, you're my road sign only I need you to say, Harry, don't think about what you're doing. Just come and rescue me." He pulled his handkerchief out of his pocket. "Open your mouth."

Millie shook her head and tried to turn away. He grabbed her by the throat and squeezed. When Millie opened her mouth and gasped for air, Byrd shoved the wadded handkerchief into her mouth. There was plenty of rope left to tie the gag in place. He gave Millie a long, appraising look. Anyone coming into the cove could see her tied to the post.

"What do you think, Kanji? Think she looks helpless enough to make Watkins lose his mind and come racing in to save her?"

"Byrd, do you enjoy tormenting the helpless? Leave the girl alone."

Frankie stepped back to examine his road sign. "You're right, Kanji. It's missing that final touch."

With her hands tied the way they were, there was no way she could hold her coat closed. Byrd spread the garment wider, then pushed the torn remains of the dress away from her breasts.

Millie kicked and squirmed where she was tied, then made a muffled attempt at a scream.

"Yeah, I think that will do it," he said. "I'm sure it will because it's damn sure starting to do it for me."

A bird chirped somewhere in the trees behind them. Sunrise was coming.

Frankie scooped up the case stuffed full of cash from the old wharf and turned for the trees. "Let's go, Kanji."

"Where are we going?"

Frankie didn't answer. He continued down the rickety old wharf and onto a dirt path leading into the woods. Joe looked at the small boat and McAllister's bag stuffed full of the P-26's secrets. Millie yanked at the rope holding her to the iron ring.

"Not a good idea to keep me waiting, Kanji," Byrd yelled over his shoulder.

"Insanity," Joe whispered, as he turned away from the boat to follow Byrd.

The path was an overgrown road that ran up the hillside. There was a dilapidated building just inside the trees that might have been a small warehouse at some time. One side of it, the side facing away from the ruined wharf, had burned completely away. Joe walked slowly across the floor of the half burned building. The roof was unsteady, and the whole structure looked like it might slide into the water at any moment. It was damp and musty inside and half filled with fallen leaves that came in through a hole in the roof. The burned out wall gave a sheer drop to the water below. There was a single shuttered window facing the wharf and its pylons. The shutters protected what was left of the window. Most of the glass was broken and what wasn't, Frankie knocked out with the barrel of the shotgun. He pushed against the old wooden shutters until they were opened wide enough to see Millie. He pulled an empty crate over against the window. Sitting on the crate, he pushed the shotgun through the window and lined the barrel up on Millie and her post. It was a long shot for a shotgun, but close enough. He grunted, satisfied with the distance.

"You are going to shoot your enemy from here when he goes to untie her," Joe said.

"You catch on fast."

"It is too far. The pellets will scatter and you will hit them both."

"Might," Frankie said. "Not my issue."

"She is just a girl."

"She's bait and I am going to kill the man who put me in McNeil Island." A board squeaked behind him and Byrd quickly spun around on his crate. The shotgun was pointing at Joe Kanji's stomach. "If you feel like dying this morning, just keep coming towards me."

Joe froze where he stood. "She cannot be more than eighteen or nineteen and you would kill her just to take your revenge on this man?"

"Kanji, you look down there and see a pretty little thing that some part of you wants to save. Me, I look and I see a witness for the prosecution. Witnesses are bad in case your spy training never told you that. Are we on the same page now, or do I need to draw you a picture in the dirt?"

Frankie waved the barrel of the gun to the corner next to the broken window. "Sit over there. I need you where I can see you."

Joe's cane tapped slowly across the floor of the old abandoned warehouse. He took a seat on one of the crates. "This building is not safe."

Frankie rested the shotgun's barrel on the empty windowsill. "It will do."

"How long are you going to wait for this man you hate so much to arrive?"

"Told you to eat something back at Blue's," Frankie replied.

"How long?"

"It won't be long."

"You do not even know if he is coming."

"Sure I do. Roscoe told him. Why do you think I didn't cut that old bastard's throat?" The crate squeaked under Frankie as he adjusted his position. "It won't be long at all."

He hadn't meant to fall asleep but sitting on the case in the corner, the night without rest caught up with him. Frankie's sudden shout of delight jerked him awake.

"I knew my instincts. It's like I told you, Kanji. You got to have instincts."

Joe eased himself up from the wooden crate and leaned forward far enough to see out the broken window. A large white yacht was making its way into the cove. It was the same vessel he saw tied to the pier back on Lake Union. The man Frankie was hunting had arrived.

"Looks like Roscoe did it." Frankie slapped the stock of his shotgun. "I knew he would." He laughed. "Trust Harry Watkins to show up right when I was about to go take a piss."

The yacht completed the turn into the cove and was slowly edging closer to the burned out wharf. The sun cleared the steep hillside and its blanket of tall trees. The bright rays shone directly into *Scarab's* wheelhouse windows turning the glass into a brilliantly bright mirror.

"Get back to your box, Kanji. I don't want any foolish last minute heroics from you spoiling my aim. Screw this up and I'll blow your good leg to pieces."

"He means nothing to me, Byrd. Your revenge is your business."
Joe dropped heavily onto the crate.

The white yacht continued to slowly edge its way into the close
waters of the cove. Both men heard the rumbling echo of the boat's
engines change from a barely heard idle to roaring full power.
Scarab lurched forward no longer dawdling in the cove's entrance,
and powered straight ahead.

This wasn't what she was supposed to do. She was supposed to
round the headland, enter the cove and get just close enough to get
their attention and she was early. The clock screwed to the wall said
eight thirty seven. Harry said nine o'clock, but when she saw her
sister tied to the post on the corner of the pier, Lucy did everything
Harry told her not to. Too late, she remembered boats didn't have
brakes. *Scarab* plowed into the space between the fishing boat and
the wharf. There was a great tearing sound as the half burned wood
of the wharf cracked, splintered and split. The smaller boat, its bow
line snapped by the impact of the much larger yacht, swung towards
the open sea. The stern line, the one tied by Byrd, held the boat fast
as it floated away from *Scarab's* hull. Lucy shifted the boat into
neutral. The boat's screws stopped turning and Harry's boat
stopped driving itself into the wharf.

Scarab was stuck like a cork; wedged firmly in between the
burned and broken remains of Frankie Byrd's old loading dock.
Lucy didn't care about any of that. Her sister was all she was
thinking about. Leaving the boat in neutral, she flew down the steps
from the wheelhouse and into the main salon. She was out the port
side door in an instant and onto the main deck.

"What the hell," Frankie swore from his position behind the
broken window. It was the blonde, the woman the shoeshine boy
called him about, and not Harry Watkins at all. "Didn't see that
coming," he said out loud.

"What is wrong?" Joe asked.

"It's the dish, the blonde. She's rammed the goddamned pier and
almost sunk Blue's boat."

"Lucy?" Joe heaved himself off the crate and nearly fell across Frankie crouched at the window.

"Get off me, you stupid fuck." Frankie shoved Joe away and turned the shotgun towards him. "Move again and I'll put you in your grave."

"Millie!" The scream was piercingly loud. Both men heard it clearly inside the ruins of the old warehouse.

Frankie turned to look out his window right as Lucy launched herself across the opening. There was five feet of open space between the boat's hull and the safety of the wharf. Lucy cleared the gap and fell sprawling onto the wooden boards.

"Hot damn," Frankie said. "She jumped like a—"

The blow stopped whatever else he was about to say. Joe Kanji raised his cane for a second strike, but the killer rolled off his perch at the window and kicked the crate towards him. He had to step around the wooden box to deliver his second blow. Byrd blocked the walking stick with the shotgun at the expense of his fingers. The lacquered black wood smashed into them causing him to lose his grip on the gun. The stick shattered with the impact leaving Joe with nothing but an ivory handle. He tossed it aside, then went for the killer.

Frankie kicked outward with his leg aiming for Joe's damaged limb. Joe fell hard with a searing pain that ran all the way from his ankle to his hip as he struck the hard floor of the old warehouse. Doing his best to ignore the pain to his leg, he twisted around and scrabbled on the floor trying to grab the Winchester lying half underneath him. His hand found the cold steel of the barrel as the two men wrestled for control of the weapon. He had to shoot Byrd before the lunatic started blasting indiscriminately at that post where Millie was tied.

"Son of a bitch," Frankie snarled as he struggled to get to his feet, fight off Kanji who was trying to climb on top of him and get control of the gun. Like Kanji, he managed to grab the barrel, but he couldn't free it from the other man's grasp. The bastard wasn't letting go and lying on the floor like this, there was no real advantage for Byrd. It was a strength of arm fight now.

Joe knew his life depended on his grip on the shotgun's barrel and it was going to take more than someone like Frankie Byrd to pull it out of his hands. The two men rolled on the floor while

Frankie growled like an animal and Joe twisted and pulled doing his best to bring the business end of the shotgun in line with Byrd's chest. They fought a life and death struggle in the old warehouse with the burned out wall and its steep drop an arm's reach away. With one savage twist, Joe freed the gun enough to whirl the barrel around. Hard steel struck Frankie's broken nose. The man howled with the fresh pain but it wasn't enough. Frankie Byrd grew up fighting in back alleys and hard luck saloons. He knew there was no giving up, no quarter when the battle was for life or death. He punched and kicked at Joe throwing wild jabs and grappling for anything that would end the fight or at least give him an edge.

"Let go," Frankie snarled. "I'll kill you, you crippled bastard."

Joe said nothing. He concentrated all his strength on prying the barrel out of Byrd's hands. With a final yank, he freed the gun as Byrd rolled away from him. The open wall of the warehouse was behind him as he rose to a sitting position on the floor.

"Now, Byrd," he said, the barrel of the gun pointing at the killer, "this foolishness is over and you—"

The floor beneath him cracked. In the struggle for the gun, both men rolled far too near the ruined wall of the warehouse. Joe was inches from the precipice and the steep drop to the water below. The wide plank beneath him shifted. With a sickening feeling, he realized the only thing keeping it and him anchored to the floor was the weight of Frankie Byrd on the other end. Byrd realized it, too. In an instant, he rolled off the plank and suddenly, Joe felt gravity move beneath him. He made a sudden lunge for something solid as the old timber board unbalanced and flipped up and over. The whole thing went falling down the hillside. He grabbed onto one of the floor beams with his free hand. The other still held the shotgun. Frankie began to scramble to his feet as Joe laid the gun across the floor and tried to pull himself up. There was nothing beneath him but a steep hillside and the water below. Joe looked up. Frankie Byrd was standing over him as he dangled from the burned out edge of the old warehouse floor.

"Ain't you in a spot, Kanji." He retrieved the shotgun from the floor. "Guess I'll have to settle for that fifty grand, won't I?" Frankie took aim at the impassive face looking up at him. His thumb cocked the hammer.

Joe let go of his grip on the old boards. He disappeared

immediately, falling into the small saplings, ferns, and rocks that formed the cliff's edge. Frankie heard a muffled splash as Joe's body hit the rock filled water thirty feet below. He tried to lean over the edge of the warehouse to point the gun at where Joe dropped out of sight, but couldn't. Not without risking a fall himself. He cocked his head to listen, but there was nothing but silence coming from the water below.

"I bet that hurt," he called after the fallen man. His hat was on the floor. Byrd snatched it from the hard planks and sat it gingerly on his head, then touched his nose. "Fucking nose. Hit my damn nose on purpose."

The broken cane was lying among the crates where Kanji dropped it. Byrd kicked the pieces out of the same hole that claimed Kanji. "Take that with you to hell. Maybe the devil will give you a new one."

It wasn't a graceful landing. She came frightfully close to completely missing the soot blackened, foot wide board and going head first into the water below. Landing on all fours, she grabbed the rough wooden planks with both hands and held on. One foot slipped off the board and a long splinter ripped a gash in her pants. Beneath her, she could see the rocky bottom through the crystal clear water. If she fell, there was no way her feet would reach those rocks. She was ever much of a swimmer. Lucy had also never jumped so far in her life and was a little amazed she actually did it.

"I'm coming, Millie," she said, never taking her eyes off the blackened plank as she crawled on hands and knees towards the more substantial section of the wharf.

Millie, twenty feet away, moaned something through the handkerchief stuffed in her mouth. Her body twisted and writhed on the post. She was crying and yanking hard on the rope tied to the iron ring over her head. Lucy made it to the wharf proper and jumped to her feet. She didn't look up the narrow lane or hear the struggle going on between Byrd and Joe Kanji. All she saw was her sister.

The knot holding the gag in Millie's mouth was very tight, and her sister wasn't helping. Now that help had arrived, she thrashed wildly against the bindings.

"Be still," Lucy pleaded. "I can't get the knot undone." Millie moaned something, something garbled and unintelligible, and her body twisted away from Lucy.

"Please Millie, be still. I can't untie the knot if you don't keep still."

Millie's eyes were no longer looking at her sister. She was looking past her towards the old overgrown road that led up the hillside.

"I need a knife," Lucy said. "It's too tight."

Frankie Byrd said, "You can use mine."

Millie screamed through her gag as Lucy whirled around to see who was behind her. A stranger in an old hat and rumpled suit torn at the shoulder and covered in a healthy dose of sawdust approached her in slow, casual, almost friendly steps.

"Sorry about my appearance," Frankie said. "Had a disagreement with a fellow a few minutes back." Frankie leaned the pump shotgun against one of the wharf's pylons. The money filled black leather case sat beside the gun. He slowly pulled the folding knife out of his pocket. The blade clicked open with a smooth, menacing snap. Millie moaned and turned her face away.

"Untie my sister."

"Sisters?" Frankie replied, doing his best to make the question sound polite like he would if a woman was introducing him to her sibling. It almost made him laugh. No female ever introduced him to her sister. He wasn't that kind of acquaintance where introductions were made. "That's a twist, ain't it. Where's my pal Watkins?" He managed a smile when he said it.

Lucy tried to think. This was the man Harry warned her about. This was the reason she wasn't supposed to go near the wharf, no matter what.

"He's with his friend at the hospital. Some murdering dog stabbed him in the back."

"Liar, liar, pants on fire," Frankie said mockingly. "That's his boat you rammed into my property." He waved the blade in the air between them.

"I took it." She backed up until she could feel Millie's body behind her. "Harry doesn't know."

"Doubt it," Frankie said. "But even if you did, how did you know to come here?"

Lucy tried to think of a convincing reply, something to buy her more time, but she couldn't think of an explanation that would sound believable. "I'm leaving with my sister, and you can go straight to hell."

Frankie smiled, and Lucy couldn't look at him. "I will soon enough, but not yet." He took a step closer to the women.

Lucy pressed harder into Millie. There was nowhere for her to go except into the water.

"Harry's coming," she blurted out. "He went ashore on the other side of the cove and is coming up behind you. You can run now and get away before he gets here." She pointed to the *Scarab*. "Take the boat and go away."

Frankie stared straight into the eyes of Lucy. She wasn't lying anymore. Glancing at the tall spruce trees surrounding the cove, he said, "Harry doesn't know this place very well. All he ever saw was the cove and the wharf. I guess he figured he could hike it overland and approach it from the road." He ran his heel across one of the old scorched planks. It made a dull scratching sound as he continued. "Not bad thinking on his part. I wasn't covering the road, but the road cuts south, not north, and he'd have to do some hard climbing to get here anytime soon."

A cold, killing look drilled into Lucy's pale blue eyes. "I guess you could'a dropped Harry off in a row boat about anywhere but I don't remember seeing one onboard when me and Squeaky cut up Roscoe." Frankie sucked air between his teeth. "I notice those kinds of details. The only spot you could put him ashore in a boat that big," Frankie motioned with his chin towards the white yacht a few feet away, "is a good four miles south of here. Watkins would need to swing way inland before he found the road if he didn't get himself lost first."

Lucy saw the friendly smile melt away from the man's face. It changed into a leering, disturbing grin.

"I got time," he said.

"You're wrong," Lucy stammered. "He'll be here any minute." She knew what the look in Byrd's eyes meant. A blind woman would recognize it for what it was. "Please, just take the boat and go away." Her back pressed hard against her sister. Millie went very still.

Byrd took another step towards her. The knife in his hand caught the morning sun's reflection. Frankie held it in a casual grip like it was perfectly normal to hold a conversation with two women on a burned out dock in the middle of nowhere.

"I've never done it with a woman as pretty as you before. Got a real classy look about you. Bet Harry likes that." Byrd glanced around the cove as if he needed confirmation of who was and who wasn't here. "Yeah, I got time. Plenty of time. You know, I never had sisters before. You can be my first."

Millie wailed something unintelligible through the gag.

Lucy's hand went quickly into the slit pocket of her borrowed leather coat. It came out again almost as fast. The shiny automatic she found lying near Roscoe was in her hand. "I never shot a dog before," she said with cold determination in her voice. "You can be *my* first."

CHAPTER 14

If the dead could feel, Joe Kanji certainly felt like one of them. The water was ice cold and if he didn't get out of it soon, he would be joining the unfeeling dead. His heavy overcoat spared him the worst of the scrapes and scratches as he fell through the brush. Even so, the fall down the hillside cut and bruised him. The limb of a larger bush ripped a long tear down the front of his shirt and he felt the burn of a deep scratch running the length of his chest. When he finally hit the icy water, the same heavy coat that protected him in the long slide nearly drowned him. His arms tangled in the sleeves as he tried to pull it off. He nearly forgot himself and panicked as the heavy wool sucked him down deeper and deeper. He freed himself from the heavy wool before he was completely drowned and kicked his mostly useless legs as his arms pulled his body towards the surface.

He was lucky. If he landed three feet to his left, he would have smashed onto a massive gray boulder larger than the boat that brought him here. But he hadn't landed three feet over. Fate was with him. He was alive for now, but he had to hurry. Hypothermia was beginning to set in. He swam around the rock, using his arms and kicking with his one good leg and into the cove itself. Keeping as close as he could to the bank and its covering of overhanging limbs, he moved beneath the wharf using its boards as cover from

Byrd and his gun.

He was cold. The water felt like melted snow against his skin. He had to get out of it and he needed to do that in a place where Byrd would not see him from his hiding place in the old warehouse. The hull of the big white boat was to his right. It was wedged into the wooden beams like an arrow driven into a target. Every time his arms stopped moving and his head went under the water, he could hear the rumbling growl of the boat's engines. He thought about swimming to the side of the yacht, but knew that would do him no good. The sides were far too high to climb, but those same high sides might hide him from Byrd's view. The boat that brought him here didn't have high sides. It sat low in the water and he just might be able to pull himself up and over.

If he hurried.

He heard voices above him or thought he did, and he thought of Millie and her sister. There was nothing he could do for them now. His one attempt at stopping that maniac Byrd failed. Joe remembered the sight of the diamond necklace and the vision of Lucy McAllister in her scandalously bare green gown. Had that really happened hardly three nights ago? Joe swallowed a mouthful of saltwater and almost choked. Visions of half naked blondes vanished as he concentrated on moving his bruised and battered body. He had to keep going. The path, he heard the voice from far away Japan say. Keep to the path.

His head went under again and he struggled to regain the surface. This wasn't the path he bargained for, but it was what it was. The hull of the yacht was behind him now and he was almost to the spot where they tied the dead man's boat. Half frozen and nearly drowned, he held on to one of the pylons for a moment to catch his breath. His teeth were chattering and he wasn't sure if he could feel his legs anymore. At least his hip quit hurting. The planks above him blocked out most of the light as he swam or crawled through a freezing gloom inching his way closer to the boat. He had to make it. He had to. The P-26 was waiting for him in that boat.

His half numb fingers brushed against something in the water. It was a rope. One of the lines they used to tie the boat to the wharf. Joe dragged himself along the line hand over hand until his head bumped into the wooden side of the boat. Feeling the sides of the hull with frozen fingers, he slowly swam towards the stern. It was the lowest part of the hull and the only place he was likely to have enough strength left to drag himself out of the water.

Frankie Byrd ran his tongue across his lips. His mouth had gone dry. "First time I ever had a woman point a gun at me," he said at last.

"Step one more inch toward me and I'll shoot you."

"I'd rather you didn't do that," Frankie smirked. He folded his knife and dropped it in his pocket. Bending, he lifted the valise containing the fifty thousand dollars. Frankie opened it, showing Lucy the stacks of twenty dollar bills inside. "Let's make a deal. I'll give you enough money to keep you in high heels and peroxide for the rest of your life, and while you're busy counting it, I'll just ease over there to my boat and be on my way."

Joe Kanji, squatting painfully beside the wheel of the murdered man's boat, shook his hands. They were stiff with cold, so he blew on them to try to get some feeling back into his fingers. He wasn't having a lot of success with his attempt to find the right wires to start the boat's engine. He touched two more wires together and suddenly the engine turned over. The motor revved, then backfired with a belch of blue black smoke before it died.

Lucy could taste the adrenaline rushing through her blood. Where was Harry? She wasn't sure if she could bring herself to shoot the evil looking man standing in front of her. She wasn't even sure if the pistol was loaded. The loud backfire coming from the fishing boat's exhaust startled her. She jumped and half turned towards the sound thinking maybe someone was shooting at them.

Byrd dropped the valise full of cash and lunged. He caught her wrist in his hand and pressed her hard against Millie and the pylon. Millie screamed through the gag. Frankie Byrd wrapped a hand around her throat. Lucy couldn't scream even if she wanted to. She felt the pressure of his grip when the hand squeezed tighter. His grip on her wrist felt like a hard vise. The pistol fell from her hand and clattered onto the wooden boards of the wharf.

Byrd bent to pick it up but before he could reach it, the blonde kicked it away with her shoe. The shiny automatic slid across the scorched planks and fell into the water. Straightening, and with his hand still around the struggling female's neck, he said, "Why can't you women stay out of my business?" His voice was a scratchy growl. The engine of the fishing boat revved behind him. "Guess my former partner didn't drown like he was supposed to." The boat's engine died again. Swinging his arms around, he flung Lucy onto the hard planks of the wharf. "I'll be right back. Don't go away, now." He turned for the Winchester still lying where he left it. A movement behind him made him pause for a moment. The moment was all it took.

Gripping the rope tying her hands above her head, Millie lifted her legs. She bent her knees, then pulled her legs up as high as she could. All her weight hung from the knotted rope as the cord bit painfully into her wrists, forcing her to bite down on the gag. Muscles toned by endless hours chasing a little white ball with Clarence Chandler rippled and flexed. With her back braced against the pylon, she kicked out with both feet. It was like serving a tennis ball only her legs were the racket and Frankie Byrd's back was the ball.

Frankie, arms flying out to either side of him flew off the wharf like a child's kite caught in a strong wind. He landed with a loud splash in the icy cold waters of the cove and came up spitting saltwater and with arms flailing. Slapping an open palm against the surface of the water, he yelled, "Again, I'm back in the frigging drink." Treading water, he looked for a spot where he could climb out. Several broken planks leaned into the water's surface. He swam towards them, cursing with every stroke of his arms.

Lucy got up from where she fell rubbing an elbow. Millie was trying to say something to her while nodding her head at the swimming man. She removed the gag from Millie's mouth.

"Run, Lucy. Hide in the trees."

"I'm not going anywhere without you."

Frankie Byrd slowly and carefully clawed his way up the burned planks.

"That's twice that little bitch has kicked me. There won't be a third time."

Lucy turned her back on Byrd and attacked the knot holding her sister.

Millie squirmed, kicked, and twisted. "Hurry. He's coming."

Lucy pulled at the knot, trying to work the line one way and then the other. She heard something behind her but didn't bother to look. The knot loosened. Another moment and…

Millie screamed.

A cold, wet arm went around Lucy's neck. It yanked her away from the unyielding knot and her screaming sister.

Joe blew on his fingers again as he tried to get some kind of warmth in them. He was having trouble holding onto the small metal wires. He heard shouting and the sound of something hitting the water and thought of Lucy and her sister. Byrd was there. He saw the brown valise filled with blueprints sitting on the deck of Blue's boat. Keep to the path, the voice in Japan said. "I am sorry, Lucy," he muttered and tried again to press the bare ends of the copper wires together. Sparks jumped, and the starter responded. He touched it again and the boat's engine cranked for the second time. Standing as quickly as he could, he untied the remaining line holding the boat to the wharf and tossed it into the water. The little boat pulled away from the dock.

An icy wind sliced across the hillside as if the world needed a reminder that winter hadn't given up its hold on San Juan Island. Harry could feel the cold eating its way through his clothes. It wasn't the best of plans, but it was the only one he could think of that would upset whatever scheme Byrd had waiting for him. Like most plans, it went wrong from the beginning. He hadn't been able to keep to the schedule and now he was almost an hour late.

When he jumped from *Scarab's* deck onto the gray stone ledge jutting out from the island, his plan seemed simple enough. He told Lucy to drive the boat farther north, look for the turn into the cove and keep the boat sitting just off the dock to hold Byrd's attention. He would come down the road, from behind, and surprise Byrd. If anything happened, if Byrd had a boat and tried to board her, she was to turn west and run at full power all the way to Victoria. He wasn't sure Lucy could find Victoria, but he was confident in his boat's engines. If Byrd chased her in another boat, *Scarab* wasn't a slow vessel. She could probably outrun him long enough until she could bring the boat to the first harbor she found.

Unfortunately, the road wasn't where he thought it would be and the route across San Juan Island wasn't an easy one. His clothing was soaked by the rain sodden terrain and the mud caked onto his shoes like wet cement. He was forced far out of his way to circle an impassible mountain of rock that sent him even farther away from his objective. Finally, after a hard hike through the forest, he was able to turn north towards Mosquito Pass and Byrd's old loading wharf. He knew he was close when, stumbling into a clear patch in the middle of the forest, he saw the blue waters of the Haro Straits a mile or better off to his west. Victoria itself was lost in a heavy mist rolling in from the Canadian coast.

He was winded from his long push through tangled branches and muddy trails that were never very level. The canopy of the island kept his line of sight down to less than thirty yards as he pressed on towards the wharf. Everything around him was a sea of green. When he cut the road at last, he paused to catch his breath and think about what was in front of him. Not for the first time, he wished Roscoe was here.

The dirt road was easier than the forest and he broke into a run hoping against hope Lucy did what he told her. Topping the last hill, the path twisted away towards the water. Almost there, he thought. The warehouse and dock he'd last seen filled with burning liquor and coast guard searchlights were very close now.

Then he heard it. At first, he thought it was a gunshot, but it didn't have that powerful echoing sound made when a gun goes off. It was a flatter sounding bang. Whatever made the sound, it was close.

The trees thinned and he could see down the sharply sloping road. The monolithic prehistoric spruce trees blocked most of the view of the small cove, but he could see the old wharf clear enough. What he saw made his stomach turn. Lucy hadn't done what he told her to do. At the end of the road, his boat was rammed deep into the blackened timbers of Byrd's old wharf. He sprinted another twenty yards so he could see the whole scene from end to end.

Lucy's bright blonde hair was easy to pick out. Millie stood beside her, but there was something wrong with her posture. It looked like her hands were above her head. He swiped the back of his hand across his nose to wipe away the efforts of running full out in cold weather. Then he started running again because Frankie Byrd just stepped out of the old ruined warehouse and was walking towards the two women.

Frankie pulled Lucy backwards with one wet arm around her throat. He held her near the edge of the broken wharf. Lucy struggled, but there was no getting out of his grasp.

"I should throw you in the drink and see how you like it," he yelled.

The engine on Blue's boat started.

"That you, Kanji?" he shouted. "I didn't know—"

Whatever he was about to say ended as his wind was suddenly cut off. He let go of the woman and grabbed at the arm that was fastened around his own throat.

Harry didn't talk. He didn't ask. He didn't question. He just struck over and over until Byrd crumpled onto the dock.

"Hello, Watkins," Byrd said after a while. "Told Kanji you'd come."

Joe cursed. The engine that ran so faultlessly the night before died. Quickly, he crouched beneath the small helm and fumbled with the wires. Touching the bare ends together again caused the starter to whirr, but that was all. He was drifting less than a stone's throw from the stern of the white yacht on a dead engine. Shuffling his way aft, he found the stick he used the night before to check the fuel tank. Opening the fitting in the deck, he plunged the wooden rod into the tank. The stick was dry when he pulled it out.

The stern of the boat was filled with discarded ropes, broken crab traps, and something that looked like a canvas sail. He pulled it all out of the way. Underneath the canvas were a pair of red cans. He removed the cap and smelled the contents then poured the gasoline down the pipe. There was no funnel, and fuel sloshed around his feet as he poured. He grabbed the second can and dumped its contents down the pipe. The tank replenished, he went back to his copper wires and tried the starter again. The battery's power faded as Joe prayed it wouldn't fail him. Not now. With the last of the starter hardly able to turn the engine over, the motor caught and roared to life.

"Joe," a woman's voice called from the direction of the wharf. "Stop or I'll shoot."

It was Lucy. Her sister stood beside her, holding the buttonless coat closed before her. Byrd's shotgun was on Lucy's shoulder and she was pointing the barrel straight at him. Joe caught his balance on the wooden mast as the small boat rolled with the motion of the water. Lucy put her cheek to the stock and sighted down the barrel. He put the engine in gear and reached for the wheel.

"Stop, Joe. I said I'll shoot."

Joe nodded his understanding, but he didn't take the boat out of gear. The shivering that racked his body stopped as he gazed at the two women. If Millie was free, then Byrd's plans had gone badly awry. He smiled at that. His hand squeezed the wooden mast harder as he waited for Lucy to make her decision.

Lucy turned her head to say something to her sister.

Joe waited. He had no intention of stopping the boat. The distance between him and the shotgun increased with every second. Whatever Lucy said to her sister, Millie didn't like it. Ignoring the coat when it fell open, she grabbed the shotgun from Lucy's hands and pointed the barrel at him.

Joe let go of the mast, then, standing very straight, waited.

The younger sister didn't hesitate. The gun boomed.

Joe didn't move.

Pellets struck the wooden boat and something that sounded like a bee flew past his ear. Millie worked the pump action, sighted again, and fired a second time.

The boat moved farther out into the cove. Millie fired twice more before the shotgun was empty. Lt. Yoshiro Kanji of the Imperial Japanese Navy bowed at the waist before turning his back on the women, the ruined wharf and the man called Frankie Byrd.

Pulling the small black suitcase out from under the protective cover of the forward cabin, he opened the brass clasps. The radio inside was dry and as unharmed as he was from Millie's attack. He wound the wires around the battery terminal, affixed the copper antenna in its slot, and placed the earphones over his head. Pulling the soggy itinerary out of a pocket, he carefully opened the folded pages. The ink was smeared by the wet, but he could still make out the numbers. Comparing the times on the sheet with his watch, he read across the paper to the correct column. Fingers still half frozen, he adjusted the frequency dial to match the fake itinerary, then spun the knob on the directional antenna until he found the signal in his earphones. Flexing his fingers against the cold, he slapped his hand against his thigh a few times before touching the telegraph key. The message wasn't a long one.

Lieutenant Kanji adjusted the boat's course and headed into the thickening mist forming in front of him. It wouldn't be long now.

"I missed him," Millie said with a frustrated voice. "He didn't even duck."

Lucy put her arm around her sister and pulled her closer. "I don't care about Joe. I've got you back now."

The rain clouds finally reached them, making both women look for somewhere to get out of the weather. There were only two choices. There was the dilapidated old building at the top of the hill or the boat.

"Think we can get on the boat?" Lucy asked. She examined the high bows of *Scarab* wedged in among the splintered and broken boards of the wharf. It wouldn't be easy.

Millie ignored her. Instead, once more clutching the front of her dress closed, she went to where Harry waited before the cowering Byrd. The gray .45 was in Harry's hand and pointing at the creature who brought her here.

"You picked up extra shells back in that man's cabin," Millie said. "I saw them. Give them to me."

Byrd looked first at the shotgun in Millie's hands and then to the .45 in Harry's. "Watkins," he said, ignoring Millie's demand, "there's a small fortune setting in that case over there and another one out there in Blue's boat. We could—"

Millie let go of her dress and, taking a two handed grip on the shotgun, swung the barrel at Frankie Byrd's head. Blood spouted from his forehead after he hit the wooden planks.

"The shells," she said again. "Give them to me."

Frankie sat up slowly with one hand on his bleeding scalp. Looking at Millie open front, he said, "Ain't those a pretty sight."

Millie struck him again, then pulled the fabric of the dress closed across her bared chest.

"Harry," Byrd began as he struggled to sit upright on the wooden planks and not looking at the female with her iron barreled club, "listen to what I'm saying. There's more money to be made here than either one of us has ever seen. All we have to do is—"

Millie swung her steel bat again. This time Byrd was able to put an arm up to protect his head. The metal slammed into his forearm.

"God damn it," he yelled. "Harry, stop that crazy bitch."

Millie turned fire filled eyes on Harry. The Winchester held before her like a batter standing at the plate made slow circles in the air.

Harry didn't look at the dress. He kept his eyes on Byrd. "Want me to hold him?"

Millie swung. Byrd collapsed on the dock with a loud groan. Digging into a pocket, he rolled a pair of red shells across the planks. "That's all of them. Take them and stop fucking hitting me."

She scooped up the shells and examined the shotgun. "How do I load this thing?"

"Are you going to shoot him?" Harry shoved the .45 into his shoulder holster, then took the shotgun from Millie. He fed the two shells into the magazine.

"Yes. He stabbed Mr. Harrison, he killed a man last night with this very gun and he tried to, he hurt me so yes, I'm going to shoot him."

"Millie," Lucy said. "We can turn him over to the authorities."

"Your sister's right," Harry added. "It's an option."

Millie worked the slide on the pump shotgun.

"Harry, listen to me," Byrd said. He struggled to his feet. His scalp still bled from where Millie's blows struck him and he had to wipe the back of his hand across his face. "I could of killed you, but I didn't. I was going to let her go once I got you here. That was the deal me and Kanji made."

Millie steadied her aim. The blued steel barrel pointed straight at Frankie Byrd. The rain started falling harder, forcing her to wipe it away with one hand. Rainwater mixed with blood ran down Byrd's face. He didn't bother to wipe at it.

The barrel wavered, then slowly lowered until it was pointing at the planks.

"I can't," she said, "I can't do it. I'm not a murderer like you."

Frankie smirked, tried to shake some of the water out of his clothes, then turned to Harry. "I'll be on my way then. No hard feelings."

Harry didn't like the smirk. He didn't like it at all. The .45 came out of his shoulder rig. Swinging it in a backhanded arc, the pistol made painful contact with Frankie's head. Byrd landed flat on his back with a fresh green welt across his forehead. He didn't move.

"Roscoe says hello," Harry told the motionless body lying on the boards.

Frankie groaned. "Old bastard deserved it."

"Say that again and I'll kill you where you lay," Harry said. "Millie might not do it, but believe me, Frankie, I will."

Lucy put an arm around her sister and pulled her away. "Come on, we're both going to get pneumonia standing out here." She took the Winchester out of Millie's hands. To Harry, she said, "We need to get inside. I need to get my sister out of this wet." She looked at the stretched out body lying motionless on the boards. "Then do what you think's best with him."

Harry ran his hands through Byrd's pockets. He found the knife, then used it to cut a piece of the rope from the binding used to hold Millie to the post. He tied the man's hands in front of him, giving the knot a good shake when he was finished. He was good with knots. "Get up."

Byrd's eyes rolled in his head as the focus slowly came back. "Harry," he mumbled. "You got to listen to me. For once, listen."

"No Frankie, I don't have to do anything. It's your turn to listen. I'm sure they saved your spot in McNeil." Pulling Byrd to his feet, he stepped to one side to see around the stern of *Scarab*. The smaller boat, the one the man named Kanji was in, cleared the cove. It was heading out into the Haro Straits. Seeing his boat with her bruised bows stuck tight in the broken wharf made him sigh. She wasn't brand new anymore.

"It's a good thing Roscoe isn't here," he told Byrd. "If he saw our boat looking like that, he'd peel your skin off your bones with your own knife."

Byrd mumbled something through a split lip. "Chance of a lifetime and you're letting it slip away."

Pointing at a spot halfway down the boat's side, Harry said,

"We'll have to climb that broken part to get back aboard."

Frankie blinked stunned eyes. The welt on his forehead was a greenish blue knot. The blood from Millie's attacks ran around it like a red river. "I wasn't going to kill them, if that's what's worrying you."

Harry grabbed Byrd by the front of his shirt, then pushed him towards *Scarab*. "Walk. Before I decide to see how long you can swim with your hands tied."

"You're making all the wrong decisions. I'm telling you, we're sitting on a gold mine and you're throwing it all away."

Harry shoved him down the half burnt planks of the wharf until they came to a more solid part. He pointed to the boat. "Get on."

Lucy and Millie watched as Byrd struggled to haul himself onto the boat's deck. "We can't get on," Lucy said.

When Byrd finally managed it, Harry said, "Give me a minute."

He motioned Byrd farther down the deck with the barrel of his pistol before he climbed the boat's side. He kept pushing Byrd forward until they were standing on the bow. Opening the pocketknife, he cut a length from Roscoe's neatly coiled mooring line. Dragging Frankie all the way to the prow, he tied Byrd to the anchor.

"C'mon, Harry. At least get me out of the weather. I'm half froze already."

"I like you where I can see you."

"Just listen to me. Please. I'm telling you, that sap out there running around in Blue's boat is the golden goose." His tongue touched the split in his lip before going on. "He'll do anything for a bunch of blueprints he's got in a leather bag. He's loaded, Harry. All we got to do is take that bag away from him and he'll pay. Real money. Money people like you and me never see in this life."

Harry checked the knot holding Byrd tied to the anchor. "Wasn't that Blue's boat I saw just now? If Kanji has it, where's the owner?"

"Blue got greedy. I had to cut him out of the deal."

"I bet you did."

Frankie shrugged. "If you were standing in my shoes, you'd have done the same thing. Blue would'a done terrible things to that girl if I hadn't taken charge of the situation."

"Shut up, Byrd."

"I didn't mean to hurt her. It just happened and to tell you the truth, she went along with it."

"I could tell that by the way she nearly beat you to death with the barrel of that shotgun."

"I'm sorry about Roscoe," Byrd continued. "He jumped me and Squeaky before I could explain. Next thing I know, Roscoe's drowned Squeaky, the girl is screaming lies, and I had to defend myself. Roscoe's a mean bastard. I had to slow him down."

"Squeaky. That the name of your partner?"

"Old friend of mine. Swell guy. Roscoe beat him up real bad then drowned him in the lake before I could explain. I thought he was going to drown me next. I swear I did."

"It was all one big misunderstanding. That your story? I heard about the night at the roadhouse. The night you told your swell friend to shoot Roscoe."

Frankie tried to smile. The blood on his teeth made him look like a ghoul. "That was alcohol talking." He flexed his fingers. "Look, I admit I overreacted. I should have thought things through a bit more, but I'm telling you, Harry. We can be rich men before sundown."

The knot was tight. Byrd wasn't going anywhere.

"Remember when the revenuers jumped us, Frankie? You fell in the water right there." Harry pointed to a spot in the cove. "You wanted me to stop and give you a rope right when Millie's brother was trying to sink me. Didn't know that was her brother out there on the water that night, did you? Well, I'm a little late, but I'm going to see you get that rope. The state's going to put it around your miserable neck, cinch it up good and tight, then drop you about ten feet. You're going to hang, Frankie. Kidnaping and murder."

Harry turned to leave. "If you don't freeze solid before we make it to Elliot Bay, I mean."

"Watkins," Frankie shouted. "This is your chance to get rich and you're going to throw it away. For what? A half grown girl and a blonde doxy? Harry," he shouted again.

Harry wasn't listening. Instead, he leaned over the bows to examine his boat's soot smudged planking. *Scarab's* engines, still idling in neutral since Lucy made her jump, rumbled in the background. The damage didn't appear to be too bad. None of the hull planking was stove in, but the boat had ridden high up on the ruins of the wharf before crashing down onto the charred timbers.

She was stuck fast and it would take some time to work her free.

Lucy, followed by her sister, walked to the spot where he and Byrd climbed aboard. Harry left the trussed up Byrd still talking about missed opportunities.

"Harry?" Lucy asked as she eyed the side of the boat some distance above eye level.

"Give me your hand," he said. He lifted her off the wharf and hauled her aboard. "Your turn, Millie."

Millie looked at the high sides of the boat, at Harry standing above her with his hand stretched out for hers, and hesitated. She held Joe Kanji's leather case out to him. "It's heavy."

Harry took the bag and tossed it on the deck. "Let's get you somewhere warm and dry." He stretched out his hand again.

"I have to hold it closed."

Harry looked at Lucy for help.

"Her dress," she said. "Her front's open."

"Give me your hands, Millie. I'll keep my eyes closed."

Millie looked past Harry to the crouched over and tied up Byrd twenty feet away. "I don't want him to see me again."

Lucy stepped between Harry and the man that nearly killed her sister to block his view.

"Promise you won't look?"

"Promise," he said. With eyes tightly closed, he reached out his hands. Millie grabbed his, and he pulled her aboard.

The three went into the boat's salon. Millie went straight to the liquor cabinet. She turned one of the crystal glasses over and poured herself half a glass from Harry's bottle of *Black & White*. Nobody stopped her this time.

Harry struck a match and lit the room's heater. The two women took the same positions in front of the heater as they had on Sunday night. Lucy tried to take off her sister's sodden coat, but Millie stopped her.

"Don't. The buttons are gone and," she glanced at Harry, "my dress."

"There are blankets in my cabin," Harry said. "I'll get them."

"No," Millie cut him off. "Lucy can get them. You need to get us off this dock and after Joe Kanji."

"I won't be able to follow him in this weather," he said. "He could have gone anywhere. Victoria, most likely."

"He's not going to Victoria. He has a radio," Millie said. "A special kind. I heard him tell all about it after Byrd killed that man, Blue."

Lucy came back into the salon with her arms full of blankets. "He killed a man?" She held one of the blankets up like a screen while her sister removed her sodden coat and dropped it on the deck. The torn remains of her dress followed. Lucy wrapped her in the blanket, then hugged her arms around her.

"Killed him for a boat. The one Joe Kanji is in now. He said he had a way out, a way back home. He has a suitcase with this electric thing in it. Like I said. It is some kind of fancy radio. He said they could find him with it and they're going to come pick him up."

"Who's picking him up?" Harry asked.

"A ship," Millie said. "He's not going to Victoria. He has to get to Juan de Fuca. They're waiting for his signal to come get him."

Harry was skeptical. "A ship?"

"He told Byrd," Millie pointed in the general direction of the boat's foredeck. "He told him there was a warship waiting for his signal." Millie looked at her sister. "He said he's in the Japanese navy and they'll come get him when he calls. I heard him say it."

"They'll never bring a warship into American waters," Harry said. "He was probably lying to throw Byrd off his trail."

Lucy watched Harry. "Supposing he wasn't lying. Can we catch him before he gets to the Strait?"

"That's a hundred miles of water and the weather's getting worse by the minute."

"But he can't be that far away, can he?" Lucy asked.

Millie said, "I don't care about weather or a hundred miles of water or taking Byrd to the police or anything else right now. Joe Kanji has something I accidentally gave him. I need you to get it back. You can do it, can't you?"

Harry could see a bruise circling Millie's neck. He looked at the crumpled dress lying on the deck beneath her feet.

Bring my little girl back to me. That's what Bertie told him. "Get what back?"

"He's got a suitcase full of blueprints that belonged to my father. They're important."

"I heard something about that from our passenger," Harry said.

Millie told them about the plans for the P-26.

"That's what all this is about. That other suitcase sitting out there in the rain, the one I handed to you, it's full of money." Millie pointed out the salon window. "Fifty thousand dollars. Catch him and you can have it. All of it. I won't tell a soul there was ever any money and neither will Lucy."

Lucy said something too low to be heard. Millie held up her hand. "That's what we're doing," she said, "and we need to get moving."

Harry went outside to get the case. When he picked up the bag, Byrd called from the bow, "That's not even half, Harry. Not even half."

Harry ignored him and, carrying the bag back inside, sat it on the deck in front of the two women. When he opened it, he whistled. "If this guy Kanji is going where Millie says he's going," he looked at the bruise circling Millie's throat again, "we might catch him."

"Come on Millie," Lucy said. "You're shivering, and we need to find you something to wear."

Harry pointed down the aft companionway. "Can't promise anything fashionable, but there are dry clothes in my cabin."

Lucy led her sister down the narrow passage. When they were behind closed doors, Millie, cold, sore, bruised and exhausted, dropped the blanket onto the deck.

"Here's a dry shirt," Lucy said.

Millie pulled it on, then stuck out her arms so that Lucy could roll up the sleeves. She buttoned the shirt while Lucy pulled and tugged at the blanket. Lucy began to vigorously rub a towel through her hair.

"Okay, okay," Millie said. "Don't rub so hard."

"Let's get you in bed."

"I'm so tired," she said as she crawled onto the cabin's bunk. "I fought him off. He didn't get to." Her voice trailed away. "You know."

Lucy nodded. She knew.

"He would have. Almost did, if Mr. Harrison hadn't stopped it."

Lucy nodded her head. "Just like in the cathouse. Good old Roscoe."

Millie made a halfhearted attempt at laughing. The laugh died and the tears started. "I think they killed him. Byrd, he stabbed Mr. Harrison in the back." Millie shuddered. "I saw it. It was awful."

"Maybe not. Harry said he was hanging on."

"He's alive?" Millie asked. She sighed. "Of course he is. That's why Harry knew where to find me."

Lucy nodded.

"That man, Byrd, he said Roscoe wouldn't die before he told Harry. He knew."

"Of course he wouldn't," Lucy agreed. "Not that old buzzard. He's tougher than that backstabbing convict hooligan. Don't you worry about Roscoe." She remembered the words Harry told her father. "I got a feeling."

Lucy removed her own wet clothing while rummaging through Harry's things. "Did Joe do anything to you? Or to Roscoe?"

"He kidnapped me, threatened to shoot me dead if I didn't go with him, but he didn't touch me. Just the other one."

The boat's vibration changed. Harry was doing something.

Millie told her story to Lucy, beginning with the overheard conversation outside her father's study and finishing with Frankie Byrd tying her to the post.

Millie asked, "What's Harry going to do with him? I couldn't pull the trigger with him standing right there in front of me. I shot at Joe, but I couldn't shoot the one I needed to shoot."

Lucy wanted to ask questions, a lot of questions, but the listless look in her sister's eyes told her now was not the time.

"Can't wait to see Mr. Harrison again," Millie said softly.

"We'll thank him together. Maybe take him for a ride in my car. I'll let him drive. He'll like that." She tried to smile.

"We have to catch Joe," Millie said. "It's all his fault."

Harry, once more behind the wheel of his boat, looked at the dark gray mist that was blowing down out of the north. Visibility was falling fast and the man Kanji had a big head start. If they found Kanji in this weather, it would be more luck than skill. He reversed his helm and gave the engines more power. *Scarab* made a long, protesting groan at the damage being done to her hull. He spun the wheel the other way. This time, the stern swung a little farther. He gave the engines more power. Roscoe would be screaming profanity if he could see the deep black gouges the burned wood was putting in the side of his boat. They moved a few more inches.

He reversed his wheel twice more, each time gaining more freedom. Frankie Byrd was huddled in a ball still tied to the anchor. The gangster gave up yanking at the rope wrapped around his wrists and curled himself into a ball against the falling drizzle. Harry straightened the wheel and gave the boat full power on both engines. Wood scraped, the boat shook, and then backed a few more inches out of the wrecked wharf.

"What do we do about him?" Lucy asked.

Harry hadn't heard her enter the wheelhouse. He didn't need to ask who Lucy was talking about. "They'll hang him."

Lucy looked out the window at Byrd huddled on the bow. "Do they allow witnesses to hangings? I'd like to see that."

Scarab shuddered with a prolonged vibration. Slowly, the boat slid backwards.

"We're out," Lucy said. "You did it."

"We're out," Harry confirmed. He steadied his wheel and eased his throttles as the boat picked up speed. *Scarab* floated free of the demolished wharf and reversed into the cove.

Lucy leaned forward to stare at the damaged wharf sliding past the hull. "Sorry, Harry. I panicked when I saw my sister tied to a post."

"We got her back," Harry said. "The rest is just paint."

Something out of her field of view scraped its way down the boat's side. Lucy cringed at the sound. "Don't tell Roscoe it was me."

Kanji had a long head start.

*****

It was the best birthday present of the young flyer's life and the best he would ever have. Twenty-two years old today and he was going to be a hero. Ensign Hideki eased the throttle of his Nakajima E4N2 to full power. The Kotubuki radial engine screamed as the floatplane's power plant spun the prop at just under the engine's red line. The voice in his headphones shouted the one word he loved hearing the most.

"Launch."

The steam catapult blasted the open cockpit reconnaissance plane away from the side of the *Takao* the moment the ship climbed

353

a steep Pacific swell. Eighteen hundred kilograms of wood, steel and canvas rocketed away from its seaborne tether. The long, single float slung below the fuselage skimmed above the wave tops before physics took over and the biplane climbed into the sky.

Hideki worked the controls with the ease of someone born to fly. Retracting his flaps, he pulled the stick gently back towards his seat and the Nakajima climbed away from the waves.

The flight was like any other he did more times than he could remember except this time, Hideki was flying solo. His backseat was empty because this time, he was doing something never did before. He was going to land in foreign waters and retrieve one of his countrymen who pulled off an amazing feat of daring and skill. The *Takao* was alive with the secret. Everyone in the wardroom knew he was going to pull a spy out of the jaws of a wolf. Hideki had no idea what feat the man he was going to save had accomplished. Whatever it was, it was great enough to risk such a brazen intrusion into the home waters of another country.

The mission sounded easy enough. Keep his bird skimming along the wave tops. Avoid any contact with other traffic. If approached by enemy fighters or patrol craft, he was to immediately abort and return to the *Takao*. Easy enough in the dark of the night when the moon was on the other side of the earth. But it wasn't dark. The mission was changed. A message had been received from the spy.

Hideki had to go now.

They wouldn't have considered the rescue mission but for the weather. Visibility was less than half a kilometer and getting worse.

"Good," Hideki said to the screaming wind blowing past his ears. "The thicker the weather, the better."

The altimeter showed his plane to be sliding through the sky at less than one hundred meters. Hideki leaned his head out of his cockpit to check the distance to the swells below him. He edged the stick forward making the floatplane move closer to the wave tops. Satisfied, he adjusted the dial on the Nakajima's radio compass. The electronic chirping was loud and clear in his headphones as he steadied his floatplane's course to match the direction of the signal.

"Patience, my friend," Hideki told the chirping. "Soon, we shall be drinking sake together and telling each other outrageous lies."

The floatplane's engines droned on in a murky, mist filled sky.

*****

Mother Nature wasn't on Harry's side. *Scarab* was making sixteen knots in a sea state more suited for five. Every three or four seconds, the boat's bows would plow into the crest of a wave sending spray as far aft as the wheelhouse windows. Frankie Byrd, still tied fast at the boat's prow, suffered with each drenching. Between the spray from the waves, a clinging cold mist and the drizzle, visibility was near zero.

Harry remembered Blue's boat. He'd seen it many times tied up at various out of the way Canadian wharves just like the one he left behind him almost an hour ago. Blue had been much like him. Hauling illegal hooch from somewhere in Canada to somewhere else in America. He didn't know the man well. Roscoe did, he thought, but he wasn't sure. Harry hoped Roscoe was still breathing.

The window fogged, and he leaned forward to wipe at the condensation with a rag. How was he supposed to see a boat in this gunk?

The arithmetic was against him. The man Kanji had almost an hour's head start. Millie said he was heading for Juan de Fuca and the open sea. Maybe he was. Maybe he wasn't. It could have all been some lie to fool Byrd but somehow, he didn't think so. Frankie, despite his faults, wasn't easily fooled. He believed Kanji. At least according to Millie. But an hour's head start in these conditions wasn't going to make it easy.

The door from the salon opened. Lucy joined him at the wheel.

"How's she doing?" he asked.

"Still asleep. The whiskey helped, I think." Lucy cleared her throat before going on. "She's told me quite a story. Now I know why Papa didn't want to involve the authorities."

Lucy reached for a brass rail to steady herself as the boat dipped into another swell. They both heard Byrd's yell from the bow as seawater washed over him.

"It's because they would have arrested him as soon as he called," Lucy said.

Harry adjusted his course with the wheel before replying. "If it wasn't your father, I'd call the papers."

"I can't hurt my family."

Harry yawned. He couldn't remember the last time he'd slept. "If we catch this guy Kanji, the proof of your father's involvement could disappear."

"And if we don't?"

"Then Byrd swings and your father will need a good lawyer."

"I can't believe all this has happened."

"You mean about Byrd?"

"About Joe and my father." She leaned forward to look at the man tied in the bows. "He looks half frozen."

"He does," Harry agreed.

"I think he is probably going to freeze to death out there," Lucy said.

"I think you are probably right."

"You don't care?" she asked.

"Not even a little bit."

Lucy nodded. "Neither do I."

"Going to tell me the details?" Harry asked.

She told him everything Millie had told her. The drawings, her father's involvement, Millie going first to his boat, then the hotel, then being forced back to his dock. All of it.

"Why was she bringing the plans to me?"

"Same reason I would have. You would have known what to do."

"Who says?"

"Millie and I say."

Harry checked the time on the clock screwed to the bulkhead over the small chart table. He turned the boat onto a southwesterly course and made a correction on the paper chart with a pencil.

"I guess I should feel flattered," he said at last. "I wish I had been there when she showed up. Somehow, this all seems like it was my fault."

"You were with me. If it was your fault, it is just as much mine."

Neither spoke for a while. He wiped the condensation from the windows again and kept his eyes peeled for a small green hulled boat with a forward cabin and a tall mast.

A particularly big wave struck the boat and Lucy nearly lost her footing. "Millie says Roscoe stopped Byrd before he was able to," her voice went lower, "you know."

Harry watched Byrd cowering where he was tied. "We got her back. That's what counts and Byrd is going to get what's coming to him. If Roscoe was here, Byrd would never have made it off the dock."

"What about Joe? Will we find him?" An upholstered bench ran across the back of the house. Lucy took a seat on it.

"If he's here I will." He slowed the boat as a dark shape materialized in the gloom on their port side. It was a northbound tug. Its captain sounded his foghorn as they passed. Harry accelerated away. They weren't looking for a tug. "Want to help?"

"What can I do?" Lucy hopped off the bench seat.

He showed her the chart spread out beside the wheel. "We're about here." He touched a spot four miles due south of Beecher Bay. "See that line?" Harry's finger traced a penciled drawing from the Haro Straits to their position.

"Yes."

"When I change my course, you mark it on the chart." He handed her a set of brass dividers. The points were locked about an inch apart. "I change course every fifteen minutes. These dividers represent fifteen minute's worth of distance. Got it?"

"Got it," Lucy answered. She took the dividers from Harry's hand and touched the sharp point to the spot on the chart where the penciled line ended. "Just tell me the direction and I'll mark the chart. Is this how you and Roscoe did it back when you were keeping everybody's liver happy?"

"Sometimes. Back in those days, it was all about going fast and not being seen doing it."

"He might not be out in this weather. He might have gone to Victoria or Port Angeles to wait it out," Lucy said.

"I'm trying not to think about all the ways your man Kanji might give us the slip."

"Is there any good news?"

"The good news is he's caught in a narrow hundred mile long strait and we're probably three times as fast as he is. This weather has to be screwing with his plans. It just has to be."

"They can't come all the way into the Straits and get him, can they? I mean, this isn't international waters and somebody would know. The Navy or Coast Guard. You can't just come in."

"I've been thinking about that," Harry said. "He might try to take Blue's boat all the way out to sea into international waters."

"Can he do that?"

"If it's this rough here, it will be worse out in the Pacific. I wouldn't do it, not in that boat of Blue's. Is Joe experienced with boats and the sea?"

"Joe?" Lucy thought a moment before answering. "I can see Joe on a luxury liner seeing the world. First class tickets all the way. I can't see him doing it in a small boat, especially in weather like this."

"Hell," Harry said, "maybe the Japanese navy sent a submarine."

"A submarine?" Lucy turned to examine the windows in front and along the sides of the wheelhouse. For the next half hour, every wave top looked like it had a periscope sticking out of it.

*****

Blue's boat was no speedster, but the engine had muscle. The undersized craft was slowly yet surely pushing its way through the hard rolling waves. The pounding of the sea against the wooden hull was causing the planks to work and twist. The boat was leaking and the water that froze Joe's feet on the ride to San Juan Island last night was now above his ankles.

He found a canvas bucket floating in the interior of the boat and, after tying the wheel with a piece of rope, spent a half hour tossing bucketful after bucketful of water back where it came from. At least the ordeal of bailing kept him from freezing. The chart he found the night before said the boat had made it to the Strait of Juan de Fuca, or at least he thought so. The fishing boat didn't have a way to measure its speed. It only had a compass to tell him his course. Without visual landmarks, it was more guesswork on his part than navigating. A half hour earlier, he heard the far off clanging of a bell and thought it was the buoy marking the point Blue's chart called Race Rocks. If it was, he had found the path to the Pacific.

Joe dumped another bucket full of water over the side as the boat pitched wildly. How long could he last? How far did he have to go before the floatplane reached him? Was he close enough now? He untied his wheel and steered the boat due west. Was he a mile off the coast of Canada or a mile off America? There was no way to tell. The gray skies, howling wind and incessant drizzle told him nothing.

After he lost sight of Lucy and her sister standing on the wharf, he tossed most of the contents of the small, partially enclosed cabin into the sea. He needed a dry place, or as dry as he could get, to set his radio. The long antenna was extended as high as it would go. Joe pressed the telegraph key all the way down and wrapped a small piece of string around it. He made it tight enough to hold the key in contact with the brass button. The radio would send a constant signal to the cruiser's floatplane and the floatplane would come straight to him. All he had to do was stay afloat long enough for it to get here.

Hideki's eyes were on the small white dial set into the dash of the E4N2. An arrow inset into the dial was lined up directly with the nose of his plane. He was flying on instruments and praying there was nothing solid between him and the signal his radio was receiving. His plan was to skim the water until the arrow in front of him spun to either the left or right. That would tell him he had passed the spy and it was time to turn around and make his landing. He was hoping the dial would spin to the left and not the right. He wanted to be south of the target so he could turn into the northern wind. Either way, it was going to be a very difficult landing. With only a handful of kilometers of open water from north to south to maneuver in, everything about the landing was going to be difficult. If he overshot the waters of the Strait, there were the mountains. Hideki doubted he would even see the side of the mountain before he slammed head on into it. He smiled. He was going to have an amazing story to tell one day.

Even over the boat's clattering engine, Joe heard the plane passing over him. He jumped from the cover of the small cabin to peer into the gray canopy.

There it was.

For a moment, he saw the double wings of the biplane and the float slung beneath the fuselage. The pilot was so low Joe could have tossed a hat into the air and hit it. The Nakajima screamed past him and disappeared into the gloom in his wake. Immediately, Joe pulled the kill switch on his engine. The motor coughed, idled down very low, then died. The welcome buzzing of an airplane's engine was still clearly audible over the sound of the wind. Joe closed his eyes and tried to track the sound with his ear. It sounded like it was turning.

"Here I am," he shouted into the rain. "I am right here."

"New course," Harry told Lucy. He spun the boat's wheel. "Three two five degrees."

"I've got it." Lucy was excited. She had never navigated before. Her face was a half a foot from the chart table, the pincers of the dividers measuring the point of their turn. She found the compass rose on the chart, laid the parallel rulers on three hundred and twenty-five degrees then walked the rulers across the chart to meet the point of the dividers. Straightening from the table, she pulled a wayward strand of blonde hair away from her face and smiled. It was her fifth course change.

"Don't get us lost," Harry said.

Lucy tapped a finger against the side of her head. "Stanford. Class of '28."

"Three semesters as I recall," Harry said. She looked good, standing at his chart table. She still wore the leather jacket she borrowed, and something told him he probably wasn't going to get it back. He opened his mouth, intending to enquire about his coat. "Holy Jesus," he yelled instead. Directly ahead of him, a seaplane suddenly materialized out of the rain filled mist. It was aimed straight at the windows of the wheelhouse and in another instant, was going to collide with his boat. Harry did the only thing he could do. He ducked.

Lucy screamed. She dropped the brass dividers and grabbed the rail in front of her. She couldn't move. Death was flying directly at her, and her life was about to end.

Hideki watched the face of his radio compass as the little red arrow suddenly spun around one hundred and eighty degrees. It meant he had overflown the target. Hideki touched his rudder control intending to bring the seaplane around in a slow circle to the north then set the plane down on the water. His eyes went wide with surprise. A yacht, a big white monster, was sitting directly in front of him. He pulled the stick towards his stomach and pushed back against his seat as if his body's strength could lift the heavy floatplane by sheer effort. It was going to be close. The E4N2 wasn't a nimble flyer. The long float under his fuselage and the two smaller floats below the ends of his wings ensured that.

Hideki closed his eyes at the last moment certain his death was upon him. Thoughts of future stories and sake toasts vanished from his mind.

The Nakajima responded; changing the angle enough to clear the high structure of the boat. The E4N2 roared over the top of the white yacht with its central float all but scraping the superstructure.

"Happy birthday, me," Hideki mumbled to himself.

He put the floatplane into a tight counterclockwise turn while keeping one eye on his airspeed and the other on the left wingtip. The Nakajima made a long, circling turn, then lined up on a western course. The luxury yacht that nearly killed him disappeared somewhere behind him as Hideki leveled off for his landing. The radio compass arrow pointed to the southwest. Close enough, Hideki thought as he concentrated on his landing and the hard blowing crosswind. A wave came up to greet him as he skimmed across the water. His airspeed slowed more and Hideki settled the plane onto the waves. Instantly, the plane, now more a boat than a flying machine, rocked in time with the sea. He maneuvered the Nakajima until the arrow on the compass pointed straight ahead. The floatplane eased forward pitching and rolling as the prop blast washed over him.

"What the hell was that?" Harry yelled. "What kind of idiot flies in this weather and only ten feet off the water?"

Byrd was yanking at the knot holding him pinned to the anchor. He was yelling profanities at the gray skies above him.

"Harry." Lucy still had a hard grip on the railing in front of her.

"Shouldn't he be grounded or something?" Harry continued.

Lucy grew up around airplanes her entire life. She had been to Boeing Field more times than she could count and had seen who knew how many desktop models in her father's study over the years.

"Harry," she said again. "What's the flag of Japan look like? I mean, what do they use for an insignia?"

Harry exchanged a look with his navigator. "What did you see?"

"A big red ball on the bottom of each wing."

Harry pushed the double levers of *Scarab's* throttles all the way forward.

"It was Japanese, wasn't it? They didn't send a submarine for Joe." She rubbed at the glass window in front of her. "They sent a plane."

"It had to come from a ship somewhere offshore," Harry said. "Guess your man Kanji told Frankie the truth after all."

The door to the wheelhouse burst open. Millie, wearing Harry's last clean shirt and a pair of old cotton trousers with the cuffs rolled up, tore into the small compartment. "What was that?" she yelled. "What was that sound?"

Lucy went to her sister and put her arm around her. "You should go back to bed. Look, you're barefooted and it's freezing in here."

"Never mind my feet." Millie grabbed Harry by the arm and pulled him around. "Harry?"

Lucy tugged the front of the oversized shirt closed and buttoned two of the buttons. "It was an airplane flying very low, that's all. C'mon, let's get you back where it's warm."

The trousers were too big for her and she had to hold them up with one hand as she scanned the gray skies outside the windows. "Don't baby me, Lucy." She went to the chart table and, leaning close to the front windows, said, "Where did it go?"

Harry, making his own scan of the gray skies, answered. "It was a Japanese seaplane," he said in a monotone voice, as if Japanese planes buzzed his boat close enough to make the windows rattle every day.

Millie nodded her head. "It's coming for him, isn't it?" She didn't need to add what him she referred to.

"Looks that way," Harry answered.

Millie, a girl a few days ago and a changed woman today continued nodding her head again. "I'll get the shotgun."

Joe shouted with all his might. "*Imasu!* Here!" He waved his hat and jumped up and down, or jumped as much as his injured hip would allow. He could hear the engine of his rescuer somewhere to the east. The fishing boat, its engine dead, floated like a piece of driftwood without the propeller to shove it through the water. He grabbed the wooden mast to steady his footing as the boat rolled. He was soaked to the skin, shaking with cold and fatigued almost beyond endurance. He didn't care. The rhythmic chop of the radial engine somewhere out there beyond his range of vision made it all worthwhile.

Looming like some kind of ghost ship in the haze, the Nakajima drifted into view. It was so close he could see the goggles of the pilot sitting in the cockpit. Joe's screaming yells died away. His head cocked slightly to one side. There was another sound, heavier than the radial engine and lower, like a boat coming across the water at high speed. He only heard it for a moment before his comrade in the beautiful reconnaissance plane drowned out the sound. All he could hear now was the scream of its engine. Joe tossed the black case with the radio over the side. He wouldn't need it anymore. McAllister's valise filled with the secrets of the P-26 was tucked under his arm. The floatplane was almost beside him. The pilot raised a hand and waved. Joe waved back. He would have to start the boat's engine again and use the prop to keep the boat parallel to the airplane. Setting the valise next to the boat's wheel, he touched the starter wires together. Sparks jumped and, the same way it had earlier in the day, the engine cranked to life. He gave the boat enough throttle to keep the bow pointed due west.

"There," Lucy said. She pointed to a spot out the port side window.

Millie squeezed in beside her. "Where?" She had made a fast dash to the aft cabin to put on her shoes and tie a blue necktie around her waist to keep the oversized trousers from falling to her ankles. "I see it. Harry, turn the boat."

"I'm turning. Don't tell me how to run my boat."

"The plane's landed, and he's, oh shit. That's the fishing boat." Millie placed a hand on Harry's arm. "I knew you could find him."

"What are we going to do?" Lucy asked.

The gap between *Scarab* and the floatplane closed rapidly. Whatever he was going to do, Harry knew he would be doing it in a matter of seconds.

Joe coiled a length of line in his hands. He threw the rope towards the floatplane. The hemp line splashed into the water.

Almost there.

He coiled the line again for a second try as something in the corner of his eye caught his attention. He turned to better see whatever it was. It was the white yacht. The same vessel he left behind him at the murderer's wharf. It was easily recognizable by the black smears on the white hull. It was the man Watkins, and he was coming on fast. Joe threw the rope again. It landed across the empty rear cockpit of the Nakajima.

Hideki unclasped the catch on his harness. He needed to stand up and turn around to reach it. "Keep clear of the wing," he yelled. The fishing boat was so close to his left wingtip, the spy could almost touch it with his hand. If there was a collision, neither he nor the spy was going anywhere. The spy turned the boat's wheel and the craft veered off. Hideki waved his hand up and down, one finger pointing at the water. "Jump," he yelled. "I'll pull you to me."

The spy said something, but his words were lost in the roar of the propeller and Hideki dared not kill his engine. The floatplane would lose all control on the water if he did that.

Joe wanted to scream his frustrations. It was impossible. He needed a raft or lifeboat to row himself across, and he possessed neither. There was no way he was going to be able to get close enough to climb into the cockpit. McAllister's valise had to stay dry. The drawings would be ruined if he tried to swim across. It would have to be the wing. Joe eased the wheel over. The boat drew closer to the fragile wingtip of the Nakajima. The pilot waved his hands. He wanted Joe to jump. Joe pointed across the water to the white yacht bearing down on them.

The floatplane's pilot turned to see what he was pointing at. It was the yacht. The same one he nearly collided with moments ago and it was coming towards them fast enough for the bows to throw up a frothy wake. Hideki cupped his hands and shouted to the spy one last time. "Jump," he screamed. "Tie the rope around your waist and I'll pull you to me."

The spy pointed to something. A bag. He wanted to bring his luggage? Hideki gave the yacht a quick glance. It would be on them in minutes. The spy waved his arms and shouted. It was pointless. He could hear nothing over the sound of his engine and the spinning propeller, but he understood the gesture the spy made clear enough. The man pointed to the boat, then drew his finger along his throat in a slashing movement.

Hideki reached for the clips holding the machinegun. The oiled clasp came free and he swung the gun around in the turret. He worked the slide and chambered a 7.7mm cartridge. Nothing in his orders said he was allowed to shoot at anything, but the spy was clearly agitated and that yacht was apparently an unexpected problem that needed a solution. Ensign Hideki pointed the long barrel of the machinegun at the yacht and pulled the trigger.

Harry saw the muzzle flash before anyone else. Not that it mattered. The bullets hit the *Scarab* before he had a chance to do anything. The windows in front of him shattered into hundreds of flying shards. Lucy and her sister screamed. Icy air flooded into the small wheelhouse as Harry drove his body into the two women. He hit them hard, driving both down and onto the deck as *Scarab's* beautiful mahogany woodwork, the pride of Watkins Yacht Building, was shot to pieces. Without his hands on the wheel, the boat lost its course and heeled sharply to one side. The impact of dozens of bullets slamming into the side of the boat sounded like someone beating on the hull with a hammer. A very fast hammer.

Frankie Byrd screamed. Millie flattened her body onto the wooden deck with both hands over her ears. Lucy sprawled across her looking at the blood on her hand as if it belonged to someone else.

"Are you shot?" Harry yelled.

"I don't know."

Millie pulled her sister's hand towards her. "It's just a cut. Glass."

Harry reached for the wheel. One of the wooden spokes was blown off by a bullet that would have hit him if he hadn't lunged for Lucy and her sister. The floatplane that was in front of him when the shooting started was now on their right side. He cringed as more bullets struck the side of his boat. A long line of splashes passed near them and danced away among the wave tops. The glass windows that lined the front and side of his helm were gone. Cold rain soaked everything around him. The chart was gone; an unrecognizable lump of paper lying beneath Lucy. Broken glass and pieces of splintered mahogany were everywhere. The upholstered bench seat running along the back of the wheelhouse had an almost perfectly level line of holes running from port to starboard.

The gun fired again; long, steady bursts that did terrible damage. Something crashed behind them as the machinegun found the salon. Bullets ripped through the leather furnishings and more glass shattered. Paneled bulkheads were punctured dozens of times. Harry knew he had to do something. The gunner in that plane had them dead to rights in open water. Any moment now, he would turn his sights back to the three of them and kill them all.

Joe saw the white yacht withering under the fire of the gun. He prayed Lucy and her sister had stayed back on that sorry burned out wharf and he hadn't just told the pilot to kill them. The gun still fired as his countryman swung the weapon around the turret to follow the yacht. He could see pieces flying off the white boat as the bullets destroyed the planking near the waterline. The boat was sure to be sinking now. Joe pulled on the rope in his hands. The fishing boat edged closer to the floatplane. Right before the wingtip was about to make contact with the hard wooden side, he jumped. It wasn't a graceful jump. More of a fall in the direction of the plane, but it served the purpose. He landed on the smooth skin of the lower wing; one hand holding fast to the handle of McAllister's valise, the other holding onto the N shaped strut between the wings. The plane rolled high on a wave before plunging down the trough. The force tossed Joe around on the sloping, wet surface of the wing. Pulling as hard as he could, he dragged himself closer to the wing's strut.

The machinegun fired on.

The gunner switched his fire from the superstructure to the hull.

Harry could already feel the difference in the way the boat rolled on the waves. *Scarab* was taking on water. An engine died. He couldn't tell which one and its twin was having problems. They were also making a slow clockwise turn around the floatplane and Blue's stolen boat. He risked a quick look through the shattered side window before ducking down again. Joe Kanji was holding onto one of the wings. Blue's green hulled boat was bobbing in the water beside the plane. He mentally measured the angles. It wasn't good. The odds were bad, about as bad as finding Kanji in the first place.

"What do we do?" Lucy asked. She was sitting on the deck and holding her sister in a corner of the wheelhouse.

He wondered if he looked as terrified to them as they did to him. "The boat's sinking and he's shot up the engines."

"I don't want to die, Harry. Do what you were thinking about doing just now. We're with you," Lucy said.

Harry turned the wheel. The broken spoke passed through his hands as he turned. Blue's boat was just about right.

"Cut me loose," Byrd screamed from where he was still tied to the anchor.

Harry ignored him, concentrating instead on the much smaller boat in front of him.

Hideki let go of his trigger and the gun fell silent. Steam rose from the heated barrel as it sizzled in the rain. He couldn't shoot anymore. The yacht had managed to put the spy's boat between him and his target. The spy jumped onto his wing and was struggling to gain his footing as the plane pitched on the waves. He was still holding onto his luggage.

"Hurry," Hideki shouted, pointing at the yacht. The big white boat was lumbering towards them. The spy's boat was drifting slowly out of the way. He put the gun's stock against his shoulder and waited. This time, he would destroy the wheelhouse and be done with them. The spy's boat drifted another meter. His finger touched the trigger.

Joe was up now and standing on wobbly legs. He waited for a wave to pass, then lunged quickly for the fuselage of the plane. The backwash from the prop hit him like a wind tunnel as his feet began to slide beneath him. He was about to slide into the sea, luggage and all.

"Help me," Joe yelled. He stuck out his hand towards the pilot standing in the rear turret. The wind from the turning propeller made him feel like he was caught in a typhoon. His fingers lost their grip on the slippery fuselage as he was slowly pushed towards the edge of the wing.

"Take my hand," Hideki shouted. He leaned over the edge with an outstretched hand. "Grab on."

A gloved finger touched Joe's. The pilot must have abandoned his gun and made it to the front cockpit. Joe lifted the brown valise to his countryman. "Save this," he shouted. He couldn't tell if the pilot heard him over the roaring radial engine or not. He felt the valise pulled away from him.

Hideki took the bag and flipped it into the rear cockpit. It struck the machinegun and landed on the rear gunner's seat. Hideki looked up. The oncoming yacht was about to ram the spy's boat and drive it into the side of the Nakajima. Forgetting the spy struggling to claw his way up the fuselage, forgetting everything except the gun, he jumped for the rear turret.

Freed from the valise, Joe, using two hands, found his footing. He pulled himself up the side of the fuselage as the pilot again climbed into the rear turret. He twisted around to see what was coming up behind him. "Shoot him," he screamed.

Scarab rammed Blue's boat with its bows, knocking the stern of the smaller craft closer to the outer edge of the plane.

"Back the engines," Harry yelled as loud as he could. He was standing on the open exposed foredeck of his boat with Frankie Byrd's pump shotgun in his hand.

"Harry, cut me the fuck loose," Frankie shouted.

"Shut up."

Lucy heard him easily enough through the shattered windows. She yanked the transmission levers backwards all the way. *Scarab*, moving on one engine, slowed its advance towards the Japanese plane.

"Better duck, Joe," she whispered.

Harry pointed the shotgun, braced his feet against the rolling deck, and tried to steady the dancing barrel on his target.

Hideki couldn't clear the gun. In his panic, he tangled himself in a knot of parachute gear, luggage and gun stock. He yanked the valise out of the way and tried to get behind the weapon.

It was Harry's turn to pull the trigger. He fired once with the barrel of the gun pointing straight at the flyer's chest. The recoil took the barrel of the pump upwards and he lost sight of the man standing behind the machinegun. When he lowered the barrel again, the gunner was slumped to one side and holding an arm across his chest. The man they were chasing, Joe Kanji, threw a leg over the side of the forward cockpit.

The shotgun had one round left. He worked the slide ejecting the empty casing into the sea.

The gunner pulled himself upright then set his shoulder to the stock of the machinegun. He aimed his weapon.

Harry fired again. This time, when he brought the barrel down, the rear cockpit was empty and the machinegun pointed at the sky.

Joe reached across the empty cockpit.

Lucy saw the man hit by the shotgun. "Dear God," she prayed as the flyer tumbled out of the seaplane.

Joe pulled himself over the divider between the two cockpits.

"Don't do it, Joe," Lucy said from her vantage point behind *Scarab's* broken wheel.

Harry waved an arm over his head and yelled, "Get closer. Go forward. Forward." He dropped the empty Winchester on the deck and pulled his Colt from the shoulder holster under his slicker as water washed across his ankles. He looked down. *Scarab* was settling into the sea. The machinegun opened too many holes in her hull. There wasn't much time left.

"Harry," Frankie said, "we got to swim for it before this tub sinks. You got to cut me loose." Frankie got his legs under him and tried to stand. His hands, still tied to the anchor, made him bend at the waist.

Lucy pushed the levers forward again and gave the remaining engine more throttle. Even she could tell the boat wasn't responding like it should.

"We're tilting," Millie told her. "Are we going to capsize?" She leaned across the shattered wooden console nearer the open hole where the windshield used to be. "Harry," she yelled, "are we going to roll over?"

Harry didn't have time to answer. *Scarab* edged closer to the plane in front of him. He brought the pistol up with a double handed grip.

Joe watched the lifeless body of the young pilot drift away on the waves. He had been knocked free of the Nakajima as if a horse kicked him. The valise, balanced on the edge of the rear seat, had been damaged by the pellets. The leather was ripped and a sizeable hole was in the side. He reached for the bag and pulled it towards him. The valise's top yawed open in the fiercely blowing wind from the engine's prop. Half a dozen sheets of paper blew away in the maelstrom like pieces of giant blue confetti in a victory parade. Quickly, he sprawled across the rear seat as he scrambled to close the bag's lid before he lost more of the P-26.

"Papa's airplane," Millie said. "It's right there."

Their boat drew closer to the floatplane.

"Ram it, Lucy. Run right into it," Millie said. "Sink him."

Lucy pushed the twin throttles all the way forward, but instead of a high powered answering scream from *Scarab's* engines, all she got was a choking rumble from somewhere beneath her feet. The boat sounded like it was strangling.

The wingtip of the Nakajima came closer. Harry, standing behind the tied form of Frankie Byrd, tried to brace himself on the sloping foredeck as best he could. The empty shotgun slid down the deck and vanished over the side.

Joe Kanji reached for the machinegun. The weapon was mounted on a large steel ring that circled the cockpit. He pulled it towards him. The gun rolled along the ring on ball bearings.

Harry, the .45 in both hands, took careful aim.

Kanji settled the stock against his shoulder as Harry fired. Something struck him very hard. He lost his grip on both the weapon and McAllister's brown leather traveling bag. Sheet after sheet of blue paper blew out of the rear cockpit. Joe flapped at the drawings with one hand managing to grab a fist full of paper before sliding down into the pilot's seat. The wind from the propeller ripped the sheets of paper in his hand to ribbons before he could shove them out of the wind. With nowhere to put them, he wadded them into a ball and sat on them. He saw the blue paper was spotted with bright red blood.

"Hit him, Lucy," Millie yelled. "Now."

"I can't," Lucy yelled. "The engines won't go."

Scarab, once all power and grace, barely had weigh on now. The black scars on her bows were hidden by the lead colored water. But still she crept steadily closer. Harry readied for a second shot at Kanji. The rapidly submerging bow touched the small float beneath the seaplane's wingtip. The impact caused him to lose his footing on the water sloshed deck making his feet slide out from under him. He fell with a grunt beside Frankie Byrd who was yanking at the bindings holding him fast to the anchor like a madman. The bump by *Scarab* caused the floatplane to change its angle. It rotated around far enough to point the propeller at the boat's prow. Harry scrambled backwards and away from the spinning blade. Water swarming over the side made it harder to push himself away from the fast turning prop. The float mounted below the plane's center rode over the submerged bow of his boat. It was coming straight towards him.

Frankie Byrd screamed. Harry didn't hear it.

Joe saw the blood spots on the drawings and wondered for a moment if it was his or the unfortunate airman's. He didn't feel any pain. At this moment in time, he wasn't feeling anything. The drawings were gone except for the handful of torn papers he grabbed. He looked up from his study of the blood drops on the wadded up paper. The big white boat was sinking. Her foredeck was already awash. The man, Donovan's gangster, was trying to slide backwards like a crab caught by an incoming wave. Lucy was making her way forward grabbing handholds where she could as she tried to get to the man, Watkins. What had the killer Frankie Byrd told him about the two of them? He hadn't believed it; was sure Byrd was lying and yet there she was making her way towards the very same man. The propeller was almost on him. It would be over in a moment. Lucy looked at him. Her lips moved, saying something impossible for him to hear over the roar of the floatplane's engine. Joe nodded his head, saying something equally impossible to hear then pushed his foot against his rudder pedal. The Nakajima skewed sideways as the propeller turned away from the man who shot him.

Scarab was going fast. Harry could feel it. She was sinking, bow first, and the angle was going to send him sliding straight towards the propeller. The plane turned. The whirring prop no longer pointed straight at him. The long, slender pontoon beneath the plane moved away like a pendulum finding the opposite arc.

Towards Byrd.

"Harry," Byrd screamed. It was a long, drawn out yell. The plea of a doomed man. Bent double and waist deep in water, he yanked helplessly at the rope tying him to the anchor while jerking his bound hands and trying desperately to free himself from the knot. The pontoon, completing its swing across the submerged bow of the boat touched him. Byrd yanked harder at the rope binding him to the anchor.

"Shoot the engine," he screamed. His voice was high pitched and full of terror as the spinning blade edged slowly towards him. "The engine," he screamed again.

The Nakajima followed the incessant pull of the propeller.

Harry tried to stand, slipped again, and felt *Scarab's* deck sliding under him. Something grabbed the back of his collar.

"I've got you," Lucy said. She pulled backward as Harry kicked with his feet pushing himself away from the spinning propeller.

The floatplane continued to turn.

Kanji saw Lucy dragging Donovan's gangster away from the front of his engine. Then he saw something else. Byrd, waist deep in water, was bent double in the bows of the yacht and yanking at his hands. The killer disappeared from his view behind the high cowling of the Nakajima.

Lucy stopped pulling. Harry found his feet as the sound of the airplane's engine changed into something else. To Harry, it reminded him of those days tied up next to the sawmill; the sound one of the big saws made when it bit into a log.

Joe watched as a red spray was thrown into a giant spiral in front of the Nakajima's cowling. The engine missed a beat, its rhythm changing for an instant, before the floatplane continued to slide away from the sinking boat.

"Jesus," Harry said. Byrd disappeared before his eyes. Parts of some bloody human remnant were still tied to the anchor, but it wasn't Byrd. Not anymore. He looked at Lucy. She didn't say anything. Just stared at what the floatplane's propeller created, then turned to one side and retched.

Scarab's last engine died as the floatplane pulled away.

Kanji, sitting on his cache of ripped and bloody drawings gave the Nakajima's engine more rpm's. The gap between him and the boat widened quickly. He glanced over his shoulder at the broken white yacht. He could see a dark haired woman standing behind the wheel. The gangster and Lucy were making their way aft. He saw something red and ugly staining the water around the submerged bow. It made him smile. "Goodbye, Lucy."

The Nakajima lurched across a wave, bounced hard once then freed itself from the friction of the water. Lieutenant Yoshiro Kanji, his body exhausted beyond endurance, frozen nearly stiff and with a bullet hole in him somewhere held the stick in a half numb grip. Pulling the dead pilot's headset over his blowing hair, he checked the frequency of the radio, then keyed the mike. It was time to go home.

"He got away," Millie said. "He got clean away."

Harry turned to see Millie holding a still very ill Lucy. The plane disappeared into the gray skies as only the fading buzz of its engine giving proof that it was ever there at all. Millie had one lifejacket half on and another in her hand. She gave the spare to her sister. "How do I hook this?"

Harry ran the straps through the buckles, then helped Lucy into the other jacket. The three of them had to hold on with one hand to *Scarab's* superstructure to keep from sliding into the Strait.

"I didn't see a third one," Millie added.

Lucy had a wild, fearful look in her eyes. "I'm not a very good swimmer."

Harry tried to think of a dozen things at once. Kanji got away. His boat was sinking. Byrd was turned into chum; parts of some gnawed thing still tied to the anchor were floating half submerged in his bows. Two life jackets. Cold water. Lucy couldn't swim very well. He pushed past the two women to the salon's open hatch. Going inside, he tried not to notice the ruin that was his boat's interior. What the machinegun hadn't destroyed, the seawater was. Sloshing across the deck, he found what he was looking for. The suitcase full of cash was wet but still intact. He made his way back to the deck and the two women.

"Take this," he said, handing the bag to Millie.

"I don't want it."

Harry pushed it into her arms, then quickly tied one end of the lifejacket's straps through the handles of the bag. Then he tied one of Lucy's straps to Millie's lifejacket.

Blue's stolen boat was a hundred yards away turning in very wide, very slow circles.

"I'm going to try for the boat." He pointed at the low green hull. "If you sink before I get back, the lifejackets will keep you afloat."

Lucy looked across the water. "It's a long way. What if you can't make it?"

"Stay on the boat as long as she floats." Making his way forward, careful to avoid the red thing tied to the anchor, he pulled his slicker off, dropped the heavy pistol over the side then jumped into the water. Lucy yelled something he couldn't understand before he lost himself in a battle with the swells.

The water was cold. Too cold. Killing cold. He swam harder. Blue's boat was sometimes visible and sometimes lost as he dipped into the trough of a swell. He put his head down, forgot about everything, forgot about the numbing cold, and swam. After a small eternity, he stopped and treaded water. All around him was nothing but steep swells with gray skies above. He tried to get his bearings, but he wasn't even sure if he was swimming in the right direction anymore.

The boat had been making a slow circle.

He should be close, but he couldn't see it. Putting his head down, he swam some more feeling his body getting heavier with each stroke as he fought the swells for some sign of the boat. If his legs cramped now, he knew it would drown him. Treading water again, he spun around in place as a swell lifted him.

The boat was thirty strokes away.

With the cold draining the last of his reserves, he put his head down and swam. The green hull nearly ran over him as his hands felt for something to grab on the algae slicked hull. For a moment, he was afraid he was going to end up like Byrd; sucked into a turning prop. His fingers found a rope. Quickly, he wrapped a turn around his wrist. The hull eased past him as the rope played out until it snapped him around, ten feet behind the boat. Inch by inch, one frozen hand over the other, he pulled himself up the rope. He had to close his eyes and hold his breath because the wake was trying first to blind him and second to drown him. Finally, his hands struck wood. He made it to the boat's low transom. He held on as the boat pulled his near dead body through the water. Beneath the waves, his legs kicked as his arms pulled. He tried not to think about the screw turning somewhere underneath him. At last, he rolled himself onto the deck of the dead man's boat.

The mast helped him as he climbed atop the small forward cabin. Scanning the waves, Harry looked for some sign of *Scarab*. All he saw were long swells and empty water. A wave broke against something to the south. He looked harder, but couldn't make anything out. Jumping down from the cabin top, he turned the boat towards the spot where he'd seen the wave strike something. It didn't take long before he saw it. *Scarab's* polished wooden stern was just visible. The blue letters were all that told him the floating wreckage was his boat. Holding on to one corner were Lucy and her sister. The swimmers waved.

*****

"No more," Roscoe said. "I can't take another drop."

Millie ignored the protests. "Just one more," she said, deftly maneuvering another spoonful of Aunt Bertie's homemade chicken soup into Roscoe's open mouth.

Roscoe snatched the empty spoon out of her hand and threw it across the room.

"Well, I never," Millie crooned sweetly as she blotted his mouth with a napkin. "Are you feverish?" She felt his forehead with the back of her hand.

"Harry," Roscoe yelled. The effort made him wince.

Millie winced with him. She sat the nearly empty bowl on the bedside table. "Shouting's bad for the stitches."

The door opened and Harry, a concerned look on his face, stuck his head around the door. "What's the emergency?"

"The nurse said," Millie began.

"The nurse can go screw a fireplug. Harry, I ain't swallowing another drop of chicken soup. How am I supposed to get my strength back on soup?"

Millie rose from her perch on the invalid's bed. "We aren't feeling at all ourselves this evening."

"Dear god," Roscoe moaned, "it ain't human."

Harry retrieved the spoon from the carpet. There was a B for

Bergonian engraved on the handle. He had a new room now, one with a second bedroom for the recovering invalid. Handing the spoon to Millie, he said, "The nurse did say no solid food. Soup and juice for now."

"That nurse can go screw—"

"Fireplugs," Harry cut in. "We heard."

Roscoe whistled. "Get a load of you. A tux?"

Harry pulled at the tuxedo's cuffs. "Lucy has a thing to attend."

On cue, Lucy came into the room dazzling in an all black evening gown, white elbow length gloves and her mother's diamond pendant.

Roscoe whistled again. "Didn't Harry fish you out of the Straits a week ago? Look at you now. Somebody take a picture."

Lucy came to his bed and kissed him on the forehead. She whispered something in his ear which turned his cheeks a bright pink. "Still time to go with us," she told her sister.

Millie shook her head. "Bedpan duty."

"Dear god," Roscoe said again.

"Is it time?" Millie reached under the bed and came up with a large porcelain dish.

"I'll just step out now," Harry said.

"I ain't using no bedpan," Roscoe shouted, his face screwed up into the kind of grimace that made feral cats hiss. "I'm not paralyzed, girl."

Millie lifted the coverlet, meaning to slide the pan beneath her patient. "The nurse said you are not to leave this bed for at least another week."

Roscoe snatched the pan out of her hand and sent it flying across the room. "Nurses be damned," he shouted. "Where are my britches, girl?"

Millie frowned. "Now, Mr. Harrison. We've talked about this. I'll just put it under you and you can tell me when you're done."

Harry grabbed her by the arm and pulled her towards the door. "Let's give the invalid a moment to compose his dignity and consider the situation." He closed the bedroom door behind him.

Millie stared at the closed door with a look of apprehension. "I need to help him."

"Trust me," Harry said, "you don't."

"I've never seen such peevishness. Does he think I'm shy? I

babysat the Ogden triplets for ages before they were potty trained. Talk about diaper duty," Millie rolled her eyes.

"You should probably keep diaper duty comments out of Roscoe's hearing," Harry said. "He wouldn't like the implications."

"I don't know," Lucy piped. "I'd pay hard cash to see that."

"The nurse said he isn't to get out of bed," Mille countered. "The poor man nearly bled to death."

Harry shook his head. "Five bucks says the poor man will be walking by sundown tomorrow."

"My money says before noon," Lucy added.

Millie was about to correct her when the room's phone started ringing.

"We're going to be late, even for me," Lucy told Harry.

He helped her into a fur wrap as Millie answered the phone. Lucy found her purse, then checked to make sure the monkey's fist keychain was inside. Her sister was talking to someone on the other end of the phone as they headed for the door of the suite. She waved a hand at her. "Back before dawn," she said with a smile.

Millie waved the receiver. "It's for you, Harry. He said it was important. Somebody named Drake."

Harry smiled as he turned towards Millie and held out his hand for the phone. "Hello, Drake." He listened to the voice on the other end of the line. "Sure, I can do that. Just say when and where."

Lucy dropped her purse on the sofa and sighed. "Something tells me I'm overdressed."

Millie nodded. "Yep."

The End

Historical Note

Like most novelized works of fiction, I have mixed in bits of real history with the imaginary. All characters used in the story were purely the product of the author's imagination as were any affiliations with companies, occupations or manufacturers. Except one. In 1932, a reserve U.S. Army Air Corps pilot by the name of Robert Short, while flying a Boeing built biplane did attack a flight of Japanese aircraft in the skies above Shanghai. The aircraft were launched from the Imperial Japanese Navy's carrier *Kaga Province*. Lt. Short lost his life in the attack.

The Bergonian was a real hotel although there was never a speakeasy called "The Pharmacy" located anywhere on the property.

Prohibition, that great American experiment in forced sobriety, ended in January, 1934. However, in Washington state, bars would not be able to operate in the traditional manner until the 1940s. I embellished or ignored this fact, depending on your point of view.

Most of my information about pre-Interstate 5 Seattle came from old maps. The streets, ferries, streetcars, bridges and locations were described as accurately as I could determine. No doubt, longtime natives of the area might pick up on a geographical mistake here and there.

The U.S. Coast Guard did operate patrol boats in an attempt to prevent the illegal trade in alcohol. If you want the real story, I highly recommend "Rum War: The U.S. Coast Guard and

Prohibition" by Donald L. Canney.

The P-26 was Boeing's first all metal monoplane fighter. At the time of this story, it was truly revolutionary. During the battle for the Philippines, post Pearl Harbor, a P-26 would score the first aerial victory against the attacking Japanese forces.

And finally, the Nakajima Aircraft Company did design and build the A2N, A4N and E4N2 biplanes mentioned in the story. In 1934, they would go on to build the Ki-11, an all metal low wing monoplane. Many experts in the field have remarked upon how the design was very similar to the P-26. The aircraft proved unsuccessful as a fighter and was quickly withdrawn. I suppose one could speculate the Ki-11 might have been based on actual P-26 blueprints stolen in some nefarious prewar shenanigans. But that would be the stuff of novels.

ABOUT THE AUTHOR

A. C. Foster is a Texas native currently living not far from Galveston Bay. He has seen a good bit of America, about forty states and counting, and has worked and lived in four countries, five if you count a long distance dalliance with Canada. He holds a degree in History from the University of Texas at Austin.

www.ingramcontent.com/pod-product-compliance
Lightning Source LLC
Chambersburg PA
CBHW070631180626
46817CB00006B/2094